The Ivory Star

by

Travis Heermann

Commonwealth
Publications

A Commonwealth Publications Paperback
THE IVORY STAR

This edition published 1996
by Commonwealth Publications
9764 - 45th Avenue,
Edmonton, AB, CANADA T6E 5C5

ISBN: 1-55197-361-8

Designed by: Tina Boer

Printed in Canada

The Ivory Star

The old man lowered the point of the arrow to Hamilton's chest, which was laid bare by the mangled tunic. A bewildered gasp flew from the man's throat, and he staggered backward, eyes bulging. The bow clattered to the floor. The arrow flew from the released string to bury itself in the dirt floor a finger's breadth from Hamilton's toes. The old man took a step forward, staring transfixed at Hamilton's chest.

Hamilton took a hesitant step backward, lowering his hands, mouth open in uncertainty.

The old man's mouth worked, but no sound came forth. He seemed to be mouthing words, but his breath would not obey him. Then he whispered, "The One!" He approached until his nose was inches from Hamilton's chest.

"Sir, I..." Hamilton stuttered.

"The One!" the old man barked, his stare nailed to the birthmark on Hamilton's chest. His fingers reached up and touched the smooth, lightly haired surface, touching the white mark emblazoned there in the angle between breastbone and collarbone. The birthmark shaped like a four-pointed star, with one point slightly longer than the others.

The old man sought half-heartedly to rub the mark off, his effort coming to naught.

"Arnor be praised!" he exclaimed. He threw his hands into the air and cried out in exultation as he began to dance crazily about the small room like one barefoot on hot coals.

To Cheryl,
for her love and encouragement
and
for Ma and Pa
for their love and support.

The Prophecy of The One

The One shall come
When The Sun becomes Blood.
The One shall come
Riding but not riding a silver Dragon that is not a Dragon.
The One shall have The Ivory Star in his Breast.
And he shall free
Mankind from The Ultimate Evil.

Prologue

The dagger glinted, half-concealed in the sagging folds of the scarlet and black robes. The wickedly curved blade soared high, then fell, effortlessly splitting flesh. The man lashed upside down to the pillar spasmed, and gurgled his last breath through the deluge of blood pouring from the monstrous wound in his throat. The thing gleefully twirled the dagger in his sickly yellow claw, and a dry terrible sound akin to laughter rattled from the recesses of the deep, black hood.

He raised his rotting hand to lick away the blood with a long, black tongue, then plunged its other claw into the man's chest. Ribs snapped like twigs, and gore splashed the black flagstone floor as it tore the steaming heart from its home. It raised the dripping fruit into the darkness of the hood, and devoured it in two massive bites, feeling strength surge through his withered limbs.

He stepped away to allow his servants room to catch the crimson spring in their large, golden bowls. The two small men with eyes like empty glass held their hammered bowls under the bubbling fount.

A suppressed whimper to his left snagged the monster's attention. His ghastly repast finished, he turned toward the woman, tied upside down to another pillar as the man before her. He towered above her. Her eyes bulged in terror. Her body trembled like a leaf, too paralyzed to shriek her terror. He paused, touched her face with his thin, moldering hand, admiring the creamy skin, the lithe firmness of her body. He leaned down, drew her lush scent into his nostrils, savoring her. With great amusement he watched her nostrils flare and her throat constrict as she drew in his own stench. Had he still been human, his desire for her would have been merely carnal. But now, it was far, far more.

He rose to his full height and tore back his hood. Her face opened up into a shriek of primal terror. He plunged the dagger between her breasts. Blood gushed from her open mouth. Her eyes went dull.

Now the final element in his grisly feast. He concentrated for a moment, gathering his will. Then his ravenous essence reached out, seeking its prey.

****

The woman gazed down from far away. She saw her body, and the inhumanly tall monster standing before it. She saw him wrench the dagger free, scattering her blood across the stone. The image darkened as her departing spirit receded. She listened carefully, and heard her name being called as if from a chorus of a thousand distant voices. One voice rose above the others, that of her mother, calling her to come, come toward the light, and she felt the love awaiting her there. She reached for the voices, to the blazing light.

Then the emotion of the voices began to change. They became fearful, urgent. Hurry! Faster! She looked back toward her far distant corpse, and her spirit screamed a soundless scream. A black *thing* pursued her. A portion of it stretched back to merge with the body of her murderer.

The voices grew nearer as she strived to reach them. And so did the thing draw nearer with its pursuit. She knew that once she was *there* she would be safe. It could not reach her there.

She was on the threshold of the light now, when suddenly the light was blotted out by something huge and impenetrable, blacker than the cosmic depths of deepest space. Formless, ethereal tentacles groped for her, hungry, relentless. She felt the nearness of her ancestors, calling for her to join them, but their hope was fading.

Substanceless pseudopods suddenly engulfed her, drawing her into the writhing black mass. It descended upon her spirit, devouring. Devouring.

****

He felt the power of her spirit surge through him like lightning. He had not devoured a human soul in at least a generation. He paused, savoring the feeling of her energy as it coursed through him. He snatched a nearly filled bowl from one of his servants, burying his face in the hot, frothy gore, and sucked a long draught. The power flowed into him, and he laughed again, licking his face with a long tongue as he handed the bowl back to his servant to capture the last of the bubbling vitae.

As the last drop fell, the servants knelt before him, chanting in their dead voices, offering their treasures. "By thy command, O omnipotent Uhr."

He took the bowls and strode away across the great circular hall, his heavy robes whispering with his movement.

The floor was a subtle pattern of obsidian mosaics, inlaid with silver and gold. He paid this beauty no heed, and ignored likewise the marvelous stonework above his head, the gorgeous cobweb-misted frescoes of gold, gray marble, and alabaster, the faded, dusty tapestries, moldering where they hung.

The hall narrowed to a long corridor. The far terminus was a thick, steel-bound wooden door, without latch or handle. The door swung inward in obedience to his muttered command, allowing the eerie red glow within to bathe him in its diseased heat. He crossed the threshold into the dark, low-ceilinged room beyond.

The stone awaited him just as it had for a thousand years, pulsing, alive. The Bloodstone's luminous scarlet pulsed like an obscene heart. Roughly the size of two fists together, its lower third was embedded in a craggy black stone pedestal jutting from the floor.

Uhr's voice rumbled like distant thunder. "The time has come." Laughter broke his words as he roared, "A thousand years! The Time...has come!"

****

The foggy sphere of Sirius III flashed beneath the nose of the streaking scoutcraft.

Lieutenant Commander Hamilton Corbin watched it disappear from the forward viewport, then verified their heading from the starchart. "Any more signs of our friends, Angus?" He cranked his head around to look back at his black bearded friend in the G-seat just behind his.

The tight pressure suit creaked in protest as Angus leaned forward to adjust the sensor sweep. Commander Angus MacTavish growled. "Bloody 'ell, no! I been scannin' for nearly an hour, and they ain't poked their ugly faces back through our sensor window."

"Course plotted and laid into navi-com, Commander MacTavish," Hamilton said, smiling slightly at his unaccustomed mention of rank. They had been friends too long for such things.

Angus grinned broadly for a moment at Hamilton's comment, then his face turned serious again. "Thank you, helm. Noted. But let's not engage the stardrive yet. I want to see if they show up again. Defense status, Commander Corbin?"

"Shields up, cannons charging. Full defense mode."

"Shut 'em down. Let 'em think we've relaxed. On my order, re-initiate full defense mode."

"Aye, aye, sir."

"Good God, man, will ye quit that already. Makes me feel like an officer."

Hamilton smiled and followed Angus's requests. His grayish-blue eyes danced over the console surrounding him as he glanced at the engineering station. He ran his fingers through his shock of sandy-blonde hair. "Need any more power to boost the sensor sweep?"

Angus shook his head. "Let's look nice and relaxed."

Hamilton stretched his wiry arms and yawned. It had indeed been a long two cycles since they had left their starcarrier. He gazed out the viewport into the cold, velvety starscape.

A tiny flash at the corner of his eye snagged his attention.

"What was that?" he wondered aloud.

Instantly attentive, Angus asked, "What was what? I didn't see anything on the scopes."

Hamilton's gaze searched the darkness outside. There, a twinkling. "Sorry, Angus. Only a star."

"A star!" Angus snorted, gesturing in mock disgust. "There you go, looking at stars again! Like we don't see 'em every minute of every day!"

Hamilton grinned at him, then turned his attention back to the far-away stellar body. There it was, one in billions, winking just at him alone, enticing him to come closer, just to see. A thrill rippled through him, and a smile stretched his lips. This was what he loved! Always something new, something that no human had ever seen in quite the same way. The longer he studied the star, the more it seemed to be the color of polished ivory, perhaps a little blue, a little yellow, and shining white. An ivory star. As he stared into the infinitely distant flames, he absently scratched at a peculiar twitching, tingling on his left breast.

Suddenly a blinding flash exploded in the viewport. Hamilton heard Angus's bellow. "Helm, full evasion mode!"

Hamilton blinked, trying to clear his vision as he hauled on the controls. The hull groaned in protest and the G-seats hugged their bodies at the violent direction change. The engines surged to full power, and the scoutcraft leaped to evasion velocity.

Angus was speaking, "...phantom proton pulse! Must have fired clean from n-space so we couldn't see them coming..."

"ID coming through. Four Asps, Mark IV fighter sleds."

"Smugglers," Angus said. "Tactical mode."

"Aye, aye," Hamilton said, touching his control console. A smooth black helmet descended from the cabin ceiling, settling over his head. The interior of the helmet hissed into place, snugly fitting his skull. Hamilton let his hands release the controls, and allowed his mind to take control of the ship's systems.

He heard Angus's voice in his ear speaker. "Do

it like only you know how, Hamilton."

The clear crystal faceplate came alive with alert messages and enemy blips. The blinding globes of the Dog Star and its Pup blazed to their right and below.

Hamilton said, "Eight hundred kilometers and closing."

"They're saving up," Angus said, "they won't miss again."

"Screens up."

"Cannons charging."

"Counter-measures enabled."

"Engines maxed."

"Four hundred klicks, Angus. Coming about to one-eight-zero, mark two-two. Missiles inbound! Two!"

Angus swore a blood-red streak.

* * * *

The stone's glow intensified as Uhr approached, its hunger growing with the blood's proximity. The blood in the bowls began to sizzle and hiss as the ravenous Bloodstone's ethereal touch caressed the precious liquid. Uhr's ancient lips began to drip the words of the incantation as he gathered his strength and will. With a rising voice he poured the rapidly congealing gore onto the pulsing surface of the stone.

The blood disappeared into the crystalline surface, and the Stone roared silently for more. The chant's unpronounceable words and unearthly tones seemed to coalesce upon the swirling air. The Bloodstone screamed the desire of its payment for power.

Uhr felt the agony of the ivory sun outside his palace as it turned the color of blood.

The bowls were empty, and the Bloodstone

blazed like a sun itself. Uhr crushed the heavy bowls like foil in his hands and cast them away from him. He thrust up his arms, howling, screaming, shrieking the last phrase of the horrible spell. A thunderclap rocked the entire palace, the city and the surrounding countryside, centered upon this very room. Uhr staggered under its impact, leaning against his black throne for support.

He felt the populace outside, sensed their screams, their utter panic at the sight of the blood-red sun. No matter. Soon the sun would return to its normal hue. But most importantly of all, he sensed that the Great Conjunction had been drawn nearer by his sorcery. The distance between the Day Stars had dwindled. The heavens had realigned themselves in his favor.

The Bloodstone slowly dimmed, slipping the chamber into darkness.

****

Hamilton Corbin leaped forward in his seat, straining at the straps. His ivory star had suddenly turned a horrible, red! Never had he heard of a star suddenly changing color in such a manner. And on his left breast, he felt a searing pain. Suddenly the ship convulsed and shuddered as if struck by a god's fist. Angus's voice roared in his ear. "...sus Christ, 'Amilton, wot're ye doon!"

Hamilton had been distracted by that star, and had hesitated just long enough for the missiles to hit them, when any other time he could have avoided them easily.

"Rear screens are doon. One more 'it and we're a debris field! Get us out o' 'ere, Ham! Engage star-drive!"

The ship leaped forward, and the nearer star-systems became streaks of bluish iridescent light as they flashed by. Hamilton heard Angus's sigh of relief, his Scottish accent slipping away. "They won't catch us now."

Hamilton looked at a flashing red light on his tactical screen. "We're off course," he said.

"What do ye mean we're off course? I thought the course was calculated and entered."

"It was, I swear." Hamilton concentrated. He could not seem to remember giving the command to engage the stardrive. He heard an alarm beep in his ear.

"Our drive isn't rated for this n-factor, Ham. Wot's goin' on?"

Hamilton could not answer. He stared at the single motionless point of light in the viewport, a sick scarlet beacon, directly before them.

Angus's voice began to lose composure, letting the Scottish brogue back in. "'Elm, disengage stardrive, re-enter normal space and recompute."

Hamilton shook off his fascination. "Aye, aye." He gave the mental commands. No response.

The ship suddenly shuddered with a muffled explosion behind them. The console exploded into fountains of smoke and sparks.

"Stardrive is gone!" Angus cried.

"Then why are we still in n-space!"

Angus's reply was masked by another explosion.

Hamilton felt himself pulled back into his seat with a sudden acceleration. Hamilton tried to speak and found he could not. The instrument console and viewport began to look stretched and warped. His hands grew long and thin.

A stabbing pain in his left breast flared almost to ecstasy. He curled over like a dry leaf.

The last thing he saw as they hurtled through space-time was his bloody ivory star.

Chapter 1

The little man dreamed. He dreamed of power, and of riches beyond imagining. He dreamed of powerful men squirming like bugs under his omnipotent thumb, and an army of little boys to serve his whim. His magnitude shadowed the land itself, and he was master of all he surveyed. Then a shadow even larger than his fell across him, a figure that bestrode the world. His small body erupted in a clammy sweat like it always did in the Master's presence, and he squirmed like a child in his bed. Blood-red eyes blazed in the monolithic darkness. And a nameless dread, like the feet of an icy rat, scuttled up and down his crooked spine.

Lord Sneev sat bolt upright, gasping for breath. A single droplet of cold sweat left a moist trail across his liver spotted pate, across his wrinkled forehead, down his hooked nose. He stared wide-eyed for a moment at his trembling hands, then glanced at the lumpy figure snoring fitfully beside him. His wife, Prilla, rolled over in the darkness.

The cold hand of the Master's presence still sent trembling chills through his gaunt frame. Uhr had contacted him in his dreams, as he was often wont. But what had the message been? Ah, well, it would come to him soon enough. It always did.

He threw aside the silk bedcovers, parted the velvet curtains and slid out of bed. The stone floor was cold on his small feet, and he stepped gingerly over the rug beside the warmly glowing hearth. He rubbed his misshapen hands together for warmth, and shivered as a stiff night breeze slammed open the shutter. Pale moonlight splashed a silvery shape on the floor.

He cursed quietly, careful not to wake his wife. The last thing he needed now was to hear her wagging tongue. Rubbing his thin arms for warmth, he stepped towards the window to close the shutter. He paused to look out over his domain, the land of Ophidia, sprawling far below. The lush forests and valleys were black in the moonlight. Sneev's chamber window, indeed his fortress, rested on a towering stone crag, jutting like a dark sentinel above the valleys below and the sleeping town of Cragmoor hunched at the base of the stone crag. He looked toward the east, toward the neighboring land of Armond, the holding of Lord Valerion. Someday, Valerion's domain would be his as well. Sneev alone would rule half of Irth. Under the Master's guiding hand, of course. Of course.

He dabbed at the sweat slicking his pate with the sleeve of his nightrobes. Ahh, the message was coming...

All Holy Chaos! The One had come! The Time of Uhr's Reckoning, as prophesied in ages past, was at hand! All the scheming the Master had done to avoid the fulfillment of the ancient prophecy would come to naught unless the Master acted quickly. For him to do so, Sneev must act expeditiously, and secure The One before any damage could be done to the Master's plans.

His brow furrowed in thought as he weighed the possibilities. The One and his dragon had arrived somewhere in Armond.

Sneev rubbed his forehead with a still-trembling hand. If Ophidian soldiers were caught in Armond, at the very least Lord Valerion would require an extensive explanation and a public apology. The thought of that filled Sneev with revulsion. But The One must be captured, and quickly. Then he realized that the Master had planted The One's location in his mind. He could take a small force of warriors, ride hard, take The One, and get out of Armond before Valerion was any the wiser! He slammed the shutter closed, turned and sought out his riding clothes.

His wife stirred as he dressed. Her voice was dreamy. "Sneev?"

"Yes, my dear."

"What are you doing?"

"Nothing, my Prilla, go back to sleep."

"Yes, my lord."

He buckled his rapier to his hip, thrust open the bedchamber door, stepped into the hallway. "Brudge!" he screeched. His short, bowed legs carried him down the corridor as best they could.

"Brudge!" His voice echoed down the empty hall.

A door whipped open just ahead of him, and a massive, ungainly shape appeared, scratching his backside. "Aye, my lord?"

"At last. You're to come when I call."

The rotund man flinched at the acid in his master's voice. "Yes, my lord." He bowed low, his bulbous belly dangling below him.

"Up, oaf. Heed me carefully."

Brudge straightened, and threw back his mop of greasy brown hair. "Yes, my lord." His voice was low and nasal. Slaver trickled from the corner of his mouth, which he wiped with the back of his hand.

Sneev grimaced, once again repulsed by his servant's appearance. As a child, Brudge had been mauled by a bullock. His nose had been crushed, his cheek split wide from the corner of his mouth to his shattered cheekbone. Breath now whistled through the lump of flesh that was his nose, and his mouth was twisted into a perpetual sneer.

"Rouse the stable boys, and bid them prepare twenty mounts. And waken the First Watch. They will accompany me."

"Accompany you?" Brudge blinked. "May I ask where to, my lord?"

"No, you may not. Obey me."

"Aye, my lord." At that Brudge spun and trundled away, leaving Sneev to rouse his servants. His tongue lashed his pages to wakefulness as the groggy boys buckled up his chain mail chausses and plate greviere, pulled the chainmail hauberk over his head, rattled the loose plates of demi-brassart into place on his upper arms. They buckled the breastplate into place, covering it with a bright green jupon embroidered in gold with three intertwining serpents. Sneev fidgeted and scolded with his acid tongue throughout the process. Finally he was fully prepared, and left his chambers for the stable, armor jangling, rapier rattling at his hip, spurs ringing on the stone floor, gleaming bascinet under his arm with the attached camail dangling below.

He stepped out into the night, taking the chilly air into his frail lungs in a deep, wheezing breath. The night was beginning its submission to the sun's approach, still and quiet. The only sounds were the noise of his accouterments and the voices emanating from the orange-glowing stable doorway a few dozen paces ahead of him. As he neared the stable, he saw two agitated stable boys standing in the torchlit opening, watching some commotion within.

Suddenly a sickening snap echoed in the dark silence, followed by a shriek of agony. A horse screamed in terror, and the stable boys bolted back into the stable out of sight. Sneev hurried toward the stable as best he could. He heard Brudge's voice, whimpering, cursing, crying in pain. He stepped into the flickering orange light within.

Two squires dragged on the reins of a rearing, terrified gelding, its sharp hooves thrashing the air. Brudge lay in the straw, curled in a ball, clutching his sickeningly bent leg. Steaming crimson stained the golden straw from the wound in the side of Brudge's lower leg, made by the protruding spear of blood-smeared bone.

Sneev's sword was in his hand. The horse's eyes bulged in terror, the whites gleaming in the darkness of the stable corner. The tip of Sneev's rapier drew a thin red line across the horse's quaking belly from shoulder to flank. The thin line exploded into a spill of gushing entrails, and the beast squealed in agony. Its thrashing legs tangled in its frothing guts as it went down into the straw. After several moments its movement slowed, and finally stopped. Its breath wheezed through the gore frothing from its nose and mouth.

Sneev licked his lips, wiped the smile of pleasure from them before he turned. He looked at Brudge's quaking form, and pointed his finger at two stable boys. "You and you. Take this lump of offal to the leech. He will not be accompanying me."

Just then, a fully armed and armored man-at-arms stepped into the stable. "First Watch is assembled and awaiting your command, my lord."

"Very good, sergeant. We have experienced but

a brief delay here."

Sneev saw the sergeant's hard eyes flicker towards the mutilated carcass, saw the instant of utter contempt on his scarred features.

Sneev stepped around him, out into the darkness. His gaze swept the group of warriors lined up before him. He chose one, the largest and fiercest in the front row. "You," he said, pointing.

The man-at-arms stepped forward. "Aye, my lord."

"Your name?"

"Rivat, my lord."

"Sergeant Rivat, strip the former Sergeant Lugh of his weapons, and escort him to the dungeon for insubordination and treason to our noble person."

Sergeant Lugh snarled, hauling his broadsword free of its sheath. "Yer a bloody horsekiller!" His sword leaped into an arc of destruction with Sneev's bare head as the target.

Another blade flashed downward, cleaving through mail and wrist. A thin, warm spray misted Sneev's face. Lugh's sword clanged onto the cobblestones, still clutched by the severed fist. Lugh's roar of pain was cut short as Rivat's blade hacked again, this time into the back of his neck. The heavy steel shore through steel links of chain, deep into Lugh's neck. Lugh groaned and tumbled onto his face. His bascinet tumbled off his head, and wobbled slowly away across the cobblestones.

One of the men-at-arms coughed uncomfortably in the tense silence.

Rivat wiped his blood-smeared steel on Lugh's surcoat. "What are your wishes, my lord?" he said.

Sneev grinned in pleasure. "Most excellent, Sergeant Rivat." He raised his voice. "All of you, take heed of what happens to those disloyal to me." He turned back to Rivat. "Prepare the men for departure. Their mounts are nearly ready."

Two stable boys, assisted a whimpering Brudge out of the stable, one under each round arm.

"Brudge, you dolt!" Sneev slapped the hideous face. "You knew not how to handle a horse! And now, you've forced me to kill a good mount! Let this be a lesson to you!"

Brudge's voice was faint and strained. "Aye, m'lord."

"Take him away," Sneev said. "And, Brudge, have someone dispose of Sergeant Lugh before sunrise. I do not wish to disturb my family."

Brudge mumbled something as the squires half-dragged him away.

"Well now, Sergeant Rivat, let us be off," Sneev said nonchalantly. He raised his voice, "Open the gates!"

The men-at-arms mounted their horses, and two squires hoisted Sneev's armored body into the saddle. The mounted warriors formed a double file line behind Sneev and Rivat inside the slowly opening gates. The drawbridge rattled down just beyond the rising spikes of the iron portcullis.

"Forward!" Sneev cried, raising his spindly arm.

The column crossed the thick wooden drawbridge. Sneev was careful not to glance down over the side of the drawbridge. Below the heavy wood and iron was two hundred feet of empty air. The road spiraled down, around the outside of the towering crag into the dark, sleeping village of Cragmoor.

After they had left the boundary of the village, Sneev urged his men to speed. They must be quick, and discreet, oh, so discreet.

More speed. Faster. They barreled down the road cut through the surrounding forest, to the east, toward Armond. They spurred their mounts to full gallop for as long as the animals could bear it, and beyond. Late morning found them crossing the border, leaving the lush woods of Ophidia for the bare, grassy hills and plains of Armond.

****

Consciousness slowly returned to Hamilton Corbin. With consciousness came pain, joined like Siamese twins. His eyes opened to pitch darkness. His hand groped for the strap buckles, and he winced with every movement. The control helmet's interior neuro-sensor sheath had not retracted, and was squeezing his battered skull like a fist. His ears burned in pain as he tried to work the tight-fitting helmet off his head. Finally he managed it, and tossed the worthless lump aside.

"Angus?"

He twisted his body, spasms of hot pain shooting through his bruised muscles, to grope where he knew Angus would be. He found Angus's knee, and shook it. "Angus!"

The big Scotsman stirred in the darkness. "Christ alive, I hurt!"

"Yeah," Hamilton said, "me, too."

"Where are we?"

"God knows. Ship's totally dead."

"What happened?"

"I...don't remember."

"I mean, how'd we get here? Where are we?"

"I haven't a clue."

"I remember Sirius..." Angus said, his voice trailing off.

"Then nothing," Hamilton said. Somehow Hamilton knew that they had landed somewhere. How long they'd been unconscious he had no idea. All the chronometers had apparently died with the ship's power. He heard Angus's straps snap open, and Angus rummaging through the emergency supply case beneath the seat. A tiny, feeble point of light appeared, spearing into Hamilton's eyes.

"I found a light," Angus said. The beam diverted into the supply case briefly, then darted about the cabin. Then its light began to die. "Be damned if it ain't almost dead! And with a fresh fuel rod at that!" The dying beam flashed around, illuminating the melted, blackened instruments and control panels about the cabin. "Every damn thing," he muttered hopelessly. He cast the spot of brightness about, holding it for a moment on a shattered glass case just behind them. They both looked hopefully inside the niche. Inside were two vacuum helmets and their accompanying rebreathers. The helmets were spider-webbed with microfine cracks, and the rebreathers were blackened by fire. Angus groaned, "We're dead."

"Not so fast, Commander," Hamilton said, trying to keep Angus from a fit of brooding. He grabbed Angus's wrist to direct the dim beam toward the forward viewport. "Soil, at least. See the roots? We've landed somewhere."

Angus paused, a glimmer of hope appearing on his face for but an instant before it disappeared. "Yeah, but where?"

"Right now, who cares? With the ship dead, our atmosphere's gonna go stale any time."

"Aye, I guess ye're right, ye damned optimist." At that he heaved his bulk out of the seat, stepped around to the hatch just behind it, pressed the release control. Nothing happened. "Damned hatch!" He punched the metal, slipping further into his ancestral accent, "Open oop, ye bugger!"

"Angus," Hamilton said, speaking quietly and evenly, moving past the seats to him, "The ship's totally dead. There's no power to open the hatch.

Use the manual release."

Cursing, Angus fumbled with his rapidly dying light, trying to work the crank.

Angus paused for a moment, then said, "Well, Ham, just in case the environment's deadly, it was good knowing you."

Hamilton said, "We'll be all right." He smiled crookedly, and clapped Angus on the shoulder, trying to put his friend at ease even though he himself was not.

Angus took a deep breath, held it and spun the crank. There came the hiss of air, and brilliant white sunlight flooded the small chamber.

"Hah!" Angus said, grinning. "Real air! At least no death by suffocation!" He disappeared out the opening. "A Terra-class planet."

Hamilton hurriedly followed. As he climbed from the dead craft, a warm, fresh breeze touched his face, and he looked about. The small scoutcraft had plowed a long furrow across a vast expanse of green, rolling hills. An exquisite blue sky streaked with ribbons of fluffy white stretched above them, and a huge white sun rose from the horizon.

Hamilton released a slow breath in perfect awe. Then he looked at the sun for a moment, shielding his eyes, and blinking away the spots. Its color was familiar.... Could this be?

Angus disappeared back into the ship. Hamilton heard him curse again. "Emergency beacon's dead as hell, too, " Angus said.

"Then we're stuck here," Hamilton said dreamily, admiring the magnificent landscape around them.

"'Odsbodikin, man, are ye daft?" Angus said incredulously.

Hamilton turned and looked at him squarely. "I don't see a spaceport anywhere, do you?"

Angus's eyes scanned the horizon. "I suppose not."

But as Angus looked out at the landscape again, Hamilton was pleased when he saw his eyes flash with the old determination that had gotten them both through the Academy, the will to conquer, to succeed, to pioneer. Whatever happened now, Hamilton thought, Angus would take it in stride. "Let's dig out the rations, Ham," Angus said, ducking back inside. Hamilton followed him.

Then Hamilton heard a sound that was vaguely familiar, one that he had never before heard first hand.

Angus's head jerked up, "Did you hear that?"

"Yeah, what was it?"

"A horse."

Hamilton suddenly glanced about. "Angus! There!" He pointed toward the ridge of a hill overlooking the valley where their ship lay. At least twenty mounted warriors stood along the ridge of the hill.

****

As his phalanx of armored horsemen crested the ridge, Sneev raised his gauntleted hand to gesture a halt. He raised himself up in the stirrups, shielding his eyes against the late-morning sun as he surveyed the grassy valley and hills below them, looking for anything that might mark The One's location. He knew he was close, he could feel it.

"My lord," Sergeant Rivat said, pointing toward the crest of a hill on the opposite side of the valley before them, "what is that?"

Sneev turned his beady eyes. "Ahh!" he breathed when he saw the beginning of a deep furrow gouged from the sod. "Very good, Sergeant.

Excellent eyes!" He raised his hand again, giving the signal to proceed.

Soon their party reached the spot where the furrow began. Sneev looked down the length, and spied no opposite end for at least a league off in the hazy distance. The furrow was ten feet deep in places, gone in others, as if that which had made it had bounced and skidded like a flat stone. Sneev motioned his men to proceed.

After at least a league's travel, they topped the final ridge. Sneev raised his hand, and the column halted, surveying the wide grassy sward below. A beast such as Sneev had never seen lay nose down at the end of the furrow. The thing was perhaps forty paces long from the point of its silver-metallic nose, half-buried in the dirt, to the heat-blackened, tailless rear end. A single fin rose into the air along its metal backbone, and, like the two wings sprouting from the sides, was hard metal. A black, toothless mouth gaped on top of its head, and there were markings on its sides, unintelligible runes scribed around a circle and peculiar emblem.

"A silver dragon!" Rivat breathed, his eyes wide.

"Silence!" Sneev hissed. Too late. The other men-at-arms gasped almost as one, and began murmuring among themselves.

Sneev laughed suddenly, "Hah! 'Tis no dragon! Merely a large wagon, or a chariot! Doubtless one of the Master's contraptions. We are here to capture one of the Master's escaped slaves. The slave stole this contraption in his escape. We want him alive, but beware, he is powerful."

"Then where is he, my lord?" Rivat asked.

Sneev shot him a glare. "Obviously inside this contraption. Forward now."

Then two men emerged from the mouth of the

thing. Two men? Sneev thought. Which was The One?

"Obviously there were two slaves," Sneev said quickly.

The two men were clad in some strange cloth that resembled the hide of this massive thing, with no clasp or buckle in view. Sneev appraised them as his band slowly approached. One of them was tall, well over six feet, well-muscled, with a handsome black beard and strongly chiseled features. The other was a sandy-blond, about six feet tall. Sneev mused that this other was not overly handsome, but neither was he ugly. The man enjoyed an attractive mediocrity.

The two men had noticed their approach.

Rivat barked orders to the men-at-arms, and they fanned out to slowly encircle the strange object.

Hamilton and Angus could only watch their approach.

"Too bad the weapons are drained, too," Angus sighed.

"What if they're friendly?"

"What if they're not? They don't look very friendly to me."

Their scoutcraft was ringed now by fierce-looking humans wearing medieval-style mail and helmets, carrying large kite shields. Their weapons were safely in their sheaths. One of them, small and ratlike, clad in the finest armor and a surcoat of forest green embroidered with gold, stepped his horse into the ring. The man smiled broadly, baring his crooked yellow teeth. The smile did not reach his eyes. His gestured widely for them to come down from the top of the craft, speaking in a language they had never heard before.

Hamilton smiled, stepping forward with his open hand upraised in greeting. "Hello," he said, in English. "We are friends." He received no response, even when he tried the greeting in three other Standard languages.

"What are humans doing here?" Angus said.

"Who knows where 'here' is?"

Angus shrugged. "Maybe some lost colony. I haven't ever heard of one of this nature."

"I didn't have time to chart the star I saw. I know this sun, but I don't know where it is."

"What're ye bloody talkin' aboot?"

Hamilton shook his head. "Never mind. I'll tell you about it later."

"I hope you have a chance," Angus said, as the ring of horsemen began to tighten.

The small leader of the men-at-arms said something else, then a look of bitter frustration flickered across his face as he saw they did not comprehend.

Then the man next to him cocked his head, listening, and now Hamilton heard it also. A low rumble just over the ridge, opposite the direction from which these men had come, growing louder.

The little man barked an order as he watched the close horizon.

The soldiers suddenly pressed close about Hamilton and Angus.

"Wot th' bloody—" Angus ejaculated before the spear shaft cracked across the back of his skull, and he fell senseless into the grass.

"No, plea—" Hamilton began before he, too was struck.

Two men slid off their mounts and quickly hoisted them onto their horses' backs, lashing them behind the saddles.

"Haste, men!" Sneev cried, "Valerion's men are upon us!"

"Round 'em up, lads," Rivat roared. "They're coming!"

A cloud of dust rose like a great bird of prey over the ridge.

As the prisoners were secured, Sneev cried, "Let us away!"

But it was too late as their enemies broke the skyline. With a fevered glance back, Sneev wiped the cold, terrified sweat from his eyes. The phalanx of enemy riders bore down upon them. He wheeled his steed, pulled his rapier free of its scabbard. "You with the prisoners, flee! The rest of us shall detain them!"

The two soldiers raced away with their burdens, up over the ridge.

The wedge of enemy horsemen crashed through Sneev's men, sending horses and men screaming into the dirt. Steel rang on steel, hacked into bone and flesh, splattering the grass with hot scarlet.

Lord Sneev cast about him. The enemy's first charge had downed nearly everyone. He saw a familiar face in the knot of the enemy glaring at him with pure hatred. "Not today, Robinton!" Sneev cried, wheeling his mount, gouging his spurs into its flanks. The horse screamed and leaped into a gallop away from the battle.

But there stood Sergeant Rivat, broadsword in hand, directly in his path, trying to direct the men under his command, unaware of Sneev's impending flight.

Sneev shrieked, "Out of the way!"

Rivat's hard eyes fastened on him, and in that instant Sneev read the warrior's loathing for his fleeing lord. As he galloped past, Sneev drove the point of his rapier into Rivat's eye socket, and the corpse toppled backward from the saddle. The sounds of battle died away as he crested the ridge, running for home.

Chapter 2

She watched in puzzlement as the men-at-arms carried the two strangers up the tower stairs. The house was abuzz with the news of her step-father's early morning excursion with a score of his best men-at-arms. Only her stepfather and two of the men-at-arms had returned, and they were carrying two senseless strangers with them.

She watched Lord Sneev as he stepped into the great hall from the daylight. His eyes were downcast, darting nervously about the room. She smiled inwardly. That was the expression his face bore when he was hiding something. She tossed back her waves of auburn hair, smoothed her gown, put on her best smile and approached him. Her inward smile broadened at his grimace of dread when he noticed her.

"Fair morrow, my dear," Sneev said, his voice betraying his distaste for her conversation.

She gave him an uncharacteristic curtsey, "Fair morrow, my lord. I trust you had an...adventurous morning."

Seizing the opportunity, Sneev unraveled his tale of their terrible ambush by Valerion's finest warriors, of how Sneev's stalwart men had killed nearly all the filthy Armondians, of how he himself had slain the last of Valerion's men-at-arms. But alas, all his men had been slain in the battle, leaving only Sneev and two of his men to return home.

He attempted to step around her and make his escape, but she moved almost imperceptibly to block his path. "But who were those two strangers your men carried through here?"

Twin surges of pride and malice rose up in his gullet. She had done that so masterfully, but how he hated it being done to him! "Ah, merely two escaped bandits, my dear. Nothing more."

"Bandits? Taken to the *tower*, my lord?"

"Yes, yes, yes, my dear. Now, if I may, I have business to attend." He took a step around her.

"Of course, my lord." She moved aside, and watched him stride away as quickly as his stunted legs would carry him. Bandits, indeed! The tower room had been empty for years. There must be something special about these men for her stepfather to open up the tower room. A burning curiosity fired her will to answer these questions. She would find the answers somehow. She had her ways.

Sneev stepped into the tower room, breathing heavily from the long climb up the steps. The two men lay senseless upon plain straw pallets hastily thrown down in the center of the circular room. A brilliant square of white sunlight streaming in from the open window framed them. He drew his poniard, tested the needle-sharp point with his finger, and approached them. His first target was the most likely One, the burly, black-bearded man with the handsome features. He touched the point of the blade to the man's chest, against the strange silvery cloth that wrapped both of them so tightly, and drew the point down toward the waist. The strange garment split neatly open, revealing the torso black with fur, and the thin line of blood welling from Sneev's cut. Sneev's fingers and eyes searched through the thick, curly hair on the man's chest, seeking the birthmark that would seal his doom. But this one had no birthmark! He searched again in bewilderment, then snorted in disgust.

"Bah! This is not The One," he grumbled.

Sneev stepped back from this one, looking at the other. Could the Master have been mistaken? This other could not be The One. He looked so...terribly plain. Sneev shook his head, turned away to leave. This man couldn't be The One. He slipped the poniard back into its sheath.

But his hand paused on the door handle. The Master had never been wrong before, and if he found that Sneev had been less than thorough, the punishment was likely to be severe. The Master's punishments were *always* severe.

He stepped up to the other, whipped out his blade. A quick slice bared the lightly tufted chest, and even a cursory glance spied the bold white birthmark emblazoned on the man's left breast. Gods and the Master, but it was true! He never truly believed that he would see The One with his own eyes, much less have The One completely in his power. A thrill of power-lust swept through him, and his dagger-hand twitched, pricking the skin. Oh, how his hands quivered to carve the flesh off this one, little by little! His ears burned to hear the sizzle of blood on hot coals.

But wait. He must not allow himself to become too enraptured. This man was the Master's private meat, to do with as he pleased. His hand fought returning the dagger to its scabbard, and he quickly left the room lest his urges overcome him.

"Aldive," Sneev shouted, struggling to be heard above the kitchen's clamor. He peered through the milling people and clouds of roiling steam and smoke, and daubed sweat from his liver-spotted pate with a kerchief. "Aldive!" he repeated.

Faintly, from across the room, he heard an answer. "Aye, m'lord!" The lanky old butler turned away from the steward he had been tongue-lashing, and attended his master, threading his way through the throng of sweaty bodies. Aldive bowed slightly, his moist gray hair falling before his eyes. "At your service, my lord Sneev."

"What is the condition of the noble Brudge?" Sneev inquired.

The sarcasm in Sneev's voice was not lost on Aldive. He looked down his aquiline nose suppressing an arrogant snicker. "The, ah, noble Brudge is faring quite well for one of his, ah, size. The leech has set his leg, and the squires have fastened him a crutch that he might hobble about."

Sneev grinned crookedly, amused by the thought of the sight of Brudge struggling about on crutches. "Very good. Very good."

"Have you any more wishes of me, my lord? I must have a cook flogged before noonday."

Sneev lowered his voice so only Aldive could hear. "There are two men in the tower room"

"Aye, my lord, I had heard."

Sneev winced. Already the news was everywhere. He continued, "Strip them of their strange garments, and leave clean dress for them. It's my wish that they believe themselves honored guests while we keep them under tight lock and key."

"May I inquire of my lord why?"

Sneev glanced about, opened his mouth to speak, then stopped himself. He shook his head. "Too much has been spread about them already. It is best that you know not, at least right now. I will answer your questions in due time."

Aldive straightened. "As you wish, my lord."

Sneev continued. "It is enough that you know I await orders from the Master. They must not be in the least suspicious."

Aldive snapped a bow. "As you wish, my lord."

Sneev turned to leave, then spun back. "And have a messenger sent to my sitting chamber."

"Aye, my lord."

Angus stirred. He groaned and opened his eyes, squinting as the bright sunlight pouring over him from the wide window compounded the ache of the knots on his skull. He saw bare wooden rafters, old and cracked in the shadows above, supporting the conical roof. The walls were bare stone blocks, as was the floor.

"Wot th' 'ell...!" he jerked erect. He was naked, lying on a crude straw mat. Hamilton lay unconscious and naked on another mat a couple of paces away. A pan, a cloth, a platter of food and two neatly folded sets of clothing rested on a rickety-looking table sitting against the wall. A brass chamber pot squatted enticingly in the corner, and Angus did not hesitate to use it.

The tremendous ache between his ears was dying, albeit slowly, leaving him free to notice the stinging pain in his chest as clotted blood tugged at his curly hairs, and stiffened the flesh around the shallow cut. He swore in anger and amazement at the rust-colored line running straight down his chest. And his pressure suit was gone.

He heard Hamilton's voice, groggy and confused. "You alive, Mac?"

"As ever, mate," Angus replied dryly, stepping up to the window.

Hamilton moaned, fingering his scalp. "Where are we?"

Angus leaned against the stone sill, gazing out the open window, smiling wryly. "We're in a bloody castle, imprisoned in the bloody 'ighest tower room, with bloody knights in shinin' armor kippin' aboot below."

"You're joking."

"Would I lie to ye, laddie?"

Hamilton stood up, pausing for moment to gain his equilibrium in spite of his pounding head, and joined Angus at the window. Hamilton's breath left him in a whistling gasp. He stared down the sheer tower wall, to the featureless cliff side below, to the road winding down around the crag five hundred feet below. The clangor of arms turned their eyes toward the courtyard below, just barely in sight, where a few men-at-arms drilled and practiced. But nothing compared to the sight of the sprawling valley below, sparkling with a hundred hues of green, lush forest and fields, stretching to the horizon, with the brilliant white sun high overhead. A cool breeze fresh with the smell of healthy greenery wafted into their faces from far, far below.

"I've never seen land like this before," Hamilton breathed.

"She is pretty, ain't she?"

"There's nothing like this left on Earth is there?"

"There is," Angus said, "but not much. Parts o' my homeland still look thisaway. Small parts. Nothing like to this, though."

"I'd given up on ever seeing anything like this."

Angus scowled at him, "Ye ain't startin' to like it here, are ye? We're bloody prisoners!"

"Then let's enjoy what we can then, eh, Angus?" Hamilton said, still looking outside.

Angus searched his face, and found him dead serious. He could not help but smile. "Yeah, I suppose. But my stomach is about to eat me. There's some food over here. There's bread, and I think this substance is cheese." Angus took the loaf of hard, fresh bread, broke it into equal portions and tossed a share to Hamilton, who gnawed on it absently as he stared out the window. The slab of orange cheese soon followed, and a ceramic carafe filled with water washed it all down.

As Angus ate, he examined the iron-bound wooden door, and found it quite sturdy. "They sure know how to build a prison."

Hamilton said, "I don't think this room is a prison. Look at the dust all over everything. I don't think it's been used in a long, long time." Just then a draft of chilly wind raised gooseflesh on his body, and he was suddenly conscious of his nakedness.

"Well, maybe they haven't taken any prisoners in a long, long time."

Hamilton ignored Angus's sardonic tone, and quickly dressed himself in the clothes provided. He found himself garbed in coarse brown breeks and a dull red tunic, both of which were a little too loose, but he did not care. Angus followed suit, and just in time.

There was scuffling on the opposite side of the door, and the door abruptly swung inward. A small weasely man stepped tentatively into the room, and seeing they were awake, smiled broadly, baring his crooked yellow teeth. He spread his arms in a magnanimous gesture, as if very pleased to have them as his guests. Hamilton immediately remembered him as the leader of the men who had captured them.

They merely watched him in suspicion for a few moments. Then Angus stood at attention, and spoke up formally. "I am Commander Angus MacTavish of the League of Worlds Interstellar Navy. This is Lieutenant Commander Hamilton Corbin. We request proper treatment under the authority of the League of Worlds."

The man merely stared at them blankly, obviously uncomprehending of anything Angus had said, still smiling like a crocodile. He was beginning to struggle to keep his lips properly stretched.

Seeing this, Angus relaxed, and said to Hamilton conversationally, "Well, what do you think the little weasel wants?"

"No idea."

Finally the little man cordially beckoned for them to follow him. They glanced at one another.

"What the hell," Angus said, and they followed him out of the door and down the tower stairs.

Lord Sneev brought them into a large serving hall, where Sneev's house and court sat at the noon meal.

The two Terrans marveled at this sight straight out of Earth's Middle Ages. Long wooden tables laden with heaping platters of crude food. Men and women dressed in medieval European garb chatted and ate about the tables, seated on long wooden benches.

Hamilton surveyed the room, his eyes catching two notable women seated at a table raised above the floor on a three foot platform. One of them was a slightly plump, rusty-haired middle aged woman, who, in her youth, might have been pretty.

Seated beside her, however, was vision of loveliness. Hamilton's jaw fell open. He heard Angus's hiss of breath as he spotted her, too. She had seen them enter, and her eyes locked with Hamilton's and he felt his stomach flip as he fell into those bottomless green caverns framed by luscious auburn hair and flawless alabaster skin. Her eyes quickly swept away, a frown of puzzlement creasing her shapely brow.

Sneev saw Tamarra's interest, and tugged quickly at Hamilton's sleeve to draw him away. He took them to his library, where he intended to made them as comfortable as possible. He shut the tall, brass-bound door behind them.

He smiled at them again. Gods, how he hated that. He pointed to himself. "Sneev."

He saw their faces animate with comprehension. "Hamilton Corbin," said The One.

"Angus MacTavish," spoke the other, thumbing his furred chest.

The little man nodded, reaching back to tug a long cord dangling from a hole in the ceiling. Hamilton thought he heard a bell ring somewhere. In a few moments, the door opened to admit a tall, austere figure. Arrogance dripped from him like slime. He spoke something to the one called Sneev, never taking his eyes from the lowly strangers before him. After a brief conversation, Sneev curtly nodded to them and left the room.

Hamilton glanced about, trying to ignore the tall, lanky man glaring at them. The room was not too large, but was filled from floor to ceiling with rows of dusty books. The man spoke, introducing himself as Aldive, and began to pull books down from the shelves to place them on a table in the center of the room. Aldive impatiently beckoned them nearer, and gestured that they pay close attention. Immediately they realized that he was trying to teach them his language. They looked once at each other, then set themselves to the task.

Chapter 3

Hamilton and Angus made outstanding students, even though Aldive made a poor teacher. Over the course of several days, they managed to develop a rudimentary vocabulary. Aldive's amazement at their proficiency for learning managed to show through his miasma of arrogance. He was not necessarily pleased, just amazed. The many long hours were fraught with countless harsh stares from Aldive if a word was mispronounced, or the wrong verb tense used, but the students quickly learned to ignore him and concentrate on the language.

The spoken language was remarkably similar in structure and vocabulary to the ancient Germanic Terran languages, such as English and German, but had many pronunciations similar to Gaelic. The written language was again similar, with an alphabet of twenty characters, which appeared to be a mishmash of descendants of Roman, Greek and Nordic characters.

With this information in mind, Hamilton and Angus managed to come up with several wildly different theories on the origins of the people on this world. Perhaps this was some long lost human colony from the early days of space exploration, gone to the medieval dogs. But if that were true, they would have needed stardrives much more powerful than any in existence even now to reach a system as remote as this one must be. Perhaps he and Angus had passed through a space-time rift to this area of the galaxy, and by some freak of fate landed on an Earth of some alternate reality. Perhaps this world, totally isolated from Earth, had evolved a species and culture so remarkably similar to Earth that differences in the scheme of things were insignificant. This latter idea was thrown out when they found that the people called their world 'Irth'. This lent more credence to the first idea, and so on, and so forth. The ramifications of any of those theories were staggering. So they gave up, at least temporarily, on trying to solve the mystery, and concentrated on learning as much as they could.

One of their most intriguing discoveries about this culture was the legends of the Day Stars, The Prophecy, and The One. They discovered these when Aldive mentioned The Prophecy, apparently by mistake, because he quickly changed the subject, pressing on with lessons, and was careful never to mention it again. Hamilton, his curiosity piqued, read more on those subjects when Aldive was not present. The entire culture seemed to revolve around the movements of the Day Stars, three stars visible even during the day, and their future conjunction. The Prophecy was the foretelling of the coming of some great savior, called The One, who would rid them of all evil. His rudimentary knowledge of the written language prevented him from completely understanding what was written.

On the evening of the fifth day, after Aldive had left them to prepare the evening meal, Angus and Hamilton relaxed in the padded, high-backed chairs in Sneev's library. Since their arrival, they had been completely isolated, confined either to their tower room or this library. Of course, Sneev had been very cordial, trying to make them feel comfortable, but it was confinement nonetheless. Angus stretched his thick arms and legs, groaning in pleasure. He said in English, "Strange how they first club us, then teach us to speak."

Hamilton nodded, his voice nearly hoarse from the long hours of speaking. His mind had turned to the beautiful woman he had seen, she of the gorgeous auburn hair.

Angus, heedless of Hamilton's reverie, continued, "I don't trust a single person we've met so far. Sneev is a two-faced lyin' bastard, I tell you."

Hamilton nodded, only half listening.

Abruptly the door opened, and a squire came in. "Will you come with me, my lords?"

They followed him to the dining hall, where the evening meal was in progress. Hamilton and Angus looked out over the sea of bent heads, to see Sneev grinning and beckoning them to the high table. Two empty chairs waited beside a porcine man on Sneev's left. On Sneev's right hand sat his rather plump wife, and then the beauty that they had glimpsed days earlier. Hamilton's eyes fixed on her. Shining auburn braids framed her perfect face. Two large green pools turned towards him, then quickly averted, alabaster cheeks reddening.

Hamilton and Angus made their way to the high table, climbed the steps.

"Ah, my friends, I am pleased to have you dine with me. Please enjoy my hospitality." Sneev smiled graciously with a magnanimous gesture.

"Thank you, Lord Sneev," said Hamilton, using a very formal form. "May the Sun shine on your house."

"My thanks, too, great lord, " Angus said, following Hamilton's example. "May your lands prosper under the Sun's care."

Sneev smiled, impressed at their fluency. "May the Sun light all your journeys." He bowed his head slightly. "Sit and eat, my friends! You are guests in my house."

Hamilton took the chair beside the hideous man seated next to Sneev. He noticed the rude crutch on the floor next to the man's chair. The man glared at him from under heavy brows, as if measuring him somehow, then looked away as if unsatisfied. The court finery and perfume that swathed him did little to conceal the stench.

Hamilton muttered to Angus in English. "Obviously they haven't invented bathing."

Angus suppressed a guffaw, then saw the curious, frustrated looks from both Sneev and Brudge. He spoke in their new tongue, which these people called Common. "Yes, Lord Sneev is most generous. We are in his debt."

This seemed to satisfy them, and they turned their attention elsewhere.

Servers circulated through the room, and heavy wooden plates clumped down before Hamilton and Angus, each laden with a massive chunk of roasted meat, and a fist-sized loaf of bread. A bronze goblet followed, brim full of a thick, honey colored liquid. Angus raised the goblet to his lips and tasted the syrupy wine.

"This is good," he said, and Hamilton quickly agreed. It tasted something of honey, with a faint spicy flavor. The meat was excellently roasted and seasoned.

"I've never had food like this, Angus," Hamilton said in Common. They had been fed on bread and cheese and water thus far. He raised his goblet to Sneev in salute. Sneev nodded, and seemed to relax slightly.

They consumed their portions with relish, and the sweetcakes that followed, and more wine, and more wine, until when the troupe of musicians and acrobats began their performance, the two strangers thought it was the most incredible thing either of them had ever seen. The musicians stood next to the cavernous fireplace, strumming lutes and citherns, piping on reed flutes, their melodies chasing each other about the room like the dwarfish acrobats who cavorted on the tabletops. Hamilton and Angus laughed until their sides ached, fully enjoying themselves, in spite of their distrust of Sneev.

Hamilton's glance wandered toward Tamarra over and again, and he felt a peculiar quivering in his belly that was not the wine. It was her. She thrilled him to the marrow of his bones.

Hamilton, the wine beginning to loosen his tongue, leaned forward and spoke across Brudge. "My Lord Sneev, this is a wonderful performance."

Sneev answered, "Thank you, sir. I am glad you find it to your liking." He turned his attention back to the performers.

"You have strange customs in your land, Lord Sneev," Hamilton said.

Sneev turned his beady black eyes on him. "Oh, how so?"

Hamilton noticed that the beautiful woman at the end of the table had cocked her head almost imperceptibly, to perhaps better hear this exchange. "Do you always bring honored guests to your house by force?"

Brudge stiffened.

Sneev's surprise was almost obvious, quickly shrouded by caution. "We brought you here for your own safety."

"From what?"

Sneev gulped at his goblet before answering. "Valerion's men would have killed you."

"We thought that's what you had planned for us. Why were we knocked senseless when we would have come willingly?"

The woman's eyes widened in excitement.

Sneev's small hand clenched the goblet. "For speed," he said quickly. "The Armondians would have slaughtered us all out of hand. Valerion and his people are savages. You would not have understood our intentions in time. As it was, only myself and the two men who carried you lived to tell the tale."

Hamilton nodded, silent but unappeased.

Then Angus leaned forward, looked Sneev dead in the face. "I do not believe you."

Hamilton saw a small flash of mischievous pleasure sparkle in the beautiful woman's eyes.

For the barest moment, Sneev's eyes flared with rage. Then another serpent's grin painted his face as he stood up, making a sweeping gesture with his hands. "Please, sirs, you wound me. If I wanted you dead, my friends, you most certainly would be. If I wanted you as prisoners, you would be in the dungeon. But instead, my friends, you sit at my family table, and break bread with me and mine. Please, sirs, I implore you to accept my hospitality without all this suspicion. You are safe here." He leaned forward, stretching his grin to almost ludicrous proportion.

He leaned back to sit once again.

Angus muttered for only Hamilton to hear. "I guess we'll see, won't we."

Brilliant silvery moonlight poured in through the open shutter of the tower room. A chill breeze brought Hamilton suddenly alert. The cobwebs of drunkenness were gone, blown away by the wind that had raised gooseflesh under his thick blanket. He vaguely remembered coming back up to the tower room after the feast, but that was all. He was not sure how long ago that had been, as he got up to close the shutters. The moon was a shining disc in full view outside the window, dropping towards the horizon, so morning was near. As the cold breeze cut through him, the residue of his wine bade him empty himself. He found the chamber pot and did so, to his great relief. The pale moonlight splashed his chest as he stepped up to close the shutters, and briefly, unexpectedly, subliminally, he felt as if something flitted past him into the room, riding a current of icy wind. But he had seen nothing. "Too much wine," he mumbled, as he shut the window and shuffled back toward his mat, rubbing his arms for warmth.

Angus's deep snoring guided him back to his pallet in the pitch blackness. He began to settle himself again when a sound caught his ear, bringing him instantly alert. The nape of his neck bristled.

It had been the sound of a carefully placed footstep, one that was not meant to be heard. His eyes searched the ebony blackness, seeing nothing, yet seeing…something, something moving silently toward him.

Then he heard a whispered word, the likes of which he had never heard before. He quickly tried to stand, and found that his legs would not obey him. Neither would his arms, nor his head. Not a single muscle would obey his command. His eyes would no longer move or focus, and he realized that he was no longer breathing. Then Hamilton saw the blacker figure in the darkness moving toward him. His every muscle shrieked to obey his commands to leap away and breathe, but they could not.

He heard the dry rasp of metal on wood, like that of a dagger being drawn. He could not cry out or scream. Tears of helpless terror burst from his eyes.

Angus snored blissfully.

Suddenly the window shutters smashed open, and a warm gust of wind washed through the clammy chamber. A glowing cascade of moonlight flooded the room, and the intruder stood revealed.

A waspish, ebon-cloaked wraith stalked toward him, silently as a cat. He tried to scream, but his voice was not his own.

Angus's snoring trailed off to silence.

A strange sensation rippled through Hamilton's body, almost like weightlessness, and his body rose from the floor.

Suddenly a deep-throated cry broke the silence, and something flashed through the air to clang against the side of the figure's head. The chamber pot. Hamilton fell back onto the pallet, sucking desperate breaths, his muscles suddenly free.

Angus stepped into the pool of silvery light, growling.

Like lightning, the cold, steely glint of a wickedly curved dagger flashed in the figure's pale hand.

The apparition made no sound as it lunged toward Angus, the razor-edged dagger slicing the air. Angus effortlessly caught the black-swathed wrist and splintered the arm across his iron-hard knee. The sickening snap was followed by a soft groan from the recesses of the ebon hood, and the clang of the dagger on the stone floor. But Angus did not expect the flailing fist from the opposite direction as it smashed into his jaw. He sprawled back into the small table, crushing it to the floor, and did not move. The figure turned to Hamilton, and with a word from the figure, the paralysis gripped him again.

Then Hamilton felt a strange tingling on his left breast, warm and pulsating. Suddenly he was free again. He lunged toward the startled wraith, spying the dagger on the floor. He snatched it up, and brandished it in a quivering fist.

The intruder paused, its shattered arm dangling limply at its side. Hamilton saw another flash of silver in a pale hand emerge from the folds of the black robe, and disappear into the hood. The figure shuddered once, gurgled quietly and crumpled on the floor. Hamilton leaped forward and tore back the hood, revealing the long, lipless mouth below the pale chin spewing gore onto the floor. Dead eyes stared upward. The man's thin hand still clenched the tiny blade sticking in his throat.

Hamilton stood over the corpse for a long while, staring at it. The features were those of a normal man, but the skin was unnaturally pale, even in the moonlight. The scalp was shaven clean, and a coin-sized circle was branded in the center of the forehead. The mouth hung open in a soundless scream of death, revealing the peculiar-looking tongue. Hamilton looked closer, and recoiled in horror when he saw that the tongue had been split, and was now forked like a serpent's.

He heard Angus stirring. Angus sat up and groaned as he fingered his jaw, gingerly working it around. "You alive, Ham?"

"Yeah."

"Is he?"

"No."

"You killed him?"

"No."

"He did himself?"

"Yeah. He had another knife." Hamilton stared. He had never before seen death so intimately.

"How did ge get in?" Angus asked.

Hamilton shrugged. "I don't know."

Angus got up and began to beat on the heavy wooden door. "Help! Murder!" he cried over and over, until he heard heavy footfalls on the steps.

The door burst open, and Brudge limped into the room, propped up by the crutch, a naked shortsword in his other hand. Lord Sneev rushed past him with a blazing torch aloft. He looked once each at Hamilton and Angus, then at the stiffening corpse. "Already they know," he mumbled.

Sneev glanced furtively between the two men, Hamilton absently holding the intruder's dagger, Angus stroking his sore jaw. "I am sorry," he said, "I will have this...carrion taken away immediately."

But no sooner had the words passed his lips than the hem of the cowl licked into flame. Suddenly a red flash of brilliant flame engulfed the corpse, blinding them. When their vision returned, all that remained was a large circle seared into the stone floor. Hamilton and Angus could only stare.

Sneev, wiping the look of frustration from his features, said to Angus and Hamilton, "Come with me. I've another room near to mine where you will be in no danger."

He turned and led them down the tower stairs. Brudge tottered along behind, grumbling something about being awakened at such a late hour. Soon they reached the main floor of the castle, and Sneev ushered them into a lushly furnished bed chamber adjoining a well-traversed corridor. "I hope this will be satisfactory. Good night," he said, and shut the door before they could answer.

Immediately Angus tried the latch. He cursed.

"Locked again?"

"Bloody 'ell!"

"And, of course, if we ask, it'll be 'for our own protection'."

"Aye, this whole scenario's wearin' bloody rammin' thin! Christ's Guts!" He ran his fingers through his thick black hair.

Hamilton sank into a nicely padded chair near the dark fireplace. "Think we dare try sleeping again?"

"I do'na care," Angus grumbled, and threw himself across the large, canopied bed. "I ain't much fer kippin' nuh'moor t'night!"

But when sleep finally did come, they were both too exhausted to notice.

Chapter 4

"You sent for me, m'lord?" Brudge gasped, his breath whistling through his mashed nose.

Sneev cast him a heedless glance through the spears of morning sunlight filled with motes of dust slanting between them through the tall window of Sneev's library. "Aye, Brudge, I did." His eyes narrowed. "And you took your time coming."

Brudge blanched, stuttering, "My apologies, Lord Sneev"

"Never mind. Save your platitudes this time." He leaned forward, resting a thin elbow on a spindly knee. "Now, we need to make sure that the prisoners are comfortable and content, and ignorant of us for a little while longer. I expect my reply from the Master to be forthcoming. But these men are not fools. Last night's attack proved that the Red Priests already know of The One's coming. They most certainly will want to use him for their own purposes, perhaps a power struggle with the Master."

"May we assume then, my lord," Brudge said, "that the Eagle Knights know of his coming as well?"

Sneev stroked his narrow chin. "I hadn't thought of that, my dear Brudge. Hah, but that is why I keep you in my service! You have a sharp wit! Yes, that is probably the case. Therefore, we must strive to put The One and his rather large companion at ease. They mustn't bolt before the Master informs me of his wishes. Who knows what powers The One possesses, after all."

"Begging my lord's indulgence, but why not kill them yourself, right now, or have them killed. No one would ever find them, or even know they were here."

"Maxha knows, I would much like to slit their throats myself." He sighed heavily. "But they are the Master's meat. He may have something special planned for them." He waved an indifferent hand. "In any case, the messenger is due any time. Then it will be out of our hands."

"Aye my lord."

Sneev thought for a moment, then said, "Bring them to me."

"Why is this bloody door locked!" Angus roared, as he slammed his fists into the groaning wood. "Honored guests, my arse! Ye gods, I feel like shit!" He stepped back, grabbing his aching skull.

Hamilton stood back, finishing the last of his calisthenics, an amused smile crossing his face as he watched the hapless door absorb Angus's rage and frustration.

Their bodies had protested greatly the previous night's overindulgence, heads throbbing from the wine, bowels bulging from the food. And both were exhausted from a nearly sleepless night.

"What next?" Angus grumbled, "Is some fire-breathing dragon gonna come doon outta the clear blue and 'ave us fer lunch?"

Hamilton cracked a smile. "Perhaps."

Then they heard the key fitting into its hole,

and the click of the lock.

"About bloody time!"

The door opened a crack, revealing the hideous face of the man outside. "You're disturbing the ladies with all this pointless ruckus, sirs. You are not prisoners."

Angus began to seethe, his anger having found a breathing outlet, his face reddening. "Then why was the door locked?"

Brudge did not flinch. "There is but one lock on this door, and it is on the outside, and there is only one key. Either your door is locked from the outside, or it is not locked at all, and after last night's events, we merely assumed that you would prefer to have your door locked."

"Well, you assumed wrong," Angus growled.

"My apologies, sirs. It will not happen again. But if you will follow me, please, my lord wishes to speak with you. He awaits you in the library." Brudge bowed deeply, a ponderous gesture indeed as his paunch hung low.

"Take us to him," Hamilton said.

"Ah, my friends!" Sneev smiled as he stood, arms outstretched. "Come, fill your bellies. I have a proposition for you."

Hamilton and Angus sat down at his table. Large platters of food awaited them. With bellies that were empty but not quite hungry, they sat down at his table. As they began to eat, Sneev spoke. "You have learned our tongue well, so well that Aldive was quite pleased with you, and you both know how difficult Aldive is to please. Before I present my offer to you, I must ask of you what your plans are." His smile was perfectly gracious.

The two Terrans were so stunned that they stopped chewing their food. Angus managed to speak first. "We hadn't really discussed it. We had assumed until now that we were well-treated prisoners."

Hamilton nodded in agreement, his mouth full of fruit.

"As I said last night, you judge me too harshly. I was merely taking care of you for a while."

Angus looked squarely at him. "Why? Why take care of us?"

Sneev just shrugged. "I am simply a very caring man."

Hamilton suppressed a choking reflex.

Sneev continued, "If you have no other plans, here is my proposition. You are both strong, able-bodied men. Our clash with Valerion's men cost me a goodly portion of my personal guard. My offer is this. Join my personal guard, and I will see that you are well cared for. You will be paid ten silver wheels per month, more than a simple farmer makes in a year. You will enjoy an elite status as one of my personal guards, and my men will train you to your best fighting ability. What say you?"

Angus began, "Well, we, uh..."

At that moment, a page hustled into the room, bowing to Lord Sneev.

"Yes, my boy," he said, leaning over enough to let the youth whisper into his small ear. Sneev's black eyes sparkled, and a genuine smile of relief flickered across his lips. He turned to Hamilton and Angus. "Please excuse me a moment. I have most urgent business. You may think about my offer. Brudge, come." And they were gone, leaving the baffled Angus and Hamilton sitting alone in the library.

After a few moments, Hamilton said, "Do you believe him?"

Angus rubbed his beard, eyes narrowed. "I

don't know. Do you?"

Hamilton pursed his lips in thought, searching his instincts for the answer. Then he shook his head. "No, I don't. What do you think he's up to?"

"No good," Angus growled through a mouthful of roast fowl.

Then they heard footsteps approaching the half-closed door. Not Sneev's ungainly shuffle, or Brudge's limping scrape. It was light and soft-soled and graceful.

"My lord?" came a smooth contralto voice from the hallway beyond the half-closed door. The door swung farther inward, gently pushed from outside, "My lord?"

Hamilton's heart thrilled. Could this be her?

The opening door revealed a beautiful face peering around the wood. Luxurious auburn tresses dangled far below the exquisitely carved face. Seeing them, her lovely almond-shaped green eyes flecked with gold widened. "Oh! My apologies, sirs." The head quickly disappeared.

Hamilton jumped up. "No! Wait!"

She stepped tentatively into the room on soft, slippered feet, delicate hands clasped demurely at her waist, eyes respectfully downcast.

Hamilton struggled to regain his composure, to quell the fire within him, an uncomfortable warmth rising in his ears. He stammered, "I do not believe we have been introduced, dear lady."

She took a hesitant step into the chamber, her thick glossy hair tumbling down her shoulders and back, full red lips slightly parted. A glistening gown of exquisite forest-green silk flowed behind her, and did nothing if not accentuate her tall, sweetly curved figure. She was tall, almost as tall as Hamilton. Her large eyes flared with what appeared to be a mixture of curiosity and excitement.

Angus stood up, mouth agape.

Hamilton steeled himself and approached her. "My name is Hamilton Corbin, dear lady. The Sun truly shines on your beauty." He bowed courteously.

"Your accent is strange. I have never heard the like..."

Angus bowed also. "I am Angus MacTavish."

She dipped a light curtsey and replied with true warmth. "I am Tamarra, step-daughter of Lord Sneev."

Hamilton smiled, "A beautiful name for a beautiful lady."

Her eyes sparkled as she smiled, and a soft flush of red spread across her shapely cheeks.

Then Hamilton made his mistake. He took her hand in his and kissed it lightly.

She gasped in outrage, tore her hand away, and with it slapped him across the face. Her eyes flared, and the flush of her cheeks turned to the crimson of anger. "Impudence!" she gasped. She stormed from the room, in a flurry of silk and auburn tresses.

Hamilton touched a light finger to the growing welt on his stinging cheek.

Angus suppressed a snicker. "Ye gods, what a blow! Ye've finger welts!" Then he exploded into a roaring gust of laughter.

Hamilton merely stood rooted to the spot, hand touching his cheek. He took an uncertain step toward the door. His heart screamed to go after her. "I should go apologize," he said, glancing at Angus for support.

"Forget her, my lad," Angus chuckled, waving off the incident. Then his laughter burst out again. "She's too tough for you!"

Hamilton nodded and sank into his chair in dejected silence. He was a storm of unfamiliar feelings. He could not be in love with her. He did not even know her. It was just infatuation. He had never been in love before. He did not know what it felt like. He couldn't be in love with her, he told himself over and over. But then why did he feel this way, as if his heart had been ripped from his chest? But she hated him now anyway, he thought with a sigh of resignation.

He pushed away his plate.

Fleeing in outrage, Tamarra slowed and halted a few paces down the hallway, standing just around a corner, out of view of the open door, her breast heaving. Angus MacTavish's guffaws echoed after her, stoking her anger. She spun, expecting to see Hamilton stumbling after her, babbling his apologies like all her other suitors would. But he did not follow, and this puzzled and intrigued her.

The man's boundless audacity! she fumed, as she spun and stomped down the corridor. Only those betrothed could kiss! Her noble body had been violated by a total stranger. But he was a stranger, after all. Perhaps he was totally ignorant of Ophidian ways. Perhaps men in his country kissed all the maidens on their hands, however risqué such a custom would be. Perhaps she had made a dreadful mistake. But strangely now, as the surge of outrage disappeared, she felt only a strange sensation unlike anything she had ever felt before. She sighed heavily, wishing he had followed her, and she would have treated him differently this time. A warmth fluttered in her belly like a captive songbird, just as it had the first time she had seen him, and she found that she rather enjoyed it. But he hated her now. It was too late to cry about it now, no matter how much she would have liked to do it all over again differently.

Lord Sneev cried, "Ah, the Master's wisdom is boundless!" He crumpled up the parchment and tossed it into the fireplace, then he turned to the messenger, a tall thin man with the dull, glassy eyes and pale skin indicative of one who had served the Master for many years, clad in tight-fitting black trousers and shirt.

"Give the Master my regards, and my thanks," Sneev said.

The man said, tonelessly, "The Master also bade me to warn you against failure. He expects nothing less than perfection."

"As always," Sneev said. "Have I ever given him less?"

The messenger did not answer.

"You may go."

The man turned and left the room.

"Now," Sneev said to himself, "Now to attend to The One."

Hamilton and Angus stood up as Sneev entered, bowing to him courteously. Sneev bowed in return.

"Well, my friends," he said, "have I an answer?"

"We've discussed it," Hamilton said, "and although your generosity is greatly appreciated, we have decided to leave."

Sneev's eyes widened. "But, my friends, I cannot allow you to leave!"

Angus leaned forward, his eyes narrowing. "What?"

Then Sneev smiled crookedly. "I cannot allow you to leave on foot. If you will accept my gift of a horse and tack for each of you, then you may leave with my farewell."

"Excellent," Angus said, "when can we go?"

"I'm afraid, not until tomorrow," Sneev said, shrugging apologetically, "I lost several mounts in our little skirmish with Valerion's men, therefore I can spare none today. However, I will take your steeds from the levy of horses I am due to receive from one of my landholders on the morrow. You may take your leave then."

Hamilton and Angus glanced at one another, unsure of whether to believe him or not.

"Please, my friends," Sneev said, "allow me to help you this one last time. I do hope you will grace my house with your presences often in the future."

Hamilton shrugged and looked at Angus. Angus sighed, and said, "Then we accept your generous offer, Lord Sneev."

"May the Sun warm your house, Lord Sneev," Hamilton said.

That evening, after the evening meal, Hamilton and Angus retired to their room. And the door was indeed left unlocked as they had requested. The maiden Tamarra was terribly absent from the evening meal. Hamilton and Angus had again shared Sneev's high table, and Hamilton's heart ached every moment, knowing why Tamarra was not there.

Angus stretched out comfortably on the bed, staring up at nothing in particular. "You think his offer's good? You have an instinct for such things."

Hamilton rubbed absently at the faint tingling in his left breast that lately seemed to be there more and more, almost a constant throbbing. "I'm not sure. But I definitely feel he's hiding something."

"Hmm."

"What?"

Angus said, "Let's just entertain the thought for a moment that Sneev actually does let us leave." He stroked his beard, brow furrowed. "What then? Where do we go? What do we do? How will we eat? Where will we sleep?"

Hamilton answered him straightforwardly. "I haven't given it much thought. All I've been able to think about is that I don't feel we're safe here, and I will never feel safe here. Therefore, we must leave. And the consequences be damned. Besides, we're not exactly helpless."

"Aye, I'm all agreement there. There's just one thing."

"What's that?"

"That's not *all* you've been thinking about." Angus suppressed a grin.

Hamilton could not help but smile outwardly, even though his heart wrenched at the memory of her hand across his face. He stared into the lone tallow candle flickering on the bed table, suddenly feeling like a pining schoolboy. Countless times he had regretted the morning. He hardly noticed when Angus blew out the candle, leaving him bathed in the orange warmth of the fireplace as he sat in the chair, elbows on his knees, hands dangling between them. The sole vision of his mind's eye was her. The lovely tilt of her head. The glow of her eyes. The music of her voice. And his fondest wish was that he could take her with him. Finally he went to bed, where he lay staring up at nothing.

Suddenly he was awake, startled to realize that he must have been sleeping, for the fire had burned down to glowing coals. But what had awakened him? Had he heard something? Then it came again. An almost inaudible grating noise, like stone on stone. He kept his breathing slow and steady, feigning sleep as he scanned the room with slitted eyes. The darkness was thick and windowless. No moonlight would come to his aid tonight.

Then he saw it. A shadow moved silently, silhouetted against the feeble glow of the hearth coals. Even in the dim glow he saw the glint of steel clutched in the shadow's hand. But this assassin was not hooded and cowled, like the previous night. The intruder moved to the foot of the bed, seeking his prey, his face obscured by the fold of the canopy. The lanky shadow circled the bed to stand beside Hamilton. The dagger began to rise, point down for the fatal stab.

Then Hamilton acted. With a cry pulled from the depth of his guts, he lashed out with his bare foot, burying it in his assailant's abdomen. The figure gasped, doubling over as he staggered back. Hamilton leaped out of bed toward his attacker. But the man was quick, seeming to recover easily from Hamilton's powerful kick, leaping back out of reach, flipping the long, straight poniard upright in his grip, dropping into a half-crouch.

The intruder stood silhouetted against the glowing fireplace as he leaped forward, the glimmering sheen of metal flickering forward like a serpent's fang. Hamilton dodged clumsily aside, out of the blade's arcing path. The two men circled one another like two snarling dogs looking for an opening. The fire was at Hamilton's back now, and as the figure stepped out of Hamilton's shadow, he saw the face of the assassin. Aldive's lips were twisted into a savage snarl, and his eyes burned with a fanatical glee.

Then came a loud thud, and Aldive's head snapped forward. The dagger skittered away, and Aldive tumbled forward to fall limply on his face.

He did not move again.

Angus, his leg still extended from the devastating kick, lowered his foot and stepped forward. Hamilton rolled Aldive over cautiously with his foot. Blood bubbled from between the butler's lips, and his head was twisted at an unnatural angle.

"'Od's bodikin, that was a blow!" Angus exclaimed proudly.

Hamilton managed a wan smile. "I owe you one, Mac."

"Ye owes me twenty-seven, m'lad, but who's countin'?"

Hamilton glanced about, spying the dagger lying near the chair. He retrieved it, turned it over and over in his hands. The hilt and crossguard were fashioned in the likeness of a coiled serpent, and the pommel was a serpent's head with emeralds for eyes.

"Wot's all this then!" Angus exclaimed, as he noticed Aldive's means of entry. A narrow opening gaped like a black mouth near the fireplace, where there had been only a blank wall before.

"You think Sneev set this up?" Hamilton asked, already knowing the answer.

"Stupid question."

Hamilton nodded. Checking a hunch, he moved to open the door to the corridor outside. "Locked."

Angus nodded. "Sneev still can't 'ave us wanderin' aboot."

No more words passed between them as they mutually decided what they must do.

Angus lit the candle in the fireplace, then looked at Hamilton. "Trade?" He offered the candle.

Hamilton looked at Sneev's dagger, nodded. "You'll be better with this thing than I would." He took the candle and gave Angus the poniard.

He approached the secret passage, holding the candle into the blackness. The passageway was cramped and low and narrow, like the door, and no one was in sight. They traveled quickly down the straight tunnel, finding the rough hewn wall unbroken by any openings. After several minutes, they saw a dim glow just ahead. The tunnel opened into another room, lit by a warmly crackling fire. Angus followed his poniard into the room, ready for anything. Finding no one, he relaxed and motioned Hamilton inside. Aldive's well-known housemaster garb was draped over the back of a chair.

"Aha!" Angus hissed, spying the pair of crossed longswords hanging over the fireplace. He took them down with relish, then grew a bit uncertain. "I've never used one of these before," he whispered, "but it's better than nothing. 'Ere ye go, Ham." He handed one to Hamilton.

Hamilton examined it. The blade was about three feet long, single-edged with a slight curve near the point, similar to a saber, with cancerous rust spots beginning to grow along the sides. The hilt was plain and leather-wrapped, with a short, flat crossguard.

Angus thrust his bare blade into his leather belt. "Ready?"

Hamilton nodded, and they went together into the dark unknown.

Chapter 5

The passage sloped steadily downward. The square-cut blocked stone of the castle's interior walls gave way to raw, rough-hewn rock. They moved down a passageway that burrowed down into the crag upon which Sneev's castle rested. Hamilton, holding the flickering taper above his head, followed Angus, who led the way with the poniard down the long, spiral curve. The floor was rough and rather uneven, which was a blessing as the grade of descent steepened.

"These walls aren't natural," Hamilton said.

"I wonder how many slaves Sneev killed digging this," Angus growled.

"This wasn't done in Sneev's lifetime. This is an old, old passageway," Hamilton said.- "Look at this slime on the walls, and the small stalactites. This tunnel is hundreds of years old."

Water trickled down the walls with a quiet rustle, dripping to the floor, providing the only other sounds in the cool silence.

They made their way slowly down the passage for perhaps an hour. The way was narrow and often slippery, forcing them to move slowly.

"Ah, blast it all!" Angus clenched his fists in frustration.

"What?"

"Look!"

Hamilton peered around him, and his heart sank.

Directly ahead of them, the tunnel was filled to the ceiling with fallen stones. The cave-in was ancient, slicked with wet slime.

"Now what?" Hamilton said, trying to remain calm. "We don't dare go back."

"Give me the candle," Angus said, and took the flame to closer examine the debris. He stepped carefully up to the fallen rocks. "I think there's an opening up there." He leaned forward, reaching up the pile, and began to pull the smaller stones down to enlarge the opening. He looked back at the expectant Hamilton. "It'll take some time, but I think we can clear a path to get through."

"As long as Sneev isn't waiting for us when we come out."

"Then he won't take us ali—Oww! Jesus Christ!"

Hamilton heard a terrible squealing hiss emanate from the opening Angus had enlarged. Angus slipped and fell on the rocks, pulling the thing attached to his hand into view.

Red eyes gleamed in the candle light as the thing growled and hissed, its long, needle-sharp teeth buried in Angus's hand. Angus kicked at it. The dog-sized rodent somehow dodged, maintaining its grip, chewing on Angus's hand. He jerked it into the air, and dashed its body against the stone wall.

"Die, you bastard!" Angus roared as he slammed the squealing thing again and again into the wall, onto the rocks, until it was little more than a pulpy mass of bone and gore. In death, the rat's powerful jaws finally relinquished their grip. And Angus stood cursing, holding onto his bleeding hand tightly. “Big blighter,” he hissed.

“Here, let’s bind that up.” Hamilton ripped a long strip of cloth from the hem of his tunic, and bound Angus’s hand. “We’re going to have to clean that as soon as we can. Who knows what diseases that thing was carrying. Feel okay?”

Angus nodded. “Let’s go to work.”

For two hours, they worked to clear a space large enough for them to crawl over the cave-in. They encountered no more of the huge rats, but they did hear the skittering of dozens of small feet moving away from them. Clothes, elbows, shins and knees were torn and bloody as they slid painfully down into the open passageway beyond the cave-in, finally able to move on.

They rested momentarily. Hamilton said, “It has to be close to daylight outside. The days are a little shorter here.”

Another fifteen minutes of travel found them at the end of the tunnel. But in the floor of the tunnel was a vaguely circular opening about three feet in diameter, leading downward like a chimney.

Angus immediately sat down on the edge and slid his legs into the opening. Bracing his feet against the rough walls, he wedged himself in and began to inch down. Hamilton held the stub of candle aloft as he watched Angus’s descent.

Angus called up to him, “It ends right here. There’s another tunnel leading out, I think! Come on down!” He was about twenty feet down, and already crawling out of sight.

Hamilton took a deep breath and dropped the candle. It sputtered out as it hit the ground below, but after a moment’s adjustment, his eyes could detect a thin gray light coming from the passage leading away. He descended after Angus, inching his way down the rough stone chimney. Finally he reached the bottom. He saw the opening Angus had disappeared into, and about thirty yards away Angus's dim outline knelt in the gray light of a small circular opening.

"Ham! Hurry! It's dawn!" Angus's whisper rang down the low tunnel.

Hamilton scurried down the tunnel, favoring his battered knees. As he reached the opening, he saw it was masked by a dense growth of brush outside.

"Let's go," Angus said. He wormed into the dim gray light of dawn, forcing his way through the thicket outside. Hamilton followed him.

The bush lay hunched against the base of the crag, wide and deep and tall. Finally, with their clothes in ruin and their flesh scratched and sore, they reached the outer edge of the thicket, and scanned the surrounding area. Sneev's fortress stood like a dark gray sentinel high above them. Before and beside them stretched a wide open field that separated Sneev's crag from the surrounding forest.

"Two hundred meters to the forest, do you think?" Hamilton said.

"About," Angus said. "Let's catch our breath for a moment, then run for the forest."

"Aye, aye, sir."

They scanned the surrounding field. No sign of any pursuit. Or ambush. Gray puffs of cloud, lightened on one side by the rising sun, scudded across the brightening sky.

They waited about a minute, then Angus said, "Let's go!" And he bolted out of the bushes, sprinting for the tree line with Hamilton two steps behind. Hamilton cast about, looking for pursuit. A quarter of the distance covered. No one following.

Halfway there. Hamilton's breath pumped in and out of him like a bellows. His blood roared in his ears. And his left breast throbbed warmly.

Then suddenly hoofbeats, coming closer. Four mounted warriors galloped into view from around the crag, bearing down fast. The horses' hooves sent clumps of sod flying behind them. And the two men did the only thing they could do. They ran.

Fifty meters to the forest's edge, and the men-at-arms were nearly upon them.

Angus slowed down and pulled the impotently flopping sword out of his belt. He turned and raised the blade barely in time to catch the nearest horseman's slash at his head. He roared in anger, and slashed the horse's front legs out from under it. The animal screamed in agony as its forelegs collapsed, sending the rider flying over its head to land in a crumpled heap a few feet away. Before he could recover, Angus was upon him, and drove the point of the longsword through the chain mail coat into the man's chest cavity.

Hamilton stopped and readied his blade for the next assailant. He saw the thundering form of the horse bearing down upon him, the dull glint of mail and steel in the early morning light. He rolled aside, blindly slashing with the longsword. Horse and man screamed as Hamilton's miraculous stroke gutted the horse from foreleg to flank. The horse flopped onto its side, rolling over on top of its rider, crushing his bones under its weight.

A tingling on his left breast grabbed his attention, and his arm convulsed upward, out of control, as if seized by a powerful nervous twitch. The sword flung back, and, to Hamilton's shock, a blow fell upon the blade, and was turned aside. The blow sent a ringing shock up Hamilton's arm, and he dived away, stunned. His assailant reined up, and the horse skidded to a halt, ripping up the turf. The rider hauled on the reins to spin the horse around, but Hamilton somehow gained his feet, lunged and impaled him through the side before he could bring his weapon to bear. The horse reared, dumping its mortally wounded rider from the saddle, and fled before Hamilton thought to grab the reins.

He turned in time to see Angus's sword slice deep into the fourth rider's thigh. The man-at-arms howled in pain and tumbled from the saddle as his mount reared under him. He hit the ground with a heavy thud and jangle of mail. Angus dispatched him in short order.

"The trees, Ham!" he cried. "There're more coming!"

Hamilton spun to see. Eight more mounted warriors appeared, coming from the opposite direction at full gallop. But the tree line was too close now for the horsemen to catch them. A few seconds later and both of them were within its boundaries. The dense brush growing under the towering trees would keep the horses from entering in any swift pursuit, but foot pursuit would come shortly.

They flung themselves through the underbrush. After several minutes of blind flight, they stopped to listen for signs of pursuit and catch their breath. They heard nothing save the beating of their own hearts.

"Angus, where are we going anyway?" Hamilton puffed. "What now?"

"I thought we might head for Armond. I got a look at some maps in Sneev's library. Sneev and Valerion are obviously enemies."

"'The enemy of my enemy is my friend', huh?

That logic's pretty thin."

"As good a choice as any, no?"

"I suppose so. Or we can at least lose ourselves in this forest for a while."

Angus grunted his assent as he hacked through a low-hanging vine.

They traveled quickly, seldom stopping to rest. The lofty, vine-festooned boughs teemed with thousands of birds, all voicing their wondrous melodies. The undergrowth which had so impeded their passage began to thin and allow them easy travel. Perpetual gloom shrouded the forest floor, fostering the growth of countless tiny mushrooms, which made their tread easy and quiet. Scattered shafts of brilliant silver sunlight speared through the thick canopy high above their heads.

Soon after what must have been noon, the two men came upon a well-kept road that cut cleanly through the forest. They stood on the side of it, looking both ways as the road bent out of sight in the trees. A breeze rustled the treetops above, but the air on the road was still, filled with birdsong.

"Shall we take the road?" Angus asked.

"I..." Hamilton began, when suddenly a tingling heat caused his arm to twitch violently. Without thinking, he spun and hooked Angus across the chest, and flung both of them back into the bushes out of sight of the road.

Barely an instant later, the rumble of many approaching hoofbeats filled the air. Angus and Hamilton scrambled to get further away from the road, and at least a dozen mounted warriors thundered past, a green banner flapping above them which bore the golden symbol of three intertwining serpents. As quickly as the noise had risen, it died away, lost in the foliage and birdsong.

Hamilton sat up, brushing the old leaves off

his torn, soiled tunic. "Think they saw us?"

"I doubt it," Angus said. "Good ears, though, Ham. I didn't even hear them."

Hamilton was not sure whether to tell him that he hadn't heard them either.

"Anyway," Angus continued, scraping dirt and rotten foliage out of his matted beard, "let's stay away from the road. We might not be so lucky next time."

The two stood up and fought their way out of the thick roadside brush, back into the relatively open area under the ancient trees, resuming their eastward course.

Soon their nostrils caught the sharp whiff of wood smoke, and with little effort followed the scent to a small thatched roof sprouting above a large clump of bushes. A thin wisp of wood smoke drifted from the stone chimney as they approached. Hunger had begun to gnaw at their bellies, and made them bold. The two approached the ramshackle structure, and stopped just on the edge of the clearing. They peered cautiously about, searching for signs of anyone nearby. No one was in sight, and they heard no activity.

The windowless wall facing their position was fashioned of logs chinked with mud. Angus gestured with his head, then leaped up and raced to the back wall, stopping with his back pressed against it. Hamilton followed suit, and together they crept along the side of the shack, around the corner. The side wall was also bare and windowless. The two men silently slipped their swords from their belts, inching their way along the wall. Angus thrust his head around the corner of the hut. Still no one in sight. A small chopping block with an ax buried in it rested on the ground, not far from the open door, beside a small pile of freshly split wood. The front of the house sported two windows, broken shutters hanging limply open. Angus stepped around the corner, sword point leading the way, Hamilton close on his heels, warily watching behind them. Angus ducked below the open window to stand between the small opening and the door, and Hamilton peered into the darkness of the tiny hut through the window.

He could see little in the interior darkness, but the warm, rich smell of food wafting from the window made his stomach roar. Hamilton's mouth watered like a gushing spring, and he looked at Angus and saw the flare of hunger in his eyes. The big Scotsman said not a word as he spun and barged into the room beyond. His eyes swept the room.

Crackling flames danced on the small hearth, over which stewed a pot of soup. A small, rough wooden table rested in the center of the room, beside which sat a crude wooden stump used for a stool. A mat of dry grass lay on the floor in the back corner. With speed that belied his great size, Angus darted across the room and snatched the stew pot from its bracket above the fire. He searched about and spied the large wooden ladle resting on the table, and traded his sword for the ladle. Lifting the lid, he closed his eyes and let his nostrils absorb the succulent aroma. He buried the ladle in the pot, and lifted it laden with stew to his famished lips.

Suddenly an angry hiss split the air, and the ladle flew from his fingers. The hiss ended with a dry thunk on the far wall. Angus's eyes bulged as they followed the sound, and saw the ladle dangling from a feathered clothyard shaft quivering in the thick wall. Angus snatched at his sword resting on the table.

Hamilton stiffened, a warmth tingling on his breast with increasing familiarity. His throat tightened. That arrow had flashed not two inches from his own ear.

A firm masculine voice rasped from behind him. "There you are now, boy. Drop the fark-sticker."

Hamilton's sword fell from his fingers, and he slowly raised his hands above his head.

The man chuckled, then barked a command, "You, too, in there, Blackbeard! Drop that food! I worked hard for that!"

Angus reluctantly dropped his sword again, and set down the stew pot.

"Steal my food, will you! Why, today's young folk are just going to Hell, I say! Now there, Yellowhair, step you inside slowly or you'll be sproutin' a shaft twixt your shoulder blades." Hamilton slowly stepped into the dirt-floored hovel. He heard the tread of soft-booted feet shuffling in the dirt behind him, into the house. The door closed them into semi-darkness.

As their eyes adjusted, Hamilton slowly turned around to face their captor. His gaze followed the length of the arrow, with its razor-edged point a finger's breadth from his nose, down the straight wooden shaft, to the neatly arranged fletching, past the taut bowstring, into a pair of piercing gray eyes. Hamilton took a stunned step backward. The piercing eyes were like chips of ice framed by a lean, hard, time-carved face. A thin leather headband tied back an unkempt mop of silver-streaked black hair. He wore a sleeveless leather vest and loose-fitting breeks of soft hide.

Hamilton decided that this old man had been quite imposing in his younger days, but now age had slumped his shoulders a bit, bowed his knees, weathered his skin, but had taken no strength from his stout thews nor clouded his alert mind. Age had only refined his handsome features.

Hamilton stuttered in his new language, "We are sorry, sir, for trespassing in your home, but we have not eaten. I apologize for the actions of my friend, but he is fairly mad with hunger. If you can excuse our rudeness, we will be on our way, and trouble you no longer. May the Sun warm your home."

The old man lowered the point of the arrow to Hamilton's chest which was laid bare by the mangled tunic. A bewildered gasp flew from the man's throat, and he staggered backward, eyes bulging. The bow clattered to the floor. The arrow flew from the released string to bury itself in the dirt floor a finger's breadth from Hamilton's toes. The old man took a step forward, staring transfixed at Hamilton's chest.

Hamilton took a hesitant step backward, lowering his hands, mouth open in uncertainty.

The old man's mouth worked, but no sound came forth. He seemed to be mouthing words, but his breath would not obey him. Then he whispered, "The One!" He approached until his nose was inches from Hamilton's chest.

"Sir, I..." Hamilton stuttered.

"The One!" the old man barked, his stare nailed to the birthmark on Hamilton's chest. His fingers reached up and touched the smooth, lightly haired surface, touching the white mark emblazoned there in the angle between breastbone and collarbone. The birthmark shaped like a four-pointed star, with one point slightly longer than the others.

The old man sought half-heartedly to rub the mark off, his effort coming to naught.

"Arnor be praised!" he exclaimed. He threw his

hands into the air and cried out in exultation as he began to dance crazily about the small room like one barefoot on hot coals.

Hamilton's face was a puzzled grimace as he glanced back at Angus, whose black brows were furrowed in bewilderment. Hamilton stepped sideways away from him, feeling the table behind him as a guide.

The man's dance subsided, and he turned to them, his grizzled face split by an ear to ear grin. "I know not whether to believe my own eyeballs! You have finally come! You have finally come!" Then he turned away, muttering, "I believe it not! I believe it not!" Suddenly he spun to face Hamilton, and rubbed his eyes, peering at the mark, rubbing, peering. Then he grew deadly serious as he whispered, "In sooth, The One has come!"

Hamilton merely stared at him, mouth agape.

Angus whispered in English, "He's deranged!"

Trying to make sense of what was happening, Hamilton implored the man, "What are you talking about, sir?"

The old man suddenly ejaculated, "The One has come!" And he began to dance about again.

Hamilton, who had taken two steps backward, discreetly kicked the bow out of reach. "Yes, we know. You keep saying that. Who is The One?"

The man snapped out of his dance, looking suspiciously between Hamilton and Angus. His eyes stopped on Hamilton. "You act mighty daft, you being who you are, you know."

"What?" Hamilton said, as he glanced back at Angus.

Angus shrugged, a faint smile growing on his face.

The old man said as if it had been obvious from the beginning, "You are The One, aren't you?"

Hamilton's eyes grew wide. "I'm not The One! I can't be!"

The man's face sobered, and he reached out to take a dusty, moldering, leather-bound book from a rough wooden shelf crooking out from the wall. He reverently began to thumb through it. He paused at a dry, yellowed page. After he cleared his throat, his voice quavered with emotion as he read.

"The Prophecy of The One.
The One shall come
When The Sun turns to Blood.
The One shall come
Riding but not riding a Silver Dragon that
is not a Dragon."

The old man's voice rose in emphasis.

"The One shall have
the Ivory Star in His Breast,
And he shall free
Mankind from the Ultimate Evil."

Hamilton had listened intently, chin grasped between thumb and forefinger. Pure reverence glistened in the old man's eyes as he fastened them on Hamilton, as if reading that passage had reaffirmed his own faith.

Then, like an anvil falling on Hamilton's head, the purpose of the old man's raving crashed into his mind. He stared down in fascination at the birthmark that had recently become more pronounced.

Angus stared at him in outright disbelief.

Hamilton stuttered, "This has to be some astronomical coincidence! I've got a birthmark, yes, but...!"

The old man broke in, "What's all this jabbering now? Some tongue of the gods?"

"That star turned red, Hamilton," Angus said quietly. "This sun, that star, turned red. Blood red."

"What are you saying?" The old man stepped between them. "Speak Common!"

"Could all this have to do with me?" Hamilton said. Then he shook his head, "No, that's too unbelievable! It has to be a simple coincidence!"

"Simple?" Angus said. "This is a little too big to be simple. But I can't believe you're some great Messiah either, Hamilton."

Hamilton stared at him. "Neither can I."

The pitch of the old man's voice rose in frustration. "Stop your babbling!"

"A silver dragon?" Hamilton said.

"The scoutship?" Angus said.

"This is too much." Hamilton's voice quavered with the enormity of all this. Could this truly be such a huge coincidence? Or could he really be here for the sole purpose of saving these people from some great evil? Or was he some dupe in a cosmic-scale game of chess between as yet unknown players?

"No!" he said, grasping the back of his neck, running his fingers through his hair.

"'No', what?" Angus said.

"I can't believe this."

"Neither can I. You can't take care of yourself half of the time, although I must admit you've been impressing me since we got here."

"It can't be my destiny to save an entire planet."

"Maybe this prophecy is exaggerated. What can be so terrible?"

Hamilton shrugged. "It just has to be some freak occurrence. Has to."

Angus grunted in agreement.

The old man had set the book back on the shelf, and stood looking at them both squarely. "If you are finished jabbering, sirs, sit down, and fill your bellies at my humble table."

Angus's eyes brightened at the mention of belly-filling, and swiftly seated himself on the stump next to the table. The old man moved gracefully about the room, humming a joyful tune. He removed three dust-covered bowls and wooden spoons from a shelf above the hearth, rinsed them in a basin, and set them on the table. He retrieved the ladle dangling from the arrow, leaving the shaft where it stuck. He chuckled, thumbing over his shoulder at the arrow. "You cannot be too careful these days, with all the brigands and thieves about. Sneev bothers not trying to control the pillaging by his own men, much less the professional thieves." He ladled some stew into Angus's bowl. "You must be Ophidian," he said, glancing between them for reactions. Angus ignored the comment and snatched up a wooden spoon and began to shovel his mouth full.

Hamilton took the old man's bait. "What makes you think we're Ophidian?"

"Only Ophidians use those stodgy 'Sun' formalities, and you're carrying one of Sneev's personal daggers."

Hamilton cringed; he had forgotten about the dagger. "We stole this dagger, and we weren't aware that the 'Sun' formalities were stodgy."

"So you are Ophidian." He was not accusing, merely making conversation. "I don't care if The One is Armondian, Ophidian, Allahnian, Tyberian, or Uhr's brother, as long as he does what he came to do. Forgive me, my lords, for the humbleness of my table. I am but a lowly huntsman."

Angus grunted, not looking up from his meal.

Hamilton studied the old man carefully as he spoke, and his instincts told him that this old man was far more than just that. He rubbed the birthmark absently. "We thank you for your hospitality."

"Fah! It is the least I can do for one such as you, my lord."

"By the by, sir," Hamilton said, "what is your name?"

"I am Garth, Son of Arnor, my lord."

Hamilton said, "Please, Garth, do not call me that."

Angus grumbled in English, "I rather enjoy it."

Hamilton ignored him. "I am no more or less a man than you or any man."

Angus mumbled in English, "That's very egalitarian of you, One."

Hamilton focused his attention on Garth. "Like you, I am hungry. Forgive me, I am Hamilton Corbin, and my rather brutish friend here is named Angus MacTavish."

Angus looked up from his meal, and interjected, "Now listen here!"

Hamilton's burst of laughter cut him off.

A grin tugged at the corners of Angus's mouth, and he returned to sating his ravenous stomach.

Garth, Son of Arnor, spread a strong, intelligent smile, dipped some stew into Hamilton's bowl and motioned him to eat. "I'll wager you're fleeing the Snake on the Crag."

"Sneev? Yes."

"Aye," Garth said, "he is Uhr's lackey to the core."

"Uhr. You mentioned him before," Hamilton mumbled, his mouth full. "Who is Uhr?"

"You know not?" Garth frowned, covering Hamilton with a severe, measuring stare. "Strange that The One knows not Uhr."

Hamilton squirmed. "And you think Lord Sneev is Uhr's lackey?"

"Hah! Sneev is Uhr's very lapdog! Did he try to kill you?"

Hamilton and Angus looked at each other, then at Garth, astounded, chorusing, "How did you know?"

Garth cracked a grim smile. "I know Uhr, and I know Sneev. Sneev wouldn't hesitate to flay his own mother at Uhr's command." His eyes narrowed, like those of a beast of prey. "You killed his assassin, stealing his dagger, and escaped. Ah, the gods know how I'd like to get Sneev's throat right here." He clenched his fists. "And throttle him like the worm he is. It was Uhr who ordered your deaths, you know. I'll stake my life on that. Sneev doesn't have the backbone to kill The One on his own. I'm surprised that Uhr didn't want to kill you himself, and devour your souls as he did it."

Hamilton stared at him incredulously. In English he said rhetorically, "What kind of person is this Uhr?"

Angus said, wiping the stew out of his beard, "The idea of a soul devouring monster seems a little ludicrous, but we can't be too careful now, can we."

"There you go with that annoying babbling again. You know how to talk, don't you? But ho! Let me bore you not with an old man's rambling! Eat. When your stomachs are full, then we shall talk. My house is your house as long as you wish to stay here. Or as long as it is safe."

Angus sat up suddenly straight as a spike on the floor of Garth's hovel, where he had been excruciatingly close to drifting off into a much appreciated nap. The muffled clattering of hooves, and the metallic jingle of mail and accouterments, sounded through the open door.

A deep voice bellowed harshly from outside, "Ho there, you old buzzard!"

Garth had gone hunting, leaving Angus and Hamilton alone in the hut. While Angus had just stretched out to snatch a few winks, Hamilton had laid down on the opposite side of the hut, where he now crouched below the window, sword in hand. Angus crawled toward the wall and knelt beside the door, grabbing his sword from where it rested against the wall.

The command came again, "Old man, come out!"

Of course, no answer came.

Hard-heeled boots thumped onto the ground, with the jingling of armor and spurs. The two sets of spurs began to walk toward the house. Angus's knuckles whitened with his grip on the sword hilt. Sweat beaded his forehead, slicked his palms. His legs tensed under him as he readied himself for the ambush. The dry rasp of steel drawn from its sheath. Angus bit his lip, fixed his gaze upon the opening. The men outside were silent now their suspicion. The tip of a blade inched through the open door. Suddenly the man leaped full into the house, spinning as he moved to scan the room. Had his reflexes been an instant quicker, his long sword would have deflected the glinting arc that speared through his shirt of chain mail and leather, into his chest. The warrior stared at the blade but a moment before his eyes rolled up in death, and he sank to the ground.

The other man-at-arms leaped back from the door, and Angus threw himself out after him. Hamilton was hot on his heels. The blades of Angus and his antagonist met with a stinging clang as the man parried Angus's savage thrust. The man lunged into a lethal riposte. The only thing that saved Angus from being spitted was a third blade that sliced across the man's wrist, nearly severing the hand from the arm. The man screamed in shock and agony. Blood spurted from the dangling member in a hot fountain, spattering them both. The man's sword dropped to the red-stained grass, his hand flopping from a shred of flesh.

With only a second's hesitation, Angus slashed his blade across the man's throat. The man's good hand reached up to try and close the second mouth that had opened below his chin. Blood spurted between his fingers and he sank gurgling into the grass.

The two horses stamped nervously a short distance away. A round, green-painted shield hung from each saddle, emblazoned in yellow with the standard of three intertwining serpents.

Angus cursed quietly to himself.

Hamilton said what they both knew. "We'll have to get out of here quickly now. These men will be missed."

Garth burst into the clearing, nocked arrow half-drawn. He surveyed the carnage. "What happened?"

They told him the tale.

Garth nudged the stiffening corpse with his boot. "Looking for you, I'll wager." Then he looked up at them, trading his gaze between the two. "It's time for you to go. Before more of these mongrels arrive searching for you. An' they find you, they'll spit you like newborn lopedeer."

Garth hurried into the house. He soon returned carrying in one hand four large leather bags, one thonged shut with a drawstring, the other three stoppered by wooden plugs and leather stoppers, and in the other hand the shirt of chain mail formerly worn by the dead man inside the house.

He handed the hauberk to Hamilton, holding heavy shirt of steel and leather as easily as if it were a cloth tunic. He stripped the other corpse of its armor and gave it to Angus. Then he showed them how to buckle the armor in place. The hauberks were padded leather inside, and covered the upper arms, torso and thighs. Circular roundels protected the shoulder creases and hips.

Garth held up the leather bags. "Here is some jerked meat and enough water to last for a day or two." He pointed to the east. "If you travel straight east you will pass through Ryvan Marsh, and finally come to the edge of the forest, the frontier between Ophidia and Armond. Keep going east, and you'll come across the Trade Road, which will take you straight to Lakeside. Beware of Ryvan Marsh, though. It's not large, but it's treacherous. There are some terrible bogs, holes with no bottom. Try to find the path beaten through the middle of it, where there is little danger of sinking and drowning in the muck. Once you find the path, do not leave it. If you do, the swamp will claim your lives within thirty heartbeats. Oh, and another thing. A tribe of Marsh Men lives in the bog. I know little about them, other than they are savages, so have a care. Just be sure to reach Lord Valerion."

Hamilton said, "Why him?"

"He will help The One."

Angus put in, "But what about the men who'll come looking for these?" He pointed at the cold corpse lying on the grass.

Garth grinned wolfishly. "Oh, I know of a hungry tree-barr holed up not far from here. If anyone comes looking, they came and were gone again."

Angus and Hamilton laughed gratefully. Then

they uncertainly mounted their horses.

Hamilton said, “Fare you well, Garth!” And they spurred their mounts away into the forest.

Garth stood alone in the clearing, leaning on his bow, smiling. “I'll wager that you will be seeing more of me in the future, lads.” He chuckled as he watched them go.

Chapter 6

“But my husband is your loyal servant, Master!” the woman sobbed. “His loyalty is boundless, Master, as is his love for you. He would never—”

The voice rumbled over her like a chariot wheel. “Silence, cow.”

Uhr gazed down from his throne at the two naked women chained at his feet. Their smooth skin glowed as the blue-white fingers of lightning flickered across the open sky above. Two scarlet coals burned into them from the depths of the shadowy hood. Excitement rippled through Uhr in a dark wave. He gazed up through the opened roof of his highest tower, past the upright roof sections as they splayed toward the open sky, sensing the power gathering with his will in the elements above. He sucked a deep breath, savoring the cool moist air as it mingled with the lovely succulence of their trembling flesh, the lush warmth of their surging blood.

The other woman, the young, beautiful one, did not speak, but her bare shoulders shook as the sobs burst from her. She knelt curled up in her shackles, her shining auburn locks falling to obscure the exquisite softness of her sensuous alabaster flesh.

The first woman, plump with age, glanced at the younger, and her eyes grew wide with horror, as if realizing something for the first time. "My lord Uhr," she pleaded, "My daughter has done nothing against you. Oh, spare her life, I beg of you. Do your will with me, Master, but spare her life!"

Uhr leaned forward in the darkness. "You presume too much, woman. Your life is mine to use as I will. Perhaps I will spare her life, perhaps not, but your mate's incompetence has spent yours." He leaned back. "Take her."

Two pale-skinned servants rushed out of the darkness. She screamed in mortal terror as they took her by the soft, thick arms and drug her across the stone floor toward the block of black stone in the center of the chamber.

"No! Mother!" Tamarra screamed.

The two men, clad in tight-fitting black, heaved the pitifully writhing woman onto the altar like a goat for slaughter, fastening the shackles to black iron rings on the corners of the obsidian table, and Uhr drew the knife as he rose to his full height. He stretched his dry, creaking arms to the sky.

"Watch girl," Uhr rumbled. "Ever disobey me, and the same shall happen to you." Suddenly an invisible fist grasped Tamarra's face, and wrenched her head into position to watch the horrible spectacle. She tried to close her eyes, but she found she could not, and the sobs bubbled out of her like a gushing spring, and tears of terror and helplessness stained her lovely cheeks. "Oh, mother, mother, mother, mother, mother..."

Uhr stepped up to the altar, dagger clenched in his rotting claw. Tamarra watched the terror in her mother's eyes die as Prilla's mind snapped, and she plummeted into merciful insanity.

Tamarra remembered little of what she was

forced to watch. Her mind went elsewhere for a time, while Uhr performed unspeakable acts on the living body, and then finally the ensanguined corpse of her mother. She dimly remembered Uhr's servants with the bowls of blood, and the stripped, red-smeared bones in their bone-white fists, and the blazing scarlet jewel, and the horrifying syllables with which Uhr smote the heavens. And the cyclone of noxious black and scarlet smoke swallowing the savaged mass of flesh that had once been her mother whom she loved, the smoke slowing its movement, spreading. And she remembered the massive hulking thing materialize in the eddying currents of scarlet smoke, as scarlet as the Stone. The thing that slobbered and rumbled, scaly, like a serpent, like her step-father's crest. And its yellow idiot's eyes, and its limp crimson wings, as it heaved itself about the tower room floor on stubby legs at its Master's bidding, its obsidian talons dragging sparks across the stone floor, its long, spiked tail. This monstrous thing kneeling at Uhr's feet and nuzzling his black and crimson robes.

And she remembered Uhr's voice in her head, his bloody breath in her face, in her ear. "You may have her now, General." And she heard the metallic rattle of plate armor, and the thump of heavy boots as they stepped up to her. And the cold gauntlet gouged her flesh as she was jerked to her feet and dragged limply away.

****

Night fell quickly under the canopy of leaves. Hamilton and Angus traveled quickly all day long, riding when the way was open enough, learning the skills of horsemanship, leading their mounts when the underbrush grew too thick. But when darkness fell it did so with little warning. The travelers just stopped where they were when it became too dark to travel safely, tethered their horses to nearby trees, and lay down on the grass. They had no means of making a fire, so they just gathered bundles of fresh grass and dead leaves to nest themselves in for warmth.

Angus threw down his armful of grass, and spoke his mind about something that had been bothering him for days. "I don't know what to think of all this, Ham. I'm not a man who believes in prophecies and portents. My parents raised me in a good Scottish home, where such things were passed off as nonsense."

Hamilton looked at Angus's dark shape standing near him in the deepening night. "What do you mean?"

He was calm, rational, as he spoke, his accent suppressed. "I'm talking about everything that old man said. About you and The One. Are you supposed to be this great savior?"

Hamilton shrugged. "I don't know. I find it hard to believe myself."

"Whether you are or not is irrelevant. The more people who believe that you are—and I'm talking about this Lord Valerion—they may force you into a position to get yourself killed by those who stand to lose by your presence. And those who stand to lose seem to be running the show."

"I see what you mean."

"So, Great One," Angus said, with sarcasm notably absent from his tone, "What should we do now? Do we listen to the old man, and look for safety with Lord Valerion, or do we just strike off on our own. What do your instincts tell you?"

"My instincts tell me that whether or not I am The One, it's not going to matter. People will think

I am, and we can't run from what's going on. We're gonna get caught up in it no matter what we do. I've a feeling whatever is going on here is a little bigger than a feud between Lord Sneev and Lord Valerion. All we can do is stick together, and try to stay alive, come what may."

Angus grunted his agreement, toying absently with a dry twig he had picked up.

Hamilton continued, "I do know one thing. We'll never see Earth again. This is our home now."

Angus's accent crept back into his rising voice. He waved the twig like a wand. "They can 'ave bloody Earth! Or wot's left of it! I've always imagined that Earth used to look this way!" He raised his arms to the forest. "A third o' the bloody surface is uninhabitable now. I was one o' the lucky ones who got to climb a blessed tree as a boy! And you! Christ, 'Amilton, you never even saw Earth until the Academy! Pinin' away fer the birthplace o' humanity are we, son? We're waxin' a little romantic, ain't we?"

Hamilton shrugged. "I guess so."

The twig in Angus's hands snapped loudly in the darkness. "For my part, I will live and die at me own choosing."

They awoke shivering in the early morning chill, each covered by his dewy mound of vegetation. They got moving again quickly to get their blood flowing. By the late morning, the ground was beginning to soften with moisture, the vines started to grow thicker, the moss more prevalent, indicating that Ryvan Marsh was close.

Shortly after midday, Hamilton and Angus stumbled across the path into Ryvan Marsh that Garth had mentioned. It adjoined the main road cutting through the forest, presumably the same road over which their pursuers had traveled. The main road angled off to the north, while a narrow, tunnel-like path split straight towards the east, into the misty dimness of the bogs. The path was firm, but the ceiling of overhanging boughs, moss and vines was low and threatening. Hanging vines drooped nearly to the road, and the edge of the path was a wall of tree trunks, keeping back the multitude of swamp noises skreeking and chirping and rattling out of the surrounding bogs.

They traveled quickly, wishing to pass through the eerie marsh as quickly as possible.

A few hours into the bog, they were leading their horses down the path. Hamilton stopped, halting his horse.

Angus, who had been leading, stopped and turned. "What is it?" he said.

"Something's wrong," Hamilton said.

Angus's eyes scanned the edges of the path. Their horses began to stamp and snort. Suddenly Angus's horse reared, screaming in terror, thrashing at the air with its front hooves. It jerked the reins out of Angus's grip, and galloped back the way they had come. Angus swore vehemently as he started after it, "It's got all our supplies!"

Hamilton was having trouble keeping a grip on his own horse as it whinnied and jerked on the reins, cinching the leather painfully tight around his hands and wrists.

Then a massive, tawny bulk exploded out of the bushes beside the road, and landed full on the back of Hamilton's horse, crushing it to the ground. The horse screamed as the thing's huge jaws ripped deep into the side of its neck, and its rear claws shredded both the saddle and the horse's back. Then the monster fastened its jaws onto the horse's head, and broke the animal's neck with a tremendous wrench.

Hamilton and Angus watched transfixed in horror as the beast lifted its gory fangs from its kill, and looked at them with blazing yellow eyes. The beast stood six feet tall at the rippling, black-striped shoulder. Its black-tufted ears lay down against its huge feline head. A tawny tail lashed back and forth as it began to stalk toward them, leaving behind the horse's twitching carcass.

Hamilton grasped Angus's arm in a gesture to stand still.

"Wot?" Angus hissed. "Are ye daft?" But the great cat's muscles relaxed just a little, as if no longer tensed to spring.

Suddenly a weird, ululating cry filled the marsh air, seeming to come from everywhere. The great cat lay down in the middle of the path, and began to lick the blood from its paws and muzzle with a broad, pink tongue.

A few moments later, the bushes on either side of the path began to move, and several bizarre figures emerged. Five men, short and stocky, wearing leather loin-clouts and numerous layers of gray mud and slime, each carrying a bronze-tipped javelin. Their hair was long and dark, matted with mud, and their deep-set eyes small and black under thick, bushy brows.

"You will come with us," one of them said.

"Like hell!" Angus said.

The same one made a clicking noise with his tongue, and the cat sprang to its feet hissing and bristling.

Hamilton said, "We seek only to pass through your lands unmolested, sirs. Please let us pass."

One of them pointed into the marsh. "Step where we step. Stray, and die."

Two of them faded into the dim wild off the path. Hamilton and Angus reluctantly followed.

The two Marsh Men were waiting for them just off the path. "Walk where we walk, and you will live." The other three fell in behind, and the huge cat disappeared, as they began their trek through the swamp. The Marsh Men moved like ghosts floating over the bogs like wisps of smoke, while Hamilton and Angus slogged laboriously along with them. Marsh mists swirled at their ankles as the soft ground sank beneath their every step. Ancient trees rose above them, gnarled branches reached down for them like moss-dripping fingers. Countless swamp creatures croaked and growled, skreeked and hissed around them, scuttling and leaping and swimming away in the alarm of passing men. Sounds echoed eerily amongst the towering boles and sprawling bogs of still, reed-choked water. The Marsh Men moved flawlessly among the treacherous muck pits and head-high rushes. They skirted a pond, and something uncomfortably large thrashed out in the middle, whipping the water to a slimy green froth, and the Marsh Men steered quickly away.

Suddenly Hamilton and Angus were alone. One moment their guides were all around them. The next they were gone. Panic surged into Hamilton's throat, then died away as he looked about. They were on the edge of a wide clearing of firm ground, dotted with more than a dozen massive trees. The branches above formed an interlocking ceiling about twenty feet above the ground. The trunks were elevated by pillars of gnarled roots poking like fingers into the ground. The spaces between the thick roots were chinked with mud, and several small fires burned about the clearing. Lazy coils of smoke meandered from open knotholes on the sides of some of the tree trunks.

Then they appeared. The tribe of Marsh Men

emerged from their tree-houses. Short, stocky people, men and women and children, caked with layers of gray-green mud, clad only in filthy leather loin-clouts. The tribe stared at the strangers with a mixture of curiosity and distrust. Mothers quickly ushered their brood back into the concealment of the root-homes. Warriors hefted their javelins, thrust out their chests, flexed their hard, wiry thews.

Hamilton and Angus stopped at the edge of the clearing.

"Make a run for it?" Angus hissed.

"We wouldn't stand a chance. Why don't we see what they have to say." He began walking forward again, surveying the village as he entered. He noticed that all the trunks in which houses were built were offshoots of a huge mother tree-trunk standing directly in the center of the clearing. It was massive, at least twenty feet in diameter. The boughs of this monstrous tree stretched out, and then down, to form the younger trees in which most of the tribe made their homes.

Angus noticed this great bole also. "That place looks rather important. Perhaps we should visit."

"Aye, aye, Commander." Hamilton forced the uneasiness he felt behind his quip.

"Bloody stop that!"

They approached the central trunk. A warm glow shone from within the large hollow in the base of the tree-trunk, and a loud voice echoed across the clearing. "Enter!"

The opening in the wall of roots was just wide enough for one of them to enter at a time, and Angus led the way down into the hollow. A stone-ringed fire pit crackled with orange flames in the center of the large hollow. Across the flames was seated an imposing figure. He was short and stocky like the rest of his tribe, but his skin was clean except for the blood-red lines tattooed down his square-jawed face, continuing down his chest, down his arms and legs, ending in elaborate designs encircling his thick wrists and ankles. Taut muscles bunched and writhed under supple, swarthy skin. His hair was coal black, streaked with silver and square-cut to shoulder length, and two gray eyes danced over them in appraisal. He sat cross-legged on a mat of striped, tawny fur, with a red-painted steel battle ax resting across his knees.

The chamber was about fifteen feet in diameter, and half as tall. An old rope ladder dangled from a hole in the ceiling, the edges of which were worn shiny. Primitive armor fashioned of leather and overlapping bone plates, brilliantly painted, hung from pegs on the wall, and several javelins leaned against the walls.

"I am Canayoga Blood Ax," the man said. "What manner of men are you?"

Angus spoke first. "My name is Angus MacTavish. My companion is Hamilton Corbin. We seek only to pass through your domain unharmed."

"That was not my question. What manner of men are you?" The hard eyes barely flickered.

Hamilton and Angus stood before him, looked at one another in bafflement. Finally Hamilton answered, "We are travelers from a far-away land."

"You lie." Canayoga Blood Ax's fingers tightened around the haft of his wicked-looking ax.

"No," Hamilton said, "We tell you the truth."

"You are Ophidians. You are Lord Snake's." A vicious edge rose in the man's eyes as he spat on the floor.

"No!" Hamilton protested. "We are not Sneev's men. We were merely passing through his lands."

Blood Ax fingered the edge of his ax. His eyes were granite. "Your horses were Ophidian stock. Your arms are all Ophidian made. You speak with an Ophidian accent. Therefore, you are Ophidians. Therefore, you are of the Snake. Therefore, you shall die."

"No, wait!" Hamilton protested again. "We are not Sneev's men! We are trying to escape him!"

"Then you are either criminals or deserters, and therefore, still worthy of death."

Angus leaped to his feet, struggling to pull his sword free.

A spear shaft from behind shattered against the back of his skull, and he hit the floor again, unconscious.

Canayoga Blood Ax growled like a swamp cat. "Strip them and kill them."

Marsh Men flooded into the room before Hamilton could move or protest. His armor was torn off his body, and before he knew it, he was lying naked beside an equally bare but unconscious Angus in the center of the room. Spear points pressed into Hamilton's back, holding him prostrate on the floor as his hands were painfully bound behind his back with thin cords.

"Great Blood Ax!" Hamilton gasped, "Please, don't do this! We're not Sneev's men! We were just travelers that he captured!"

"Enough talk! Take them outside."

The Marsh Men dragged Hamilton and the limp Angus outside by their ankles, and dumped them on the ground. Canayoga Blood Ax raised his head, gathering his voice with his hands. That strange, ululating cry issued from his quivering throat, filling the clearing, echoing into the marsh. Except for the stout guards, the rest of the tribe retreated into their homes. Then the great cat appeared, shouldering through the veil of rushes bordering the clearing. With a low growl it stalked across the open ground.

Canayoga cried out in a strange note, "O Great Akk, friend and protector of the Men of Ryvan, we offer thee the fruits of our war with the Snake!"

It padded toward them, its tufted ears laid back, its muzzle wrinkled into a savage snarl.

As if sensing something was about to happen, Angus began to stir.

Hamilton's mind was a flurry of desperation. Suddenly he had it. With all the power he could muster, he roared, *"Blood Ax, STOP! The One commands you!"*

Canayoga raised his hands to stop the beast's advance. His heretofore inscrutable eyes flashed with anger. He stepped in front of Hamilton, and slapped him across the face with the back of his corded paw. "You dare to profane the name of the sacred One!"

Hamilton, knowing this would be his only chance, gazed squarely into the chieftain's deep-set eyes, and licked the blood nonchalantly from his lip. "How can The One profane himself, Blood Ax? I am He."

Canayoga Blood Ax's hand was a fist this time as it crashed across Hamilton's teeth. "You lie! The One would never allow himself to be defiled by anything Ophidian."

Hamilton blinked the pain into tears, spat blood onto the ground. Then he took a deep breath and said, "Is it not The One's duty to save *all* men, even Ophidians? So says the Prophecy."

Blood Ax seemed taken aback for a moment. Only a moment. "Bah! Ophidians are Uhr's own lackeys! What need have they to be saved?"

"Must not all men be saved from the Ultimate

Evil? So says the Prophecy."

Blood Ax shook his head. "Silence, impostor. You confuse me with your yammering." He raised his hand to the cat.

"Wait, Blood Ax," Hamilton said, "The Prophecy says who The One will be. 'He shall have the Ivory Star in His Breast'. Come, look at my chest, Blood Ax. See with your own eyes that I speak the truth."

Reluctant, but driven by some wild curiosity, Blood Ax stepped up to Hamilton's naked body. It took but a moment for his eyes to lock on the white birthmark emblazoned on Hamilton's left breast.

"By Manogan and Lludd, 'tis true."

A collective gasp rose from the crowd of warriors who had gathered about them. As one, they fell to the ground, kneeling in reverence.

Blood Ax's wide, staring eyes slowly fell as the enormity of what he had done dawned upon him. He dropped to his knees, pressing his forehead to the soft ground. "Forgive me, Great One. I knew not who you were. My tribe and my life are yours!"

The great cat had stopped several paces away, and was watching in feline puzzlement. Angus groggily lifted his head to look around. He saw the Marsh Men kneeling at Hamilton's feet, and after a moment of realization, he stared up in amazement at Hamilton, the only man still on his feet.

"Stand, Blood Ax," Hamilton said.

"I struck The One!" he said, his voice even, with an undertone of shame and resignation. "My life is forfeit."

"I give you back your life, Blood Ax. You may keep it. Now all of you stand up." He glanced down at Angus, and whispered in English, "Get up, Mac. We're getting out of here."

Canayoga Blood Ax stood up, careful to keep

his eyes downcast. The surrounding warriors stood up as well.

"I have only one request of you, Blood Ax," Hamilton said.

"Anything, Great One. If it's within my power, it is yours."

"Guide my friend and I out of the swamp, back to the path."

"It is done. Barak, Thuul, Trar, get up." Three of the stocky warriors leaped up and stepped forward. "You will guide these men back to the path, and protect them from all harm."

"Thank you, Great Blood Ax," Hamilton said, bowing his head. "You are a good man, and a wise leader."

Angus growled, "And bring us our clothes."

Hamilton smiled to help put Blood Ax at ease. "Yes, and bring us our clothes."

Chapter 7

Hamilton glanced over his shoulder at the majestic explosion of color as the great, silver sun slowly buried itself below the skyline of the forest behind them. This world did indeed have some of the most beautiful sunsets Hamilton had ever seen on any world. Angus plodded evenly beside him into the grassy, rolling hills of Armond. The forests of Ophidia were probably a league behind them now.

As they walked, Hamilton said, "What do we do if Valerion is just like Sneev?"

Angus's face was a grim mask. "I don't know."

"He may just try to kill us outright."

"Then he'd better not be too close when he does it."

"But what if—?"

Angus cut him off. "I will not allow what happened with the Marsh Men to happen again."

Silently Hamilton nodded, seeing the rage and humiliation in the set of Angus's jaw.

Twilight cloaked the land, lending long, deep shadows to the valleys below the hills, darkening the tough grass rustling at their mounts' passage. A slender stream gurgled at them from far below as they wound down into the large valley. The stream bubbled from beneath a small rock escarpment below a particularly tall group of hills. Small, bushy trees lined the banks of the stream. The two men knelt and drank their fill from the cool, sweet water. The night began to darken, so they decided to halt and rest there beside the stream. They fashioned themselves some makeshift beds from the springy prairie grass and settled down for a night's rest.

Hamilton lay awake on the ground, listening to the noises of the night creatures, staring up at the stars, vainly trying to recognize just one of the many constellations he was familiar with. He saw nothing even remotely familiar. The silvery splash of the galactic arm was low on the horizon, and instead of a streak, it was more a disk. The vast, unimaginable gulf of space seemed to draw him up as it always did, and he floated among the twinkling beads of color sprinkling the black abyss. Among the stars he drifted forever and ever, enthralled and enticed by their beauty...

Wakefulness came violently.

His eyes snapped open to stare through the web of a stout net. Instinctively he began to thrash about, trying to throw off the tangling strands, but only succeeded in firmly embedding himself within it.

His hand fought for his sword hilt, and he found it, trying to pull the blade free and cut himself loose, when a sudden gripping paralysis seized him, a horribly familiar paralysis. His eyes searched the darkness, and he vaguely saw several waspish, black-cowled figures moving around them.

He could not move a single muscle, and as the time before, he could not even breathe, but he heard Angus growling and cursing not far away. Their attackers bound their hands and feet while they were still enmeshed in the net. Hamilton felt himself hoisted into the air, and draped across the back of a stamping horse. He heard Angus's breath driven from him as he was slung across the back of another horse. The horse beneath Hamilton began to walk, jolting his netted body to and fro. He sincerely wished that this would not be a long journey, but somehow he knew it would be. Then a cold finger touched a nerve in his neck, and he felt nothing at all.

Hamilton's senses seemed to be immersed in some sort of sticky blackness that drowned out everything. Then this tar-like blackness began to leave him, and he could feel the slowly moving horse beneath his body. His eyes would not open yet, but the black thickness was gone from his ears, and he heard the rustle of feet slipping through the thick grass. Gradually he could distinguish the slow, rhythmic plod of the horses' hooves from the soft tread of sandaled human feet. He had no idea how many pairs of human feet walked around him. Sluggishly his vision began to return. The first thing he saw through the ropes of the stout net was the lathered brown belly of his transportation. Next came the grass moving along below. Occasionally a particularly long blade of grass would snake up to tickle his face through the coarse cords. Then, bit by bit, he was able to move his eyes and head. He craned his neck and saw a pitch black robe drifting through the stiff brown-green switchgrass, a thick wooden staff gripped in a thin, white hand, the head hooded in purest black, like the rest of the body. Hamilton craned still further to see a half-dozen more identical figures, among three more horses. Across one of the horses was draped another netted body.

The sun stared down at them from its zenith. As Hamilton's body slowly came back to life, he painfully felt the aching bruises now covering his abdomen and thighs. He moaned softly, involuntarily. The hooded face of the man walking beside him glanced quickly at him and then away.

They traveled on. He realized that they were traveling northeast through the hills, toward a towering mountain range that jagged up into the sky. He twisted his head, trying to see Angus. A cold fear whispered through him that Angus was dead, but somehow he knew that Angus remained alive.

The sun grew hot on his back, and he slipped in and out of consciousness.

By mid-afternoon, the sun was a blacksmith's furnace. Sweat poured in a steady stream across his face, dripping down out of sight among the grass. The sweltering heat taxed the horse, too, judging from its choked, labored breathing. He looked groggily up at the black-robed man walking beside him who seemed unaffected by the heat, walking with a steady stride. Not once did Hamilton see a water bottle or a food bag.

His tongue became a lump of dry leather in his throat, as the blazing heat reflected off the thick grass.

Then the small party stopped.

Their captors looked about, as if they had heard something. They looked up with some excitement in the direction of a nearby hill. The air was quiet, save for the heavy breathing of the horses.

Now Hamilton heard hoofbeats, fast approaching. The black figures looked at one another. They gripped their hardwood staves in their fists and moved toward the sound, to stand between the approaching sound and their own animals.

Hamilton could not see all of them, for they

were hidden by the horse's body. The muffled sounds became suddenly clear as the oncoming horses broke the crest of the hill, galloping down upon them. He heard the accompanying jangle of armor and accouterments and the throaty cries of the men who wore them. No sound came from the eight cowled figures. They merely stood motionless, like obsidian statues, staves in their porcelain fists.

The approaching riders came hard upon the small party. Hamilton caught a glimpse of one of the wooden staves carried by their captors, and thought he saw a crimson glow appear at its tip as the man holding it stepped out of sight. The horses reared, and if Hamilton had not been lashed across the back of the horse, he would have been dumped onto the ground. Screams of rage and agony split the air. Sod flew high into the air, torn by trampling hooves. Something crashed into Hamilton's horse, spinning it around, just in time for him to see a mail-swathed warrior pile onto the ground. The man jerked and twitched, spraying gore into Hamilton's face from an unseen wound.

The men in black faced the mounted warriors with eldritch staves upraised. A mounted warrior galloped into them, broadsword upraised to split the nearest black-hooded skull. A red-glowing staff licked out like a serpent's tongue, and seemed to brush the man's mailed throat. He suddenly flew back off the saddle as if struck by a hammer, and landed heavily on his back, where he kicked and thrashed spasmodically in an agony of death. He clawed at his throat through the coif, gurgling and coughing, spraying a froth of blood from his mouth.

The remaining warriors were among the men in black, iron-shod hooves ripping up the tough sod, blades slinging crimson across the grass. The eerie staves licked here and there, and men flew from the saddle, dying in excruciation like the first. Razor-honed steel sheared through wood and bone. The black figures sank to the earth in death. Then it was over.

Eight ebon robes lay in heaps in the grass. Twelve soldiers remained.

One of them slid from the saddle, shoved his blood-smeared bastard sword into its sheath, and approached Hamilton's shivering horse. Hamilton felt himself pulled from the animal's back. His numbed legs collapsed under his weight, and he toppled to the ground, gasping in pain.

"They live," the man said to his men.

As Hamilton lay in the grass only half aware, the net was cut from him, and water poured into his mouth. He gulped at it frantically. Strong hands pulled him to his feet, as he gazed stupidly about him. He looked around and saw Angus guzzling water from a bottle.

Two of the warriors were examining one of their dead. They peeled back the blood-soaked mail coif, and stared in astonishment at the man's throat. Where the staff had touched his neck, it looked as if a huge bite had been taken from it. His throat was torn almost through, baring one side of the backbone. And not so much as a scratch was detectable in the armor.

Meanwhile, another of the men tore off the hood of one of the black corpses, revealing the shaven head with the scarlet circle branded upon the man's forehead. Suddenly the hem of the ebon robe began to smolder, and a tongue of fire licked up. In an instant, a blood-red flash consumed the corpse. When it faded, a burning circle smoldered in the grass where the corpse had been. Then the other corpses erupted in balls of crimson flame.

The fourteen bedazzled men shielded their eyes from the glare, and when they opened them again, they saw seven more burning circles etched in the sod.

Hamilton and Angus stood quietly leaning against each other, rubbing their legs, wrists and arms to restore circulation and flexibility to their muscles, regaining their equilibrium. The twelve warriors paid them little attention as they began to lift their dead onto the riderless mounts, securing the corpses with rope. The soldiers were armored with chain mail hauberk and coif, thick leather chausses and iron-banded leather helms. They tethered the horses used by the men in black to their own saddles.

The man who had spoken climbed into the saddle of his dappled gray mare, turned and regarded Hamilton. This man had a strong, handsome face, framed by a gray-striped red beard and mustache. Two intelligent green-blue eyes flickered behind the iron nasal of his helm. A fierce scarlet dragon writhed about an ax and sword on his soiled white jupon, identical to that of every man with him. A pair of vaned metal wings adorned his helm.

Hamilton looked up at him, and said, "We seek Lord Valerion."

The man's voice was firm as he replied, "And you are?"

"Hamilton Corbin."

"Angus MacTavish."

"You can ride."

Angus and Hamilton promptly climbed onto the horses used by their former captors. They rode bareback, but it was preferable to walking. Their leader raised his arm. The troop started forward, men-at-arms falling behind him in double-file.

They traveled through the day. The sun gradually sank nearer the horizon behind them. Hamilton could sense the warriors' anger and frustration over the bizarre deaths of their comrades. They were also very distrustful of Hamilton and Angus. No one spoke. The only sounds were the steady plodding of the horses through the rustling grass, the clink and rhythmic jangle of armor and weapons. The sun beat down, and the men doffed their helmets, loosened their hauberks to let the cooling breeze through them. Nothing larger than a bush or shrub provided respite from the monotony of the heat and the long rolling hills. Here and there a small stream trickled through the valleys, forming ponds or continuing on their courses. A scarce few trees grew near the water but only the small scrubby sort. As the great orb above just touched the hills behind them, they came upon a well-kept, stone-paved road that shot straight as an arrow from west to east. They traveled east along this road as the day shifted mellowly into dusk, and the parching heat of the day faded into a wonderful breezy sweetness, touched gently by the scent of grass and distant wildflowers.

As the party topped the crest of a hill, they saw a fair-sized town nestled in the valley below. Hundreds of sod buildings lay spread across the deep valley. Hamilton saw little activity in the deepening dusk. The group of warriors clopped casually down the stone road, which formed the town's principal thoroughfare. A few tethered horses stood along the street, and an occasional open window cast a yellow square onto the main street. Here a light winked out, there another.

The leader of the band raised a hand in signal to halt, beside a wide open brightly lit doorway. Above the doorway hung a wooden sign, painted white with a red flaming dragon on it. Not far from the door loomed the open front of the stable. The men came to a halt, and dismounted with the creak of leather.

The man with the winged helm strode toward the door, spurs clinking on his heavy boots. Everyone followed him into the large sod building. The room beyond was lit by the brightly crackling fireplace and several smoky oil lamps placed about the hazy room. Tables and chairs filled the room, with a short bar along one wall. Farmers and business-keepers stared past their goblets at them as they entered. The low-raftered ceiling deepened the smoky heaviness of the air, and the savory scent of roasting meat and the tang of wine filled their nostrils. Hamilton's mouth watered in anticipation.

The leader of the band of warriors removed his winged helm, shaking loose his matted shoulder-length mop of gray-streaked reddish-brown. "Fortine, you fat fool!" he barked. "Get you out here!"

A balding circular head, fringed with wisps of gray, popped out of the brightly lit kitchen door to ascertain the cause of ruckus in his tavern. His eyes bulged at the sight of the armed and armored men standing in his doorway. He quickly regained his composure and strolled out of the kitchen. A furry belly hung out merrily from beneath his sweat-and-lard-stained shirt. A double-chin draped his hairy throat. Powerful arms, now sheathed in a layer of fat, swung at his sides, and a long, vicious chopping knife was thrust into his belt.

"Robinton, you witless sword-swinger," he roared, "what do you in my tavern? Causing trouble?" The two men stalked toward one another.

Suddenly both laughed and clapped each other

into a fearful embrace, swearing and battering each other's backs with gusto.

Fortine stood back and held Robinton at arm's length. "Ah, Robinton, you old devil dog! What do you in Dynorr? No trouble on the border is there?"

Robinton grinned through his beard. "Nay, nay. No more than usual with Sneev I suppose. Just a routine patrol today."

Fortine lowered his arms and looked askance at the taller Robinton. "Now tell not a lie, man, nay, not even a bent truth. There's still enough sense in this fat head to know that a mere patrol would not be made entirely of Red Dragons, and with you in command no less."

Robinton lowered his voice. "Not now. Later, after our bellies are full and our horses stabled."

Fortine nodded. "Aye, I understand. By the by, how is my lord Valerion these days?"

"I wouldn't know," Robinton said, "I haven't seen Lakeside in well-nigh two weeks. And a bloody two weeks it's been."

Fortine cocked his head in concern, then shrugged. "Well, find yourselves someplace to rest your bones. I'll dig up some food for your empty bellies." With that he turned and strolled back into the kitchen.

Robinton and his men, Hamilton, and Angus traced their way among the closely spaced tables toward the rear of the tavern, near the cold fireplace. The men relaxed, loosening their sword belts, leaning back in their chairs, stretching their tired muscles.

Hamilton and Angus sat comfortably in the chairs, saying nothing, just surveying their surroundings and taking stock of the people around them. Robinton sat next to them, as if to watch them more closely. Nevertheless, Hamilton and

Angus began to relax for the first time in days. Somehow, they felt they were safe here.

Soon Fortine and two serving girls brought several platters laden with roast haunch and fresh bread, jugs of thin wine, polished wooden plates and drinking jacks. The hungry men dug into the meal with relish.

After they finished, Fortine took away the plates, and then returned. Sitting down backwards on a chair, his belly hanging low between his thighs and his meaty arms crossed atop the back of the chair, he said, "Now, Robinton, let's have it."

The soldier leaned forward, resting his cordiere-covered elbows on the rough table. "You were correct, Fortine, about the nature of our mission. After what...what happened to the sun, Lord Valerion received word of something big happening. He didn't tell us what. He just sent us to patrol the Ophidian frontier. Apparently his source was accurate, because several days ago we intercepted a band of Ophidian fighting men quite a distance within our borders. Sneev himself was with them."

"No," Fortine said in disbelief, "I thought Sneev never left his little burrow."

Robinton shrugged. "He got away before I had a chance at him. A couple of others escaped, but we otherwise slaughtered the lot of them."

"Hah! Good!"

Then Robinton's brow creased. "But there was...something else."

"What else?" Fortine asked, his eyes widening in curiosity. "Where?"

"There. Where we fought. It was the strangest creature..."

"Yes? Yes?" Fortine prodded.

"But it was dead. It was huge and made of metal, but unlike anything I've ever seen. The words fail me to describe it."

"A creature made of metal?" Fortine said.

Some of the warriors began to shift uncomfortably in their seats, obviously uneasy about even discussing the matter.

"In any case, it was dead." Robinton tried to change the subject. "Several days later we met with a trader caravan on the Trade Road. One of the merchants told us they had seen a band of Red Priests traveling through Armond carrying two prisoners with them, so we went off in pursuit of them."

Fortine growled, perhaps too loudly, "What in the name of The One were Red Priests doing in Armond?"

The heads of the nearby patrons turned to stare at them, eyes wide with surprise and fear. Several of them made peculiar gestures to ward off evil.

Fortine lowered his voice. "What were the Red Priests doing in Armond? We've heard nothing of them for years."

"In sooth I wish it would have remained so. As I said, they had these two men captive," Robinton said, gesturing toward Hamilton and Angus, who fidgeted in their seats, uncomfortable being discussed as if they were absent.

Then Hamilton said, "They were after us."

"Well, Robinton, I hope you slew the black bastards in any case," Fortine said, apparently ignoring him.

"Aye, that we did," Robinton said, and his men nodded proudly in agreement.

Suddenly Fortine turned to stare at Hamilton. "Did you say they were after you?"

Angus abruptly stood up, his hard knuckles resting on the table. "Aye, they were."

Fortine's eyes peered at him askance, eyes

narrowing, as he pulled the long, wide chopping knife from his belt and toyed with it, spinning it like a lethal child's top on the rough table top. He glanced at Robinton. "And what think you of their growing boldness?"

Robinton glared at Angus as he answered Fortine's query. "I am uneasy. Something has lent them reason to suddenly show themselves. I just wish I knew what."

The tankards of wine jumped as Angus's fist struck the table. He was tired of being ignored. "Damn you, I know why they were—" His sentence was cut short by a gasp of terror from one of the patrons.

Nearly a score of black-hooded figures now stood within the room, simple wooden staves clutched in their thin, pale fingers. Robinton and his men were on their feet in an instant, frantically tugging at their sword hilts. The wraiths in black began to move forward.

Chapter 8

The ebon swathed figures glided forward, eerie red lights shining on the tips of their brandished staves. Robinton's men threw their chairs out of the way and drew their blades. But the Red Priests stopped, and the two groups faced each other silently, each waiting for the other to make a move, with the common folk caught cowering the middle.

One of the Red Priests wore a long scarlet strip of cloth draped around his neck and down his chest, and his staff was laced with patterns of intricate carvings. "Hold!" he cried, "Men of Valerion, we quarrel not with thee. We have come only for those taken from us. Return them to us, and we shall allow thee to live."

Fortine hissed to Robinton, "Let 'em have 'em then."

"Silence, Fortine," Robinton muttered.

Hamilton and Angus, swords in hand, glanced uneasily about them, knowing these Armondians were seriously considering the Red Priests' request.

Robinton growled in defiance. "We have nothing of yours."

The figure in black spoke. "Thou art sorely mistaken, vassal of Valerion." His split tongue distorted the words hideously as he spoke, raising the staff to point at Hamilton and Angus. "These slaves were stolen from us, and we mean to have them. Return them to us, and we shall forgive thee the slaughter of our brothers."

"We did mankind a service in their killing!" Robinton spat in return. "And what is your business with them? They are now under the protection of Lord Valerion."

"They are our prisoners."

"No longer."

"Then we have no choice but to kill you all."

Robinton howled, and leaped toward the figure in black. "Have at them, lads!" His bastard sword whistled up and down in a glittering arc that at once clove deep into the Red Priest's hood and crushed the gurgling corpse down into a heap on the floor.

As one, the Armondian warriors charged, thirsty for blood, leaping over tables with blades glinting in the smoky orange firelight. Wine flew through the air from a thrown tankard. A Red Priest ducked reflexively, distracted enough to allow Robinton's blade to punch through his bowels, and bare two feet of gore-smeared blade behind his back. Robinton dragged his steel from the crumpling body as he darted lithely inside the reach of one of the ghastly staves. He caught the carved wood with his arm just above the wielder's grip, ripping the staff out of the pale hand, smashed his steel-plated elbow across the black-hooded face. As the Red Priest staggered back, Robinton's heavy boot snapped his knee backward with a sickening crunch, and the battered Red Priest collapsed into a whimpering heap.

The Red Priests moved forward with the clash and clatter of melee. The townsfolk ducked under the tables or edged towards the door. Hamilton and Angus were left standing alone in the corner.

Then Angus said, "These men are fighting for our lives!"

"You're right!" Hamilton cried, his sword quivering in his fist. He had never had to think about entering a deadly fray before. Until now they had been thrust into them.

"Stay close to me," Angus growled, as he circled the tables toward the nearest black figure.

Two Armondians screamed terribly, their heads falling unnaturally aside as they collapsed.

Hot gore suddenly sprayed Hamilton's face, and he cringed reflexively, as the force of a nearby Armondian's blade slung an arc of sticky scarlet from its deadly sheen before it crunched into the skull of another Red Priest.

A Red Priest stepped forward, his staff spinning in a red-glowing whirlwind of grisly death. Angus waited with hard-clenched weapon for the figure to attack. The staff licked forward, and Angus clumsily batted the stroke away, but would have been caught by the other end of the staff, if not for Hamilton. Hamilton had skirted the Red Priest, and, as the other deadly end of the staff flew for Angus's throat, he hacked through the Priest's hamstring: The collapsing leg threw the blow off enough for Angus to dodge. Angus wasted no time in taking advantage and chopped down into the figure's shoulder in the crease between neck and torso. The corpse fell, dragging Angus's sword with it. He cursed as he struggled to jerk the blade out of the dead man's breastbone. Hamilton saved his life once again, stepping before him to block the attack of another enemy aiming for Angus's head. An Armondian sword blow from behind dispatched his adversary.

Suddenly it was over, and the only people left standing were Armondians, and Hamilton and Angus.

Before anyone else could say anything, Fortine bellowed, "Get their filthy carcasses out of here, before they start my tavern afire!"

The other Armondians heeded quickly, dragging the oozing bodies outside into the street. No sooner was the last thrown onto the pile of dead than they began to burst into dazzling scarlet flames, leaving their smoking rings forever etched on the cobbled street.

"Be damned," Fortine said, "I'm going to have to cover that up." He rubbed his stubbled chin as he stared at the slowly cooling circles. "Else I'll never get another patron."

Robinton strode up to Hamilton, eyes blazing. "Now, stranger," he said, standing barely a hand's breadth away. "Why in Hell are you and your companion of such importance to the Red Circle that they are willing to sacrifice a score and more men in an effort to fetch you?"

"I..." Hamilton began.

"And why," Robinton demanded, "have I lost fifteen good men to save your worthless hides?"

"Well..." Hamilton stuttered.

Robinton's voice rose. "And *why*, above all, do you seek my lord? Speak!"

Hamilton took a step backward, unbalanced at this outburst.

Angus strode forward. "Now listen here!"

The flat side of Fortine's chopping knife against his belly stopped him short. "I'll hear what he has to say, large one."

Robinton did not take his eyes from Hamilton. "Speak, damn you, or I'll finish what the priests began!"

Hamilton swallowed hard, then said, "We were told to come here to meet Lord Valerion."

Robinton's eyes narrowed. "By whom?"

"A man," Hamilton said, struggling to gain his composure. "A man named Garth, Son of Arnor."

Robinton took a step backward, a disarmed scowl knitting his red brows. "How long ago?"

"Two days."

"Two days! Are you sure?"

"I am quite sure."

"Then he still lives?" Robinton looked away in obvious disbelief.

The Armondians began to mumble amongst themselves.

"He lived when we stayed with him in his cottage not three days gone."

Robinton shook his head. "You lie."

Hamilton straightened his shoulders. "I do not lie. His cottage lies half a day's ride west from Ryvan Marsh. He told us to seek Lord Valerion."

Robinton took his red-bearded chin thoughtfully between thumb and forefinger.

Hamilton recognized his wonderment and did not ease off.

"He said that Valerion would help The One."

"The One!" Robinton exclaimed. Then his tone grew skeptical. "What know you of The One?"

"He is here."

Several of the men laughed.

Robinton laughed humorlessly. "You?"

Hamilton nodded soberly.

"That is absurd. There have been many through the centuries claiming to be The One, and all of them Uhr has quickly eaten. Why has he not eaten you? Are you still too small a fish?" Sarcasm dripped like scalding water from Robinton's tongue as he crossed his mailed arms across his chest.

"Several days ago," Hamilton said, "a strange silver dragon landed in Armond. Robinton, you yourself said that you saw it. Am I correct?"

Robinton's eyes widened in surprise, then hardened. "Aye, I was there. Were you one of the men who escaped with Sneev? If so, I'll simply gut you right here, and be done."

"My friend and I," Hamilton said, "were not one of the Ophidians who escaped, but the men they carried on their horses tied behind them. We were Sneev's prisoners." Hamilton glanced at Angus and winked.

Angus cocked his chin in acknowledgment, waiting for Hamilton to finish.

Hamilton continued, "Sneev took us from the 'silver dragon' and kept us prisoner in his fortress for several days. He tried to kill us, and we managed to escape. Tell me, Sir Robinton, did The Sun recently turn the color of blood?"

Robinton stiffened. "Aye...it...it did. Two days before..."

Hamilton sensed the upper hand now, and pressed, "Tell me, Robinton, did that great chunk of silver look much like a dragon?"

"Indeed, no, as I said. It wasn't like any dragon I'd ever heard of."

"Then its resemblance was, perhaps, a resemblance only?"

"Aye, perhaps." His eyes narrowed, searching Hamilton from head to toe, measuring him somehow, also wary to being duped. Then his gaze switched to Angus, measuring him also.

"Angus and I were riding inside that dragon. Not riding it, but riding in it."

The warriors were murmuring again.

Hamilton smiled inwardly. "Garth, Son of Arnor, read to us a passage from an ancient book.

He said, 'The One shall come when The Sun turns to Blood. The One shall come riding, but not riding, a silver Dragon that is not a Dragon. He shall have the Ivory Star in His Breast, and He shall free Mankind from the Ultimate Evil'."

"The Prophecy, of course," Robinton said dryly. "Every man knows the Prophecy almost from birth."

"That's what he called it," Hamilton said. "Now I have something to show you." He unbuckled the straps of his hauberk, and pulled it off over his head. Slowly he began to lift his soiled tunic and pull it off. He straightened and faced Robinton barechested in the evening breeze. The fourpointed star blazed whitely on his breast.

Robinton took a step back. His face was taciturn, but his eyes betrayed him.

Gasps of excitement escaped the Armondians.

Fortine whispered, "Well, broil my guts in barr-liver oil, it may just be true!"

Hamilton merely stood there, his visage firm, without arrogance.

Robinton stared at Hamilton's chest. Then he said solemnly, "My lord." He knelt on one knee.

Without hesitation every other Armondian followed his example.

Hamilton shook his head in sudden embarrassment. He had to stop all this groveling to him. "Up, men! You are warriors! I am not a lord or a king to pay obeisance to, nor will I ever be! I am a man, like you."

Robinton and all his men slowly took their feet, gazing upon Hamilton with unquestioning awe.

Angus stepped around Fortine, leaning into Hamilton's ear, and whispered in English, "I'm with you, my friend."

Hamilton looked at him, smiling warmly. His blood pulsed with excitement. "I know, Mac. You always have been. More often than not you've been in front of me, protecting me."

Angus grinned and snickered.

Hamilton felt his chest swell with both love for his friend and a new-found strength. Even as he had been speaking, Hamilton felt his own strength rising like a tide, like he had merely opened a floodgate to a power that had been with him all along.

"What is your wish, my lord?" Robinton asked.

"First of all, my name is Hamilton. My friend is Angus. Secondly, sir, you do not need my leave for anything. What is your wish?"

Robinton smiled in pleasant surprise. "Well, Hamilton and Angus, I wish to go inside and fill my belly with Fortine's swill, and sleep in a much-craved bed."

"So we shall," Hamilton said, picking up his hauberk and gesturing Robinton to lead the way.

By noon the following day, the town of Dynorr and Fortine's inn were far behind. At first light Robinton roused his men and began to make their preparations for departure. Fortine agreed to see to it that the dead were properly cared for, and Robinton secured their accouterments to their saddles for return to their families. Their clamor awoke Hamilton and Angus sleeping in one of the other rooms, and before the sun broke the horizon, the party was on the road.

The brilliant white disc of the sun rose from between the squatting hulks of a distant mountain range before them. The land began to rise and fall in the growing foothills of the faraway black mountains.

Hamilton and Angus rode beside Robinton. Hamilton said, "Sir Robinton, I have some questions to ask you."

"If I can, I will answer."

Hamilton took a deep breath. "Who is Uhr?"

Robinton shot him a look of amazement, at once accompanied by distrust and skepticism. "Do you say that you don't know?"

Hamilton nodded. "That is the truth. I don't know who Uhr is."

"How can The One be so ignorant of his destiny and purpose?"

Hamilton scratched his head. "As I told you last night. We are merely travelers. We are not from your world."

Robinton waved his hand in disbelief. "Yes, yes, you said that last night, about your dragon actually being a sky ship, but I didn't believe you then either. Some of our more far-fetched scholars believe that there are spheres other than ours but those with any credibility are killed by Uhr, and those without any are simply mocked."

Hamilton repeated his question. "Who is Uhr?"

Robinton sighed, shaking his head in disbelief. "He is the Evil One himself. Demon made flesh. Necromancy incarnate. And worst, he is the ruler of the world." At that moment, Robinton happened to glance up. He cursed under his breath, then said, "And he is Master of that thing!"

Hamilton followed his gaze. Floating sluggishly through the azure sky high above was a beast such as Hamilton had never seen. It looked vaguely reptilian, with vaned, batlike wings. Blood-red scales reflected the droplets of sunlight like spattered gore. A long tail trailed the creature's lumpy body, and massive hooked talons dangled limply at its front. Its wide, toadlike head leered down at them from its dizzying height, watching.

Hamilton shuddered.

"Uhr knows of you," Robinton warned. "However little you know about him, you can stake your mother's life he knows all about you."

"Why is everyone so frightened of him?" Angus asked, "If he is merely one being—man, beast, demon, whatever—why not simply kill him? Surely if he is so terrible, you could raise an army large enough."

Robinton hissed, "Lower your voice, man! We know not how sharp of hearing is that thing!" He lowered his voice still further. "No worldly means will take Uhr's life. He has lived for a thousand years, almost from the beginning of time. He has his own demonic army of Slayers that enforces his wishes. It is said that the Slayers are men whose souls have been devoured by Uhr." His tanned face grew pale as he spoke.

Hamilton stared forward. "I had no idea," he whispered.

Robinton continued, "And then bastards like Sneev follow him like puppies. Sneev is Uhr's informant and ally. He keeps close watch for Uhr on all the other lords."

"But if Uhr has so much power, why can't he watch everyone himself?" Angus asked.

Robinton shrugged.

Angus said, "Can Valerion trust the other two lords to help him if a war with Uhr is coming?"

Robinton's face regained its color, as if this was a subject more suited to a warrior's blood. "Skaand will help us, I think, but Erastus values the lucrative trade routes, which Uhr has allowed him to keep, therefore he treads the dividing line between loyalty to Uhr and rebellion. It would take some major event, such as the coming of The One with the Ivory Star in hand to tip him to our side."

Hamilton took a step back in the conversation. "You said earlier that Uhr could be slain by no worldly means. How then is The One to destroy him?"

"With the Ivory Star."

Hamilton regarded him. The Ivory Star was what he himself had called the sun above his head.

Robinton noticed Hamilton's expression and explained, "The Ivory Star is a mystic talisman, forged when Uhr was young, to destroy Uhr when the time is right."

Hamilton asked, "What is it, specifically?"

"No one knows."

"Where is it?"

"No one knows."

Angus broke in, "Then how is The One supposed to use it?"

Robinton shrugged. "That is for The One to discover."

Angus humphed in disgust.

Hamilton asked, "Who are these Red Priests?"

Robinton spat on the ground. "The Circle of Red Priests is an order of monks who make their home in Vicorian Mountains north of here. No one really knows much about them. But it seems they want you badly."

"They are allied with Uhr?"

"No. For centuries they have been his deadly enemies, which, I think, is why they want you. They want to use you to destroy him."

"Isn't that what everyone wants?"

"If the Red Priests managed to kill him themselves, with you under their control, they would then have enough strength to simply usurp Uhr's throne and rule in the same manner."

Hamilton nodded. He found himself trusting this man, with his forthright nature and easy conversation. They continued over the road toward the east. The iron-shod hooves of the horses clip-clopped steadily along. A few trees dotted the vast expanse of hilly grassland, but so sparsely that only two or three could be seen at one time. Occasionally a gurgling stream crossed their path, and they rode across the small stone bridges. They passed by peasant families laboring in the golden fields of rippling grain, and draft horses bearing wagons full of vegetables, a shepherd and his flock of sheep.

As the sun fell and dusk began to deepen, they reached a roadside inn called The Cool Tankard. The tall, well-built innkeeper welcomed them as his three giggling tots cavorted around his legs.

They dismounted and made their way through the gate into the walled compound that comprised the center of the structure. The house itself was built into one side of the outer wall, with the stable built into the other half.

The men dismounted, stretching their legs and massaging their rumps from a long day's riding. As they filed through the gate into the yard to take care of their horses for the night, Angus passed one of the innkeeper's children.

Two saucer-sized blue eyes stared up at him in wonder. Flaxen curls framed her small, copper-flecked face, with her thumb planted firmly in her mouth. Her thumb popped out as she said frankly, "Yer biiiig!"

The tall, barrel-chested Scotsman squatted beside her, resting his elbows on his knees. "And so are you, my lady."

She twisted at her skirt, twirling her little frame back and forth. "But not as big as you are."

"That is true," Angus said, "I am bigger, but your beauty far exceeds mine."

Her freckled cheeks flushed, and she fled with a giggle. She found refuge behind her father's leg, and the innkeeper laughed as she hugged it, the thumb back in her mouth. He tousled her flaxen hair.

"My lord Robinton," the innkeeper said, "I have room enough for all your men, and supper is in the kettle."

"Most welcome news, Master Leonidas," Robinton said, "and I have news for you, sir, most welcome news indeed."

Chapter 9

Hamilton sat bolt upright in his bed. The sound and sting of the slap were fresh on his cheek, and the dreamworld scent of a gurgling stream and a woman's perfume fresh in his nostrils. He had been sitting beside a giggling brook, surrounded by cataracts of milky flowers that glowed in the moonlight. Someone sat next to him. The sweetness of her scent, the music of her voice as she laughed with him, the silky touch of her hand on his. The dark sheen of her long hair, and her alabaster flesh.

He knew who she was without looking at her face. They were just laughing and talking wordlessly, as people do in dreams, and it was comfortable, natural, as if they had done it a thousand times. Slowly, imperceptibly, Hamilton began to move closer to her. Their voices faded. Their eyes locked. Their lips brushed only for an instant, and she gasped in outrage, drew back and struck him across the face. The stinging smack jerked him from sleep.

He lay back on the mat, touching his cheek with gentle fingers, and lay awake until the cock crowed.

The party left the roadside inn early that morning. Robinton called back to the innkeeper as they rode away, "Don't forget, Leonidas. When the Great Conjunction draws near, pick up your family and head for Lakeside. You will be safe there!"

The inn was left far behind, and the sun grew warm again, sweltering the men in their padded metal hauberks.

They crested a hill to hear a cacophony of growling, yipping and barking. They saw a writhing mass of small brownish-red canine beasts clustered about something a few paces from the roadside. Roughly a dozen of them, feeding on what looked like the remains of some large carcass.

"Filthy farracs!" Robinton snarled, drawing his sword. He spurred his mount toward the writhing mass of wild dogs, howling. "Away, you filthy sons-of-bitches!"

The farracs scattered like rats, yipping and snarling in protest at the interruption of their repast. Robinton's horse reared at the sight of the mangled carcass, its hooves beating the air.

"Away, blast you!" His bastard sword flashed down, cleaving one of the animals nearly in twain.

Hamilton glanced at the other men, who did not seem the least bit interested in Robinton's outburst.

The farracs disappeared in the tall grass, and Robinton returned to the ranks.

"I fail to understand your hatred of those animals," Hamilton said.

"Are you daft?" Robinton asked, shoving his bloodied sword home. "They're but filthy carrion eaters!"

"But don't they serve a purpose?"

Robinton snorted in disgust, and said, "And what possible purpose could that be?"

"They are carrion-eaters, correct?"

"Yes, but what of that?"

"Do they not remove the carrion?"

Robinton opened his mouth to speak, then shut it again in a moment of realization. He said nothing for a while.

Angus said in English, "Ham, I thought you were supposed to be merely a military leader."

Hamilton shrugged. "Maybe The One is supposed to be more than that."

The column's journey continued through the rest of the day and most of the next. As they traveled, the land grew progressively rougher. The low, rolling hills began to climb higher and higher, with steeper grades and more bare rocks pushing through the thin layer of soil. Cool breezes from the mountains ahead of them made the heat bearable. Their path led them parallel to a river, narrow and fast-moving, a hundred paces or so from the road, flowing toward them out of a large lake that came visible a league or so ahead.

The lake lay like a flawless jewel at the base of the first towering mountain peaks. As they crested a final hill, the town of Lakeside came into view at the far end of the glimmering expanse, not far from the base of the mountains. The setting sun behind them cast a dazzling silver ribbon across the glimmering surface of the water. And there, just visible beyond the cozy-looking town of Lakeside, sitting on three small islands near the shore, sat a fortress with walls of grim, gray stone. The fortress of Lord Valerion.

Robinton traced his party around the shore of the lake, approaching the town and the imposing fortress looming behind it. As they neared the edge of the lake, Hamilton could discern several small rivers flowing from crevices in the adjacent mountain-sides. The nature of these streams ranged from muddy-flowing trickles to bursting cascades of showering water.

As they neared the town and fortress, Hamilton could see that the town was surrounded by a wooden palisade about twelve feet tall, made of upright logs with the ends sharpened to crude points. The wall ended its rough semicircle at the sheer rocky shorelines on either side of the town. Several men-at-arms patrolled the top of the palisade.

The party approached the simple wooden gates of the palisade, and the sergeant in charge hailed them. He quickly recognized Robinton and his force, and ordered the gates opened for them.

The cobbled street beyond was flanked by shops, taverns, inns and houses on both sides. The buildings were fashioned from various combinations of wood and sod. Most were only one or two stories, although a few stretched up to a bare three. The weary riders passed into the shadows of deepening dusk along the main thoroughfare. They saw few people. At this hour, most of them would be sitting down to the evening meal.

As they neared the shore of the lake, the street's curve straightened to expose a large, thick-walled structure with its raised portcullis waiting like a black-fanged mouth at the end of the street. Hamilton saw that this was a long tunnel reaching out from the bank, to the bridge leading out over the water to Valerion's fortress. The four men-at-arms standing watch at the entrance greeted them as they passed by into the structure. The inside of the tunnel was fraught with murder holes above and beside, with a heavy portcullis at each end. Hamilton mused at how many men could be slaughtered wholesale if trapped within this structure.

Beyond the tunnel was a stone bridge reaching to a fortified island about fifty paces from the shore. The stone walls of the fortress met the sheer edges of the island about ten feet above the level of the water. At the far end of the bridge was a lowered drawbridge leading into a barbican. This barbican was flanked by thirty foot crenelated towers on either side. After they passed through the barbican, they entered a wide open area with a long, low building nestled against the far fortress wall. Ahead and to their right was another gate. Another bridge stretched beyond this gate, which in turn led to another island, this one a hundred paces from the shore. This wide outer ward they were crossing lay deep in shadow from the falling sun, with the long shadows of three more towers along the southwestern wall falling across the northeastern wall to their right. Sentries were black silhouettes against the red sky, patrolling the battlements with their crossbows across their backs. Ballistae were just visible nosing over the edges of the flanking towers.

They passed through the far gate, onto the stone bridge beyond, towards another drawbridge awaiting them at the far end. Across this they rode, the hooves of their mounts thundering on the thick wood, echoing against the lapping water below. Under the raised portcullis, through the barbican, into the middle ward. Dozens of small cottages filled this wide area, and they rode down the path through the center of the middle ward, towards yet another wall about one-hundred and fifty paces ahead of them. The walls of the middle ward were about twenty-five feet tall, but those were dwarfed by the height of what could only be the defenses of the last bastion, the final barrier against invasion. The walls of the inner ward stood a full fifteen feet higher than those it adjoined, glowing slightly silver in the light of the setting sun.

Angus and Hamilton were speechless with awe as they surveyed the magnificence of this impenetrable edifice, hardly noticing at first the people who came out of their cottages to greet them in the silvery twilight.

Little ragamuffin children scurried about, scolded by mothers who thought them too close to the horses' stamping hooves. Old folk, young, and in-between came out for a view of Valerion's best warriors, or perhaps get a glimpse of a friend or a loved-one returning from expeditionary duty. The hopes of many were dashed at the sight of so many riderless mounts, so many saddles that had once carried their sons and fathers and husbands. Robinton had once again created a few more widows and orphans. Several of those hopeful faces fell in sadness, or suddenly contorted with anguish and disappeared into the cottages.

Hamilton heaved a deep sigh at the sight of their pain. Their loved ones had perished to save the lives of both him and Angus. He hoped that someday he would be able to repay them all for their sacrifice.

A narrow moat separated the wall of the inner ward ahead of them from the middle ward. Another drawbridge waited for them to cross, pass into yet another barbican, through massive wooden gates into a small courtyard. And if everything Hamilton and Angus had seen so far looked impregnable, the Keep was the coup-de-grace. Forty feet high, cylindrical, built into the rear wall of the fortress, its back to the lapping waves. Only arrow slits broke its sheer surface. There was no visible entrance to the Keep, but it formed one of three connected buildings, with Valerion's house on one side, and a stable on the other. Off to the right hand was an inner wall about eight feet tall adjoining Valerion's house, beyond which they could see several trees and flowering bushes reaching high enough to make their presence known.

Valerion's house was a long, low structure of only one story. The front doors were opened wide, casting a warm square of firelight on the courtyard cobbles. Hamilton could see a large open room just inside filled with tables and people. The rich scent of baked bread and roasted meat filled the courtyard. His belly roared in ravenous desire, having had only Robinton's harsh rations of dry bread and jerked meat for two days.

"Looks like we made it just in time," Robinton said, sliding off his horse.

The thick, triple-bolted gates began to swing ponderously closed with the heavy creak of hinges and clank of massive chains. Several men cranked on large windlasses within the barbican to pull the gates closed.

The rest of the column dismounted, and the stable boys appeared and led their mounts away.

Robinton said to his men, "Fall out for the evening meal." He pointed at Hamilton and Angus. "You two," he said, "follow me."

He led them across the courtyard toward the wide open door. As they stepped into the dining hall, Hamilton's gaze swept the room. A gigantic fireplace took up a great portion of the right-hand wall. The floor was lined with long tables and benches filled with dozens of people waiting for the evening meal to be served. Where Sneev's people had been largely reserved and silent, these Armondians were boisterous. Lord Valerion's standard, a red dragon writhing about an upright, wide-bladed dagger on a white field, hung above the high table, which sat conspicuously empty.

Robinton led the two men to the right, past the warmly burning fireplace, which, Hamilton noted, he could have stood up inside. A door in the far corner awaited them, opening to a long corridor. They passed several closed doors before stopping at one near the end of the corridor. Robinton knocked firmly on this one.

A deep baritone voice sounded almost unmuffled by the thick wood. "Enter."

Robinton pushed the door inward, and motioned for Hamilton and Angus to enter ahead of him.

Hamilton could not but stare at this powerful man whose presence alone filled the room. Lord Valerion regarded them with deep-set eyes that blazed like azure stars. His heavy black brows furrowed as he scrutinized them. He stood at least half a head taller than even Angus, with an unkempt mop of coal-black hair hanging square-cut just above his shoulders. Bulging thews sprung from his thick arms like rippling steel bands. Battle-scars criss-crossed his arms, and a few minor ones marked his handsomely chiseled face. A full, black mustache adorned his upper lip. A great broadsword resting in its simple wooden scabbard leaned against a chair beside him, its worn leather-wrapped hilt proclaimed its long-time use. He wore tight-fitting brown trousers and a short-sleeved purple tunic with his standard embroidered into the front.

He stood at the foot of a four-posted canopied bed. A window stood open behind him, overlooking a lush garden. A caged dove rested on a pedestal near the window, and a writing desk sat against one wall.

"Aye, Robinton," Valerion rumbled.

"My lord," Robinton said, kneeling.

Valerion's voice seemed to resonate in the very walls. "Up, Rob! You know to bend your neck not before me!" Robinton stood, and Valerion laughed a deep chuckle. Valerion took a step forward, and clapped Robinton into a powerful embrace, dwarfing him as he did so. "Hah, man, it's good to see you!" he said, as he released him.

Robinton's face was all grin. "I can only say the same, my lord."

"Now, my friend," Valerion said, turning his attention to Hamilton and Angus. "Who are these you've brought before me?"

"My lord, we intercepted a small band of Ophidians, and did battle with Sneev himself. We killed the entire band, save Sneev and two others, who these two men claim were carrying them off as prisoners. They escaped from the Crag, and came to Armond, seeking your protection, whereupon they were again captured, this time by Red Priests. A merchant caravan informed us of the Priests' presence in Armond, so we decided to track them down. When we caught up with them, they were quickly dispatched, and we succeeded in freeing these men. Apparently the Priests wanted them back rather badly, and attacked us in Fortine's tavern in Dynorr."

The lord's eyes scrutinized Hamilton and Angus as he listened intently to Robinton's tale. "Well, then, who are they?"

Robinton took a deep breath, let it out. "The Prophecy is fulfilled, my lord."

Hamilton watched Valerion closely for a reaction. He didn't bat an eye. "Nonsense! The Prophecy is but an old wives' fable."

Robinton protested, "My lord, you cannot mean that. He has the mark!"

"Silence! I care not!" Valerion waved his hand in dismissal, "Get them out of my sight. Feed them, then sleep them in the stables. They can work for their supper in the morning. I want them not in my house."

"But he has the mark!"

"Bah! Get them out of here."

Robinton simply stared at him, mouth agape. His eyes expressed his betrayal. Then he snapped a curt bow, and motioned the two strangers out into the hallway. As he led them back to the dining hall, he said, "I owe you both an apology for my lord's behavior. I don't know what's gotten into him. Perhaps his mood will improve later."

Robinton seated them with the rest of the common folk in the dining hall, where they ate their meal in silence. They stared dumbly at their food, hardly tasting what they lifted into their mouths. They had come here seeking safety and answers to their many questions, and had been scorned.

Valerion never made an appearance in the hall. In fact, no one sat at the high table, a fact that was noted by mumbled comments about them. As soon as they had finished, Robinton took them out to the stables, left each of them a blanket and departed.

Angus turned to Hamilton. "Now what, Great One?"

Hamilton's gaze was calm as he patted him on the shoulder, struggling with himself to remain calm, and not lose control of his emotions, which threatened to submerge him in a wave of crushed hopes. "We sleep, Mac."

Angus snorted in disgust, and threw his blanket down on the fresh straw. "At first sign of trouble, we're leaving. Agreed?"

"Agreed."

They curled up on the straw, side by side, wrapped in their heavy blankets to keep the night chill at bay.

Hamilton lay on his back, arms behind his head, staring up into the dark rafters. "This just keeps getting worse, doesn't it, Mac."

Angus grunted his agreement as he rolled over.

"Did Valerion act like he was hiding something? He seemed preoccupied."

Angus turned to look at him. "You thought so, too?"

Valerion sat down at his writing desk with a scrap of parchment and quill in hand, and began scratching a message down. His pen halted occasionally as his mind grasped in spurts the enormity of the events that had already transpired here, and the events that would surely come. He signed his name with a long, scrawling hand.

He rolled up the parchment tightly and stuffed it in a small silver tube. Then he took the fluttering dove from the cage and tied the silver tube to its leg with a leather thong. Stepping up to the window, he tossed the bird gently into the air, and it disappeared in the darkness with an excited coo.

"Fly, little bird," he said, "fly to your master with my message."

Chapter 10

Hamilton and Angus stirred as the shaft of sunlight from an open shutter speared them.

A booted foot kicked Angus onto his side. "Up, up, up, you lazy oafs!" came a gravely voice.

Angus gasped in surprise and outrage.

Hamilton had just enough time to roll over and see Angus bluster to his feet and lash out with an angry fist. The giant caught Angus's fist in a vise-like grip, and with his own iron-knuckled projectile sent Angus rolling back into the straw. Angus didn't move.

Hamilton knuckled his sleepy eyes as the giant flashed him a tooth-deficient grin.

The giant said, "He threw first, I threw last." He ran sausage-like fingers through his straggling mop of straw-colored hair, and reached down with a hairy paw to help Hamilton to his feet. "Wake him up."

Hamilton found a bucket of water nearby, and with a mischievous grin dashed it over Angus's prostrate form.

Angus shook the water from his hair, blew it from his face and stood up, his eyes glinting like those of an animal enraged.

Glee crossed the giant's unshaven face for but

a moment, but then he raised a hand in warning. "Remember, old boy, you struck the first blow. I merely came to rouse you out o' bed. You men have work to do this fine morn."

Angus's fists clenched.

The giant raised a warning paw. "An' you try it again, I'll be forced to pound you." A hint of anticipation flickered in his ice-gray eyes for an instant, then he continued, "Come with me. Break your fast. Then you work. Oh, by the by, I am Tarl, Lord Valerion's house master. Come."

They followed him wordlessly. Hamilton slapped Angus lightly on the back as he rubbed his sore jaw. Tarl took them to the kitchen and gave each of them two loaves of hard but fresh bread.

"What are those huge doors?" Hamilton asked, pointing past the milling cooks, over the preparation tables, toward the massive steel double doors filling the far wall of the kitchen.

"The entrance to the Keep."

"This place is impregnable," Angus marveled past a mouthful of bread.

Tarl nodded. "Aye it is. In truth, enemies have never set foot in even the outer ward. Now finish your bread. You'll need your strength." Hamilton and Angus tore quickly into the bread, and Tarl continued talking. "Follow me. Eat on the go. You've a full day ahead of you, mangy fellows. First, you'll clean the stables. Then you'll haul out the manure. After all that, I've a full cart o' wood on its way for you t'split. No one eats my lord's food for nothing around here, by Tor's Teeth. You'll work your keep, sluggards, sleeping in 'til all hours of the day, while honest folk are already hard at work. Who the hell are you anyway? My lord isn't in the habit of sheltering vagabonds..." He rambled on as he led them to the stable, and there he put wooden pitchforks in their hands and set them to work.

And work they did.

"This stinks," Hamilton complained

"Ye got that right, laddie!" Angus said, as he pitched a mound of straw and horse-dung onto the pile they were steadily building.

They finished cleaning the stables about noon, when Tarl returned with two more loaves of bread and a bucket full of water for them to drink from. As they munched hungrily, a cart laden with logs trundled into the courtyard, and Tarl gestured with his thumb. "That's next."

By dusk they had finished the wood. Hamilton's arms hung numbly like wet rags at his sides, limply holding the ax in his blistered fingers. He merely stood, slowly recovering his breath, gazing up at the multi-colored sky. "Those must be the so-called Day Stars."

"What? Where?" Angus said, then he dropped his ax in disgust. "'Zounds, man, yer still lookin' at the bloody sky! I'm ready to pass out colder'n a bloody Arcturan fuzzpup! Are ye daft, after all?"

"No, Mac, just curious. They're fairly close together, aren't they?"

Angus sighed and leaned on his ax. "Aye, I suppoose."

"What's all this gibberish you're spoutin'?" Tarl demanded. "What the hell language is that? Allahnian?"

"Precisely," Hamilton said.

"Strange that you don't look Allahnian." He cast them a sidewise glance. "You finished with the wood? Looks like it. Good. Now get your lazy arses to the moat and wash the stench off your worthless hides."

"That's the best idea you've had all day!" Angus growled. He dropped his ax ceremoniously at Tarl's feet, and walked off toward the gate without a look back.

Hamilton saw the look of savage delight ripple across Tarl's face at Angus's impudence. He suppressed a smile. Angus was walking in a posture that dared Tarl to try something. But Tarl didn't. He simply unclenched his fists. Then with a warning glance at Hamilton, he turned and went into the house. Angus just kept walking.

The gate keepers of the inner ward called out that the gates were closing for the night, and Hamilton and Angus were forced to cut short their delicious bath. They walked back into the inner ward, bare feet slapping on the cobblestones, leaving a trail of water from their dripping clothes.

As the gates began to close behind them, Angus stretched his weary muscles. "Gods, that felt bloody good!"

Hamilton nodded. "It did."

"Oh, bloody wonderful," Angus snorted when they saw Tarl approaching.

Tarl was carrying two bundles, one under each arm, and he tossed one to each of them. "Dry clothes. My lord Valerion says that you may eat in the hall again tonight."

Angus's voice dripped with sarcasm. "We are honored."

Tarl spun on him, and stuck a huge finger in Angus's face. "There will be NO disrespect to Lord Valerion by anyone within these walls! I've slain better man than you over disrespect to my lord!"

Angus opened his mouth to retort, but Hamilton laid a hand on his arm to cut him off.

"Master Tarl," Hamilton said, "my friend meant

no disrespect. We would be pleased to dine in the hall as one of Lord Valerion's guests."

Tarl stepped back out of range of Angus's arms before he relaxed. He grunted once and walked away. "Supper begins."

Hamilton released his breath and turned to his friend. "You came that close to getting your ass kicked." He held up thumb and forefinger to his eye and looked at Angus between them.

"Ah, I coulda taken 'im." Angus looked down at the cobbles. "Let's get dressed, eh?"

Tonight, the high table was occupied. Valerion and his family and Robinton sat up there waiting for the meal to commence.

No one paid Hamilton and Angus the slightest heed, except for Robinton, who nodded to them and smiled in acknowledgment. They found an empty space on a bench near the huge fireplace.

"He's got a beautiful family," Hamilton said.

"What? Oh, Valerion you mean."

Valerion sat the midsection of a long table. On his left sat three beautiful women. The closest to him had to be his wife. Her face no longer held the sparkle of youth, but had passed into that realm of older women who, like fine wine, grow finer with age. A golden-threaded net contained her glistening golden hair, and her deep brown eyes regarded her husband with pure love and devotion. The low-cut gown strained to contain her luxuriant bosom. As she spoke and moved, she became grace incarnate, and it was plain she was dam to the young ladies seated beside her.

One was somber, raven-haired like her father, sloe-eyed, breathtakingly beautiful, whose eyes surveyed the crowd as if searching for someone.

The other was a pretty doppelganger of her

mother, except this one possessed her father's azure eyes.

On Valerion's right reposed a lad whose features could not be mistaken. He was Valerion, except thirty-odd years younger. The resemblance was uncanny, though he could not be more than eight. He dexterously played with his knife, spinning it in his hand, deftly tossing it back and forth in a flurry of hand movements.

After all the preparations were finally complete, Tarl seated himself on the end of the table next to Robinton. From this vantage point he watched Hamilton and Angus like a cautious bull.

Hamilton and Angus began their meal after the food was carried out, and failed to notice the scrutiny of someone at the high table. The raven-haired beauty was paying them close attention, but discreetly of course, discreetly.

In the middle of the meal, Angus chanced to glance at the high table, and his gaze immediately met with that of the dark young woman. Their eyes locked, and her luscious lips parted slightly, and smiled at Angus. He returned her gesture, and added a wink. She looked away.

Angus sighed and looked down at his wooden plate. "God, she's beautiful."

Hamilton looked up at him, his mouth full. "Who?"

"That dark-haired girl."

Hamilton glanced over his shoulder. "Yeah, so? Aren't all princesses?"

Angus cracked a smile. "So far, anyway, but this one just gave me a look to melt a glacier."

Hamilton raised an eyebrow, and glanced back again. "She's gone."

"Damn." Angus looked down at his plate again. "Suddenly this meal we worked too damn hard for isn't very appealing."

Hamilton smiled ironically and continued his repast.

After the meal was finished, and everyone was beginning to disperse, Tarl stamped up to where they sat. "Out to the stables, fellows!" he bellowed.

Hamilton and Angus grudgingly went out to the stables. Angus threw his blanket down on the fresh straw. "The boudoir smells much fresher t'night!" he quipped.

"After a while you don't notice it," Hamilton said dryly.

"Greetings, Lord Valerion," the voice said from the darkness.

Valerion gasped in surprise, but did not bother to turn. "Greetings, Master. I hadn't expected you so soon."

"News travels quickly on the wings of doves, Lord Valerion."

The silvery square of moonlight splashed across Valerion's chest as he opened the meeting chamber shutters.

The soft tenor voice in the darkness said, "It has been a long time, my friend."

"Aye, my friend, it has." Valerion turned on his heel.

"He is here?"

Valerion could see the man now, like a disembodied shaven head that glowed in the moonlight. His body was swathed all in deepest back, leggings, hooded tunic, soft boots. His face was handsome, passive, with high cheekbones, a long, straight nose and intelligent black eyes.

Valerion's ears caught the rustle of clothing just behind the man, and only then did he spy the other two standing just behind him. They were identically clothed, except that black masks and hoods covered their heads.

"Aye," Valerion said, "he is here. He has a companion, a large man. Tarl tells me that one has the strength of a bullock."

"That is quite a compliment, coming from Tarl."

"They sleep in the stable."

"I know," the man said. A flicker of amusement crossed his face. "I have been watching them since dusk."

Valerion smiled in amusement and admiration. "Of course you have." Then his voice grew serious. "You will take them then?"

"Not the large one. I cannot train him. He has not the patience or temperament. You train him yourself, as one of your Red Dragons. He will make a mighty warrior, but not as one of the Order. I will take The One and train him, prepare him for what he must do."

"Will he be as powerful as one of you?"

"Less, and more. He has not had a lifetime to learn all the skills of the Order. But he is The One, and therefore, more powerful than only of us."

Valerion nodded, turning away to look out the window at his garden.

"The One will be gone in the morning," the man said, "and you will no longer need to worry so about spies."

Valerion looked back over his shoulder. "How fares Capian?"

"He is well and strong. His skills have much improved."

"It's been a long time..."

"Yes."

"Give him my love."

"I will," the man said, "but there is more. I have foreseen many things of the coming days."

Valerion faced him again, crossing his arms.

"The future is murky, even murkier than the present. But I have foreseen great things for Capian. One day he will be Master of the Order."

Valerion's mouth fell open. "Such an honor...!"

"There will be very little honor in it, I fear."

"What do you mean?"

"I have seen much, but not that much. Catastrophe is coming. Death will reap heavily the living when Uhr's wrath has risen. Fire. Blood. Famine. Plague. This much have I seen."

Valerion's fist crashed onto the table. "Damn you, Sorde, you've always been cryptic, but never like this! Is there no hope? Nothing we can do?"

"Your hope is in the hands of The One, and your own inner strength. Remember this, Valerion. Flesh and bone can be made as steel, if the will is strong enough. You will need your deepest reserves of strength to see Uhr defeated."

Valerion nodded. "It's coming then. There is no stopping now," he said, as he looked up into the aloof face of the moon.

"It begins here," Sorde said. "Farewell, my friend. May Arnor aid you."

"Farewell," Valerion said, looking back, but they were already gone.

Chapter 11

Angus awoke with a stabbing ache in the back of his skull. He groaned, cranking his head around. Where was he? In the stable. Where was Hamilton? Gone. Morning light sprinkled the straw.

"Those bastards took him," he snarled, "those damned Red Priests!" Rage boiled up in him. "Someone's gonna pay!"

They had taken Hamilton, three shadowy black figures. Angus vaguely remembered trying to fight them, but he couldn't remember the blow that had felled him. One moment he had been on his feet, the next, nothing.

He struggled to his feet, his anger shoving aside the pain in his head, allowing room for little else. He stormed out of the stable, across the courtyard. Denizens of the fortress hurried out of the path of this fearsome apparition, with his face twisted by rage, eyes shot with red ribbons, matted with dust and straw.

Angus lurched into the house, through the Great Hall, down the corridors toward Valerion's chambers. There Valerion stood, standing in the corridor, watching Angus's approach with surprise and anger.

Valerion faced him. "Now what are you doing

in my house at this hour!"

Angus stamped toward him, fists clenched. "They took my friend," he growled. "He's gone."

"I know." Valerion's steely blue eyes gazed evenly at him.

Unnoticed by either of them, a door just down the hall cracked open, with a watchful eye and nimble ear within.

"What do you mean, you know?"

"Aye, just what I said. I know. Now step into my meeting chamber where we may speak privately."

"We can speak right here!" Angus's voice rose. He stepped forward, fists clenching.

"My meeting chamber, man!" Valerion growled, his eyes blazing with impending rage. With that he spun and entered the nearest door.

Warm sunlight poured into the room from the open shutter, and Valerion faced Angus with his arms across his broad chest. "Shut the door."

Angus slammed the door as hard as he could, and the echoes shook the building. Then he spun to drill his gaze into Valerion. His voice was ice. "My only friend is gone. And you know who took him. And you will tell me where he is. And you will tell me who they were. And you will tell me why! Or Robinton will pry my cold dead fingers from your cold dead throat."

The veins crossing Valerion's arms and neck throbbed with the effort of containing his rage. "No one threatens me in my own house," he growled. His callused paw stopped halfway to the leather-wrapped hilt of his broadsword.

Angus's teeth clenched. "We had no one to trust but you! An old man in the Ophidian forests told us to come to you, and we trusted him because he helped us. But you!" Angus spat on the floor.

"You're no better than Sneev. At least he's not in league with the Red Priests"

"Hah!" Valerion's outburst cut him off like cold steel. "You think I'm in league with the Red Circle? You are truly mad! And you are a fool."

"Then who were those men who hammered me and took my friend away?"

"They were not of the Red Circle. They were Knights of the Eagles."

"Who in hell are—?"

Suddenly Valerion looked past Angus, towards the door. "Silence!"

"What?"

"Did you hear that?"

"I heard nothing..." Angus said.

Valerion moved tigerishly toward the door and flung it open. He looked up and down the hallway outside. "Hmmm..."

"What did you hear?"

"A stealthy footstep. Clothing against the door. A quick breath."

"What, are you scared of spies in your own house?" Angus said.

"Above all, my own house. Uhr's tentacles can reach into the darkest corners, or the brightest." He took a few steps in each direction, looking for a sign of anyone who may have heard. "There is no one now." He stepped back into the room and shut the door.

Angus repeated his question. "Who in hell are Knights of the Eagles?"

"They're a clan of warriors, scholars, philosophers. Only they know where the Ivory Star is to be found. Only they can train The One for his task."

"You knew?"

"Of course! I am no fool. I take nothing Robinton says lightly. I only suspected at first, then

Robinton told me everything." He toyed with his mustache, looking directly into Angus's eyes. "Robinton tells me this old man you met in the wood, he called himself Garth, Son of Arnor."

"That is true."

"Interesting."

"Why so?"

"No matter." He shook his head, closing the subject. "In any case, the Eagle Knights did not take you because your temperament is not their way. It is better for both you and your friend if you remain here and train yourself as one of my Red Dragons. You certainly have the temperament for that. Rest assured The One is in good hands."

Angus's rage began to subside. "Why didn't you say all this that first night?"

"It was better that I didn't. The walls themselves may have ears." He gestured around him. "If that is so, much is already lost by our conversation. I can trust no one, not even my family, not even Robinton. Uhr knows my 'loyalty' falls not far short of open rebellion, but I think he just toys with me, playing his demonic games with me and my people. But when his ire is raised, fear not. We will suffer. Our hope rests in your friend's hands. He is The One. I hope he is up to it."

"So do I," Angus said, looking at the floor. "But this castle looks like it could withstand anything."

"Aye, it does, but don't think we could hold it against the full might of Uhr and his army of Slayers. They are all very devils."

Then a knock sounded on the door.

"Enter," Valerion said.

Robinton stepped inside. "My lord. I was informed there was a problem…"

"Ah, Robinton, just the man I was looking for."

"My lord?"

"Take this man out, give him a place in the Red Dragons' barracks, and start his training."

"When sire?"

"Now. This morning. Teach him everything you know, my friend, and then some. Make a warrior out of him!" Valerion grinned.

Robinton smiled. "Always good to have a new pupil. Follow me, sir."

"That is your new home," Robinton said, pointed at the long, low structure lying against the northern wall of the outer ward. It lay half beneath the ground. Steps led down to the doors on each end of the structure. Angus then noticed the straw-stuffed practice dummies hanging from posts in what was obviously a well-used training area. Angus was slightly annoyed with himself that he had not noticed any of this when they first passed through.

Then men began to issue out of the structure, and they indeed looked a motley collection of vagabonds and rogues. Days' worth of stubble darkened their faces, and sweat and soil stained the red dragons sewn across the chests of their tunics.

Angus looked askance at Robinton. "Who are these rogues?"

The old soldier glared at him. "Valerion's Red Dragons."

Angus scrutinized them more closely. Beneath all the grime and filth were the rippling thews and hard eyes of seasoned warriors.

Robinton barked, "Red Dragons assemble!"

The Red Dragons leaped at Robinton's order, and within moments had formed two perfect ranks of rod-straight warriors.

Robinton turned to Angus. "Some of them have

been on a mountain patrol for a fortnight, those that weren't with us. They just returned this morning." Then he raised his voice for all of them to hear. "I give you the finest warriors in Armond."

Angus saw their chests swell with pride as Robinton spoke, and he knew that they would follow Robinton anywhere. He was their leader.

Then he turned to the Red Dragons, and said, "I give you the newest of your brethren. His name is Angus MacTavish."

Angus nodded his head once.

"Fall out!" Robinton barked. "Aalok, to me!" Then he said to Angus, "First lesson."

A man stepped out of the loose crowd of soldiers. He was only five feet tall, but he was barrel-chested, with a thick bull-neck and hard thews. He was bald, with a square jaw and pug nose, and his beady black eyes appraised Angus up and down.

"This is Aalok," Robinton said. "He will show you the fundamentals of unarmed combat."

Angus smiled inwardly.

Aalok began to casually circle Angus, who pivoted to face him. After several moments, Aalok darted in, and Angus danced aside, out of his reach. Aalok's dark brows rose in surprise at Angus's dexterity, then furrowed in determination.

Angus attacked. He feinted low, and kicked high. Aalok caught Angus's leg and twisted. Angus's breath left him in a great whoosh as he hit the cobblestones.

A powerful arm pulled him to his feet, and slapped him heartily on the back.

"Not bad," Aalok said, his voice low and coarse as he grinned, shaking hands with Angus.

Angus smiled half-heartedly. "I'm a little out of practice, it seems."

Hearty cheers and laughter sprang from the throats of the men around him, and each one in turn slapped him on the back. Angus had been initiated.

The rest of the day was hard. After the Red Dragons had shaved and cleaned themselves, Robinton led them in a bone-breaking barrage of calisthenics, most rather different from those Angus had done at the Academy, but nevertheless strenuous. The rest of the morning was spent in weapons practice. Ax, spear, dagger, several types of sword. They ate their noon meal from wooden plates as they sat on the ground along the stone wall of the barracks.

Every Red Dragon wore the standard uniform of a plain white tunic, brown trousers and boots. Except for Angus, who wore no Insignia on his chest. And he soon noticed the pride with which these men wore this mark. They were stronger, faster and better-trained than common soldiers, and they knew it.

The next morning found Angus sore and bone-weary from the exertions of the day before. After calisthenics, Robinton shoved a blunt, iron training sword in his hand, and introduced him to Daarton, the Red Dragon sword master. Daarton was a swarthy man of medium height and hawk features. He twisted his pointed black mustache and flipped Angus a salute with the blunted point of his sword.

Robinton also handed Angus a bundle of heavy leather, and told him to put it on. It proved to be a suit of thick cuir-boulli, padded inside, and a battered iron helm with large eye-slits. After much struggling into the stiff, boiled leather suit, Angus faced the Red Dragon sword master.

He told himself, "You've done this before,

laddie. What could be so difficult?"

Daarton attacked before Angus was ready with his blade. Daarton's blade smashed the hilt out of Angus's stinging hand, and crashed into the side of the helmet.

Angus staggered back, deafened and stunned by the shock of a real sword blow. Over the ringing in his head, he heard Daarton speaking, "...first lesson. Always be ready, even when you're not!"

Angus glanced at the blade incoming again, just a moment before it smacked against his rib cage.

"Waugh!" he gasped. He would have a nice, purple bruise there tomorrow. He scooped up his sword hilt.

Daarton said, "You'd better get used to moving in armor, too. You'd be dead without it! Ho, clod! Move quickly. Excellent, you've finally managed to block a blow! Hah! And another! You're not as stupid as you appear! Listen to me and you may live to ripe old age!"

Angus was barely keeping Daarton's dancing blade at bay. How could the man use such an unwieldy weapon so deftly?

"Strength of arm, strength of wrist, strength of fingers! It will come, clod, and be assured we'll be at it until it does! Have at you!"

CLANG! Angus's arm went numb to the elbow as Daarton's blade struck near the hilt, and he nearly dropped the weapon again. This time, the point of Daarton's sword struck him squarely in the chest and drove him back a step.

"If this had been a real weapon, I'd have your heart. Where's your spirit, man? Attack me now."

"Does your tongue always wag like this?" Angus swung his blade.

"Pitiful!" Daarton scolded as he batted it easily

away. "Yes, it does! Attack again...Again!...Again!... Better!...Again!...Terrible! Economy of motion, man! Don't chase me with it. Again!...Again!... Better! Hai!"

And again Daarton's dancing blade drove Angus backward with another bruise on the way.

The dull iron clanged and banged dully in the cool morning air, as they furiously traded blows. Daarton's blade and his tongue were one, stopping only for rest when Angus dropped his blade. As they fought he explained thrust, parry, cut, block, slash, riposte, remise, economy of movement, keeping the enemy off balance, stance, dodge, feint. All morning, into the afternoon they drilled.

As they took a short break for lunch, Angus crashed down on the ground next to Aalok with his portion of roast haunch and loaf of bread. He groaned and heaved himself into a more comfortable position against the wall, adjusting the armor as he did.

"Trade you a sweetcake for that bit of meat?" Aalok said after Angus had settled himself.

Angus grunted and looked at him

"It's sweet, and you're practicing with Daarton," Aalok said. "You need the strength."

"What kind of sweetcake?"

"Honey and butter-filled bread."

"Sounds good. Here."

"My thanks," Aalok said. "Brrr!" He shivered as a chill breeze whipped through the compound. "Autumn's coming."

"I'm rather grateful for this armor. It keeps the wind off." Angus sampled his sweetcake. "Not bad."

Aalok nodded. "Padded leather like that is fine during autumn and winter, but it'll broil your balls in mid-summertime."

Angus chuckled and nodded. Aalok laughed with him.

As he munched his sweetcake and bread, he looked up at the dismal gray sky. The clouds hung above like drooping sacks of water just waiting to empty themselves.

Angus was pleasantly surprised when Daarton did not return him to practice immediately, but allowed him half an hour's respite from the grueling work. But nevertheless they took their weapons and began practice again. Angus grunted and gasped during the prolonged exertion, and the numbness and weariness of his arm masked the pain in his blistered palm.

The sagging cloud-cover finally unleashed its torrential downpour just as the day began to fade. Angus and Daarton were drenched within moments.

Daarton finally lowered his blade. "It has been a fine day, Angus. You've learned much. Rest yourself for tomorrow." He clapped Angus heartily on his bruised shoulder, and strode away through the sheets of water.

Angus smiled wearily as he took a deep breath. It had been a terrible, wonderful day, and the exhilaration of it all swept through him. Then he realized that he could not remove his hand from the leather-wrapped hilt. He looked down and saw his fingers fairly glued around the hilt of the sword, with blood congealed to a stiff crust between his fingers, like some rust-colored mud.

Chapter 12

Hamilton winced as the horse between his legs jolted down a short drop-off in the rocky path. Saddle sores tenderized his inexperienced backside. The sun warmed his back as it rose over the mountains towering above him. He rubbed his exhausted eyes.

Several hours ago, consciousness had returned. A horse was moving rhythmically between his legs, and a full moon shone brightly above. Since he had awakened, he had been trying to piece together what happened the night before.

He remembered a sudden commotion. He had been groggy from exhaustion and very near sleep. He remembered Angus's rage, and his attempt to protect him. Then someone had pinched a nerve in his neck. Nothing after that, until he awoke, deep in the mountains, surrounded by men garbed all in black, vague shadows in the ghostly moonlight. Black hoods and masks swathed the faces of his captors. Damned Red Priests! He cursed silently.

Once he had asked them where they were taking him.

The leader said, "Silence."

The voice had carried such authority that Hamilton obeyed almost by reflex. However, as the hours passed, Hamilton's active, apprehensive imagination had transmuted that nondescript but powerful command to one of evil dominance, almost as if a demon had silenced him. And their neutral disinterest in him his mind changed to malevolent arrogance. The rhythmic plodding of the horses' movement lulled him, and he caught himself dozing several times. He thought he caught glimpses of horns on the heads of his captors concealed by their black hood, patches of death-white skin momentarily revealed, red eyes that glowed in the darkness. Or perhaps it was all his imagination running away with his dreams.

So he rode on in glum, uneasy silence. Their small band traversed the valleys slicing between the mountains. The high peaks, white-capped, clothed in patches of deepest green, loomed over them, while a swift stream galloped beside.

Hamilton contemplated escape, as he had throughout the night, but like each time before, he dismissed the idea as lethal foolishness. The day wore on like the slow gnawing of water upon a stone.

The white sun had long since passed its zenith before they finally halted for rest. Everyone but Hamilton dismounted and walked toward the stream to drink. The three men began to remove their hoods and masks. Hamilton stared in uneasy fascination, expecting to see deathly pale skin, red-rimmed eyes, split tongues and scarlet circles branded into their foreheads. What he saw surprised him.

"Come down and drink, if you like. I know you must be thirsty."

The man who spoke was the same who had silenced him the night before, and was not at all the ogre Hamilton's mind had conceived. The man smiled at him, and his eyes regarded him with a sort of paternal kindness and boundless wisdom. His head was clean-shaven. He was short of stature, not particularly muscular, but his small frame radiated finely honed power. Hamilton felt small by simply looking at him.

As he reluctantly slid down from his saddle, his legs nearly collapsed under his weight. The three men watched him with a kind of bemused interest, but did not move to help him. After he steadied himself against the saddle, one of the other men, tall and slim, with bright gray eyes and light brown hair, tossed him a small leather sack. He cautiously opened it. He almost expected to find a venomous serpent within, and found instead several strips of dried meat. He grabbed one out, sniffed it and began gnawing on it hungrily.

These men lacked the small red circle between their brows!

Hamilton's jaw dropped open. Taking a step backward, he said, "You're not Red Priests are you?"

The first man answered. "You are correct." He stepped forward.

"Then who are you?" Hamilton retreated a step.

The man smiled again, not Sneev's cruel teeth-baring, but an honest, friendly grin. He spoke with infinite calm and precision. "Be at ease, friend. You are not among enemies."

Hamilton opened his mouth to speak, then stopped, unsure of what to say.

"My two companions and myself are of the Order of Knights of the Eagles."

Still suspicious, Hamilton asked, "Why did you abduct me?"

"That was not our design, but your large protector left us no choice. You are The One. We are the makers, keepers and protectors of the Keys of the Ivory Star. You are coming with us to our Sanctuary where you will be trained as one of us, to prepare you for the days to come."

"Why did you not tell me this last night?""

"We were searching for signs of pursuit, hardly the place and time for an extended conversation."

"Pursuit by whom?"

"Why Red Priests, of course."

Hamilton looked down, embarrassed at himself, the way his mind had conjured up such terrible images the night before.

"I am Master Sorde, and my two companions are Valt and Darius."

The man who had given Hamilton the food bag nodded soberly as Sorde spoke his name, Valt.

Darius was slightly shorter than Valt, with a flaming mop of red hair. His eyes were hard blue, like those of a man who has seen too much. Freckles spotted his faintly handsome countenance like specks of rust.

"My name is Hamilton Corbin."

Sorde nodded once, moving toward his horse. "Let us continue our conversation as we travel."

They mounted up and were on their way again.

"Who are the Knights of the Eagles?" Hamilton asked. "It sounds very prestigious."

Sorde smiled again. "We are warriors, scholars, philosophers, historians, magicians, the things that give mankind life, the things that Uhr has tried to suppress. We are Uhr's bane, and therefore renegades. The Order was founded many generations ago, after the coming of Uhr. History written by the early Eagle Knights tells us that Irth was once ruled by a Council of Twelve. A young philosopher named Uhr was a member of the council. Everyone loved him, as he was a kind and generous man, handsome, with thick, flaxen hair and blue eyes the ladies swooned for, not to mention being one of the greatest minds of the time.

"The records do not tell us why, but one day, he disappeared from the Council palace in the capital city of Arnath. No one saw him for five years. The people mourned his supposed death, although no corpse was ever found.

"But one day he returned, and every generation since wishes he had not. He had changed, rather drastically. The Council members hardly recognized him, and for a while did not believe him when he told them who he was. Only after he told them things that only Uhr could know did they believe it was him.

"He had changed in every possible way. He was wearing robes of somber black, whereas before he had always dressed in bright, happy colors. He had shaved all his hair, which gave him a cadaverous appearance, his nails had grown long and sharp, and he looked to have grown a hand taller. Even his eyes had changed color. Before they had been a bright blue, now they were a dull gray shot with red.

"He also carried with him, where ever he went, a leather satchel, in which we now know he carried his dreadful Bloodstone.

"He demanded to resume his old place at the Council table, so vehemently in fact that the council member who had taken his place stepped down to allow him to do so. But the other council members did not trust him now, and began to take steps to have him legally removed. It was then the dreadful things began to happen. Uhr's opponents were the first to die. Within a week, three council members had died grisly deaths. All occurred late at night. Their bodies were found in their own bedrooms, torn and dismembered as if by some wild beast. Parts of them were missing, thought eaten. Witnesses said they had seen a black, manlike shape prowling the city streets at night. The most outspoken witnesses were dead within days in the same manner, five or six in a night. Soon, no one spoke of it for fear of death, and the good people of Arnath were afraid to leave their homes after sunset.

"And no one could ever find Uhr after the sun had set. This, of course, led many to suspect him of the crimes. Before long no one was left to accuse him. All the members of the council were dead, leaving Uhr to rule alone. Everyone feared him so that none came forward to claim the other council chairs. The killing ceased after that. Uhr ruled with a cruel and ruthless hand that quickly snuffed all open opposition to him.

"After a few years, no one ever saw Uhr. He secluded himself in his empty palace, but the populace did not forget the horrors of his rise to power. One of his most powerful and courageous generals, named Arnor, sickened by Uhr's brutality and ruthlessness, rose in revolt against him. Arnor marched up the palace steps to confront Uhr alone, while the regiments loyal to him waited for him to carry out Uhr's severed head.

"One of Uhr's palace slaves later wrote that Arnor had walked into the Council Hall, ready for battle. Since this slave's tongue had been cut out, he could not warn Arnor that Uhr waited for him above the door, clinging to the wall like a ravening bat. Uhr dropped onto his back, and tore a great gash in Arnor's mail before the warrior threw him off and faced him. By this time, Uhr had degenerated into much the same form he wears now, that of a walking, rotting, inhuman corpse, and he laughed at Arnor's impudence."

Hamilton shifted uneasily in the saddle at Sorde's description.

Sorde continued, "Arnor was angered by Uhr's arrogance, and sickened by his appearance, and he leaped to attack. Before his blow could be struck, Uhr's claws had shredded his bronze shield, and most of Arnor's arm along with it. But with shield and left arm hanging in tatters, he struck a mighty blow that cleft Uhr's body in twain, from shoulder to waist. Believing Uhr to be slain, Arnor turned to leave the hall in triumph, but while Arnor's back was turned, Uhr's arm and head slithered back to the torso and reattached itself. Uhr, again whole, pounced upon his back, and ripped him to ribbons. It was Uhr who carried Arnor's head out in triumph, and what was left of Arnor's body he ripped to pieces and contemptuously threw into the faces of Arnor's friends and followers."

Hamilton stared at Sorde, spellbound by the master's tale. "This is the creature I must kill?"

Sorde nodded. "Yes, but you will have one advantage Arnor did not. You will have the Ivory Star."

"But what good will that be?" Hamilton's eyes were wide with fear. "He'll tear me to shreds just like Arnor!"

Sorde's voice was calm and reassuring. "You are The One. That is your greatest advantage."

Hamilton shook his head in disbelief.

Sorde continued his tale. "The revolt dissolved with Arnor's death, and it was on that day that Uhr's army of Slayers was born. To make sure that his armies were completely and totally loyal to him, he devoured the soul of every single man in his army, thousands upon thousands, and then did his reign of terror truly begin. These soulless husks retained a semblance of life, but all things that make us human—will, imagination, honor, desire, pride, curiosity, creativity, desire for life—all these things were stripped from them. He now had a fanatical army that was absolutely loyal to his will alone. Only his greatest generals were allowed to keep their souls, as their wills and creativity were valuable in war.

"But even though Arnor was slain, his valiant attempt to save everyone was remembered by the people and his descendants. His wife and newborn son went into hiding in Armond, and eventually, after several hundred years of clandestine hereditary maneuvering, his descendants gained the lordship. Today, the first born son of every generation is called Son of Arnor, although the identities of the Sons of Arnor are kept a secret from Uhr, to avoid him stamping out the line entirely. Now they are back in power, and we know not if Uhr is privy to this information.

"It was in the midst of the events of Arnor's time that the Eagle Knights were born. A small conclave of Arnor's closest friends and powerful associates gathered, and made a pact to preserve everything Uhr was trying to stamp out. Knowledge, free thought, poetry, alchemy, magic meant for the greater good, art. All these things he had systematically set out to destroy to keep the people cowed, all the things on which mankind thrives. Mankind of the outside world was stagnating. These men, Arnor's friends and followers, warriors foremost, but also chroniclers, scribes, philosophers, artists, alchemists, great thinkers, left the society of their fellows, and went into hiding here, in the Viderian mountains, far, far away from the horrors of Arnath, beyond Uhr's reach—at least as far as he was able to reach in that time. His reach is considerably longer now. Only by luck and utmost secrecy have we managed to survive this long.

"These forefathers of our order found a stone which had fallen from the sky, and having Irth's greatest craftsmen among them, forged the Ivory Star, the weapon that could destroy Uhr."

Hamilton asked, "But what was it?"

Sorde shrugged. "No one knows anymore. Those records were lost hundreds of years ago."

"You mean you don't have it?"

Sorde shook his head. "It was hidden when Uhr was still young, before he had lived through his second lifetime."

"And how long has Uhr been…alive?"

"Over a thousand years."

"So no one has seen the Ivory Star for almost a thousand years?"

Sorde nodded. "That is correct."

Hamilton's fear rose in him like a wildfire. His voice raised dramatically in pitch. "Then how can you be sure it even exists? What if…what if it's just a myth?"

Sorde's brow wrinkled, as if he was considering that possibility for the first time. "Then I suppose we must have faith that it does exist."

Hamilton sighed. "The burden of The One is heavy."

Sorde said, "Aye, it is." Then he added matter-of-factly, "But you can bear it. You are The One, after all. And you are with us that you may learn how to bear your burden, and finally relieve yourself of it."

Hamilton sighed again, his chest heavy, and they rode on in silence as Hamilton sorted through all the information he had been given. Then he spoke again. "Where did the Prophecy come from?"

Sorde answered, "Alas, those records were lost in the fire with the records of the Ivory Star's nature."

"What is the Great Conjunction? What is its significance to Uhr?"

"Uhr is a being of black and evil craft, with great, great power, but he receives some of his power from the heavens' alignment. Power flows more readily when the heavens are favorable for such things. A Great Conjunction last occurred during the time of Uhr's first disappearance, when Mankind still spoke many tongues. It was a time of powerful magic. The heavens show the next Great Conjunction to be imminent, and Uhr believes that at that time his power will increase a thousandfold." His voice fell to a husky whisper. "Enough for him to destroy The One, the Ivory Star and all resistance to him. He may well become a god."

Then Sorde's voice rose again as if trying to dispel his own doubts and fears. "But look, we are here!" He looked up the sheer rock face that blocked their path and towered above them.

"Where is here?" Hamilton craned his neck to see the top of the rock face.

"Sanctuary," Sorde said. "Come." He gently kicked his horse, and the hardy, mountain-bred animal scrabbled up the loose rock incline toward a huge boulder leaning against the side of the cliff.

Hamilton kicked his horse to follow, and as he did so, Sorde and his mount disappeared behind that massive boulder. Hamilton's mount followed the first as if it had traveled this way dozens of times, and Hamilton merely held on as the horse dug its bare hooves into the gravel and pulled them both up the grade. As they passed behind the boulder, Hamilton saw the opening that was completely hidden from the outside, and the rump of Sorde's mount disappearing within. Then his own horse took over, following Sorde's into the cave.

Just inside the cave was pitch blackness. Hamilton felt a surge of momentary panic, but his horse moved as if it knew the way without the need to see, and he began to relax again. The hoof-falls reverberated distantly, and Hamilton could only guess at the sheer size of the cave. Water dripped far off, its echoes as distinct as those of the horses' passage.

Soon the black roof of the cavern was split by a sunlit crevice far above his head. The crack in the ceiling soon became the sides of the cave as the cavern metamorphosed into a narrow, sheer-walled canyon.

The canyon began to widen. Then Hamilton saw the magnificent valley below.

"Home," Sorde said, looking back at Hamilton with a kindly smile.

The canyon widened into a gorgeous emerald-green valley. The gently rising sides of the valley were dotted with huts. Fashioned of logs and bark, these huts housed the several dozen people milling about the valley. The people were garbed in bright robes of various colors, and they cheerfully went about their duties, carrying firewood, gardening, herding flocks of sheep, weaving, cooking. Cobblestone walks criss-crossed the cozy valley, and a fresh silver stream chuckled beneath a stone bridge.

Sorde led them down one of the cobbled walks along the side of the gently sloped valley. The people greeted them warmly, and smiled as they passed. Then they rounded a gentle bend. Sorde pointed and said, "Sanctuary."

Hamilton felt a smile of wonder spread across

his face as he looked at the long, two-story wooden structure nestled in the crook of a grassy vale like a great sleeping hound. The smell of the grass, punctuated by the faint scent of wood smoke and seasoned vegetable soup, the sound of the birds singing in the open rafters of the Sanctuary, the loveliness of the mountain skyline, all filled Hamilton with a peace such as he had never felt.

As they stopped before the building and dismounted, four shaven-headed boys came out and led their horses away. Sorde led the three men up the steps and into the house. Hamilton could not help but notice how the planks creaked terribly under his feet, but made not a sound under the tread of the other three men.

Hamilton noticed a basket hanging near the door frame of the house, and the basket was filled with shards of crystal that glowed with a pale yellow light. He stopped to examine them more closely.

"Come!" Sorde said sharply, and Hamilton quickly followed him. The other two men disappeared down side hallways as Sorde led him to a room not far from the entrance. "This is my chamber," he said. "Remember where it is, as you will be here often. Sit, there, on the mat."

Hamilton followed him into the chamber, and sat down on the plainly woven mat on the otherwise bare wooden floor. Before him sat a low brazier of blackened iron with warmly glowing coals resting in the bottom.

A chilly wind rustled the plain white curtain over the open window. Sorde immediately got up to shut the window. "The winter is coming. It will be a hard one for you, but you are The One. I have faith in your ability."

Hamilton said, dubiously, "It's unfortunate that your faith exceeds mine."

"Henceforth, you are not The One," Sorde said, taking the mat opposite the brazier from Hamilton. "You are only my student. You will be treated as any other student, and you will learn. If you do not learn, you will die. Simple. And Irth will lose its only hope."

Then Sorde smiled that kind smile, and reached to take a small crystal from a nearby basket, a crystal identical to those in the basket outside. "Take heed. This is your first lesson."

He turned the stone over and over in his hands, then passed it to Hamilton. It fit nicely in his palm, warm to the touch, glowing softly a pale yellow.

"That is a glowcrystal," Sorde said.

"This glowcrystal is my first lesson?"

Sorde nodded. "Exquisite, isn't it. It does not soil the air like flame. Its energy is pure, and comes from within. You are that glowcrystal."

Hamilton looked at him in puzzlement.

"Every being has its own inner light, inner strength. Anything you require, you need only ask yourself. Any strength, answers to your deepest questions, anything, may all be found within yourself. You need only ask yourself for help, and you will receive it."

"That sounds easy."

"It is. However, you must learn to ask in the proper manner. That is the difficult part, and an Eagle Knight spends his entire existence in the pursuit of the best way to ask the proper questions." Sorde paused. "Now off to your quarters with you. Tomorrow for you will be either devastating or effortless. It is your choice."

"I believe I choose effortless."

"Good!" Sorde said. "Your attitude thus far is perfect." He called out, "Rolf!"

In a few heartbeats came a knock on the door,

and a voice. "What do you require, Master?"

"Rolf will take you to your room."

Hamilton sat with his chin between two fingers for a long moment, then said, "Will I learn everything about being an Eagle Knight?"

Sorde smiled again, warmly. "I am sorry, my son, but I don't have an entire lifetime in which to teach you."

Chapter 13

"Hai!" Angus leaped to the side, and the whistling iron blade slid just past him. He followed with a slashing counterattack.

"Waugh!" Daarton gasped as he staggered backward.

Angus's breast swelled with sudden pride. What a blow! If the blade had been sharpened, Daarton would have had his chest cavity cleft open. Finally Daarton had tasted of his frustrated blade. For two weeks Daarton had taught him the sword nearly every daylight hour, and never had Angus so much as touched him. He felt himself grinning, and his sword point dropped only a bit...

CLANG!

Daarton's heavy iron sword crashed into Angus's metal helm.

He was awakened by cold water dribbling into his face, and he opened his eyes to see the cold gray sky above and Aalok squeezing a rag above his face. Angus sputtered and spat and tried to sit up.

Daarton towered over him. "Fool! Never, never lower your blade if your opponent is still standing!"

Angus shook his head, trying to clear the stars

from his vision.

Daarton offered his hand, and Angus took it to stand up unsteadily, like a willow in a storm. He felt a sticky rivulet trickle down his cheek, and his gaze began to cloud again, so he closed his eyes until his equilibrium began to return. He heard Daarton speaking, "...have taught you much, sir. As much as any man can learn from a mere teacher. The rest comes with the first test of steel and battle, and scars across your body." He patted Angus on the shoulder brotherly.

Then Daarton bellowed, "Sigmunnd!"

Angus winced at the noise.

From across the yard, "Ho!"

"He's yours!"

A golden-locked lad of medium height and hardly twenty years, clad all in buckskin, strode toward them from the archery range, long bow and quiver of arrows slung across his back.

By the time Sigmunnd had reached them, Angus's vision and equilibrium had returned.

Sigmunnd looked Angus up and down, rubbing his fair-stubbled chin with a callused finger. "He is not an archer, but he will learn. Come."

The skies grew increasingly overcast, and the cold rain fell daily, rain that would be turning to snow, driven by the biting north winds.

As the weeks passed, Angus discovered that practice with the long bow found new muscles to tire, new places to blister. After a few days he was able to hit the target with some regularity. He practiced with the bow until his fingers bled, and the cold numbed his hands. After he was deemed ready, he moved on to other things, other weapons, other styles of combat.

The weeks passed in a frigid whirlwind with

the approach of winter. A thick blanket of furs and coarse blankets kept him warm in the Red Dragons' barracks during the cold autumn nights with the wind slicing through the compound outside, and a hot, though sometimes distasteful, meal always filled his empty belly. The comradeship of the other Red Dragons helped him fill the emptiness left by Hamilton's absence. The Red Dragons embraced him as one of their own. He had never experienced such a bond between fighting brothers as this, not even before, at the Academy. The lonely life of a scout was not the environment for such companionship. All he had had before was Hamilton, and now Hamilton was gone.

"No, this way," Robinton said. "The battle ax is not like a sword. It's heavier, more for brute-strength armor-bashing than a deft round of fencing."

Angus nodded, hefting the weapon again as he watched Robinton's movement. Then he gripped the weapon as Robinton had shown him and chopped into the straw dummy, neatly hacking off one of the arms.

"Much better; excellent, in fact," Robinton said, "I believe we have found your weapon."

A devilish smile crossed Angus's face. "Hah! I like it!"

Then a clattering at the barbican caught their attention. A brightly painted wagon, festooned with gaudy streamers and ribbons, trundled into the outer ward. Two old nags, their ribs protruding like sticks, pulled the wagon, and a couple of old pack mules trailed along behind. The driver of the wagon was a riot of colored patches.

Robinton smiled. "It's that time of year again."

"What time of year?" Angus asked. "Who are they?"

"Harvest Festival. In that cart is a troupe of musicians. The first of many, I'll wager. The farmers are finished in the fields, and they bring their harvest to Lakeside to sell. We have a festival every year that's part celebration, part marketplace. It's quite a grand affair."

"When does it start?"

Robinton smiled facetiously. "When everyone gets here."

Angus snorted.

"What, no mood for jokes today?" Robinton explained, "At about this time every year, people begin to arrive, and they just congregate and do as they will. It's not organized by any means. It just lasts until all the produce has been sold, and everybody goes home again, usually about four or five days."

Angus watched the wagon pass with interest. Upon noticing his gaze, a slim, bauble-bedecked woman riding on top of the wagon flashed him a generous portion of supple flesh, throwing in an alluring giggle to peak his interest. He felt a monstrous grin stretching his mouth as he watched her go.

Robinton chuckled.

"It's been a long time," Angus said, shaking his head, eyes wide with sudden excitement.

Robinton's chuckle rose to hearty laughter. "Well, perhaps your time is here!"

Angus looked out over the shore from his vantage point on the outer gate tower. "Look at all of them!" he breathed.

"Aye," Robinton said, as he approached. "Tis quite a sight."

Angus did not notice the peculiar smile on Robinton's features.

The sun was beginning to sink off to their left, turning silvery blue the hundreds of multicolored tents and pavilions and booths now covering the shore of the lake, totally surrounding Lakeside.

"And they all arrived today!" Angus said.

"Like I said," Robinton remarked, "people know when it's time. Farmers with their produce, merchants to buy it, and actors and musicians to entertain the lot."

Angus glanced at him, then looked again. "What? You've a strange look on your face."

Robinton grinned. "I've news for you."

"What, spit it out."

"Good news."

"Gods, man, what is it?"

"Valerion told me himself just a little while ago."

Angus voice rose. "*What?*"

"Lord Valerion himself is going to present his newest Red Dragon with the Insignia at a feast in your honor tomorrow night."

Angus's jaw fell open, speechless.

"Tor's Teats, Angus!" Aalok cried. "What are you *doing!*" He ran up to Angus. "Stop!"

Angus answered him, wiping off his dagger blade, and looking back into the tiny mirror. "I'm shaving off my beard."

"I can see that! But why?"

Angus shrugged. "You heard about tonight, didn't you?"

"Of course! Everyone has! But why shave it off?"

Angus shrugged. "Just an urge I guess."

"But you look more...distinguished with your beard."

Angus snorted, "What need have I to look distinguished? I'm a warrior."

Aalok grinned through his own stubbly growth, wiping the top of his bald head. "That is true." Then his face gained a mischievous expression. "Perhaps you need to look distinguished for the maid Madra, Lord Valerion's eldest daughter?"

Angus glanced at him.

"Aha! I knew it! Your ears perk up whenever her name is mentioned. She's a beauty, eh?"

Angus continued shaving, noting the pale white skin where the beard had been.

Aalok went on, "Good luck, my friend. She is very available, if you follow."

Angus smiled. "Good."

"Rumor has it she's quite…experienced in such matters. Although she still plays the part, she's hardly a maiden anymore, from what I hear. Much to Valerion's chagrin, I'm sure."

Angus said, "I'll let you know how she was."

"Haw, haw, haw! You do that! And I might just believe you! Haw, haw, haw!"

"You can laugh, stumpy. But you'll see." Finished shaving, he gazed into the mirror. "Gods, you're a handsome devil!" He glanced back at Aalok for a reaction, but Aalok was already rolling on the floor, clutching his belly with laughter.

Robinton came at about dusk to fetch Angus to Valerion's house. Angus had dressed in a brand new snowy white tunic and pair of forest green trousers, which he'd just purchased from one of the merchants thronging the fortress. He had given up too much gold for them, not knowing how to haggle, but what the hell. He should look his absolute best for this honor.

Angus and Robinton shouldered their way through the throngs of people. Angus smiled at all the decoration. The front of Valerion's house and his garden wall dripped with garlands of flowers. "That's a beautiful tapestry," he commented, referring to the tapestry hanging near the door, depicting the activities of the harvest festival, and it was indeed beautifully done.

Robinton said, "Lady Ilone's latest work. She's quite good."

They went inside the house, and more tapestries covered the walls, interspersed with more fragrant blossoms and gaious banners and bright ribbons. A band of musicians played a jig on their lutes, flutes, harps and zithers, while tumblers cavorted in every open area. The rich men and nobles of Armond sat at the tables with their ladies, conversing amongst themselves or watching the tumblers with amusement.

Angus glanced up at the high table.

Lord Valerion and his entire family sat there. More importantly, *she* was there, seated next to her father.

And she was looking directly at him.

Angus's eyes bulged in surprise, and he looked away. Embarrassed at himself, Angus looked at the floor. Then, after a moment, he hazarded another hopeful glance.

She was clothed in a silky scarlet gown, bodice cloven nearly to the waist and laced up with black ribbon, accomplishing little in concealing her high, firm breasts, round and perfect like fresh apples. Her lustrous ebon locks were bound into long braids coiled behind her head with a diaphanous white cloth dangling down her back. His eyes were drawn to hers. Her dark, inviting stare swallowed him like the depths of an unplumbed cavern. He felt his heart flip over behind his ribs. She licked her lips sensuously, stroking the nut-brown valley between her breasts with a slender finger.

He swallowed hard, and followed Robinton to the high table. Two empty seats were placed at the end of the slightly curved table and Robinton seated himself at one, motioning Angus to take the other.

Robinton was talking to him. "...the matter with you, Angus? Are you drunk already? You've swallowed not a drop, and you're in a stupor."

Angus shook his head and blinked.

Madra looked away, stroking her wine goblet.

Angus mumbled something incoherent, and tried to watch the tumblers, which did little to hold his interest. His gaze kept wandering back to Valerion's eldest daughter. Almost every time, he caught her looking at him discreetly.

He wiped the small beads of sweat forming on his brow.

He did not notice another pair of eyes watching him, those of Valerion's second daughter, Nessa. She was perhaps not as beautiful as her older sister, but Dame Pilgra always told her she was pretty, and so did her father. She tossed the rich cascade of golden hair about her shoulders, trying to gain this man's attention, adjusting her well-filled bodice. She had her mother's body, voluptuous but firm, where Madra was thin like a sapling. But alas, the man paid no attention to her. All night she endeavored to snag his glance, but his eyes had already been bought.

The tumblers ended their act with a flourishing bounce and were gone, with generous applause thrown in their wake. Lord Valerion stood up, and his movement immediately brought a hush to the room.

He raised a heavy arm, and his deep voice filled the air. "Ladies and gentlemen, tonight there is a man here who was initiated into the ranks of the

Red Dragons to be trained as one of my finest warriors. Since then he has proven himself one of the finest of the finest. Now I present him with an honor received by few, only the greatest warriors on Irth. The Red Dragons." He spread his arms wide. "I hereby dedicate this bounteous meal to the honor of Angus MacTavish."

Robinton elbowed Angus, saying out of the side of his mouth, "Stand up."

Angus did so. He was speechless.

Valerion raised his goblet. "To the health and prowess of Angus MacTavish, newest of the Red Dragons."

And all the affluence and gentility of Armond raised their goblets and drank in his honor, and Angus's breast swelled with a pride like he had never known.

Then Valerion clapped his hands, and a squire came forward carrying a white jupon, and a kite shield. The Insignia blazed on the faces of both. Angus stepped up to him.

"Angus MacTavish," Valerion declared, "I hereby present you this shield and this surcoat before all witnesses, proclaiming your place as a Red Dragon. Wear them in battle with the spirit of a dragon!"

Angus knelt before him, not knowing what else to do.

"Rise," Valerion said, and passed the surcoat and shield into his hands.

A grin split Angus's face from ear to ear. "My eternal gratitude, my lord, and my undying loyalty."

Valerion's laughter boomed across the room, and he bellowed, "Musicians."

They struck up a reel, and conversation resumed. More goblets were raised in his honor, and

Angus could only nod in acknowledgment, overwhelmed. Bottles and pitchers quenched the crowd, and the merriment rose like a tide on toes tapping with the music.

A brimming tankard found its way into his hand. Soon the cup was empty, then filled, then empty again.

Suddenly wine splashed out of his cup as a heavy hand crashed onto his back, nearly throwing him off the chair. Wine-soaked breath flooded his nostrils as a huge, yellow-haired giant leaned over his shoulder, and bellowed, "Congrajulayshuns, ol' sot!" He slapped Angus gustily on the shoulder. "Tomorrow we shall see if you can thrash my arse!" Both men laughed heartily, and Tarl wheeled away.

Lady Ilone, resplendent in a stunning lavender gown, gracefully made her exit, taking Valerion II, or Val, as he was called, away to bed.

Nessa soon followed, and Angus thought he caught a pretty pout on her lips as she glanced sheepishly in his direction.

But Madra remained for now, and Angus caught himself staring many times. She did not try to avoid his eyes. She stayed another hour, sipping delicately at her wine glass that seemed ever full. Then she stood to leave, and treaded softly across the platform behind him, stopped, patted him gently on the shoulder.

"Congratulations, Sir Angus MacTavish," she half-whispered in a rich alto voice. Her warm, moist hand lingered on his shoulder, and lightning coursed through his veins.

Then she was gone, and a small slip of parchment slid down his chest into his lap. He did not touch it right away, but after a few moments discreetly slipped it into his tunic. He excused himself from the hall, and in an empty rear hallway, pulled it out and read it in the light of a smoky yellow lamp. From the smattering of literacy he had gained, he determined that it said to meet her in Valerion's garden at midnight.

What time was it now?

He quickly returned to the hall and rejoined the banquet. He asked Robinton, "What time is it?"

Robinton drained his goblet. "Why, nearly midnight, I'll wager. Why do you ask?"

Angus shrugged. "I suppose I should be getting back to the barracks."

Robinton nodded. "Angus, once again, congratulations."

He offered his hand, and Angus clasped it firmly.

"Thank you, Robinton. I am boundlessly honored." Angus spoke solemnly and sincerely. Then he took his leave. As he stepped outside, he looked around for anyone. No one was about.

"Midnight! All secure!" cried the sentry at the gate house.

Angus looked about for an entrance to the garden. No one was in sight. A wall separated it from the courtyard. The starlit sky was patched with clouds, making the night darker. Would anyone see him?

He stole along the garden wall, and with another glance about he jumped up to grab the clammy ledge on top of the wall. He hauled himself up and over, and dropped inside, behind a well-kept hedge. He searched the darkness under the roof of tree limbs. Most of the leafery lay at his feet in a thick, noisy carpet. He hoped no sentries patrolled the garden. But would she have invited him here clandestinely if there were sentries about?

He certainly hoped not.

As he waited, the chill night air nipped at him. With a sly smile he hoped that Madra would need a little extra warmth.

There! A slim cloaked figure glided amidst the shadows. A half-moon broke through the clouds, and by its light he saw that it was her. She walked slowly, looking hopefully into the black shrubbery around her. Angus stalked toward her, dry leaves trumpeting his passage. The pale smudge of her face in the inky darkness turned toward him as she searched for a moving shape.

At that he stood up and approached her. "It is I. Angus," he whispered.

She moved silently toward him on the stone path, and he stepped from the darkness. "You came!" she said, the excitement high in her voice. "I was afraid you wouldn't."

"Aye," he said, "you needn't have feared."

She touched his cheek with a warm finger. "You shaved your beard."

His heart raced like a herd of stallions. "You noticed."

"Of course," she replied, biting her lip mischievously. "I always notice such things about desirable men."

Angus felt the warmth and energy of her closeness, and felt himself blushing.

"Come," she said, "share my cloak. You are cold." She lifted one side up over his broad shoulders. Her cloak was large, large enough for the both of them.

Angus asked, "Why did you ask me here?" Best to find out for certain early.

"I've never met a man such as you," she said, "I wanted to know you."

They walked slowly down the stone path, and

Angus slipped his arm around her waist. She suddenly came alive under his touch, molding into the curve of his mighty arm. Her soft, sensual warmth thrilled him to the fiber of his being, and his blood stirred. It had been a long time.

"Tell me about yourself," she said, her hand straying to his hip.

"What would you know?"

"How did a man such as you come here?"

"I came from the west. Robinton brought me here," he said, purposefully enigmatic.

"But you were not alone."

"No, my friend, Hamilton, was with me."

"I remember. But he is gone now. Don't you miss him? Where did he go?" Her fingers tiptoed across his hard buttock.

Passion lit like a wildfire in Angus's veins. Control was a sweet agony. "He left some time ago, and I miss him very much."

"Have you been friends long?"

"Almost our entire lives. And why do you keep asking me about him anyway?" Angus said, in a moment of suspicion. Valerion had been afraid of spies...

She laughed, a warm, sensual sound, and wrapped her other arm around his belly. "I feel that the best measure of a man is not the strength of his arm, but how he loves his friends." Her hands moved over him. "But I find that the strength of his arm has its own merits as well." Her soft breasts pressed firmly against his ribs.

She asked, "Where did he go, that you are now apart?"

Angus sighed. "He's The One. He went with the Knights of the Eagles to prepare himself." Had he felt her stiffen, ever so slightly?

"What an honor!" she exclaimed. "Your friend

is The One! How wonderful for you! I've heard rumors that The One had come, but I'd no idea he had been here! Oh, how joyous! Angus, you have made my night." She paused, then added, "In many ways." Her eyes were bottomless caverns in the darkness, gazing up into his.

He liked the sound of his name on her lips, and smiled.

Her eyes glowed with pleasure and wonderful surprise. "What is his name? I simply must know!"

He cautioned her. "You must not spread this around."

"Oh, it'll be our secret, yours and mine. Please, *please!*"

Her hands moved again, and he answered her question automatically. "His name is Hamilton Corbin."

"Another strange name," she said. "Are you from Tyberia? They have strange names there."

"No, farther away than that."

"Farther still? Arnath?"

"No, farther."

She looked up at him dubiously. "There is no place farther than Arnath. Really, tell me."

"You would not believe me if I told you," said Angus, touching a finger to her lips. "Why all these questions, anyway?"

She closed her eyes and caressed his finger with a sensuous tongue. "I am merely curious," she said. "All women are, you know." And her hands moved again, and Angus felt himself swelling. "We're curious about a great many things." Her voice was husky and moist on his neck as her lips gently brushed it.

He swallowed hard as her hand stole up his chest, caressing, toying with his hardened nipples.

"But enough talk," she whispered breathlessly.

"Let us share our warmth under yonder grove."

She led him into the darkness, and pulled him down beside her onto the cold ground, wrapped in the heavy cloak. Her warm, soft hands slid into his tunic and played across his chest. His mouth buried hers with fervid kisses, and his boiling blood raced while he feverishly unlaced the front of her gown. His hungry hand slipped inside to cup a hot, creamy-soft, hard-tipped mound.

The heat of passion kept the cold night air away from their naked flesh as she took him in like a cozy tavern welcomes the weary wayfarer.

Chapter 14

Angus crouched at the foot of the garden wall, surveying the courtyard for anyone who might have seen him. No one was in sight. Good. The grin plastering his face grew wider still.

That girl knew her way! he mused, sighing wistfully. He shook his head in near-disbelief at the passion of the recent memory, unable to wipe the smile completely off his face. He chuckled, amusing himself. "Angus, you old dog, you," he muttered.

He started across the courtyard, allowing himself to bask in the memory. He stopped in midstride. A terrible feeling suddenly washed over him. A feeling that he had somehow missed something vital, and the consequences would be dire. He searched his memory, a sick feeling spawning in the pit of his gut. Had her behavior seemed a bit peculiar afterwards? Perhaps he had unconsciously disregarded it as a young woman's foolishness.

She had seemed excited, almost frantic, although she hid it fairly well. She had wanted to get back into the house quickly, hurrying Angus out of the garden. She said that she had to return to her chamber before she was discovered missing. Angus had thought that possibility remote at this late hour, but he dismissed it. Perhaps he had been wrong to do so. But perhaps not, maybe he was overreacting. He tried to put these things out of his mind, and remember only the pleasure, at least for a while.

He strolled across the yard, whistling a tuneless melody, toward the gate.

A voice cracked the overcast darkness, breaking his reverie. "Hold! Who goes there?"

"Worry not, fellow," Angus said, continuing forward. "It is I."

The voice had come from the top of the wall. He saw no one in the darkness, but the sentry up there doubtless saw him very clearly on the light-colored courtyard cobbles. "Halt, I say!" the watchman commanded.

Angus heard the snap of the firing mechanism, and the whine of the crossbow quarrel over his head. "Move not!" the sentry ordered, "I shall not fire another warning shot!"

Angus froze. He heard footfalls coming down the interior steps of the gatehouse. Two black shapes emerged from the dense night, crossbows leveled.

He chastised himself. Think fast, dolt!

At that instant, the door of the house flung open, filled with the towering form of Lord Valerion, torch upraised. He emerged from the doorway, and stormed down the steps into the courtyard. His bare feet slapped the cold cobbles, and the autumn chill seemed to go unheeded on his all but naked frame.

Robinton and Tarl followed close behind. The three men marched across the ward, Robinton buckling his sword belt around his flapping robe, and Tarl carrying a leg-sized oaken bludgeon in his yellow-furred fist.

"Angus MacTavish!" Valerion exclaimed. "What do you here at this tender hour?"

Angus stammered, struggling to formulate an appropriate lie.

Tarl cut in, brandishing his fearsome club, "Let me beat it out of him, m'lord." His eyes were dull and red-rimmed from the massive amount of wine that had passed his gullet.

Restraining him with his free arm, Valerion ordered, "Hold your overanxious arm, my friend. Don't you recognize my newest Red Dragon?"

"Aye," Tarl growled, "I do. I should dearly love to pound him good nonetheless."

Valerion cracked a smile. "Why is that?"

"I have my suspicions, my lord."

"And what suspicions are those, my good fellow?"

"I had best not say, m'lord. But rest assured that if I come across anything more than a suspicion, I will beat the truth out of him." His eyes glinted with malicious glee as he fingered his massive club.

Valerion burst out with a gust of hearty laughter.

Angus swallowed the lump in his throat, failing to see the humor in this rather delicate situation.

The lord said to his waiting sentries, who had lowered their weapons, "Back to your posts, men, and fine work. Stay alert." He turned to Angus. "Now, let us into the house and out of this damnable cold, where you can explain to us your nocturnal meanderings over a cup of warm tal."

Angus followed without hesitation, feigning calm honesty. Valerion was shrewd. He wasn't about to let something like this slide by easily.

Inside the kitchen, Tarl poured four tankards of syrupy, spiced tal from a pot above the warm coals. Valerion inquired politely, "Now why were you in the inner ward so late, after the feast was over and the gates were closed?"

Angus looked into his cup, and had a flash of inspiration. "I drank too much. I passed out near the garden wall."

"Ah," Valerion laughed, slapping him on the shoulder, "then let us finish our drink and to bed. The night is not yet too old."

Angus eyed Valerion closely. Perhaps he had accepted that explanation a bit too readily.

Madra checked the corridor outside her chamber, then locked the door. She took a wide, shallow copper bowl from a small bureau, holding it away from her with revulsion. The bizarre runes etched upon the bowls inner surface glinted redly in the candle's feeble radiance. A shudder swept through her as she looked at those dread sigils. She quickly turned her eyes away.

She knelt before the fireplace and scooped a few glowing orange coals from the hot mound into the bowl. She set the bowl on a silver pedestal and began to precisely, purposefully arrange the coals and ashes with a pure iron rod. When she was finished, she looked at the glowing ash symbol in the center of the bowl. The ring of runes around the edge of the bowl formed the border of a perfect pentagram. She shivered again.

She tensed at the sounds of shouting in the courtyard. Taking a deep breath, she muttered, "Must work quickly." Nothing must disturb her.

She took a small leather pouch from her bureau. Untying the drawstrings, she poured out a handful of the foul-smelling crimson powder.

"Come to me, O Master," she chanted, as she threw the powder onto the glowing goals.

Noxious black and scarlet smoke rose like a terrible shadow from the bowl. Madra's eyes watered, and her throat constricted violently as a wispy tendril of smoke and corruption rose up to caress her face. The smoke ascended to the ceiling, hovering heavily in the still air, then began to swirl and coalesce. The shapeless wraith congealed into something terrible, utterly corrupt, hanging in mid-air like a black plague.

Madra knelt, forehead to the floor. "By thy command, O omnipotent master Uhr."

"What news have you for me, woman?"

"O Master, The One was here, at my father's fortress," she said.

The great black hood seemed to bear down on her. "Where is The One now?"

She swallowed hard. "He left here several weeks ago with some Knights of the Eagles."

"Knights of the Eagles!" Uhr's inhuman voice chopped the room like a cleaver, and Madra leaped back as if struck. Uhr hissed like an obscene serpent. "Why did you not learn this sooner?" he snarled, a scythe-edge of restraint tightening his voice.

Terror smote her like a hammer as she groveled at his feet. "I did not have the opportunity, O dear Master! Spare me, Master! I beg your mercy and forgiveness! Spare me, spare me, please. I beg your mercy..." Her voice trailed off into sobs of mortal terror.

"Away from me, mortal sow! I have not time to kill you properly." His hand gestured as if tossing something away. Madra was whisked into the air like a doll, and struck the stone wall of the chamber with a sickening thud. She slid heavily into a motionless heap on the floor.

The robes of Uhr lost their substance, and he dissolved into the smoke from which he came, disappearing back into the coals.

There was much to be done.

Valerion's tankard fell to the floor, sloshing tal across the stone, as the deep, booming cry shook the walls. He leaped to his feet like a cat from where he had been leaning against the chopping table.

"Our chambers!" he roared, as he bounded across the kitchen. He had nearly crossed the great hall to the opposite door before the other three men left the kitchen. Down the corridor he plunged. Doors opened about him as he ran, with curious heads peering into the corridor.

"Inside!" he ordered. "And lock your doors!"

He reached his own chamber to see Ilone standing in the corridor holding a glimmering candle, eyes wide with fear. "Madra's bedchamber…!" Her voice quaked.

Valerion did not halt, but tore a battle ax from a hook on the wall, barreling toward Madra's door. He tried the latch. Locked. Cursing, he threw his shoulder like a bullock against the solid wood and iron. With the crash of splintering wood and groaning metal, the door flew open.

In the feeble light of the glowing fireplace, he saw a last wisp of ebon smoke seeping into the coals burning in a strangely carved copper bowl. Then he saw his daughter lying in a heap against the far wall, her neck bent at an unnatural angle.

The ax struck the floor with a dull clang, and Valerion was across the room in a single tigerish leap. He knelt at his daughter's side, stretched out her broken, motionless form, and tenderly cradled her head in his hands. The back of her skull was a pulpy mush. Glazed, lifeless eyes stared up at him. His anguished scream of rage and sorrow thundered down the house's corridors.

Angus was next to reach the door, and he stepped inside. His nose recoiled at the foul stench lingering to the air. Like rotting flesh it was, only more, worse. He kicked over the copper bowl. "What's this?"

Valerion mumbled numbly. "That which I feared most has come to pass."

"What?" Angus asked.

The lord sighed, long and quivering with emotion. "One of my own family, a spy for Uhr."

Angus gasped, "Who...?"

Valerion exploded, "Are you stupid, man? Can you not see?"

Angus stared at him, uncomprehending. "Look there, that bowl! She summoned him with it!"

"Summoned...?" Angus stuttered, bewildered, unbelieving. "With magic?"

"Aye!" The word tore from Valerion's lips like a catapult stone. "Vile sorcery!"

Angus turned away, and his stomach heaved. The enormity of what he had done settled on him like a sledge. His fists clenched, and he pounded his palm in guilt and frustration. He took a deep breath and reached up to stroke a beard that was not there, and he cursed himself bitterly.

Robinton and Tarl entered the room in time to see Valerion pick up his dead daughter and place her gently on the bed.

Now, suddenly, he exploded in fury. "Damn you, Uhr!" he thundered at the ceiling, his flushed face twisted into a savage snarl. His fists clenched into iron pummels. The muscles of his heavy arms and legs knotted into steel bands. Veins in his neck leaped out like ropes. *"Damn you!"*

"A girl I knew from a babe," Tarl said forlornly, his eyes glistening with wetness. "How could this happen?"

"Anything is possible with Uhr," Robinton muttered.

"Oh, that scum!" Tarl spat the last word. "Corrupting innocent girls!"

Robinton's voice hardened. "She was a spy. So what did the spy tell her Master that displeased him so?"

Valerion's eyes turned on him angrily. "Must you ask such questions now?"

Robinton gazed evenly at his friend and lord. "Yes, my friend, I must."

Valerion looked down, his voice softening. "Of course, Robinton, you are right."

Tarl shrugged his shoulders. "The answer, I'm afraid, is lost with her life anyway."

Angus spoke up, "My lord, I must confess something."

"Well then, speak up, man!" Valerion urged. "We are not in mind for idle prattle."

"I think I know what she must have told him," he admitted.

"Speak on then," Valerion prodded.

Robinton and Tarl chorused, "Aye, speak on." Tarl flexed his thick fingers.

Angus took a deep breath. "I was with Madra tonight in your garden. After the feast, she slipped me a note as she left, bidding me meet her there. I met her as she desired. We talked and walked for a while, during which time I..." He choked out the words. "I told her of Hamilton, and that he left with a small band of Eagle Knights."

Valerion swore vehemently, his eyes blazing with azure fire.

Angus swallowed hard and continued. "I had

just left her, and was crossing the courtyard when the sentry discovered me. She seemed anxious to be away into the house, as if she had to attend some urgent business. I dismissed it as a woman's foolishness, until now."

Tarl growled, "And therein lies my suspicion, you scoundrel! What were you doing with my lord's daughter all night?"

Angus could not resist. "Were you a true man, you would not need ask."

Rage reddened Tarl's leathery face, and he stepped forward, "Why, you insolent whelp, I'll—!"

Angus's sword sprang half from its sheath into his hand as if by magic.

"Enough!" Valerion bellowed, jumping between them. "There has been enough!"

Tarl drew back at his master's wrath.

Angus's sword slid back home.

They were interrupted by the Lady Ilone's blonde head peeking around the doorjamb. She treaded softly, fluidly, on slippered feet into the room, drawing her robes about herself. Her eyes became salty wells of tears as she took in the scene for a few moments. Then she said, her voice a quavering near-whisper. "Why?" she sobbed, "Why did that monster kill my second born?"

Second-born? Angus thought. He had thought Madra to be the eldest. This thought was quickly drowned by the guilt churning in his belly like a boiling acid. He had not realized until now just how strongly he had become attached to these people and their cause. At this moment, all he desired was to plunge into battle in the name of those he was sworn to protect, to redeem himself in his own eyes for the terrible thing he had just done.

He failed to see Valerion's second daughter, Nessa, enter the chamber. Lady Ilone suddenly burst into sobs, breaking the silence, and drawing attention away from Nessa's entrance.

She approached the bed where her sister lay. She did not cry, or even shed a tear, but only stood silently, staring at the stiffening body.

She and Madra had been...well, there was no love lost between them. Nessa was the younger of the two, and always, it seemed, the least noticed. Madra had always been beautiful and charming to men. In truth, she had always flirted annoyingly with every male guest, no matter what his position or inheritance, much to their father's chagrin. Doubtless she had taken many of the more handsome and powerful fellows to her bed. But to Nessa and the house servants, she had been invariably haughty and abusive.

Nessa herself had never been close to a man. She had always been overshadowed and shoved aside by her sister. Where Madra had been outgoing, slender and beautiful, Nessa was shy, voluptuous and merely pretty. The only men she had ever known were her father, whom she loved dearly, Tarl, who looked over her like another father, and Robinton, like a much older brother.

But this stranger, this Angus MacTavish, was something wonderful! To her, he radiated a virile, dynamic strength that thrilled her to the marrow of her bones! Oh, but he was handsome! And, with the iron will of her father, she decided that he would be hers, even at her sister's deathbed.

A small figure stepped into the room in his white, dragon-crested sleeping tunic, Valerion II, bare feet slapping on the stone. "Father?" he said.

Valerion, broken from some deep reflection, looked at his son, "Aye, my son?"

"What's going on?" the raven-haired lad said.

"Terrible things, my son. Your sister has been slain."

"By whom?" the lad asked. "Are your guardsmen searching for the assassin?"

Valerion grimaced. "I'm afraid no mortal man could find him."

Val's face reflected puzzlement, then, "Uhr?"

Valerion nodded.

"But why? How did he get here? Where did he go?"

Valerion drew a deep breath, and said, "He was finished with her."

"But...A spy!" the boy exclaimed. "A traitress!" He abruptly stalked toward the bed and spat on the lifeless body of his traitorous sister.

Valerion roared, leaping to his feet and struck the lad across the face with the palm of his hand. "Nay!" he growled, as he glared at his son. "She was my daughter, your sister, and in my house there shall be no disrespect to her, living or dead, traitress or no."

Val picked himself up off the floor, and left the room without another word, his young features knit into a furious scowl.

Robinton said, "My lord, do we tell anyone of this?"

"Nay," the lord said quickly, "no one, save those in this room, shall know the true tale of her death. Everyone shall be told she fell and struck her head. If the people of the realm heard that one of my own family was Uhr's spy, I would soon lose all following. Nay, tell not a soul. The funeral pyre I will build myself. Until then, let my wife and I mourn our daughter alone."

At that, everyone left the room, save for Valerion and Ilone, where they stood embraced beside the bed, mourning until darkness was shattered by the dawn.

Chapter 15

The wind howled like an enraged banshee, and Hamilton pulled his black cloak tighter about himself, blowing on his hands for warmth. Sorde climbed on tirelessly ahead of him up the steep mountain path. Hamilton wearily followed after, marveling at the man's agility and endurance. He had believed himself in good physical condition, but after following Master Sorde up a mountain he knew himself to be mistaken.

The path spiraled high, high around the steep mountain peak. The air was thin and bitter cold, and the wind knifed through his thick cloak as if it were gauze. Snow crunched underfoot, making the walking perilous.

They had left Sanctuary before dawn to set out across the mountain range. Hamilton guessed the time to be roughly noon now.

Sorde stopped to look back at his struggling student, then said, "We are here."

Hamilton climbed up beside him, took a deep breath, and looked about. They stood at the edge of a great yawning chasm, perhaps fifty paces wide, cut by a raging icy river far below. A flimsy rope bridge stretched across the windy gap, swaying and whipping in the stiff gusts.

Sorde said, "Walk across and return."

Unquestioning, Hamilton stepped carefully out onto the bridge.

The bridge consisted of two ropes serving as railings, and one rope as thick as an arm, braided from many others, to walk on. Hamilton stepped gingerly out onto the rope, gripping the hand-ropes carefully. Sweat froze to his cold face as he precariously made his way across the bridge, one foot, then another. When he had covered slightly over half the distance, he looked back at Sorde to see what he was doing. His heart skipped a beat.

Sorde was untying the hand-ropes from their wooden moorings!

Hamilton blurted, "Master, don't!"

But, of course, Sorde did not heed.

Suddenly one rope fell, and Hamilton was left clinging like a spider to the other. Terror lent wings to his feet as he made for the other side. The other rope went slack in his hands, and he fell. His flailing hands caught the thick foot-rope, and there he dangled like a doll over the roaring river.

Then he saw the spikes. The opposite end of the bridge bristled with them, arranged in such a way that anyone trying to gain the other side would either fall or impale himself.

He swung his legs up over the rope and started his journey back, hand over hand.

Then an arrow whistled past him. He could have wept when he looked back and saw the drawn bow in Sorde's hand. Sorde was trying to kill him! The razor-sharp arrow point glinted in the gray light. Sorde's face was a grim emotionless mask. Hamilton halted where he hung, and tried to gather his scattered wits. If Sorde was actually trying to kill him, he would already be certainly dead. What then was his purpose?

"What are you doing, Master?"

"Preventing your return."

"Why?"

"This is your first and greatest Test."

"Test of what?"

"Many things. Your strength of body, of will, of spirit. Many things." His tone was nonchalant.

Hamilton took a moment to absorb this, then peered down at the river again. "How long must I hang here?"

"A while."

"I can't stay out here all day!"

"Of course you can. You are The One."

But he couldn't hang here all day! His strength would give out soon. With desperate obstinacy he inched back toward safety. Another arrow flashed between his arms and tore a rent in the fabric of his white trousers between his legs. Hamilton stopped. Sorde lowered the bow. Hamilton started for the solid ground once again, and the bow rose. So there he was, trapped on the bridge where he clung with his arms and legs for dear life.

"Listen to me carefully, student," Sorde said. "If you fall into the water, you will likely die. If you try to reach the other side, likewise. If you try to return, you will fail, and our world is doomed. This is your Test."

Hamilton's voice rose in frustration. "How long must I stay here?"

"As long as necessary to purge yourself."

"Purge myself of what?"

"Self-doubt, insecurity, anything that will get in the way of centering your mind and spirit for the tremendous task ahead of you. It is doubt that will kill you, not lack of strength. If you doubt your ability to hang on, you will fall. Simply call upon your inner strength, and it will aid you."

His arms were getting weaker. "But I don't know how!"

"Everyone knows how. They have but forgotten. They merely need to remember."

Hamilton took a deep breath, let it out slowly. "How do I remember?"

Sorde leaned toward him, his voice growing soft and earnest. "Clear your mind. Empty it of all doubt, anger, frustration, all weakness."

Hamilton observed the Master's seriousness, then closed his eyes, trying to clear his mind.

After a few long moments, Sorde said, "Good. Now focus upon one thing. Focus your entire will onto holding on. Imagine your body as a bottomless well with limitless reserves of strength. When you feel yourself weakening, focus upon drawing another bucket of strength, and pouring it into yourself. When your body begins to feel too heavy, imagine yourself a feather."

Hamilton imagined these things, focusing his will, and gradually his hanging body seemed not as heavy. The birthmark on his breast thrummed pleasantly, spreading warmth. In a flash of inspiration, he used this as his focus, imagined his ivory star shining white strength over his entire body, and felt a flood of warm energy flow through him. The aching weakness left his limbs.

"Excellent!" Sorde said, almost excitedly. He seated himself on the ground at the edge of the chasm. "You will succeed. You are The One."

An hour later, after Hamilton had changed positions about five times, trying to rest his tired arms and legs and hands, Sorde still sat like a statue blocking the end of the bridge, observing with calm scrutiny. After another hour, Hamilton's arms were limp rags and his hands were useless, but still he clung to the thick rope.

Sorde called out of him, "Come to me in my chamber tomorrow, immediately upon your return. There is much you have yet to learn."

Hamilton mumbled to himself, "That's a little premature, isn't it?"

Sorde said, as if he had heard every word, "You will succeed. You have but to trust yourself. Trust the immense power that is within you." And he said nothing more for a long time.

More than once, Hamilton's resolve flagged, and he weighed his chances for survival should he just let go and plunge into the river below. His chances, he judged, were slim to nil. The water was freezing, and he heard the deeper echoing roar of a raging cataract and waterfall farther downstream.

After another hour, he no longer felt his arms. They were just locked mechanically around the rope, and his concentration was a constant ordeal. But the light within him never dimmed, and his arms did not let go. Then his stomach began to growl its discomfort at being empty. He had not eaten since the day before. This he easily pushed away as unimportant. For now, survival was paramount.

The next hour, cold had numbed his entire body. He believed that he must have slept, or blacked out, because the next thing he knew, darkness had fallen, and still he hung on the rope. He looked back. Sorde was gone. Cold white flakes touched his face, disappearing as they did.

He tried to move his arms to pull himself back to the side, and spasms of pain shot through them, nearly dropping him into the river. Slowly, agonizingly, he began his torturous journey, nerveless arms locked around his life-line, using his legs to inch himself along. Blackness.

He awoke lying on his back in a couple inches

of snow, the silvery face of the large moon looking down at him. He tried to move, and pins and needles shot painfully through every limb. He glanced around. He lay less than a foot from the edge of the chasm, his right leg still draped over the rope. Somehow he had reached safety, blacking out somewhere along the way. He sat up, suddenly seized by a violent shivering from the cold. He stood up unsteadily, fighting his way erect, his limbs all but collapsing, rubbing his arms and legs to restore circulation and warmth.

He glanced down the path. The falling snow had obliterated Sorde's tracks. He knew that he must get down the mountain into the warmer valleys or soon freeze to death, so he began to stumble back down the path. His legs were dead stumps, and he knew his hands and face were on the verge of frostbite.

Midnight came and went before he finally reached the foot of the mountain, nearly frozen, collapsing from exhaustion, and weak from hunger. He could not remember which way the Sanctuary was. His rapidly dimming mind had long since lost sight of the strength-giving light. He decided that he must find shelter as best he could for the night. He would search for Sanctuary in the morning. The snow began to fall harder, coin-sized white flakes falling and blowing in the light wind. He looked about him, finding no discernible cover. Not a cave, not a boulder, and the snow was waist deep in places.

Blindly, aimlessly, he wandered in the direction he thought Sanctuary might be, hoping to stumble upon a cave or something. The deep snow greatly hampered his exhausted legs. He knew his strength was waning rapidly, with his mind unable to focus for long on anything. If he stumbled and fell, he would never get up again. Through the steadily increasing snowfall he walked for what seemed an eternity.

Suddenly an unseen hole opened in the snow beneath his feet, and he plunged beneath the surface. Then his feet hit something solid but yielding. Just as suddenly he was thrown back into the air as the snow erupted like a geyser around him. He landed on his back in a cushioning snowdrift, with the back of his neck packed with new snow.

A grim black shape reared up, towering above him. A sinister roar echoed like a muffled storm in the cold black night. The beast shrunk down on all fours and lumbered through the deep snow toward him.

Hamilton fumbled under his cloak for his only weapon, a long-bladed knife. He tore it from its scabbard, and stood up to face the beast, adrenaline pumping him full of momentary strength. He gripped the hilt with numb fingers. If he tried to run, the beast would surely overtake him. He noted well the ease with which this thing moved through the soft snow.

He could distinguish little about its appearance, except that it looked very much like a bear, with gleaming red eyes and slavering, dagger-filled jaws.

The bear's knees buckled, almost imperceptibly, and it staggered toward Hamilton. Suddenly it roared ferociously, reared up before him, and charged. Hamilton dove under its raking front claws, trying to escape being shredded to dripping ribbons, plunging forward with the knife-point foremost. The long-blade slid to the hilt the bear's furry belly. The beast bellowed frightfully and fell backwards. Hamilton was carried by this momentum onto its belly. The beast twitched and lay still.

Hamilton gaped in astonishment. What a lucky stab!

The instinct for survival allowed him only a moment's wonderment before it clouded rationality. He pulled his blood-smeared blade from the giant carcass, got up and searched the snow for the beast's hole. There. He crawled down into the large opening. In the bottom of the hole was a small hollow. Fur and dried leaves littered the floor, and some of the beast's warmth remained. The wind howled above, but he did not feel it in the den. He wrapped himself tightly in his cloak, scraped the hair and leaves over him as best he could, and curled up in a tight ball. Darkness engulfed his mind almost instantly.

Had Hamilton examined the animal's carcass further, he would have seen the two arrows buried to the fletching in the back of the huge skull.

Sorde, on a ledge far above, pulled his cloak tighter against the cold, contemplating as he watched Hamilton below. Incredible! This one had strength such as the Master had seen only a few times before, and then only in lifelong Masters, not a student on his first Test. He was indeed The One.

The sun's radiance brought Hamilton up from the oblivion of exhausted slumber. He sat up, shaking the light sifting of snow off himself. He was warmer now, but his toes were numb. He hoped they were not frozen. Climbing out of the hole with a clear mind, he immediately knew where he was and which way Sanctuary lay. He passed the snow-covered carcass and set off across the snow as quickly as he could manage in the deep drifts.

At about noon he found his way out of the highlands and walked down the final slopes into one of the warmer lowland valleys. The sun quickly warmed him as he traveled, and he was grateful when feeling returned to his toes. At about midafternoon, weary and hungry, he trudged down the muddy slopes toward Sanctuary.

A feeling of pride and immense accomplishment rose in his breast. He had survived! He had succeeded, just as Sorde had known he would! Just as Sorde had known.

He entered the Master's chamber quietly, wondering what to expect next.

The master of the Knights sat cross-legged with his back to the door, as if in meditation. Strangely, he wore a black hood covering his entire head.

Moving not a muscle, his voice muffled by the thick hood, Sorde said, "I have been waiting for you. Take up that staff couched near the door and approach me. Silently."

Uncomprehending, Hamilton obeyed, trying his best to shake off his overwhelming exhaustion and hunger, lifting the wooden staff from where it leaned against the wall. The staff was roughly six feet long, thick as a man's wrist, tough and light.

Hamilton removed his cloak and lay it down near the door, leaving him clad only in his loose white tunic and leggings and boots. On tiptoe he slowly walked toward Sorde, trying to be quiet. The only sound was the rustle of his clothes against his skin. About three paces behind Sorde, he stopped. There was a loose board in the floor near here. He had noticed it before. Carefully, carefully, he slid sidewise around the motionless master.

Suddenly Sorde exploded into action. He leaped to his feet like coiled spring, swinging something at Hamilton. Before he knew what had happened, Sorde had struck him thrice with a three foot staff, on the leg, ribs and chest. The pinpoint accuracy stung. And Sorde was hooded. Blind. The Master said, "Had this been a sword, you would be dead. Defend yourself!"

Sorde attacked again. Thrice more Hamilton was staggered by his master's lightning fast, incredibly accurate blows, while he stood dumbly, endeavoring to ward off the strikes.

"Defend yourself!" Sorde cried, "I have killed you four times!" Again, in a flurry of movement, Sorde attacked. This time Hamilton managed to swat away two of the six blows that Sorde threw in the time of two heartbeats.

"Better," Sorde said, and threw his small body into motion again.

This time, Hamilton batted away three of the seven attacks. Sorde backed up a pace and removed his hood. He regarded Hamilton evenly. "I cannot even see you, and yet I know exactly where you are. I have killed you a dozen times. You had your sight. I had not mine." He paused to let Hamilton absorb this.

Every blow Sorde had struck had fallen precisely. Hamstring. Heart. Jugular. Back of the neck. Throat. Head. Abdomen. And he could not even see.

He continued. "You must see that which cannot be seen, know what cannot be known. To do this, you must not rely on mere sight. I heard you, heard your breath, the rustle of your garments, the sliding of your feet. I scented your sweat. But most important of all, I reached out with my mind." He touched his temple. "Beyond the realm of the five physical senses, sight, touch, smell, taste, hearing, there is another realm, the realm of the mind and spirit, of *jii*, the oneness that binds the universe together. There are mind, body and spirit. All are bound by *jii*.

"Every man has an aura of *jii* that surrounds his entire body." Sorde gestured around himself. "With proper training, one can sense when his own aura is entered, or is about to be entered, and where.

"You must focus your mind on the things you have learned the last two days. Purge your mind of all hindrance, then *feel* it. Focus on the task. Imagine yourself doing it, and you will do it. Feel your *jii* around you. Yours is the strength and sensitivity to do so. You will do it because you are The One. With training, this sensitivity will sharpen.

"I could see in my mind exactly the position in which you stood, thus I could attack."

He replaced his hood, tying it securely about his throat. "Attack me."

Hamilton obeyed, swinging the staff at Sorde. The small stick the Master held batted the blow away effortlessly.

"Attack me."

Hamilton flew forward with a whirlwind of blows, all of which were halted by Sorde's lightning quickness.

Sorde removed the hood again. Now he approached Hamilton and settled it over his head. "Your *jii* is like a beacon to me. The key is to be passive. Feel your *jii* around you like a blanket of warmth. Relax. Breathe steadily, evenly, with knees slightly bent, both feet flat on the floor. At some time I will move into your *jii*. Try to reach out with your awareness, sense your *jii* around your body, and feel when it is entered."

Hamilton concentrated. A pleasant throbbing arose on his left breast, in time with his heartbeat, and he imagined he saw an ethereal brilliance shining from the birthmark. His aura, shimmering with colors. He gasped when a shadow appeared in his aura, not a shadow precisely, but more a foreign presence, a different light.

He said, "You are standing behind me to the

left, about two paces away."

The presence in his aura suddenly flooded with Sorde's amazement, like a river of disembodied emotion.

Sorde said, "Amazing! I have never seen one use his mind so quickly! Good. Good! This permits us to move on to other things more quickly."

Hamilton, surprised at this new-found ability, removed the hood and said, "I hardly had to try!"

Sorde gazed at him seriously. "That means your spirit is strong within you. Mind, body, spirit and *jii* all feed from the strength of the others to achieve balance. Strengthen one, all benefit. Now we must strengthen all. Your *jii* is a powerful force. You are indeed The One.

"Now," he said, seating himself cross-legged on the floor, gesturing Hamilton to follow suit. "What remains is to teach you the skills of the warrior. We of the Order of Knights of the Eagles are warriors first and foremost, warriors against Uhr and his oppression. But we arc also philosophers, scholars and historians. It was us who recorded the events of Uhr's rise to power, and it shall be us who record his downfall."

Sorde paused a moment, then said, "You have doubtless noticed that no women abide in our Sanctuary."

Hamilton said, "But there are women living at the mouth of the valley."

"They are the workers and wives of workers. Their families bear the children that keep our order strong."

The door opened, and the boy named Rolf entered, bearing a tray laden with food and drink. Hamilton's stomach growled like a wild thing. Sorde smiled patiently. "You are doubtless hungry after your exercise. Eat." The boy set the plate down, and silently stood awaiting further command. Sorde gave him leave, smiling as Hamilton began to devour the food set before him. Sorde continued, "There are no women here because we will allow none. They lack the physical strength of men, and would interfere with the total concentration of the men I train. Thus, we have all taken vows of celibacy and chastity. Women are like peaches, Hamilton, so soft and sweet on the outside, but when one reaches the core of their being, one finds the stone."

Hamilton interrupted, "Master, I must disagree…"

"It is tradition," Sorde said quickly raising his hand. "It has been so since the beginning of the Order, and will be so until the end of it."

"But, Master—Enough gabble, " he said, abruptly rising. "It is time to continue your lessons. Come."

Chapter 16

He reached out with his aura, sensing his surroundings, his breath hot in the heavy cloth hood engulfing his head.

"Where am I sitting?" Sorde asked.

He "saw" the shape of Sorde's flickering, pulsating aura. "Before me, slightly to the left."

"What else is here?"

Hamilton extended his *jii* further, and located a symmetric fluctuation in his aura behind him. He scrutinized it carefully. No life. Curving symmetry. Smooth surfaces. Finely textured.

"A vase?" he said.

"Good," Sorde said, "what else?"

His searching mind probed the small chamber he was in, searching for more. An empty space. "A small fireplace," he said.

"More."

"Seven logs."

"Good."

Hamilton suppressed a surge of pride. He could sense all these things, as he sat cross-legged on the floor in the center of the small, stone-walled room.

Emotion flooded his aura of awareness. Approval. Satisfaction.

"What do I hold in my hand, student?"

Hamilton's mind reached out to feel what Sorde held. Cold. Hard. Steel! "A sword," he said.

"Correct," Sorde told him. "Remove your hood." Hamilton did so, and Sorde continued. "Your lessons have gone far better than I imagined they would. In the past thirty-day, I have seen the strength of your *jü*-sense surpass that of many lifelong Knights I have known. You've been taught in the ways of the mind, and of the flesh. The awareness of the mind and spirit is instrumental in the awareness of the warrior. For the warrior who sees nothing, life is short. It is now time for you to learn the warrior's art. Come."

Hamilton followed him into the hallway.

Hamilton had learned much in his stay at the Sanctuary. Life here was good, peaceful, as if they did not care about the very purpose behind their existence, which was Uhr's downfall. As Hamilton's lessons progressed, his dormant mental abilities manifested. Sorde explained to him that his previously untapped spirit was emerging, bringing with it a fierce independence yet subtle interdependence, an indomitable will, and an incredible physical strength.

Hamilton had grown quite comfortable with this world. He rarely missed his former home anymore. This was his home now. And over the time he had spent here, he thought with some amusement, his constant use of his new language increased his proficiency, and he often found himself thinking in it as well.

He and Sorde spent hours talking about many things. They discussed philosophy on occasion, art, history, science. Hamilton could not help but smile at Sorde's reaction when he learned of Hamilton's own origins. Hamilton told him the whole story, and Sorde believed it without reservation. Sorde was amazed at Hamilton's knowledge of astronomy and the sciences, and Hamilton delighted in telling him stories of the "wondrous machines" created by Hamilton's people.

One day Sorde was relating to Hamilton some history of the world Irth, and Hamilton asked what Sorde knew about the Priests of the Red Circle.

Sorde said, "Their Order is old, almost as old as ours. No one in the outside world is aware of what I am about to tell you. And with good reason. Once, long ago, a small band of Eagle Knights were expelled from Sanctuary, exiled for twisting good magic into evil. In effect, they corrupted the benevolence of Eagle Knight magic into unspeakable rites of black sorcery. They were discovered one night performing an arcane, intensely evil ritual. They were robed all in black, sitting within a scarlet circle painted in the floor. The Master of that time ordered them to cease their evil madness, but they defied him, condemning the Eagle Knights for using their knowledge and arts for greater good, instead of their own ends. They proclaimed themselves separate, demanding autonomy as well as access to the greater, more powerful mysteries of magic, doubtless to corrupt that as well. The Master cast them out, drove them from the Viderian Mountains. The outcasts settled in the Vicorian range to the north, sister range to the Viderians, and built for themselves a fortress and temple to their chaotic gods. Priests of the Red Circle. The very day following the outcasts' departure, the old Sanctuary was struck by lightning in a mysterious storm, and burned to the ground. It was that blaze that destroyed nearly all our records of the Ivory Star. The only records saved were those of

Uhr's rise to power, and his battle with Arnor, and that the Ivory Star indeed exists.

"The Red Priests' order eventually began to gather followers, and grew quickly. Our order saw this growth as a tremendous threat to the world's well-being, what with Uhr already in power, therefore they mounted a series of raids against the Red Priests, all of which returned nothing. Captive priests were somehow destroyed, incinerated, apparently from afar, leaving nothing but scorched circles.

"We have hated and warred with each other for centuries, and it continues. We know less about them now than we did back then. They manage to hide their activities even from us. Someday in the future they must be dealt with, but not today. Perhaps after Uhr's downfall we can concentrate on them. In any case, not today."

Hamilton spent much time with Sorde out in the mountains. He spent many a day and sleepless night learning the ways of the land, and furthering his physical endurance. Running, climbing, hanging from ropes, branches, rock overhangs. Sorde taught him to become invisible in snow, grass, trees, rocks, night and day. He stood for hours on tree branches that swayed in the wind, balancing on ropes, jumping, rolling, twisting like a human fly. Sorde taught him to scale sheer rock walls like a spider using only the strength of his fingers and toes, or, where there were no hand holds, using steel claws strapped onto his palms and toes.

Sorde hardly contained his surprise on the many occasions where Hamilton's abilities far outstripped Sorde's expectations.

Hamilton would practice something until he

succeeded at it, spending all day, if necessary, to perform a single act such as turning a somersault on a suspended rope. What was more, he discovered, he could use his will to diminish pain, dispel weakness, add strength to certain parts of his body. And all the time that he performed these feats of strength, the birthmark on his breast would pulse with a pleasant warmth.

During his stay in the Sanctuary, he saw no Knights other than Sorde. The other Knights spent most of their time away from Sanctuary, Sorde said, doing one thing or another, such as surveillance on their enemies, or practicing various facets of their art. Carrier pigeons arrived daily, bearing small tubes in which were stuffed messages scrawled on scraps of parchment concerning various things, such as the movements of the Slayer legions, activities of the Red Priests, actions of Lord Erastus, all gathered by Knights living in these regions, serving as spies and messengers.

Hamilton soon found that this was not Sorde's only means of gathering information. One particular afternoon, Sorde told Hamilton he wished to show him something. He led Hamilton down a long spiral staircase carved into the heart of the mountain, to a room far below Sanctuary.

As they entered the room, Hamilton saw the pool of water.

Sorde said, "This pool has never seen the light of the sun."

A circle of tightly mortared stones contained the calm pool. The water rippled and glistened in the glowstone light as it seeped over the sides, covering the floor with a thin layer of wetness, seeping away between the cracks in the rock. Hamilton saw the tiny trickle of the spring that fed the pool flowing down the stone wall. Centuries of flowing water had left brightly colored mineral deposits on the wall and lip of the pool.

Hamilton also noticed the two steel-bound hardwood doors that stood closed on opposite walls.

Sorde threw a handful of some ghostly silvery powder over the calm surface of the water, and closed his eyes in silence.

Ripples on the water began to fade, leaving a clear mirror surface. Hamilton watched in fascination as he saw something moving within the pool, like a scattered reflection. The reflection began to settle, to calm into an image on the flawless sheen of water.

Sorde opened his eyes and gazed at the utterly still pool.

Hamilton cocked his ear. Had he heard something? There it came again! The clang of metal on metal. The clash of arms, the gasp of sucked breath, the grunts of exertion. He stared into the water in stunned amazement.

There, in the water, was the image of two men fighting, seen as if from the top of the stone wall surrounding Valerion's outer ward. Hamilton's breath hissed in wonder when he saw, reflected in the pool, that one of the men was Angus. He battled desperately against another man. Both were clad in thick cuir-boulli, wielding heavy iron swords. They were practicing.

He glanced at Sorde, who stood stiff as a statue, staring into the shimmering water with glazed eyes. Hamilton said, "How do we see this, Master?"

Sorde's eyes focused, and the image in the pool disappeared. He replied, panting slightly as if from tremendous exertion, "A bird perched on the wall of Valerion's castle. With the aid of this powder, we have seen and heard through his eyes and ears."

"Can I learn to do this?"

"Yes, in time you could. But even with such abilities as yours, it would take years, and we have not years to spare. Perhaps later, after Uhr is dead, we shall have more time to bring you to your ultimate potential." He paused. "I have shown you how Angus fares, because I know you have wondered. Now it is back to the lessons with you."

He stepped into a dark room, following Sorde. Instinctively he inspected the room with his mind. It was very large, square, with a high, vaulted ceiling. Many things he sensed hanging on racks and hooks on the walls, sharp objects, razor-edged things of tempered steel. But there was someone else in the room also, with an aura that was unfamiliar to him.

Sorde reached out, and pulled firmly on a thick rope that hung from the ceiling near the door. Hamilton heard the clacking and clunking of weights and counterweights somewhere, and suddenly silver morning sunlight flooded into the room from several large skylights. Hundreds of weapons glinted like steel fangs in the bright sunlight.

A man sat cross-legged, revealed, in the far corner.

Sorde called out, "Brother Capian. What do you here?"

The man's eyes snapped open. He stood and approached them, silently, barefooted on the wooden floor. The Knight called Capian spoke. "I have been meditating, Master Sorde."

Sorde nodded.

Capian regarded Hamilton. A close-cropped thatch of yellow locks crowned Capian's head. His face was fair, ruggedly handsome, untouched by years. He gazed at Hamilton placidly with two deep-set eyes that blazed like chips of blue agate, eyes Hamilton had seen before in the face of another.

Hamilton stated, “You are the son of Valerion.”

Capian contemplated him with something akin to astonishment.

“I have seen your father,” Hamilton told him before Capian could speak, “and you are very much his son.”

Capian smiled, then turned to Sorde. “I do not wish to disturb your practice, Master.”

Sorde interrupted him, touching his shoulder. “We would be pleased, Capian, if you would stay and assist for a time.”

Capian nodded. “Of course, Master.”

Hamilton sensed Capian’s *jii.* It radiated respect for Sorde, admiration, perhaps a brotherly love. All this blanketed by a headstrong will and determination, like his sire’s.

Hamilton looked about him. The walls were lined with weapons of every description. Sorde took down a sword from one of the many racks. The sword was about three feet long, with a straight, single-edged blade about two finger-breadths wide, razor-keen. The hilt was about a quarter of its length, with a small square guard. Sorde flourished it with practiced ease, twirling the vicious edge around his head and torso. Suddenly he stood stock still, sword extended in a perfect thrust, motionless. Then he stood straight and took a black wooden scabbard from the wall and slid the blade into its well-oiled opening.

Sorde lifted a small wooden box from the floor and approached Capian and Hamilton, who had been watching him in respectful silence. Capian nodded as he seemed to recognize the box. As Sorde stepped up to Hamilton, he sat the box upon a nearby table, and opened it. He reached inside and withdrew a strange blade, shaped like a quarter moon, about the size of a fist, but thin like a dagger blade. Its concave edge was sharpened, leaving the thicker, convex outer edge to be gripped.

"A talon-blade," Sorde said, handing it to Capian, who received it in his outstretched palm. Capian's wrist snapped, and the blade slashed the air as it flew across the room. It sank, points foremost, into a man-shaped wooden target twenty-five paces away, exactly where the victim's jugular would have been. Suddenly a talon-blade was in Sorde's hand. It flashed through the air, and struck the one which Capian had thrown. Capian's fell to the floor, in two evenly shorn pieces.

Hamilton would have thought Capian too accustomed to such feats of prowess by Sorde to be awestricken, but nevertheless he was. Sorde smiled, not a smug smirk, but a friendly grin. He passed a talon-blade into Hamilton's hand. The student examined the weapon with interest. It was strangely light, but its tensile strength was obviously very high. He ran his fingers along the polished surface. The points were slightly thicker, heavier, to keep them foremost in flight. With a quick wrist motion he cast it. It flew surprisingly straight and strong, and sank into the target in the exact center of the target's groin area.

Sorde turned to Hamilton with an amused smile. "You have just succeeded in gelding a man."

Hamilton and Capian burst into laughter, and Sorde joined them with a quiet chuckle. The laughter subsided, and Sorde took two sheathed swords down from the wall, one of which he handed to Hamilton, passing the other to Capian. Hamilton followed the other Eagle Knight to the center of the large room, where he pulled the sword from its scabbard, finding it to be made of light hard wood.

Sorde said to Capian, "Attack."

The blunt wooden edge whistled toward Hamilton's throat. Hamilton, slightly off-balance and unprepared, barely caught the blade with his own, driving it away. Capian spun behind him, sidestepping. Hamilton's blade came up to block Capian's as Capian pulled his blade back toward Hamilton's throat. All that stopped Hamilton's mock decapitation was his own blade interposed between his bare throat and Capian's sword. Knowing not what else to do, Hamilton let fly backward with his free elbow, striking Capian in the belly. It felt like striking wood. Capian laughed good-naturedly and released him, stepping away.

"Balance is the key," Sorde told him. "Balance." He took the sword from Capian. "Mimic my actions."

He thrust forward, stopping dead still at the terminus of the move.

Hamilton thrust ahead swiftly, and nearly fell on his face.

Sorde said, "In the beginning, you must realize the uselessness of excessive speed. Trying to hit one's enemy before his sees you move is folly if one is a novice. As one becomes a master, that will happen naturally. If one tries to move too quickly, one will inevitably lose one's balance, and run oneself onto the point of the enemy's weapon. A man's body can only move as fast as his legs can carry him *on balance*. If he has difficulty stopping or changing direction once he has started moving, he is using excessive speed.

"Now," he continued, "cut. Like this." Sorde cut ahead of him at the air.

Hamilton mimicked his motion, this time retaining his balance.

"Again...Again...Again...Good. Do not move

yet," Sorde said, "now like this." He slashed into another attack from this still position, and Hamilton did the same. "Back," Sorde said, cutting to his original position. "Forth." Slash. "Good," he said finally. "Now, attack me."

Hamilton did so, using the first cut. Sorde caught the edge on his own. Hamilton slashed back. Sorde parried this, too; suddenly countering with a low gutting stroke to Hamilton's belly. The wooden blade stopped finger's breadth from his tunic. Sorde backed away and said, "A counterattack properly executed will kill an enemy before he realizes he is dead. Now I shall attack you in such manner as you did me. Counter as I did. *HAII!*"

Startled, Hamilton almost failed to block the first cut. He caught it and counterattacked swiftly, but on balance. He was astonished at how the counter flowed like water from the first position. However, Sorde caught the gutting stroke easily, and suddenly Hamilton found the edge of the hovering wooden blade a finger's breadth from his nose.

Sorde taught him this attack as well. So it went throughout the day. Hamilton learned an entire repertoire of thrusts, cuts, slashes, their defensive counterparts, and how each was interrelated. Some followed others more efficiently. Sorde told him over and over: balance, economy of motion, accuracy. Hamilton was drilled in several attacks, their counters, and shown how they were related. When he learned one or two techniques, Sorde would throw in a new one, and then drill him with those.

The days passed in sword instruction. He was introduced to dozens of techniques, such as attacking with the draw itself, "punching" the enemy with the pommel as the sword was drawn, or turning the draw itself into a cut or slash. He was taught to feint as a means of throwing the opponent off balance, thus making an opening, and how to fight against blades while unarmed, by turning the enemy's blade against him.

In the days that followed, Sorde introduced The One to a host of other weapons, several types of bows, knives, clubs, bladed chains and ropes, staves of various lengths, bladed spears. They also spent several days of practice with the talon-blades, "the patron weapon of the Eagle Knights". Hamilton became quite pleased with his growing skill with them.

Days passed quickly as Hamilton absorbed the ways of the warrior, but even in his exhaustion his nights were not peaceful. Every night, during his profound slumber, he found himself dreaming of a tall, auburn-haired beauty. He and she always sat together near a small gurgling stream. Well…he had dreamed it before, and every time he awoke, the memory of that stinging slap lay fresh upon his cheek. But his dream did little to assuage his growing longing for her.

But the day eclipsed these night-time melancholies, as hours of practice and exertion consumed him.

He learned empty-handed fighting, spending hours driving his hands and feet into a sand-stuffed leather bag, increasing the strength of his limbs, and callusing the striking points. He learned to channel his *jii* into the force of every blow until his fists and feet became like things of iron. The principles of attack and counterattack were the same with fists as with steel. Balance. Accuracy. Strength. Economy of motion. Unpredictability.

"Your enemy cannot stop you as easily if he

does not know where the next blow will fall," Sorde said, "it is up to you to read his thoughts by sensing his aura and watching his eyes, even as he tries to read yours. Thus, you must not let your eyes give you away. One with a *jii*-sense such as yours would do just as well or better to fight with your eyes closed."

Hamilton tried it, with considerable success.

Sorde continued, "Imagine your enemy's surprise if he sees you fight with your eyes closed, especially if you are winning."

As the weeks progressed, and Sorde exhaustively trained and taught The One, the Knight Master saw something emerge from Hamilton Corbin, something that he had long suspected to be there. Hamilton, Sorde knew, was a hero, as Arnor had been so very long ago. But he maintained a fervent hope that Hamilton would not die as most heroes did. He was the last hope of the people of Irth. This man alone could thrust off the yoke of evil that had burdened them for so long. The people of Irth were ready for a leader, a hero, and he truly believed that Hamilton Corbin was such a man.

The time to complete his training was nigh. Lord Erastus, Sorde's spies told him, teetered uncertainly on the brink between loyalty to Uhr and rebellion. A sign of hope, a sign that Uhr was not invincible, would tip Erastus in favor of rebellion. The Allahnian lord's only bond to Uhr was the terror that he shared with all men of that unspeakably evil being and his loathsome legions.

Yes, soon Hamilton would go on his quest for the Keys. And after that, the Ivory Star!

Chapter 17

The man knelt and pressed his forehead to the floor. The black and crimson cowled figure glared down at him, impatiently.

"By your command, O omnipotent Uhr," the kneeling man groveled.

"Up, cretin."

The man scrambled to his feet, babbling for forgiveness. Middle age had long since claimed him, and had not treated him well. His graying brown hair retreated like a routed host. Filthy rags hung on his gaunt, half-starved frame like stringy moss from spindly boughs, and his face was drawn and haggard.

Suddenly Uhr's sickly yellow claw lashed out, and gripped the terror-stricken face. The helpless fellow dangled like a doll in the vice-like clutch, and Uhr held him, arm stiff and unbent. His free hand he laid upon the pulsing scarlet surface of the Bloodstone.

A soul-rent shriek ripped from the victim's lips, muffled by Uhr's moldering palm. Abruptly the bloodcurdling scream ceased, and the fellow hung grotesquely limp in his grasp. Uhr let the body drop carelessly to the stone floor. He turned and peered deep into the Bloodstone. There, within the crimson, crystalline depths, he saw the movement of a vaguely human shape, struggling wraith-like, thrashing for escape. Uhr nodded with satisfaction. The man's soul had been sucked from his body and imprisoned within the gem. Now Uhr let his own foul essence seep into the stone.

As he gained awareness within the stone, he searched and groped for the man's bewildered and terrified spirit. He located it, and it sensed him. Uhr savored the cold, delicious terror of the soul as it tried to flee, and approached the quivering essence menacingly. He amused himself for a time, chasing it, toying with it, allowing it to remain just out of his ethereal reach. Then, as his amusement began to fade, he lashed out and grasped it. His rending, ripping, spirit claws tore a great chunk from the ectoplasmic shape, and he withdrew himself, laughing, devouring the piece of the soul as he went.

Again in his own body, he picked up the man's seemingly muscle-less form from where it lay in a heap on the floor, and touched the Bloodstone. With his mind, he reached into the Bloodstone, grasped the spirit and channeled it back into its own flesh. The man's eyes blinked once, and intelligence, of a sort, returned to those shallow depths.

Releasing him, Uhr saw that he regarded him calmly now, fearlessly, all terror that had previously possessed him gone.

Uhr rumbled, "Who is your one and only master?"

The man looked at him calmly, and answered, "You, O powerful one."

Good. He had taken away the man's emotions, thus he could not lie. This was the same process with which he had conditioned his entire army of

Slayers, excepting only the highest officers.

"Now," he said, "this is what you are to do."

****

The torch in Valerion's sweaty hand flickered uncertainly in the stiff autumn wind.

The small group stood in a solemn half-circle beside a tall mound of wood. On top of this mound stood a platform, on which rested the silk and flower draped body of Madra.

Valerion looked around him at the people assembled with him in the garden. Robinton stood beside Tarl and Dame Pilgra, Madra's former tutor and Valerion's house mother. Val stood next to his mother and his remaining sister, Nessa.

A somber-clad priest muttered prayers to the gods of Law and Good for the soul of the departed.

The droning liturgies of the priest seemed so much drivel to Valerion. Thoughts of the consequences of recent events weighed heavily on his brow as he stepped up to the pyre, and thrust his torch into the pile of oil-soaked wood. Thick smoke roiled from the flaming mound, and Valerion wiped at the wetness in his eyes. The flames licked up, enveloping Madra's body.

The flames rose high, blackening first her clothing, and then her flesh.

"As black as Uhr's soul," Valerion mumbled under his breath.

Ilone looked at him, and squeezed his hand.

Valerion looked at her, surprised she had heard. Her lovely brow was twisted into a mixture of fury and sorrow. He put his arm around her, rubbed the small of her back, squeezed her shoulder.

She looked up into his face, and her scowl softened. "We will wait and see."

Valerion smiled at her mirthlessly. "You know me too well."

She turned her gaze back into the flames and nodded.

Valerion stared into the fire. After a long while, Ilone glanced at him. "Come, Nessa, let us go in," she said, turning to her daughter.

At Ilone's urging, everyone except Valerion turned to go back into the house. Tarl wiped his eyes with a thick, hairy paw as he lumbered away. Valerion remained until the fire began to burn down, like the rage in his heart. He drew a deep breath, turned and walked away.

Then, happening to glance up, he saw a colossal winged shape, high, high in the morning sky. Sunlight shone off scarlet scales.

Now what was Uhr up to? The dragon seemed to be heading for the mountains, and, if Valerion squinted, he thought he could see something dangling from its claws. He leaped the wall of the garden and ran toward the gatehouse tower. As he reached the crenelated height, he watched the dragon spiral down into the lofty peaks, disappear for a few moments, then vault back up into the sky and away, as if it had deposited something there.

Robinton cracked the whip above the heads of the four steam-snorting war-horses as they shouldered their way into the teeming crowd in Lakeside's town square. The battle-wagon's wheels rumbled heavily on the cobblestones. Valerion stood on the roof of the wagon as it rocked along, dragon-crested helm under one arm, black mane flying in the wind, his melee-nicked broadsword resting point down under his palm. His gleaming, gold-laced plate armor shone in the sun. His people saw him, ceased their chores and stared. He had chosen to do this now because this was only the second day after Harvest Festival, and most of the people of Armond were still at Lakeside.

Valerion halted the wagon in the midst of the square, surrounded by the murmuring mass. He raised his plated arm, and silence fell like a blanket. His voice cracked the silence like a lash. "All men wishing to fling off the bloody yoke of fear that rests upon you, your women and your children, hear me!"

People emerged from houses and wagons to further pack the throng to hear their lord's words.

Valerion cried out again, "Hear me, brave, stalwart men of Armond! Bones have been cast in the past days that hold grim tidings for all of us!"

The murmur rose again.

Valerion continued, "Uhr knows of my plans for rebellion, and the Slayers are coming."

The mention of Uhr's dreaded soldiers brought more fear from the crowd. The Slayers were the very bolts that locked Uhr's despised yoke of evil upon them.

"They will destroy us!" Valerion cried. "They will enslave our women and our children, or worse!"

Cries of fear, anger and despair ascended from the throng.

Valerion continued, "But we have hope! I call upon you men, those of you who are able, to help me raise an army, that we may fight him. You are the bravest people on all of Irth! There come days when blood will soak the ground like Hell's rain, but with your strong arms and courage..." He flourished his glinting blade. "...the blood that flows will be that of the Slayers!"

A fellow far back in the mass raised his voice for all to hear. "But what of Uhr? We cannot kill him!"

Many nodded and muttered assent.

Valerion raised his arm, and the hush fell again. He looked out over the teeming thousands. "There is a Prophecy, given down to us by the Knights of the Eagles, and your hope lies there. 'The One shall come when The Sun turns to Blood. The One shall come riding but not riding a silver Dragon that is not a Dragon. The One shall have the Ivory Star in his Breast, and He shall free Men from The Ultimate Evil'."

The people were spellbound, still unable to comprehend what their lord meant by reciting something everyone had known almost from birth.

"The Prophecy has been, in part, fulfilled!"

The people stared at one another in astonishment.

"The One has come!" Valerion thundered.

A cheer such as Valerion had never heard rose to the sky. Tears of joy sprung like fountains from eyes that had known no hope for hundreds of years. Could it be that that which their great-grandfathers' ancestors had awaited had finally come? A multitude of questions flew at him. "Where is The One?" "Is he here?" "Where is he?" "Show him to us!" "Is Uhr dead yet?" "When will The One get him?"

Suddenly another voice silenced the throng. "Hold!" It was the fellow who had spoken before. "Where is The One? Is he here? Or is it, perhaps, some trick to persuade us to join your mad crusade against Uhr?"

Valerion frowned and answered, "My people. You know full well that never would I do anything to trick you. I speak the truth! Even as I speak, The One, aided by the Knights of the Eagles, seeks the Ivory Star!"

Hundreds dropped to their knees weeping for joy.

"The One can kill Uhr for us," Valerion continued, "but he cannot vanquish armies! He needs us for that. He is but a man like you and I. But he is a hero, a man that will lead us to victory, and freedom, if we will let him!"

He paused, then boomed, "Are you with me, my people?"

The crowd roared. The throats of the inflamed thousands kindled a spark of hope that had been so long denied them, the chorus fanning a flame of courage that would, gods willing, lead them to glorious freedom.

Valerion raised his arm once more, gradually silencing the raging tumult that threatened to overwhelm him. "You men," he cried, "will you take up arms and follow The One and myself to freedom?"

A chorus of thousands of deep-throated voices fairly blew Valerion from his perch. He smiled with satisfaction as he saw the man who had spoken out cheering with them.

****

The man threaded his way among the mountain valleys, stumbling, weary from hunger and exhaustion. For six days had he wandered through the Viderian mountains, eating only what he could find, searching for that which no man of the outside world had ever sought and found, The Sanctuary of the Eagle Knights.

But unbeknownst to him, he had been watched, followed for the last five of those days.

Valt kept his eyes on the strange wanderer night and day. He saw that the fellow was well-nigh starved, ready to collapse with hunger. When he did, he would take the senseless man to Sanctuary. The man's garments hung loosely on his emaciated frame, like a gunny sack over a twig.

Valt believed that the man somehow sensed his presence, because the fellow occasionally twisted his graying head about, searching the rock outcroppings. But Valt would not be detected. He was an Eagle Knight.

Abruptly the man stumbled and collapsed in a heap of skin and bones. Valt watched the unmoving figure for almost an hour before emerging from the clump of brush in which he had concealed himself. He stopped beside the motionless form, scooped it up, and slung the incredibly light, rather angular weight across his firm shoulders.

In slightly less than half a day, he reached Sanctuary with his burden, and deposited the skeletal body in a bed in one of the Sanctuary's many apartments.

Broth was poured down the stranger's throat, and he awakened as Sorde and Hamilton entered the room to stand beside Valt and Rolf.

Valt explained, "He has been wandering about the mountains for days. I think he may have been searching for us."

The man's dull, sunken eyes stared blankly at him over his bowl of warm broth, which he gulped desperately. When it was empty, he held it forth, desiring more.

"No," Sorde told him, "you have not eaten in days. More will sicken you. Now what do you in these mountains, in winter, without food or water?"

"I seek the Eagle Knights," the man rasped through taut lips. His face was a skull stretched over with thin leather. His cheekbones protruded grotesquely darkened by frost bite.

"You have found them, friend," Valt said, looking at the man with his sparkling gray eyes.

The fellow nodded weakly, as if the effort to do so took all the energy remaining in him.

Sorde questioned further, "Where do you come from?"

"Arnath," he replied.

"That is far," Sorde said. "How are things in Arnath?"

"There is famine," the skeletal being answered. His voice was slow, halting and raspy as he explained. "Uhr takes almost all the food for his Slayers. He is massing a huge army, ready to crush any resistance, by taking every man between fifteen and thirty-five years of age that is strong enough to walk and carry a weapon."

Hamilton glanced at Sorde, and tried to read the stranger's emotions. Strangely, he could detect none. He thought this rather odd, but he attributed it to the man's numbness of mind.

"But now," Sorde said, "we shall leave you to your rest."

Then they all filed from the room, leaving him alone. As soon as the door was latched behind them, the man reached down into his filthy, ragged shirt and pulled forth a fist-sized copper disk, slightly concave, inscribed in black with a pentagram and several eldritch symbols.

"Come to me, O master Uhr," he chanted, thrice.

A faint, almost inaudible hum began to emanate from the disk. The man then struggled out of bed, and staggered toward the window, the broth lending him the strength he needed. Opening the shutter, he reached out with the disk in his hand, and threw it back onto the roof.

It was only a matter of time now. His work was done. He then slipped a tiny blade from the only intact hem of his shirt, and slit his own throat.

****

The days dragged as the people of Valerion's realm settled down to preparing for the siege that would surely come. Immense quantities of food, the remnants and wares of the Harvest Festival, were carted into the fortress. Along with food, water would be of little concern; several wells were scattered throughout the fortress.

Nearly every man, old and young alike, signed the roster for temporary service in Valerion's army. Robinton oversaw the signing up. If he deemed someone too old or young to fight, he denied them service, even though it pained him to see the expressions of profound disappointment on their faces. These were given the tasks of squires, muleskinners, water-bearers and stretcher-bearers. The army was outfitted, the armories emptied, the stables and courtyard filled. The armorers and smiths were hard-pressed to produce the vast quantities of helmets, shields and weapons needed by the rag-tag militia. Many of the ladies, wives and maidens of the realm teamed with leather workers to sew makeshift leather leggings and shirts to be boiled in oil and hardened into cuir-boulli. Meat was cured and stored, along with grain and vegetables, in dozens of large pots sunk into the floors of houses and buildings. Immense quantities of firewood were piled against the walls of the castle, brought in by caravans of woodsmen from the mountains. Dried cattle-dung was stored in massive piles on the shore outside the Lakeside palisade. The impenetrable Keep was stocked sufficiently to support a small number of people for several months, if it should come down to that.

Valerion's assembled army began its training on the fields south of the lake. Farmers and herdsmen made up most of the ranks of his makeshift army, but also laborers and townsfolk. Bands of mercenaries anxious for war and gold began to filter into the fortress. The prestigious Red Dragons became the principal officers and leaders of the swelling army.

A fortnight passed, clouded by a gloomy apprehension and growing foreboding. Could they defy Uhr and live? Many thought not, but believed with some misgivings that the die had been cast.

The cold autumn sank slowly into winter, and snow fell, blanketing all with its cold, wet whiteness. The training field became a sea of mud, and sickness spread among the soldiers. Morale was high for the time being, for Valerion endured all that they did, sitting on the back of his stomping black stallion, watching over them, directing them, marching with them. He treated them well, and they were proud to follow him.

One gorgeous morning, the sun splashed its rose and silver across the gleaming surface of the lake, and the new soldiers drilled along the shore. Suddenly a lone voice rose in warning, as a monstrous shape took form in the sky above their heads. A red dragon swooped low over them, terrible leathery wings buffeting them with wind, crimson scales glinting dully in the winter sunlight, beady red eyes flicking over the field. But that which smote icy terror into the veins of every witness was the menacing figure mounted upon the back of the flying beast, swathed in robes of black and scarlet.

Uhr's malevolent stare swept the field like a scythe, impaling everyone with those baneful eyes, sending cold fingers racing up and down their spines. The beast hovered momentarily just above and before where Valerion sat astride his massive black stallion. Uhr cast him a baleful glare from the ebon recesses of the hood, and Valerion threw back an unyielding defiant gaze.

Then the monster wheeled away into the sky toward the mountains behind them. The dragon and its malignant rider dwindled to a drifting speck in the endless blue.

Shaken, the men resumed drilling. Not a hundred heartbeats later, the ground began to tremble with a distant rumble. Angus felt the vibration up through the legs of his horse. Suddenly the western horizon began to move, shifting rhythmically. The thunder of hoofbeats rose up, drowning out all other sound. A legion of mounted warriors hove into full view, galloping toward them.

Then Valerion roared, "Robinton!"

"Ho, m'lord!" came Robinton's reply from the other side of the mass of men.

"The Slayers are here! Get the men inside the walls!"

"Aye, m'lord!" Robinton called back.

And they moved the newborn army into the walls of the palisade, and to Valerion's pride, his men did not panic and flee for safety at the approach of the Slayers, who had come earlier than expected. Angus MacTavish reined up his horse and stared.

Sun glinted off gleaming steel and full suits of black plate armor. As they neared, Angus began to distinguish more detail. Black spikes bristled up and down the arms and shoulders. The helmets were the very heads of death itself, each adorned by a grotesquely unique figure. Horns, skulls, wings of a hundred different types, claws clutching at empty air, talons, hides. The barding of the horses was of deepest black, hung thick with scalps and hides and bones. The chenfrons covering the horses' heads were spiked down the center, but on the forehead, between the eyes, a painted red eye glared ahead like a third orb.

Angus watched the revulsion and fear sweep through the faces of the men around him.

With everyone inside, the gates were closed. Defenders quickly mounted the palisade as the alarm bells tolled throughout Lakeside and into the fortress. The Slayers had come.

But they did not approach. In fact, the entire legion rode right past, pounding up a gigantic swath of snow-patched ground as they veered away, galloping past as if Lakeside did not exist. They were headed toward the mountains.

After the last phalanx had passed by, Valerion's voice thundered a command. "Red Dragons, mount up once again and follow me! The rest of you guard the walls here and inform the fortress of the impending siege. Quickly now! Robinton, until I return, you rule Armond."

Robinton stepped from the crowd of men. "I, m'lord?" His eyes were wide.

"Yes, Robinton. If I fail to return, you will rule Armond in regency until another agreement with my family is reached among you."

"But, my lord!" Robinton protested. "I should go after them, not you. You are lord of Armond."

"I must see whatever is to be seen for myself. Just believe me when I say this. I know where Uhr is taking them."

"Where, my lord?"

"The Sanctuary of the Eagle Knights."

****

Hamilton Corbin snapped awake, bolting upright in bed. His mind screamed at him, *Danger! Danger! Danger!* A cold sweat sheened his half-naked body. He took a deep breath, and sensed his surroundings for any immediate danger. He found none, but the terrible unease would not leave him.

"It must be nothing," he said to himself, trying to calm his shrieking nerves.

A loud knock at the door nearly sent him though the ceiling.

"Enter," he said, hiding his quivering hands behind his back.

Rolf stepped gingerly into the room and smiled brightly. "Sorde wishes your presence, Brother," he said.

Hamilton smiled half-heartedly in return, and nodded.

The boy withdrew.

Hamilton slipped into his clothes, using the power of his will to soothe himself.

The Master sat cross-legged before a fire, facing the door, when Hamilton entered.

"Ah," he said, "Hamilton. Sit you down. I have much to tell you."

Sorde's manner, Hamilton noticed, seemed anxious and hurried. Hamilton, remembering his earlier alarm, tried to read his emotions. Sorde's aura flickered with excitement and apprehension.

"Today is the day, Hamilton."

Suddenly excited, but still disturbed, Hamilton sat down in front of him on the floor.

Sorde reached behind himself and brought forth a bundle of black cloth. "These are your garments, the customary raiments of the Eagle Knights." He handed this bundle to The One. Hamilton's pride and excitement drowned his foreboding as he took the bundle.

Sorde stood and opened the beautifully lacquered wooden doors of the small bureau near the wall. From within, he took a sword in a polished black wooden scabbard. The gleaming sheen of brilliant steel slid from the well-oiled opening with hardly a whisper, and he handed it to Hamilton hilt foremost, careful not to touch the edge with his flesh.

Hamilton took the hilt, admiring the exquisite workmanship of the blade, handle, pommel and guard. Then he pulled a few strands of hair from his head, and, as Sorde had shown him, dropped them across the upturned blade. They rested there lightly for a moment, and then fell divided on either side.

Sorde smiled proudly. "I made this myself when I was about your age. It took me over a year of constant work. This sword is my soul as a Knight of the Eagles. Its steel has been folded nearly seven-hundred times. It is now yours."

Hamilton's mouth fell open. Sorde, Master of the Order of Knights of the Eagles, had presented him with his own sword, his very warrior's soul.

"Wield it well," the Master said. "My use for it is done."

Hamilton's voice was husky. "I will, Master."

Sorde continued, "I have something else for you to bear as well." He withdrew a small roll of black velvet from the bureau, and unrolled it, revealing that which lay within. "This is the first Key of the Ivory Star," Sorde said. Hamilton sucked a quick breath.

It looked not like a key at all, but like the point of a star, glowing with a soft white luminescence. It was roughly the length of a hand, the width of two fingers at one end, tapering to a point on the other. Hamilton stared in fascination.

Sorde spoke on. "There are three other Keys, the location of which I know only vaguely. Lord Erastus has stumbled upon one, another is somewhere in the jungles south of Armond. The last, gods help us, is in the hands of the Red Circle."

****

A woodworker at the lower end of the Sanctuary's valley touched his wife on the shoulder, and pointed up into the sky. She glanced up from where she rubbed her laundry against a stone in the cold stream, to where her husband pointed. The thing looked like a huge, bat-winged flying creature, faintly scarlet in its great height, circling lazily directly above them. Then it plummeted like a stone straight at them. Straight down at them, at Sanctuary...

****

"But," Hamilton asked, "how do I find the other three Keys?"

"This Key will lead you to the others, the ancient records say. All the Keys must be joined together. When they are joined, you will know where the Ivory Star may be found."

Then the door opened, and three Eagle Knights entered the room, Valt, Darius, and Capian. "Ah, Brothers," Sorde told them, "it is time." Then to Hamilton, "Don these garments."

Hamilton removed his white tunic and trousers, and put on the black clothes, slung the sword with its belt across his back. His heart swelled with nearly uncontainable pride. He was an Eagle Knight! That for which he had been training was now at hand.

Sorde gave Hamilton a paternal smile, like a proud teacher. Hamilton sensed Sorde's emotions now. Love, pride, then...fear? Fear. He had never known Sorde to fear anything, and felt a flash of fear himself.

Suddenly an earth-quaking roar shattered the silence. A reverberating screech from the lower valley ripped through the wooden shutters over the windows, a human shriek of despair and physical agony.

Sorde's modulated voice resonated with calm authority. "You must hie hence. He has found us!"

A vase on top of the bureau began to vibrate. An instant later they felt the ground begin to tremble frightfully.

"Farewell, my son," Sorde said to him, and reached out to embrace him.

"I shall return, Master," Hamilton said, released him and stepped away toward the door.

"I think not. Nothing will be left to return to," Sorde said. "Now go!" Wetness glistened in the Master's eyes as he nodded to Capian. "Keep him safe, Capian. He is our only hope."

"I will, Master. I so swear," Capian said. Then he looked at his companions and said, "Come, Brothers."

Sorde was left standing alone in the room, bearing a sad smile. He would never see them again.

Smoke drifted in lazy wisps through the corridors as the four of them stopped at the armory. As they entered, they saw the smoke curling above, among the rafters. Capian and Valt and Darius each took a bow and quiver full of arrows. Hamilton passed on these, but joined his companions in taking a dagger and a handful of talon-blades, which they slipped into pockets hidden in the folds of their clothing.

Capian motioned them to follow him.

Another unearthly roar split the air like an explosion. The skylights were open, and they saw a huge scarlet shape flash past above, spewing flame from its gaping maw.

"Come," Capian urged, "we must hurry!"

The screams of dying horses came faintly to their ears, as they ran from the room on silent feet, down the smoke-hazed hallway. Down to the underground level below the Sanctuary they went, splashing across the water-covered floor, past the pool, to the thick door on the left side of the room. Capian pulled back on a lever, opening the bolt. They filed through the open door, and Capian jerked it shut behind them, throwing the bolt, or rather, triple-bolt, as they could see from the other side. Capian pulled a pin from the mechanism and tossed it away, so it could not now be opened from the other side.

Then they were on their way again, down the pitch black corridor. Water trickled down the rough-hewn sides. Hamilton sensed the walls at about arm's length on either side and the ceiling a few inches above his head. The passageway stretched long and straight. Soon a light appeared from around a sharp bend in the corridor. They emerged from the tunnel behind a clump of thick brush at the foot of a tall hill, the hill to the side of Sanctuary. Cautiously they made their way through the thicket by a small passage cut from the brush, invisible from the outside.

Capian pointed to a trail about a hundred paces away across the wide-open snow-spotted sward. The trail snaked up the side of a sheer towering cliff. Without a word, they sprinted into the open in a mad dash for the trail. Halfway to the cliff, the thump of galloping hooves spun them around.

Sorde's blade flashed into Hamilton's hands as he spun. He gaped in astonishment at the sight of the five monstrous figures clad in spiked black armor galloping hard down the hill toward them, weapons brandished, flying iron-shod hooves ripping up the soft soil and snow in a spray of turf.

Hamilton glanced a flash of silver in the air, and watched a black-armored warrior tumble backward from the saddle, gore spraying from beneath the bat-winged helmet.

Capian readied another talon-blade.

Valt let an arrow fly. Another Slayer fell from his mount's back, arrow quivering in the eye slit. The horse screamed, pulled to the ground by convulsing fingers still clutching the reins.

Darius raised his sword in defense of a flailing, viciously spiked mace, caught the bludgeoning stroke, and slid fluidly into a slash that slipped neatly between the black breastplate and the taces of the armor as the Slayer galloped past. The man flopped sideways from the saddle, blood pouring from beneath the breastplate in a crimson cataract.

The other two fell upon Hamilton, striking savagely with their heavy longswords. One stroke he dodged lithely, and the other he caught on his upraised blade. A moment of panic seized him as he realized he knew nothing about weak points in armor. Almost instinctively he thrust up into the nearest helmet. The blade pierced the coif and sunk easily into flesh and bone as rivulets of hot gore trickled down the gleaming sheen. He heard a distinctive "ting!" of a talon-blade, and a heavy, armored body crashed down into his, dead, nearly knocking him to the ground. Wrenching his blade from the gory recess of the helmet, wiping it on his tunic, he returned it to its sheath on his back.

Capian bounded toward the cliff, followed closely by the other three. Up the narrow trail they climbed. It was barely wide enough to safely accommodate a man walking normally, but none of them faltered, even for an instant. They were Eagle Knights.

Hamilton looked across the hilltop to where Sanctuary had stood. A pall of thick black smoke rose into the air.

Screams of agony drifted across the distance.

Master Sorde stood on the muddy hillside before the flaming ruin of Sanctuary, spiked staff clutched in his bloody fists. Behind him lay poor Rolf's body, stretched out like a slab of meat, his belly vomiting its ensanguined entrails onto the blood-soaked ground. An expression of resolute calm painted Sorde's scarlet-spattered features. The oozing bodies of a dozen Slayers littered the ground around him. Other than Slayers, he was the only person in the valley left standing.

Two of the soldiers rode hard toward him, swords upraised. He ducked beneath one whistling blade and thrust the spiked end up into the black helm. Fresh crimson poured down the staff, already sticky with gore, and the gurgling corpse tumbled backward from the saddle. But weakened as he was from loss of blood, he failed to dodge the other Slayer's blade. It sank to the bone into his left forearm. The Slayer fell over the neck of his horse with two spikes buried in the back of his neck.

A dozen wounds seeped crimson and Sorde now stood in a pool of his own blood.

"Come on then, fellows," he said. "Let me free you from your Master."

Then a huge red talon swooped down from above, snatching him up. Rumbling inhuman laughter cut the valley.

Hamilton watched the red dragon spiral high into the sky with something dangling limply from a claw.

He turned away, and did his best to put it from his mind, following the Eagle Knights up the cliff. The trail ended at the top of the cliff. There Hamilton saw a large cave a few dozen paces away, far enough back that it was invisible from the ground. Its mouth was at least twenty feet tall and half again as wide, dwarfing the four as they entered. Dozens of glowcrystals hung in sconces on the walls, clearly illuminating the interior of the cavern. A few paces inside, the cave widened considerably, divided by several wooden walls and gates. The roof was supported by thick wooden beams. The air was heavy with the smells of dust and straw, leather, dung, and...something else. It was an animal smell.... The track of countless feet had worn the floor smooth. Hamilton noticed several sets of leather straps, like harnesses, hanging on hooks from the rafters and walls.

A young man ran up to them, his face pale with fear. "My lords," he said, "your mounts are fed and saddled."

"Good, Danyel," Capian said quickly. "You would do best to leave soon, before the Slayers find this place. The Sanctuary is gone. Wait here but a short time longer for any Brothers that may have escaped, then release the rest of them."

Tears welled up in the lad's eyes. "Aye, my lord," he murmured, his face pitiful in its grief.

The three Knights and Hamilton started toward the back of the cave. There, in the soft half-light, Hamilton saw four massive moving shapes, and felt his innards tighten. Then one of the shapes shuffled into the sunlight, and Hamilton gasped.

That scent he couldn't identify before was the scent of dusty feathers.

In the dim light Hamilton saw them. One of them regarded him quietly with dish-sized brown eyes, ruffled its thick feathers. They were half-again as tall as a man at the shoulder, with razor-sharp, hooked beaks, and talons as long as a man's forearm, sheathed in serrated steel casings. Their feathers were mottled, brown, white and black. Eagles! Then Hamilton saw the leather straps buckled on each of the mighty beasts, and his jaw dropped open still further.

A heavy mass of leather slapped him in the chest. "Put that on," Valt said. "It'll keep you warm." He unwadded the heavy mass. It proved to be a heavily padded leather jacket and leggings, tight-fitting. He slipped it on and buckled it tight about him.

"Aiya, Starjumper," Capian cooed softly, soothingly to one of the birds, stroking the fearsome beak that could have torn off his arm with one bite. Grasping the reins of the huge bird with his other hand, he jerked downward. The beast knelt, allowing Capian to hoist himself into the saddle.

"Haaah, Moonlord! It is good to see you, my old friend." Valt patted the thick feathers on the side of another bird's neck.

Darius tugged on the reins of his mount, and the bird knelt. "Let me ride you once again, Skyrider. Hah! Anxious for battle are we, you old war bird?" He climbed easily into the saddle as the restless beast twitched and fretted.

In truth, there was no actual saddle, only the harness. The rider sat on the bare feathers, straddling the beast's neck just above the powerful shoulders, held in place by a leather strap buckled across the thighs, feet slung in the stirrups. Hamilton looked at this arrangement dubiously. One eagle remained, regarding Hamilton calmly. Its eyes were bright with intelligence and wisdom.

Capian said, "That is Skyking. He is old and

wise, the strongest of all, and will care for you as Sorde would have."

Hamilton said, "This was Sorde's mount?"

Capian nodded. "They were great friends. Skyking will miss him, as will I."

The birds and their riders shuffled out of the huge cave, out onto the flat crown of the cliff, preparing themselves for flight, leaving Hamilton studying the series of reins used to control the eagle in flight. The beast wore a specially fit halter on its head, with three separate reins attached one above the other.

"How do I control him?" Hamilton asked, tugging his own steed out the entrance after the others.

Cinching his own thigh-strap tight, Capian answered, "You must get on him first. Jerk down on the reins."

Hamilton did so, and Skyking knelt to allow him to climb on. The massive eagle's eyes were infinitely serene as Hamilton hoisted himself onto Skyking's back.

"Pull back on the top strap, and he ascends," Capian said, "bottom strap, he descends. The middle rein is used to turn him in level flight. By pulling on the top rein by one side, he will turn and ascend at the same time. Likewise with the bottom strap."

Hamilton nodded. "I see."

"Come then," Capian said, "let us go."

Starjumper, Moonlord and Skyrider vaulted into the air and away with a mighty rush of wind. Hamilton swallowed hard and gave the top strap a small hesitant tug. Skyking remained still. He pulled harder. Nothing. Exasperatedly he hauled back on the top rein, and the mighty bird leaped into nothingness with a single gut-lurching beat of his wings. His stomach was pulled into his feet as the ground dropped away like a plummet. The other three were already dwindling specks in the crisp winter air.

Below him, on the scrolling landscape, hundreds of black specks milled about. A sinister cloud of smoke hung like a widow's veil over the scene.

Suddenly Hamilton realized he was cold! Thin, bitter cold wind whipped by him, and he was grateful for the leather clothing protecting him. He swiftly pulled his hood up over his head, tied it in place, and stretched the black mask over his cold face. The steam of his breath disappeared behind him. Then his searching fingers found, in the pocket of the coat, two thick gloves, which he pulled onto his numbing hands. A pair of goggles would have been perfect, for his eyes watered fiercely in the cold wind, making it hard to see.

Skyking quickly attained a cruising altitude, and easily overtook the other three birds. Hamilton found it best to give him his relative head, for if he tried to overly control him, he found himself weaving a jerking, pitching course, not at all comfortable to the stomach.

Suddenly something struck him like a giant pincer, nearly ripping his leather coat off him. A huge, red, scaly monster flashed past just overhead. Only his safety strap had saved him from being plucked from the saddle like a grape. A thunderous bellow drifted back over the roaring wind.

Hamilton jerked hard on the top strap to the right. Skyking peeled up and to the right with terrific speed. The scarlet dragon executed a wide, flaring bank and turn, coming back for another pass, and Hamilton saw the black-and-crimson-swathed rider. His blood froze in his veins. The dragon banked ponderously toward Valt and

Moonlord. The smaller team turned on a pinpoint and sliced toward but slightly above Uhr and the dragon. The huge, scaly beast was infinitely slow to react to the lightning quickness of the eagles. The steel-sheathed talons raked the dragon's back and across the rider. Uhr's black and scarlet robes flapped about him in tatters. Scores of crimson scales fluttered groundward like handfuls of coins, and trails of steaming black ichor poured from the ghastly wounds.

Aerial warfare, Hamilton quickly realized, differed from ground fighting in that it involved three dimensions, rather than two. The birds strove to get above their enemies and strike with the talons at the unprotected back. A bird attacked from above could not bring its own talons to bear against its antagonist.

Starjumper and Skyrider plummeted like stones from out of the silver sun, ripping claws foremost, falling like avenging angels on the dragon and its rider. A whirlwind of motion coupled with the dragon's agonized screams. The red scaly beast began to fall, its vaned, leathery wings rent to ribbons.

Thundered curses from an inhuman throat followed the dragon's descent. The voice chilled Hamilton to the bone, as he guided Skyking away to begin the quest for his destiny.

Chapter 18

Valerion reined up. His massive black stallion snorted a cloud of steam into the cool air. A slowly rising pall of smoke obscured the morning sky, and Valerion cursed. Twisting in the saddle, he called back to his men. "Faster! But pick your way carefully among the rocks. Remember, let us not provoke them. Bare your blades only if they fall upon us!" The Red Dragons did not draw their weapons, but they made sure they were within easy reach. The men spurred their horses forward, proceeding around the mountain toward the smoke.

Valerion led the way through the hidden entrance to the valley that Sorde had shown him when he had taken Capian to be an Eagle Knight.

As Valerion and his band rode out of the cave, their eyes met with a grisly, tragic scene. Valerion would have wished his eyes blasted from his head ere he saw something like this again.

Bloody bodies and pieces of bodies scattered the valley like gory, broken sticks. The blackened beams and planks of the burned Sanctuary jutted from the charred rubble like the quills of some grotesque porcupine. All of the cottages at the lower end of the valley lay in smoking ruins.

The procession of silent warriors walked their horses slowly down into the valley. Not even animals had escaped the mauling, mutilating swords of the Slayers. Here lay the body of a small dog, its head a few feet away. There stretched the huge carcass of a mightily horned bullock, its innards spilling a long trail behind it.

The men gaped in sickened disbelief at the horrendous carnage here. Hardened warriors of a hundred battles felt their guts thrash and reel at the butchery around them. Bodies lay scattered everywhere, human and otherwise, broken, so mutilated that age and sex were best left matters of guesswork. There on a gore-spattered pike thrust into the ground hung an ensanguined net crammed with severed heads, lifeless eyes staring into nothingness. One of the Dragons reeled in the saddle and spewed the contents of his belly onto the bloody ground. A furious, sickened scowl furrowed Valerion's brow.

Then a low agonized moan floated from a small cottage nearby. Valerion leaped from his horse.

Angus exclaimed, "My lord, wait!"

Valerion did not turn as he stamped into the house. "The time for waiting is long since past!" he growled.

Angus leaped from his horse and followed Valerion into the ruins.

On the floor lay a woman, horribly violated, of possibly late middle age, but they could not be sure. Her face was but a crimson smear. Weak fingers clawed desperately at her entrails, striving to keep them within herself. Two bloodshot eyes stared vacantly. Angus doubted she was even aware of their presence. Suddenly the poor woman loosed a terrible gurgling scream. Valerion, unable to withstand any more, pulled out his sword and ended that scream with merciful finality.

"Butchery!" he growled wrathfully.

Angus stepped aside for him as he stalked outside.

Valerion looked up the hill toward the remains of Sanctuary, sighed, and walked toward it. Angus followed.

As they neared, Valerion saw four pikes jutting from the midst of the debris-strewn ashes with a severed head thrust onto the point of each one. As he approached, as yet unable to distinguish features, he prayed to the gods of Law that Capian and Hamilton were not among them.

But then he saw a face he had not expected to see. "You deserve better, my friend," he said, as Sorde's ensanguined head stared grotesquely down from its perch on the blood-smeared pike blade. The sick feeling that always came with the loss of a friend crept into Valerion's guts.

The other three heads were not those of anyone Valerion knew; doubtless they were Knights somehow surprised or overpowered. He stepped over the black-plated corpses littering the ground before the heap of scorched debris. He shook his head in sadness and disbelief.

The sound of Angus's footstep turned his head. "A tragedy, Angus," he said, "The Order of Knights of the Eagles has been wiped from existence, an order as old as Uhr himself." He took a deep breath, gazing up into the sky. "They are the first casualty." Then he stepped gingerly over the wreckage, reaching toward the pikes. He pulled them out one by one, and lay them gently on the ground. One corner of Sanctuary still burned quietly, and he threw the severed heads into the blaze.

He wiped his hands on his white jupon, smearing Sorde's thickening blood across his coat of arms. "The time has come!" he said, and strode back down the hill.

"Good work, sergeant," Valerion said. "I am pleased my orders have been followed so completely."

"Thank you, my lord," the gate sergeant replied, his chest swelling with pride.

And the band rode through the gate into Lakeside. The gates had been locked tight, and watchful sentries patrolled the battlements. Not a soul walked the streets of Lakeside. As the band crossed the bridge, the drawbridge was lowered for them, and raised again after their passing.

Valerion returned to his house, heavy of heart and soul. He closed the front door behind him to ward off the chilly evening air.

"Tarl!" he bellowed.

The housemaster walked into the great hall from the kitchen, wiping his hands on a cloth. Already the aromas of the noonday meal filled the house. The smell of baked bread clung to him as he approached.

"Aye, m'lord."

"Send a messenger to my council chamber at once."

"Aye, m'lord."

"Is Fortine here?"

"I know not, lord."

"Find him. If he remains in Dynorr, send a messenger telling him to get his arse here now."

"Aye, m'lord." Tarl bowed ponderously.

Valerion glared at him and snapped, "Enough obeisance, man! After what I have seen today, I have not the stomach for it!" He spun on his heel and strode across the hall.

Ilone met him outside his council chamber.

"Val?" she asked. "What ails you so?"

Valerion cursed himself. She could read his face and manner like an open book. He shook his head in sadness.

"What is it, beloved?"

He looked into her beautiful eyes. "Sorde is dead." His voice caught, godsdamn it all. "The Eagle Knights are gone."

She paled, her hand rose to her mouth. "Is Capian dead?"

"I think not," he said, smiling weakly. "He is our son. He would not allow himself to fall under the sword of a filthy Slayer."

She embraced him, burying her face in his chest, and his massive arms encircled her. "It has begun, hasn't it?" she said.

He took a deep, quivering breath.

"Yes."

Valerion dropped his quill as Robinton burst into his sitting room. "Dynorr has been sacked!" he exclaimed.

The lord leaped to his feet. "What!" he bellowed.

"The Slayers," Robinton said, "probably the same legion that destroyed the Eagle Knights' lair."

Valerion's fist crashed onto the table with thunderous force. The quill and parchment jumped.

"Casualties?"

"My beautiful tavern for one!" A rather rotund tavern-keeper threw himself into the room.

"Fortine!" Valerion exclaimed with relief. "I had feared for your safety! After all, I could little afford to lose my best engineer!"

They clasped hands as Fortine answered, "Hah! Your only engineer! I damned near ran my horse into the ground getting here!"

Valerion's face stiffened. "What of Dynorr?"

"It is bad, my lord," he replied grimly. "Every house burned to the ground, including my poor tavern. Several hundred women and children were dragged away. The men were ...recruited."

Valerion cursed.

Another voice interrupted them. "My lord?" A young man entered, clutching his cap nervously in his hands. "I am to bear a message?"

Valerion looked at him skeptically. "Why, you look barely old enough to grow hair on your face!"

The lad blushed. In truth, his slim young jaw was lined with a light-colored fuzz.

"In any case, I do have a message for you to carry," the lord said. He sat back down and finished the letter. Picking it up, he read it to himself.

"Most Respected Lord Skaand,
That for which our ancestors have waited has come to pass. The One has Come! He now searches for the Ivory Star that he might destroy Uhr. However, Uhr has taken the initiative by obliterating the Sanctuary of the Eagle Knights, and sacking and burning the town of Dynorr. I now must call upon the ties of our lifelong friendship and alliance. I call upon you to aid me and the rest of Irth in destroying the scourge that has ruled us for so long. I thank you.
Signed,
Valerion, Son of Arnor."

He folded the parchment, poured melted wax across the fold, and stamped it with his dragon's seal. He handed it to the waiting messenger. "Get this to Skaand as quickly as possible. Ride for all you're worth. Stop for no one. Avoid all armed men.

I'll wager they will be Slayers, or perhaps Sneev's men, and they will be looking for *you*."

The lad blanched as he took the message, swallowed hard, and nodded.

"Now, go!" Valerion commanded. "And may the luck of The One be with you."

The boy turned and bounded from the room, down the hall like a gazelle. Fortine watched him go. "Ah, to be so young again!" He turned to Valerion. "Like in the old days, eh, m'lord?"

"Aye," Valerion said, smiling faintly, "and wild days they were." Then he grew serious. "This will not be like those old times. Back then, we had a home to return to, and we could be certain our families would be there when we returned from those long campaigns. This time, if we fail, everyone dies. Everyone."

Fortine took a deep breath. "I shall begin preparations for the defense immediately."

Valerion smiled again, grimly, "Robinton will get you whatever you need. Workers, tools, materials, anything."

"As you say, m'lord," Robinton said.

"Then let us to work!" Fortine exclaimed, slapping Robinton across the mailed shoulder. "Broil my guts, but there is much to be done!"

The eagles wheeled and pitched in the afternoon sky in a precision arrowhead formation with Capian and Starjumper as the point.

The snow-bespattered green and brown and gray of the mountains drifted several hundred feet below them. Hamilton found that he could release the reins completely, and Skyking would not veer from his course, so he reached inside his tunic and withdrew the first Key. He unwrapped it from its covering of soft, black velvet, and looked at it.

Its glow had faded considerably. He turned it over and over in his gloved hands. With a twinge of curiosity he noticed that it seemed to twist in his grasp when he turned it to point a certain direction, and it seemed to lie still when the wider end of the Key pointed to the south. Sorde had told him that the Key would tell him where to go, also that another Key lay somewhere to the south...

The key was indeed telling him where to go!

He hailed Capian over the rushing wind. "We go south!" Hamilton shouted.

Capian nodded, and they flew on.

The enormous wings of the war-birds caught and held the wind with breathtaking ease. The thrill of such flight, sitting astride the beautiful eagles as they floated and soared! The wind warmed as they traveled south, and the sun touched them with warm, gentle hands.

The horizon behind them was lost in wintry haze. The shimmering surface of Crystal Lake became a silver ribbon beside the bumps of the Viderian Mountains.

Eventually the sun began to set, and they decided to halt for the night. They camped in a valley, near a gurgling stream. They released the eagles to go and feed, while the four Eagle Knights sat around the small fire.

Hamilton sat before the fire, examining the great gashes in his leather coat caused by the dragon's talons.

"Lucky," Valt said. "Your quest might have been over before it began."

"My quest." Hamilton shook his head ironically, and sighed.

"Something ails you, Hamilton?" Capian said, as he poked the fire with a stick.

Hamilton sighed again, gathering his thoughts.

"Everyone keeps telling me this is my quest, and my quest alone. The fate of everyone, I'm told, rests solely on my shoulders. Don't you think that's a heavy burden to bear?"

Capian said, "But you're The One!"

"I'm just a man, Capian!"

"No," Capian said, "you are more!"

"How can you say that...?"

"Sorde knew it, and he told me so. You have a power as great as his. All you need to defeat Uhr you already have, except for the Ivory Star. And we shall soon have that."

Hamilton looked puzzled.

"You are powerful," Capian said, "as powerful as Uhr."

Hamilton stared at him is disbelief. "You can't mean that. After what I've seen, I doubt anything can kill Uhr."

Capian leaned forward, elbows on his knees. "Your power is different from Uhr's. Uhr's power comes from outside himself, from his Bloodstone. Gods know where he got it. Your power, however," he said, gazing into Hamilton's eyes, "comes from within *you*."

"How do you know all this?"

"Sorde told me so."

Hamilton did not respond.

Capian continued, "Brother Hamilton, you've spent the last few months mastering fear and self-doubt. Why now this trouble?"

Hamilton looked into the fire. "I'd never seen Uhr before. I had no idea..." His voice trailed off as a cold chill raced up and down his spine at the awful memories burned into his mind's eye.

"Quite honestly, Hamilton," Capian said, "I had never seen him before either, only heard stories. In fact, no one ever sees Uhr."

Valt said, "Your presence has already frightened him, Hamilton."

Capian nodded. "You have brought him out of his warren. Therefore, he considers you a threat."

Hamilton shivered again.

Darius said, "You can hurt him."

Hamilton said, "If he considers me a threat, he will concentrate his power to try to kill me." By force of will he kept his rising fear in check.

"That is why we are with you," Capian said. "We are to make sure that you complete your quest. At all cost."

The other two Eagles Knights nodded solemnly. "We would die to protect you," Valt said.

Hamilton sat for a moment, absorbing what Valt had just said. Then abruptly he stood. "I need to be alone for a while," he said.

Capian moved to protest.

"No," Hamilton said, "please, I have to deal with that. I don't like the idea of friends dying to save my life. I'll just be over here by the stream."

They let him go. He left the ring of firelight to go sit on the bank of the small stream strolling down through the middle of the valley. The valley was long and wide, carved from the mountains by a glacier ages gone. He sat down on a wide flat rock, watching the rippling of the water in the rising moonlight.

Sorde had taught him to control his fear and self-doubt. They had been driven from him. But now, after the first sight of his adversary, it came creeping back like a thief in the night. But perhaps this first meeting with Uhr was fortunate, because now Uhr was no longer a story or a legend or some abstract evil. He was very real, and extraordinarily dangerous. And he was just as horrible as everyone said. He was now something real and solid that Hamilton could steel himself against. As Sorde had taught him, he entered a meditative trance, where he hardened himself against Uhr's horrors. Yes, next time the fear would not appear.

But even in his meditative trance, he was finely aware of his surroundings, acutely aware of the whisper of feet on the ground across the stream. Unmoving, Hamilton reached out with his mind to sense whatever was out there, perhaps now less than fifty paces away. A human presence. Several of them. Moving quickly.

Hamilton leaped to his feet, sword bared. "Show yourselves!" he cried.

Thick clouds scudded across the face of the rising moon, and Hamilton felt a sudden chill brush past him. He had felt that chill before!

At that moment, a bright flash behind him lit up the night for a brief instant, after which the light of the fire disappeared. Hamilton heard the startled cries of his companions behind him, and the shuffle of running feet before him, splashing as they landed in the stream.

Several black shapes stood now in the middle of the brook moving quickly to cross. They carried long staves in their pale hands.

Hamilton heard Capian's voice. "Filthy Red Priests! You brought insufficient numbers!" He caught the hissing buzz of talon blades as they sang through the night.

He pulled a talon blade from a special pouch in his tunic, and in one swift movement sent it streaking toward the nearest shape in the water. He heard the satisfying thunk as it sank into bone within the black hood, and the figure sank into the water. A low, rhythmic chant arose from the approaching Red Priests, and Hamilton felt a peculiar sensation in the air around him, like a swirling, ethereal whirlwind, building.

"Hamilton!" Capian cried.

"Here, Capian!" Hamilton answered.

"Red Priests are everywhere!"

"We're coming!"

And they were. Hamilton glanced back, saw three vague shapes running toward him. Suddenly a white flash exploded high above their heads, revealing almost a dozen Red Priests approaching Hamilton, and with his peripheral vision he saw several more in a wide circle around them.

The three Eagle Knights stopped a few paces from him, and readied themselves for the attack.

The blazing light in the air above them hovered and glowed and sizzled, illuminating the area with a stark white glow.

"What's that thing?" Hamilton said.

Capian answered, "A bit of Eagle Knight magic."

Their gleaming blades caught the brilliant white light flickering above.

Hamilton felt the whirlwind about him gaining strength, felt it tugging at him, trying to carry him away.

"*No!*" he cried, leaping down into the shallow water among the Red Priests, his Master's sword slicing three of the Red Priests into swift death. The invisible whirlwind had followed him as he moved, but had somehow been diminished slightly, but now was gaining strength once again, threatening to lift him into the air. Then his birthmark began to pulse, and he realized that he was not helpless against this magical vortex. In an instant he had gathered his strength of will, and then, with a roar of deep defiance, sent it bursting outward like an explosion. The whirlwind immediately dissipated, and he breathed a heavy sigh of relief and pride, which was all he had time for as the rest of the Red Priests closed about him.

He heard the other three Knights engaged on the bank, sensed their satisfaction at the ease with which they dispatched their hated enemies. Sorde's blade danced and bit, as the Red Priests fell about him, nearly helpless against him without their sorcery. Hamilton felt his sword arm entangled suddenly in a stout, sticky net, but a deft twist of the uncannily sharp blade quickly freed him.

The glowing ball in the air above began to die, and with it, the last of the Red Priests under the Eagle Knights' blades. The four Knights stood amongst the black corpses, gazing about for any more enemies.

Hamilton reached out with his mind, then said, "The rest have fled." He waded out of the stream toward his companions. About them, the corpses began to burst into flame and disappear. They ignored the flames and returned to their campsite.

"You see, Hamilton," Capian said.

"What's that, Capian?"

"Sorde was right about you. You have all the training you require."

Chapter 19

"You summoned me, my lord?" the young man asked, stepping into Valerion's sitting room. The lad was clad entirely in leather and buckskin, and his eyes mirrored a wise maturity that reached far beyond his meager years.

"Aye, lad, I did," Valerion said, looking up from his maps, "I am told that you know the shortest route to Albreth's estate."

"I know the Frontier like my own palm, my lord," the young fellow replied. "I grew up on the plains of the Frontier, trapping small animals with my father since I was old enough to walk and sit astride a horse. I know the way well."

"Excellent. I would have you bear Albreth a message."

The lad nodded.

"Tell him that Dynorr had been sacked by Slayers, and now the Slayers may be coming for him. Tell him he must gather an army and prepare for war. The One has come. Answer any of his questions as best you can. I will be in further contact with him. Tell him all this, and if he believes you not, show him this." Valerion pulled a short, wide-bladed dagger from his belt. Its hilt was worn with heavy use, its blade notched from countless battles.

Valerion said, "This is Arnor's dagger. Albreth will recognize it."

The messenger reverently took the dagger from Valerion's scarred hand and slipped it into his belt. He would not dare lose it.

Valerion commanded, "Now go! And make haste! The fate of Armond may ride on your horse's hooves."

The young man whisked from the room like a whirlwind. Valerion hoped Albreth survived Uhr long enough to receive the message and act upon it.

With Fortine now in charge of all defense construction, work was moving quickly on the additional catapults and ballistae to be mounted on the towers and walls. Stones for the catapults were gathered and piled along the walls. Pitch, stiff and sluggish from the cold, was brought from the tar pits north of Crystal Lake. The bridges spanning the water between the islands were modified so they could be collapsed at the pull of a rope.

On the mainland, crews worked to dig wide, deep trenches in the cold, muddy ground circling wooden palisade. The trenches were arranged in concentric half-circles from the wall of Lakeside. The bottoms of some of the trenches were lined with carefully sharpened, fire-hardened spikes. Any siege engines, such as catapults, trebuchets, springals, or siege towers would be unable to pass until the trenches were somehow bridged.

The days passed, and the people grew restless in their vigilance, waiting for the attack yet to come. Valerion wondered what had happened to the legion of Slayers that had destroyed the Eagle Knights' Sanctuary. Where had they gone? What was their next target? He could only assume it was Lakeside.

The messenger he'd sent to Skaand finally returned, horse lathered and shivering in the winter cold. Valerion took Skaand's letter from the young messenger. "Saw you any Slayers?"

The puffing lad replied. "Nay, my lord. Nary a one."

Valerion took Skaand's reply to his council room, where he broke the seal and read the letter.

"My dear friend Valerion,
I am alarmed and angered by the news of the sack of Dynorr. It would be my duty and privilege to aid you in your war against Uhr. But, alas, I must tell you that my own people must come first. Winter is here, and it is much harder on my rough land than on yours. My place is here, at least for now. I can only hope that you will understand my plight, as one leader of men to another. But should worse fall to worst, as I pray it shall not, I will throw the full weight of my own country upon Uhr's back, as I would know you would do for me. My thanks, dear friend.
Signed,
Skaand of Tyberia."

Valerion understood. He had expected little more. A lord must see to his own people first. Just as he himself would do.

"Broil my guts, but it's a cold morning out there!" Fortine exclaimed, slapping himself for warmth. He took up his tankard of steaming tal and gulped half of it down.

Valerion cracked open the council chamber window and peeked outside at the aloof gray sky, admitting a biting waft of wintry chill. "Aye, Fortine. 'Tis most strange. Yesterday was nearly like summer."

"'Twas fortunate then that we finished the trenching yesterday," Fortine said.

"I've a feeling," Valerion said, rubbing his stubbled chin with a callused finger, "that winter is here. How is the supply of firewood?"

"It is fine, I think."

"Even should winter fall hard this early?"

Fortine shrugged his shoulders.

"It's started to snow now. Damned strange..." His voice trailed off. Then he said, "Send out another firewood party."

"Aye, m'lord," Fortine said, and turned to carry out Valerion's orders.

That evening, as the fireplace in Valerion's dining hall blazed furiously in its attempt to thwart the frightful cold outside, people huddled around the serving tables, bundled into furs and cloaks and heavy blankets.

Valerion and his family sat at the high table, trying to stay warm as bitter cold drafts nipped at them.

"Robinton," Valerion said, "remember you a day any colder?" His breath puffed as steam from his mouth and nostrils as he sipped his hot tal.

"Nay, I do not," Robinton answered, sipping his own mug.

Val, seated between Ilone and his father, spoke up. "Father, how much snow is there?"

"Last measure was knee-deep."

The boy's eyes widened in surprise and pleasure. "Hah! Can I play in it tomorrow, father?"

Ilone said, "We shall see, son. Perhaps if it's not too cold."

"I hope so. I like snow."

Valerion growled, "I'm afraid we'll have plenty."

Ilone gave Valerion a long searching gaze, then lifted her son onto her lap, and slid next to him, pulling her husband tight. She knew he would need her own strength added to his in the days to come.

Angus cursed for the hundredth time. "Fine night to pull guard duty, eh, Aalok?"

The small, stocky man merely grunted, intent on preserving his own warmth.

Angus pulled his cloaks tighter about himself and looked out at the vast expanse of powdery white beyond the palisade of Lakeside, dim in the lightless night. He breath disappeared in the knifing wind, lost with the barrage of biting ice particles.

"This wind's as cold as deep space," Angus muttered.

Aalok said, "Cold as what?"

"Nothing," Angus said, slapping his fur mittens together. The bitter wind whipped and wailed about them with devilish intelligence, cutting through clothing more efficiently than the keenest blade, as they stood shivering on the battlement.

"If we stay out here all night, we'll likely freeze," Aalok said.

Angus nodded.

Suddenly something touched Angus's shoulder. He spun, startled. "What the hell...?"

Daarton's dark shape stepped back.

In the darkness, Angus saw Daarton's wide, staring eyes. "You two, come with me," he said, speaking loudly over the howling wind.

They followed him down into the tower, thankfully out of the wind. Even inside, the wind whispered and rustled, seeming to find every chink in the stone walls, every crack in the shutters. Daarton spoke as they walked. "There will be no more guard duty tonight for anyone."

Angus felt a surge of relief. "Not that I'm complaining, sir, but why?"

They came down the stairs into a guard chamber at the base of the tower. "That's why," Daarton said, pointing.

Three frozen shapes lay stiffly in the middle of the floor.

"They were the last guard shift."

Ice hung from arms and legs frozen solid, faces calm and restful, like sleeping statues.

"We have little to fear from attack," Daarton said, "no one can survive outside tonight."

Angus said, "Are winters here always this cold?"

Daarton looked at him grimly, and shook his head. Then he looked out into nothing, his eyes haunted, glazed. "Something is not right."

"What do you mean?" Angus asked.

"Something is out there," Daarton said, "winter cannot do that to a man in mere hours." He pointed forcefully at the three frozen corpses. "I've heard tales, tales of snow spirits that can..."

"Bah!" Angus exclaimed, in total disbelief, "Old wives' tales!" He glanced at Aalok, searching for agreement.

But Aalok was silent, staring wide-eyed at the three frozen men, blowing on his hands.

Lady Ilone sat on the bed, brushing her long, silky blonde hair, letting it fall in a gleaming cascade down her chest. She glanced at Valerion as he sat in a chair across the room, gazing into the fireplace, his brow furrowed in thought. A cold breeze brushed past her like an icy demon, and she shivered.

"Val, come to bed," Ilone said.

He said nothing, did not even move.

"Would you care to warm me up?" she asked.

He did not respond.

She sighed, gathering the blankets about her as she slid off the bed and approached him. "What is it that's troubling you, Val?"

He took a deep breath, let it out. "It's Uhr."

She touched his shoulder. "Uhr worries all of us."

He interrupted her. "No, I mean the storm. It is his doing."

"Are you so sure?"

He nodded, pulling his gaze away from the flames to look up at her. "Robinton tells me that three men were found frozen solid at the end of their guard shift." He felt her grip tighten on his shoulder. "Aye, three men." He looked back into the fire. "Frozen solid. No natural snowstorm can do that."

She said nothing, just stroked his ebony mane, as he continued, "His power is growing. That is my fear. He can manipulate the very sky now. What's next?"

"Come to bed, my love. Let us be warm together, for as long as we may."

He looked up at her, following her enticing curves, up to her beautiful face, her deep, sparkling brown eyes, and he smiled, touching her. "Aye, my beloved. We shall do just that."

Morning found the snow waist deep and still falling, in places burying whole cottages. The fortress was adrift in a sea of powdery ice.

People in Valerion's house moved about bundled in heavy furs, and only then to get more firewood. Valerion fumed about the house in a decidedly foul mood, in spite of the extended pleasure of the night before.

"By the gods, I loathe this!" Valerion exclaimed, "I can do nothing cooped up in here!" He pulled his furs tighter.

Ilone said, calmly, "Neither can you do anything outside but freeze." She looked back down at her needlework, as she stitched a small tapestry for Val's bedchamber.

"But, the people!"

"They can do no more than we. They must survive as best they can. We have enough firewood to last for a good while."

"But how long will this last?"

"The gods know."

"At least it's stopped snowing, for now," he said, grudgingly. "The wind just keeps shuffling it around, like it's trying to find the best place for it."

She laughed at that, and went on with her work.

Snow fell intermittently for three more days, before the tearing winds abated and the sky began to clear. Folks began to stir, as if emerging from hibernation. Shovels were broken out, and used to clear paths and dig out the houses buried under gargantuan, sparkling drifts. Whole families were found frozen to death in their homes, huddled in stiff, cold masses.

As the clouds began to disperse, Valerion made his way down a newly cleared path through the courtyard of the middle ward. Snowdrifts taller than him hemmed him on both sides. The morning air was wintry, but not bitterly cold as it had been. He saw Fortine coming to meet him.

"Greetings, my lord Valerion. Boil my fat, but

it's good to be finally outside!"

Valerion smiled at him. "Aye, it is."

Fortine sucked a deep breath. "Gods know, a man needs fresh air after so long!"

Valerion said, "What's to report, my engineer?"

Fortine's face grew grim. "At last count, twenty-three whole families were found dead, frozen in their homes."

Valerion grimaced.

"There was nothing to be done, my lord. Their houses were covered up completely. They couldn't even get outside for more wood to burn."

"And the supply of wood?"

"We're digging out what's left."

"How much?"

Fortine sighed, pausing. "Worse than I thought, damn me. Winter may be too long for what we have."

Valerion said, "More of Uhr's inhuman cunning."

"My lord?"

Valerion lowered his voice. "This storm was Uhr's doing. I am certain of that."

Fortine whistled, "May the gods strip me naked and hang me to dry, I hadn't thought of that."

"Tell no one else."

"Of course, my lord," Fortine said, "but why, if I might ask, would Uhr conjure up a storm on us?"

Valerion shrugged. "Methinks to make us use up all our firewood, perhaps kill a few of us.

"Or perhaps the bastard meant to drive us out, away from the defense of the castle, into the warmer south. And into the open. The Slayers would have their way with us then, gods know. Shall I send out another wood-gathering party, my lord?"

"Can they get out with a horse team and

wagon?"

"I suppose not, damn me for not thinking."

"Carry on, my friend. When they can get out, send them. I mean to see the full extent of the damage."

Three suns rose and fell after the clouds of the storm dissipated. Then, as suddenly as the blizzard had landed, the air began to warm rapidly. The snow started to melt in a slushy tide, run-off shooting down the gutters and drain holes like icy fountains.

Angus had been shoveling snow for three days, and he was tired of it. Today he worked barechested, knee-deep in snow, as a summer-like sun bore down upon him. The air hung heavy with damp from the melting snow. If this heat persisted, he would not have to shovel snow any longer, for it would all be gone.

Aalok, working nearby, asked him, "Angus, you're a smart fellow. What's all that snow out there going to do to the trenchwork, eh?"

Angus stopped shoveling and straightened up. He had not thought of that. "I don't know for certain. If it melts fast enough it could turn everything to soup and fill up the trenches with mud."

"Gods, I hope not," Aalok said, sincerely, "we worked hard enough on them."

Angus grunted his assent.

Aalok's voice grew excited. "Look you, Angus. The Day Stars! They're getting close."

Angus looked up at the three points of light in the midday sky, nearing one another.

"I hope The One grabs the Ivory Star soon. When those jewels touch, we'll all be dead," Aalok said quietly, returning to his labor.

"How do you know?" Angus asked.

"I've a feeling in my bones."

Angus left it at that.

By late afternoon, after a day as hot as the height of summer, all the snow melted, and the trenches filled with mud as Angus predicted. After another couple of days of sweltering heat, the mud hardened, turning most of their earthwork into folly.

As the mud hardened in one hot afternoon sun, a dot appeared high in the sky against the glaring sun. The dot grew wings and legs and glinted red light from shiny scales. Before anyone could react, the scarlet dragon swooped once low over the castle. Screams rose up as mothers hurried with their children into their homes.

Valerion ran from his house, across the drawbridge to the middle ward. As he stood on the cobbled path near the drawbridge, a bellowing roar smote his ears like a drum. An eerie, echoing cackle came from the black shape astride the beast's thick neck.

"Uhr, you bastard!" he roared.

The dragon came around again, flying low over the middle ward, its massive maw gaping. Over the rows of cottages, a gout of billowing orange flame spewed from the hideous orifice, settling over a dozen roofs. Families fled screaming from their blazing homes. Immediately men rushed forward with buckets of sloshing water to quench the conflagrations.

And still that awful mocking cackle echoed like demon's laughter over the fortress.

The dragon made another pass. This time it snatched a shrieking man-at-arms from his post on the wall. One talon dug into the hapless victim's upper body, while the other grabbed his legs. Armor, flesh and bone gave way like gauze as the man's torso came apart like a bag full of blood, raining pulped offal and hot red drops on the screaming people below. The legs and hips splashed into the lake, while the upper body splatted on the cobblestones of the inner ward, trailing mangled entrails.

The dragon flashed past above. Now it was turning again, and Valerion saw several large bags were slung across the beast's thick neck. As the dragon came around, Uhr tugged on the drawstrings of the large bags. The dragon swooped low over the castle, and Uhr flung the bags and their contents far away from him, scattering clouds of black dust high over the castle. Two more passes emptied the sacks, leaving a sinister cloud of ebon dust that floated like a black plague in the air above the fortress. Then the dragon was gone, disappearing into the sun.

Valerion watched the cloud as it began to settle on the castle, and fear gripped his heart.

The cloud settled lower and lower, slowly, as if allowing them to ponder its malevolence. People fled once again into the believed safety of their homes.

Then a stiff breeze suddenly rose in the air, and whipped the cloud into an angry frenzy. The cloud swirled and coalesced in seeming fury, as if struggling to retain its position above the castle. The wind pushed the thrashing, helpless cloud away from the castle, off toward the mountains. Still, a light sifting of the black dust managed to filter down onto the fortress and its inhabitants.

By the end of the day, the entire fortress and town was ill with a ghastly sickness. It began with fits of a terrible, hacking cough.

Everyone in Valerion's house fell sick. Valerion himself somehow seemed to shrug it off, escaping with only a day or so of painful coughing. He hoped that the rest of his family could survive it as easily as he had. Val got over it with a child's hard constitution. Nessa survived as well. Robinton and Angus seemed to have avoided the illness all together, or conquered it quickly, showing no symptoms. Tarl fell severely ill, as did Dame Pilgra. And Ilone.

After Valerion's own quick recovery, he sat by Ilone's bedside for days, caring for her. He watched her grow increasingly pale and haggard. He cursed Uhr a thousand times as he watched his once-beautiful wife become a sickly shell, eaten from the inside out.

But she tried to keep up her spirits, as her husband suffered with her. She would tell him, "I'll be up and about in a few days. I just need some rest. And I like someone waiting on me hand and foot."

But Valerion saw the agony in her eyes as she hacked and coughed up chunks of bloody phlegm. She could not eat, as nothing would stay down, and her limbs shrunk with emaciation. She burned with a terrible fever, and Valerion held her hand as she raved in delirium to her long-dead mother and father, her brother slain by bandits twenty years agone. Valerion teetered with her on the brink of grief-stricken madness. In the final days, she stared through blind eyes, aware of nothing, not even the touch of his hand, or his voice. When death mercifully descended, she succumbed, vomiting chunks of clotted blood. And Valerion wept.

Dame Pilgra gave up her ghost a few hours before Ilone did. Tarl lay sick for days, but survived somehow, and slowly recovered, his eyes haunted by the horror of the terrible malady.

Hundreds died, hundreds more nearly so.

Carts collected the dead regularly, taking them to a mass grave dug outside the trenches.

Valerion saw no one for three days after Ilone's death, taking no food, locked in his room. He appeared again at the funeral, haggard, eyes rimmed with red, clinging to his children, Nessa and Val, as if they were the only things he had left in the world.

After Uhr's deadly disease, winter's customary cold returned. For a while the days passed without incident. The winter once again captured the surface of Crystal Lake in a solid white sheet of glaring ice.

Valerion's confidence in their ability to fend off the Slayer's inevitable attack gradually deteriorated. One by one nature had stripped their defenses. The cold had taken many good fighters, and depleted their firewood. The mud had filled their trenches and hardened, then froze, effectively bridging that barrier. Now the lake had frozen into a sheet of firm, solid ice. Slayers could now directly reach the walls.

Uhr would wait not much longer. Slayers were probably on their way. Countless times Valerion wondered where The One was, if was alive or dead, or imprisoned somewhere. He prayed to every god he knew that Hamilton Corbin still lived, and that if it was so, they could hold out until he came.

They had to.

"There lies the Frontier," Capian shouted over the roaring wind. A few leagues ahead of them lay a wide, slow river that barged across the grasslands like a mile-wide snake. Beyond that was the hilly grasslands of the Frontier, craggy with vestiges of the Viderian Mountain range, sparsely dotted with clumps of trees and bramble.

Half a month had passed since their journey

had begun.

Capian pointed to the west, away from the morning sun. "In that direction lies Albreth's estate," he shouted. "It's the last civilized outpost and garrison before the jungles. Otherwise, the Frontier is dotted with a few small trading villages. The soil here is too rocky to farm, so they must trap and hunt. Further south lies jungle."

The Frontier passed beneath the eagles' wings like water beneath a bridge. At about mid-afternoon, the brown colors of the Frontier gave way to an almost imperceptible green strip growing along the horizon. As the sun began to set, the first few trees drifted below them, and they sent the eagles earthward.

The war birds lit in a wide, grassy area surrounded by tall, broad trees. The sharp hills and rolling grasslands of the Frontier were behind them.

Capian dismounted. "We must leave the eagles here. There will be no other places for them to land in the forest."

"Will they not fly away if we are gone too long?" Hamilton asked.

Capian shook his head. "They will stay in this vicinity until we return."

That evening they made certain the water bags they had fashioned were full. Food would pose little problem for them in a teeming forest.

The next morning their journey on foot began. The first few miles passed swiftly under their fleet feet. Gradually the trees grew nearer together, forming large clumps. The clumps grew steadily larger, more dense. After half a day's travel, the jungle had closed about them irrevocably.

The thick, mossy trunks screened the sun to an eerie half-light. The heavy, impenetrable canopy of leaves hung above them like a patchwork quilt of a hundred green hues. The mighty, gnarled boughs reared high, high above them, festooned with leafy vines. The soft, mushy ground sank beneath their feet, a carpet of decaying leaves, moss and fungi. The air was mild, heavy with forest wetness, cooling as dusk approached.

Birds piped in the branches above, some with beautiful melodies, others voicing long, mournful cries that echoed like the cries of lost souls. Hamilton shivered as a feeling of foreboding washed over him, similar to that he had felt on the morn of Sanctuary's destruction. He said, "Let's be careful. I've a bad feeling."

"You, too?" Valt said.

"We'll be careful then," Capian said.

As they traveled, they made sure to notch trees to mark an easy path back out.

Hamilton held the first Key in his hand. It led the way, it's soft, dim glow seeming to warm him. At sunset the daylight was gone, and the perpetual gloom of the forest floor plunged into impenetrable darkness. Hamilton's mind reached out and felt the way among the maze of trunks. The other three Knights fell in behind him as he confidently threaded his way among the massive trunks. The Key in his palm glowed sufficiently to tell its direction.

Half the night they traveled, and Hamilton found that prolonged use of his mental abilities fatigued him.

Then finally he sat down against a tree. "I must rest," he panted, exhausted.

The other men also seated themselves near him. Within seconds, Hamilton's snores broke the forest silence.

The next sunset found them several leagues

deeper into the boundless vegetation. The deeper they went, the forest became much wilder. Undergrowth tangled the trees in its impenetrable abundance now, and gnarled, twisted boughs reached down for them, forcing them to stoop in their passage. In places, the leaves above grew so thickly that they blotted out the sun's light entirely, leaving patches of nightlike darkness. Rodents and vermin chittered and skreeked just out of sight, scurrying for safety at their approach. It was these small creatures that supplied them with meat.

After a couple of days travel, strange glimmering webs enwrapping the branches above them caught their attention. The underbrush thickened, threatening to enmesh their feet in leafy tentacles. They were forced to use their swords to clear their path through the thick shrubbery.

The webs they had seen in the upper branches grew in number and size until they choked out any sunlight that happened to filter through the leaves. As the branches came lower, so did the webs. Cocoons of shimmering silver appeared in the clumps of webbing, containing what, they could only guess. A thick strand dangled from a branch and brushed Hamilton's cheek, and he shuddered with revulsion. It was cold, clammy, sticky.

Valt spoke for them all. "The sun is fading. I sincerely hope we don't meet whatever made these webs."

Suddenly their muscles tensed as overwhelming panic surged over them like a monstrous tidal wave. The Eagle Knights, unfamiliar with such unnatural, overpowering terror, reeled and staggered and cried out, striving to control the urge to run, to flee. In a terrified haze, Hamilton's mind floundered for the source of this unreasoning fear. Blindly, his trained mind sought the source. With terrified astonishment and wonder, he found it. This fear was not theirs. It was being suggested to them, forced upon them from somewhere. A thousand powerful minds with a single focusing entity.

Hamilton's training took hold of him. His mind sought the source, found it, and shattered it with a single mental blow. Suddenly the feelings of panic and fear were gone. Hamilton thought he heard a faint screech of anguish somewhere in the darkness.

They moved on quickly, wishing to leave this place behind. Hamilton had smashed the source of the assault the instant he found it, but in so doing, had failed to examine it. He still did not know what it had been, but he did know it was sentient, and telepathic, and had been very close, perhaps within arm's reach. They quickly left the clusters of webbing and cocoons behind.

Hamilton turned his attention to the Key. It looked to him as if the glow was now brighter, stronger.

Perhaps just a trick of the darkness.

About an hour later, the ground began to slope sharply downward. With his mind, he reached down into the darkness, feeling his mental way down the slope. The incline was steep, but covered with towering trees. As far down as his senses could reach, the slope seemed constant.

He turned to the others. "Let us rest here until morning," he said, "I am weary, and the slope is steep and long, possibly treacherous."

They agreed, and began to stamp beds for themselves in the grass and brush. Capian stood to take the first watch. He looked at Hamilton, and seeing he was already slumbering, smiled ironically. The weight of a world's fate was a heavy thing to rest on one man's shoulders, a heavy thing indeed. The One deserved any rest he was able to snatch.

An hour passed.

As he glanced around in his vigilance, he spied a close-set pair of tiny yellow orbs peering at him from the darkness in the branches above. As quickly as he saw them they were gone.

Another hour passed.

Sleep nagged at him like a warm, inviting bath. But he was a Knight of the Eagles. He would not sleep until it was time to do so, so he crossed his legs in vigilant meditation. He saw the eyes again several times, until he came to doubt the presence of only one pair.

Another hour came and went.

His eyelids were weighted with leaden chains that threatened to close them irrevocably, but he somehow knew that if he weakened and succumbed, none of them would ever see the light of day again. He would not sleep.

Then suddenly an overwhelming panic seized his mind like a rapidly tightening vise, a panic he had felt before only a few hours ago. Valt suddenly bolted upright from slumber, leaping to his feet, screaming in blind unreasoning fear. "*No!*" he screamed, froth flying from his lips. "*They* are out there! Coming for *us!*"

Capian, now alert, but keeping his fear in check, demanded, "Who?"

"*Them!*" Valt cried in stark terror. "Thousands of them, to get us! Eyes! *Eyes!* Tiny yellow eyes! Burn like fire! *Burn!*" The glint of utter madness sparkled like black fire in his eyes. He clutched his palm across his eyes. His sword flashed into his hand. "I'll kill them all! *I'll kill them all!*" He crashed through the brush, out into the darkness.

Darius stood awake now, gleaming steel in a

clenched fist.

Valt's insane screams and thrashing echoed eerily among the trunks and web-festooned boughs. For a moment he was silent. Then he screamed, "No! *Stay away! Nooo!*" The sound then became muffled, as if he had been gagged by something.

Capian glanced at Hamilton. He still slept like a dead man.

A dead man.

Capian, in abrupt fear, leaped to his side. He took Hamilton's shoulders and shook him violently. "Wake up! *Wake up!*"

The only reply was a long, fitful snore.

The things in the forest were excited. One of the Prey was already theirs. The Young would not go hungry this night. The one that had thwarted their Mind Hunt before, they had now forced into a deep slumber from which he could not escape.

Now they would wait, just out of sight, until the right moment. Then none of the Family would go hungry for a while.

****

Hamilton Corbin was dreaming. He knew it, and cared not to change that. A stunningly beautiful woman walked beside him along a gurgling starlit river. Her long, auburn tresses draped in a flowing cascade down her back that shimmered darkly in the moonlight. The moon glanced softly off her fair skin, and plastered a white blaze across the flawless face of the water.

They walked and talked. He apologized to her for his shameful audacity in her step-father's sitting room, and begged her forgiveness.

To his elation, she understood, and forgave

him. Then her fingers entwined his, and his heart thumped like galloping hooves. Her hand was soft and warm in his gentle touch. As he turned to gaze into her bottomless green eyes, his strength flowed from him like water. He moved to kiss her full, vibrant lips. Somehow he knew that, for the first time, she would not slap him.

****

The panic seized Capian again like a huge, rough fist. But he would not flee. Capian held little doubt that Valt was now dead, or cocooned out there somewhere. Darius knelt on the ground, eyes squeezed shut, knuckles digging into them.

Eyes!

Thousands of them!

Bearing down!

The pressure of a thousand little minds beat his skull like stormy waves upon a rapidly cracking dam. He wanted to charge them, to kill them, to make them leave him alone.

Capian fought to think clearly. He must wake Hamilton. He was their one slim hope, if he could end the assault as he had before. Capian groped blindly for his water skin, found it, pulled the plug. His entire body quivered in raving panic as he inched toward Hamilton.

****

Hamilton saw her eyes close, the subtle tilt of her shapely face, ready for the kiss, this moment for which he had so longed, every fiber of his essence moved to her in passion. His own eyes closed.

Water! He was soaked with cold water! His eyes snapped open, to see her lovely, heart-stricken face fading away, like a picture in a tarnished mirror.

Wetness stung his eyes that was not from the cold water. Her beautiful image was replaced by a vague silhouette surrounded by blackness.

"Capian?" he began, when suddenly his skull was bombarded by a wave of sheer panic.

But as before, he sensed that it was being forced upon them, projected. As before, his seeking mind lashed out and smashed the source without mercy. A tiny shriek of pain speared from somewhere in the darkness.

Darius's screams abruptly died in his throat, and he stood up, eyes clear and alert.

Capian and Hamilton gained their feet, swords in their hands.

Darius cried out suddenly, "Come then, devils! Take us!"

His taunt was instantly answered.

A silvery cocoon suddenly enwrapped his sword arm. Before his could free his sword, a stream of glittering fibers shot from the dark and plastered his left arm to his trunk.

"My arm!" he cried, "it's numb!"

Suddenly dozens of streams shot toward all of them, threatening to enmesh them quickly. The Knights writhed and dodged. Globs of sticky fiber smeared their bodies, numbing the flesh beneath.

Then the creatures showed themselves.

Hamilton froze in astonishment, almost succeeding in getting himself smothered in webbing.

They were surrounded by hundreds of small snakes. Each was about two and a half feet long, thick as a man's wrist. A pair of stringy, clawed forelimbs dangled weakly just below the fist-sized wedge-shaped head. Yellow eyes burned into them with sinister hatred. They spat the webs from their mouths like venom, in long, sticky streams.

Capian leaped among them, hacking and slashing. The web-snakes screeched and hissed in helpless rage as he cleaved ten of their number in twain with every stroke. Bodies and pieces of bodies flew in a cold ichorous spray.

Hamilton and Darius followed suit. The fight was short. The web-snakes retreated, and the three men were left to painstakingly pull the clinging, flesh-numbing fibers from their bodies.

Hamilton looked about. "Valt?"

"He's gone," Capian said quickly. "They drove him mad. He fled into the night."

Darius was pale, eyes wide and haunted. "Dare we stay here any longer? They may return."

Capian said, "Aye. Let's move on. Hamilton, are you well enough?"

Hamilton nodded. He pulled out the Key again, and they made their way down the treacherous slope. For hours they picked their careful way down the hill, using the trees as steps and braces. Hamilton used the Key to light and lead their way. He was sure now that it seemed to be glowing brighter than before.

They became aware of daybreak only because the darkness of the night gradually faded to a dim gloom.

As the morning slowly brightened, Hamilton stopped. "Wait here," he told them, "I'm going to climb above the canopy, see what I can see." Clamping the Key in his teeth, he began to scale the nearest tree with practiced ease. Strange, these trees on the slope, he thought. They seemed younger than those on the level land above. Still, they were very old, but lacked the antiquity of those ancient boles above. But perhaps it was just his imagination.

A hundred and fifty feet above the ground, he stopped and looked about. He was now high enough to see for a good distance. His perch sagged precariously under his weight and swayed in the wind. He and his companions were on the side, near the bottom of a long valley. The valley was perhaps a league wide at the top, and almost as deep. Hamilton noticed something strange about the valley with its steep, tree-covered sides, and flat bottom. He saw no river that could have eroded this valley. And the valley ended abruptly not far to his left. The opposite end was lost in the misty distance. The surrounding land was mostly flat. In truth, the entire valley looked as if it had been dredged from the planet's surface by the spoon of a god.

Hamilton quickly turned his attention to the near end of the valley, a flash of intuition crossing his mind like a flaming chariot. The vertical end seemed somehow symmetrical. Vines and creepers carpeted the smooth sides of the thing forming the valley's terminus.

Answers to many of his questions flooded over him like a swirling tide. His heart pounded in excitement as he braced himself in a crotch between branches, took the Key from his teeth, and held it out. It turned in his grasp to point directly at the thing buried in the soil.

Hamilton nodded, and made his way back down the tree. He didn't know whether to smile or cry.

"That way." He pointed, and they made a diagonal down the slope to the relatively flat valley floor. A peculiar, wispy fog clung to the cool, dewy ground, hanging no higher than their knees. Hamilton knew where to go, and led them quickly to the terminus of the gorge. The trees ended several paces from this, and the morning sun streamed down on the huge metal lump embedded in the ground. Parts of a dull gray hull peeked through the tangled blanket of leafy vines. Four huge circular caves, choked with vines, were spaced symmetrically on the portion of the lump facing them, high above their heads, each about thirty feet in diameter.

Hamilton's suspicion was confirmed.

They approached the huge structure.

"The second Key is here," Hamilton said to them. "Remain here."

"But—" Capian began.

"Remain here," he repeated. "This is my quest. I am The One."

Resorting to such words with his friends sickened him, but he had no choice. They were baffled by this monstrous structure, and more than a little afraid. As much as he would be comforted by their company, he had no idea what he might find inside. He had no intention of seeing his friends' innocent vision of the universe destroyed or corrupted.

"We obey, Brother," Capian said. "Luck of your ancestors be with you."

Hamilton nodded and walked away, toward the crashed starship. He followed the aim of the brightly shining Key. He reasoned that any hatch or port from which the passengers had escaped could not be buried by debris, masked perhaps by vines and creepers, but not buried.

The Key did indeed point him toward the section of the spacecraft just emerging from the soil. He stepped up to the scarred gray surface that curved sharply upward from the ground. The Key pointed directly into the checked and battered hull. He tucked the Key inside his tunic, and looked around. Superficial scrutiny revealed no obvious entrance. Perhaps the ship was tilted slightly, and an entrance was up around the curve, out of sight. The vines snaking up the side afforded him an easy ascent. As he worked his way up over the curve of the hull, he found what he searched for. A small hatch, standing open like a starving mouth. He approached, and looked down into the dark recesses of the ship. The vines wormed down into the small airlock, down the corridor beyond, to be stopped short by the absence of sufficient light.

He climbed down in the airlock, into the dark. He must bring his own light. He pulled out the Key. It burned more brightly than ever before, blazing with a brilliant whiteness, illuminating the passage below for several meters. He would use it to light his way.

Down into the bowels of the strange spacecraft he crept. The corridor, with its long, unbroken walls of stark gray metal, tilted crazily with the angle of the ship, treacherous with wet slime. With great care he moved down the dark passage. The white portal above him became a small spot of luminescence. The Key shed more light now than even the brightest torch.

The passage abruptly ended with a pool of stagnant water. Millennia of forest rains had filled the sharply slanted tunnel to the ceiling. He slid slowly into the pool. He hoped there was a turn or something below that would switch back above the level of the water. If there was not, his exploration would end in its infancy.

He sucked a tremendous breath and plunged into the inky depths. Down, down, down he swam, the Key lighting the way, and he saw no opening. Down. Down. His taxed lungs threatened to suck a great draught of stagnant water against his will. To his immense relief, in the white light he saw a sharp upward turn in the passage. Up, up! Past closed doorways. Up! Up! Then he burst through the surface with a desperate gulp for air and a spray of black water.

Above him was an open portal, with blackness beyond. Panting breathlessly, he climbed through the crazily tilted opening.

The water running from his clothes echoed profoundly in the vast space beyond.

He might have just stepped into some cyclopean warehouse. His eyes widened in astonishment and recognition.

This chamber was filled, row upon row, tier upon tier, wall to wall, with thousands of man-sized cylinders, standing open, empty, banks of them lost in the gigantic blackness above. Their design was unfathomably alien, but their purpose was obvious. Suspended animation capsules. Thousands upon thousands of them. As he passed rows and rows, he saw that not all of them were empty. He found one of them with the seals unbroken. Peering through the transparent frosted-crystal cover of one of them, he saw a vague, passive, sleeping human face inside. This one had not regained consciousness. And he never would. In his passage through this chamber, Hamilton found several others like this one. Some had not, after all, survived the journey from Earth.

As he neared the wall opposite his entrance, he discovered several thousand other capsules of different sizes, both larger and smaller than those that housed the humans. These had been used for other animals, livestock, pets, countless other fauna. Hamilton could only marvel at the scope of this relocation.

An interstellar ark.

After nearly an hour of making his way through the maze of rows of capsules, he reluctantly left the huge storage bay to once again follow the direction of the blazing Key. He passed into a long corridor at least twenty feet wide. Hallways occasionally branched off from the wide main, into unknown sections of the ship. But the Key led him straight down the middle. The adornment and architecture of the ship was indescribably alien, with strange glyphs and bizarre, swirling textures shaped into the dull gray metal, exuding a powerful antiquity, perhaps eons old. Or perhaps it was the sense that this ship was not dead, but only slumbering, like some cosmic behemoth. Hamilton felt a magnitude of power, of knowledge, in this place at which human beings in their present state of evolution could only guess.

For over an hour he traversed this wide way, following the Key. This ship was miles long, buried in the crust of Irth. Finally the passage ended in a wide door, intricately, subtly shaped, as if the hard metal had been shaped and molded like clay into incredible patterns and asymmetrical reliefs. Hamilton looked about, seeing nothing with which he might open it.

His hand was shivering. He glanced at it. The Key flared like a tiny white sun. And it was quivering, shaking like a thing alive. And it pointed directly through the massive door.

The second Key was beyond those doors. He could feel its presence.

He minutely scrutinized the wide surface, searching for some means of entry. After a couple long minutes, he discovered a small, diamond-shaped hole near the center of the door.

He looked at the Key, then at the hole.

The wide butt of the Key fit perfectly into the diamond-shaped aperture. A faint rumble broke the silence. A crease appeared in the formerly seamless surface, and a loud hiss of escaping air struck Hamilton in the face with its centuries-old stagnance. The crease between doors widened, and Hamilton jumped back, pulling the Key with him. The doors continued their outward movement slowly, steadily. And Hamilton glanced a separate but identical glow shining from within the chamber beyond.

When the doors were wide enough for him to step between, he did so.

The second Key was resting impatiently on a metal and glass table in the center of a large room. In an instant it was in his hand. Both Keys flared blindingly in his eyes as he brought their ends together. A flash of brilliant light dazzled him, and the two Keys were fused together as if they had never been separate. Hamilton now held in his hands a single piece of faintly glowing crystal. He then noticed that the second Key was slightly longer than the first, making the fused pair look very much like a bizarrely shaped dagger.

Hamilton now took the time to look about him. The table on which the second Key had rested appeared to be the surface of a large, detailed star chart in two dimensions. Studying it he found that one star system on the outer section of the galactic arm was brightly outlined, with a small yellow sun. He recognized its position. It was Sol, Earth's own sun.

Another part of the chart caught Hamilton's attention where another system was boldly outlined. This system was on the opposite side of the galaxy. What this other system his current location? Or perhaps the system where this ship had originated? Either way, this was the opposite side of the galaxy, an incredible distance from home.

He sighed, feeling a pang of loss at the immense

gulf between himself and the cradle of his species. After a few moments of nostalgic melancholy, he looked about the room again. The walls were some sort of crystal, blank and black. Coppery metal plates, covered with weird runes, rested on black pedestals before these massive crystals. He saw no movable controls, nothing he could recognize besides the star map, but he guessed this to be the bridge or control center of the ship. The beings that constructed this ship had perhaps some other means of achieving their wishes than mere physical movement.

Many more questions swirled like a wind-whipped fog in his mind, with so little time to seek answers.

But for him, much had already been answered. An incredibly ancient, advanced alien culture had transported men of ancient Earth here, men of all races brought here for some unknowable purpose.

Hamilton held the glowing Key before him, smiled, and began his long walk back to the outside world.

Chapter 20

The journey out of the forest was a swift one. They merely followed the path they had marked for themselves on the trees and cut from the underbrush, fortunately without any more encounters with the web-snakes. At about noon of the third day from the derelict ship, they reached the clearing where the birds had been cloistered.

To Hamilton's surprise, the four eagles were sitting peacefully in the shade of the enormous trees protecting the clearing. At the warriors' emergence, the majestic predators stood up in faithful greeting.

The three men approached their birds, cooing to them softly. Moonlord looked about with his dish-sized yellow eyes, searching for his rider, Valt.

Noticing this, Capian lowered his head sadly, and walked up to the huge bird. Moonlord backed away, unaccustomed to being approached by anyone other than his master. Capian continued to move near him, and the beast finally stopped. Hamilton heard him whispering softly to the quivering bird, as he released the buckles and snaps of the harness, reins and saddle. Capian stepped away with the bundle of leather straps in his arms.

Moonlord regarded him with sadness, as if recognizing the dreadful finality of Capian's action. With a final scream of despair, Moonlord leaped into the air with a single beat of his mighty wings, cleared the treetops, and was gone.

The moment of silent farewell was broken by an anxious scream from Skyking.

Capian smiled at the bird, "Aye, old warrior, we hear you." Then to his companions he said, "Let us away, fellows!"

Once in the air, Hamilton held the Key in his hand, loosely. It twisted gently to point west, slightly to the north, and that was the direction they went.

As dusk approached they spotted a dark smudge on the horizon, directly in their path. As they neared, they saw that it was a pall of slowly rising black smoke. The source of the smoke came into sharp, terrible focus.

Capian cried, "Albreth's estate!"

The Slayers' encampment circled the entire fortress. Black and red striped tents were pitched in wide circles around the castle. They drew closer and closer, then saw that it was not actually Albreth's castle that burned. Capian's sigh of relief was lost in the wind when he saw that the thick cloud of oily smoke rose from a burning siege tower near the wall. As they circled they saw a horde of black armored Slayers swarming about the walls. Slayers clumped like black beetles on the ladders stretching up the tall stone walls. The defenders atop the ramparts struggled desperately to repel the assault. Broken, ebon-encased bodies covered the ground at the base of the walls in great mounds of death.

Hamilton said, "Capian, who is this Albreth? I've never heard of him."

"He is my father's cousin, and runs this small holding near the border of Allahn, on the Frontier."

Puzzled, Hamilton said, "But what is its significance to Uhr?"

"Perhaps he's trying to strip away any aid my father can receive. It could also be a strategic point to strike into Allahn from."

Hamilton surveyed the scene. Albreth's castle was surrounded by a six-foot stone palisade separated from the main wall by about twenty paces. The castle itself was about a hundred yards long, eighty wide, surrounded by a forty-foot crenelated wall. A slate-shingled roof protruded above the walls, following the rectangular perimeter, covering the house, grand hall, stables, surrounding an inner courtyard. Circular towers at each corner held ballistae that sent long javelins arcing into the ranks of Slayers below. The massive gates were still standing, under assault by a great battering ram.

A small village just to the east of the fortress lay in charred ruin.

Catapults and onagers hurled stones and balls of flaming pitch. Javelins from the towers hurled into the mass of Slayers, and Hamilton saw small clusters of black-plated bodies impaled together on single spears. The wide, deep ditch dug in front on the castle had been partially filled with rocks and earth to build pathways across which the Slayers could storm the walls. Mantlets had been erected in this ditch to protect Uhr's engineers from the archers above, while they burrowed like moles at the wall's foundation.

They circled the eagles lower and lower. Capian waved his arms to the men on the wall. Suddenly a storm of arrows shot up at them like a swarm of angry bees, thankfully falling short.

"No! No!" he cried. "We are friends! Hold your fire!"

The other three men followed suit, waving their arms.

Another volley hissed skyward, and the Eagle Knights pulled up again, out of range.

Then something streaked up just off Skyking's right wing. A javelin. And another.

Darius cried over the whistling wind, "That didn't come from the fortress."

"Excellent!" Capian said. "Perhaps now my countrymen will stop shooting at us!"

Hamilton saw another ballista swivel toward them, and prepare to fire. "We've got to land, or we'll be falling soon!"

The arrows from the fortress stopped. The men on the wall began to wave to the Eagle Knights, and faint voices rose on the wind.

Capian waved back, and nodded to his companions as he sent Starjumper plunging downward toward the castle. They fluttered cautiously down into the courtyard.

They were surrounded by the faces of weary, desperate men. Dozens of drawn bows and crossbows were trained upon them as they dismounted. Capian removed his mask and pulled back his hood, revealing his handsome face and tousled shock of blonde hair.

"Albreth!" he shouted. "Where are you?"

A scarred, unshaven man took a couple steps forward with his crossbow leveled at Capian's chest. "And who are you, laddie?"

Capian gazed at him evenly. "I am Capian, Son of Arnor."

A collective gasp rippled through the surrounding crowd.

A man pushed his way through the throng. "What's going on?"

"Greetings, Albreth," Capian said, taking stock of the tall, spare man before him, comparing this one to his memory.

Albreth simply stared at him with his dark eyes.

Capian smiled, "What, do you not recognize me, cousin? You, who used to bounce me on your knee when I was but a toddler?"

A light of recognition glinted in Albreth's eyes. "Capian!" He took a step forward.

Capian grinned.

Albreth stepped forward with a smile reaching his ears, and they clasped arms.

Hamilton regarded Albreth. He was tall and spare, with skin and hair as dark as his eyes. Wisps of gray peppered his temple, and age had whittled at his thin face. He was garbed in a soft brown tunic and breeks, with his crest of two crossed crossbows embroidered on his chest.

A ball of flame burned a flaring arc over the wall down into the courtyard, splattering flaming pitch all over the remains of a charred wagon at the far end of the courtyard, thus ending the brief reunion.

"Come," Albreth quickly said, "let us into the house. They can burn nothing more out here of consequence. These walls and roof are of stone." Leaving the eagles locked alone in the stable, they followed Albreth into the house, which was actually built as part of the wall. The clamor of the outer courtyard was gone within the thick stone walls of the house. They were in the large dining hall; long tables and benches stretched in lines around the room. People hustled about, performing their duties.

Albreth led them to a small room on the far

side of the hall, adjoining the kitchen. He motioned them inside, shut the door, and seated himself on one of the bare wooden chairs. He motioned for them to sit.

Albreth's eyes, filled with an immense helplessness, met Capian's. He took a long, quivering breath, "You must leave here immediately, or die with us," he said.

Capian's jaw clenched.

"This castle cannot long stand against Uhr's forces," Albreth said. After a long silence, he continued, "Several days ago, a messenger arrived from your father. He told me that war with Uhr was forthcoming, that Dynorr was burned and sacked, that I should prepare my people and my fortress for attack. Like a fool, I thought that Uhr would disregard my tiny little estate, at least for a time. I had no idea he would use me as an example for everyone else." He wiped at one of his eyes. "Valerion sent this to seal his message. Again a fool, I failed to recognize the urgency of your father's plea. He would not have sent Arnor's dagger if that were not the case." He pulled the short, double-edged, wide-bladed knife from his belt. Its leather-wrapped hilt was worn and ancient. "Arnor's dagger must not fall into Uhr's hands. Therefore, I entrust it to the next Son of Arnor." Albreth handed it reverently to Capian, hilt first.

Capian took it, and turned it over and over in his hands. "My thanks, cousin."

A tremendous crash resounded somewhere. Albreth jumped up reflexively, then relaxed. "They throw stones again," he said tiredly. "You are welcome to rest here for a while, but you must take your magnificent birds and fly away from here before this fortress is overrun. Methinks we shall not last until morning. Slayers have pounded at our walls for two days, and have already gained them once. We managed to beat them back, but it was a terrible, bloody fight. We lost half our fighting number in that first rush. Eventually we must succumb."

Pangs of helplessness knotted Hamilton's gut. He was The One, and yet he was powerless to help these people. The supposed savior of an entire world could do nothing to save a miserable hundred-odd brave men and women.

A young housemaid carried in a platter of bread and meat. Albreth offered it to the Eagle Knights, and they reluctantly helped themselves to the platter. "We will have little use for it soon enough," Albreth said, after the young woman had left.

Hamilton said, "Is there nothing we can do?" He looked pleadingly at his companions.

Capian shook his head faintly.

Albreth had not seen Capian's gesture. He said, "Not unless you can kill ten thousand Slayers single-handedly. Or you're The One. Perhaps he could do it."

"No," Hamilton said, "He couldn't do that."

"What makes you say that? He's supposed to be some great hero." Albreth's voice carried an edge of bitterness.

"He's just one man. Just a man."

Albreth humphed. "The Savior's arrival will be too late for us."

"You must trust in yourselves," Hamilton said.

"To what, die?"

"To live, and keep the Slayers out of your walls." Hamilton almost pleaded with him. "You can! You need only believe. If you give up, then Uhr has already won."

For an instant, a fire rekindled in Albreth's tired eyes. Then it was gone, replaced by a deep, overwhelming despair. "It is too late."

Hamilton sighed, staring at the floor, feeling Albreth's immense loss and personal guilt.

Capian said, "It's not your fault, cousin. No one could have known Uhr would strike here first or so quickly."

Albreth's fists clenched as he spoke through gritted teeth. "As I said, we're to be an example to remind your father and any other would-be rebels just who they're dealing with. And you're wrong. It is my fault. Your father warned me. By the gods, he sent Arnor's dagger to impress upon me the urgency of his words. The very symbol of your line, Capian! And like a fool I ignored it."

Capian looked down. Darius stood back, silent. Hamilton felt tears welling.

Albreth exclaimed suddenly, "Oh, gods, where is The One now!"

Hamilton took a deep breath, long and quavering. "He is right here."

Albreth's eyes shot toward him, searching. His voice was quick and raspy. "What did you say?"

"Lord Albreth, I am The One."

Albreth looked to Capian for confirmation.

Capian nodded. "He is truly The One."

Hamilton said, "We are on a quest to find the Ivory Star." He pulled the Keys from inside his tunic. "These are the Keys to finding it."

Suddenly the door burst open, revealing a man on the fear-stricken edge of madness, eyes wide and rimmed with red, face streaked with blood. "My lord!" he yelped. "The main assault!"

Albreth nodded to him. "Have someone fetch my arms. I'll be there shortly."

"Aye, my lord." And he was gone.

Albreth approached Hamilton. He clasped his shoulder in a quivering grip. He said, "Sir, I believe my cousin when he says you are The One. And I am sorry for any guilt I have laid upon you with my words."

Hamilton cut in, "You have no need to be sorry. I swear I would help you if I could."

"I know." Albreth gazed dead into his eyes, his slumped shoulders straightening as he spoke, his voice gaining timbre. "I know that one man alone can not save us. And I can now go to my death knowing that Uhr's days are numbered. Sir, you have given me reason to fight again. There is honor in what happens here today. And for that I thank you."

Hamilton tried to speak but could not find the words.

"I must go now. And so should you." With that, he turned to go.

"Cousin!" Capian said.

Albreth turned, his cheeks wet with tears. "Capian, dear cousin. I do remember bouncing you on my knee."

Capian stepped forward, and they embraced.

Capian said, "I wish I could take you with us."

Albreth nodded. "My honor is here."

After a long silence, Albreth turned away. "You must hence. Now. Darkness has surely fallen by now. May the luck of our ancestors be with you."

"Give my best regards to them, dear cousin."

Albreth turned to Hamilton. "Sir, it was the honor of a lifetime to meet you."

Hamilton said, "Good luck, Lord Albreth." They clasped hands.

Albreth nodded to Darius, who returned the gesture.

Then he was gone.

"Let us go," Capian said, his voice grim and cold.

And they did. They mounted their eagles in

the dark courtyard. Blazing fireballs whizzed past overhead, and streaks of flaming javelins. The dull roar of battle filled the air, almost ethereally faint outside the walls.

As the eagles pitched up from the floor of the courtyard, the Eagle Knights saw Albreth in his battle-scarred armor, gazing out over the field from the gatehouse tower, heavy spiked mace resting beside him. As they cleared the walls in the dimness of the deepening dusk, they saw the enemy's cookfires spotting the land with small flickering circles of orange luminescence. Waves of black figures rippled about the field. Black and scarlet pavilions glowed with feeble lights from within. The crack of catapults, the thwang of ballistae, rose over the field with the staccato notes of war. Already, the ranks of waiting warriors surrounding the castle swelled for the assault. Then as the three war-birds circled high, high above, the ranks of ebon-encrusted Slayers swarmed the walls with ladders and grapnels. The stench of blood, sweat and burning pitch wafted up like death on the wind, and with heavy hearts the three companions turned their screaming steeds from the rising moon.

Chapter 21

"Tejun!" Capian cried over the whistling of the wind. "The Jewel of Allahn."

Hamilton looked out at the glittering carpet of twinkling gems sprinkled over the horizon, shining in the twilight.

"Finally!" Darius exclaimed.

Hamilton, too, breathed a sigh of relief. The journey across the Allahnian Steppes had been a long five days. Even with winter in full swing in the north, the sun here had been hot, so during the day they took shelter in the niches and crevices of the tall, rocky bluffs that spotted the hot, arid wasteland. For five nights of travel the Key had pointed, led them to Tejun, the largest city in Allahn, and home of Lord Erastus. Tejun was a great trading city, huge and sprawling, nestled in the green valley along the coast, spindly limbs of the city stretching out into the neighboring hills and lush valleys, up the Saxon River basin. The city straddled the wide, muddy river as it emptied into the moon-splashed southern ocean far off to their right.

They landed, and hid the eagles in a copse of trees about a league upriver from the outskirts of the city.

The night had fallen completely before they reached the outskirts of Tejun. A cool salt breeze whispered in from the sea. They moved like wind-blown smoke through the dark alleys and streets of the city, among the sallow, stuccoed buildings. The outlying slums stank of old urine, excrement and other garbage, tempered by the sting of wood smoke in the heavy air. They followed the river among the scattered houses toward the center of the city. Streets and alleys, haphazardly strewn among the buildings and houses, meandered about, with sewer gutters carrying away their fetid streams of human filth to the ocean. The dark streets provided ample cover for three black-garbed, hooded, masked Eagle Knights. As they neared the center of the city, the buildings became more and more closely spaced, affording them easy cover.

They passed into an older section of the city where the streets became so narrow they were scarcely more than alleys themselves. The buildings were packed together in tight masses. As the three warriors ghosted like thieves down the narrow alleys, their shoulders scraped moldering stucco from the darkly stained walls.

The alley they now traversed ended in a wide, brightly lit thoroughfare. Lights shone from open windows and doorways, even at this hour. Smells of filth and garbage and smoke filled the air, laced with undercurrents of food and spirits. Boisterous voices burst from doorways sharply defined in the night. Weathered wooden signs, garishly painted with scenes and pictures, hung above open entrances. The Dragon's Claw. The Lord's Gullet. The Serpent. The Full Tankard. The Soft Woman. A bawdy song echoed from the open doorway of an establishment named Wine, Women and Song.

Here and there, a drunken sot staggered from one of the doors to vomit or collapse in a convenient alley. A gang of swarthy neighborhood toughs lounged near a lamp post, surveying their territory, keeping an eye on a band of staggering, singing sailors swaying drunkenly down the street. Scantily clad, bauble-bedecked whores hung expectantly in doorways, waiting for customers for whom to flaunt their wares. A brawl exploded far up the street. Shouts of anger and pain echoed hollowly down the street. Ordinary two or three story buildings lined this street. Erotic voices and equally self-explanatory sounds drifted from open windows above their heads.

Hamilton glanced at Capian.

Capian pointed upward. Metal glinted in his palm. Suddenly with a cat-like leap he was halfway up the soft wall. And there he stuck like a great black spider. With quick, precise movements he scaled the smooth surface using the hand and foot claws designed for just that purpose.

Hamilton and Darius followed him as he disappeared over the edge of the wall. The sharp, curved claws dug easily into the soft plaster as they scaled the wall, quickly gaining the roof. From rooftop to rooftop they traveled swiftly and silently.

The Key pointed them toward roughly the center of the city, more specifically, to a massively walled palace that stood above the surrounding city like a swan among chickens, tall and magnificent. It shone like a beacon in the darkness. Nets filled with glowcrystals encrusted the exterior like brightly hued jewels. Its spires towered above the rest of the city, stretched like glittering needles toward the sky.

The houses over which the Eagle Knights moved now were becoming more and more elaborate, sporting stone-shingled roofs, carved marble rain gutters, lush gardens, wide balconies crusted with obsidian and lapis lazuli. This was the wealthy section of town, the merchants' section, clustered about the palace as if for protection.

Bored looking city guardsmen strolled listlessly down the streets in this section of the city, to protect the possessions of the merchants who paid their meager wages.

Midnight was nigh when the trio finally reached the palace. They surveyed the palace from their perch atop of the roof of a nearby house. The palace was surrounded by a thick, crenelated wall, perhaps thirty feet tall, with sentries patrolling the brightly lit battlements. A thick bramble lay hunched at the base of the wall around the entire perimeter. The gates consisted of spiked steel bars as tall as the wall. Two leopards, silent figures of immobile stone, crouched atop two pillars on either side of the gate. A wide, cobbled street surrounded the wall, making a large open space, a wider space than they would have desired. In the bright moonlight their black garb would stand out like flies on bleached parchment. Hamilton glanced up at the sky. Not a cloud to be seen.

They decided on a plan. Gradually circling the palace, they used Hamilton's sense to probe beyond the wall.

Hamilton stopped. "There is a garden here," he said.

Jumping nimbly down from the roof, melding with the darkness of the alley below, Capian darted away, leaving Hamilton and Darius to wait just within the shadow of the alley. Before long, a small flame arced through the air, struck the stone atop the wall, and a blinding orange fireball exploded on the walkway.

"More Eagle Knight magic?" Hamilton asked.

Darius snickered.

Cries of consternation and astonishment echoed down the wall as the guards tramped toward the sudden unexpected phenomenon. Hamilton smiled behind his black mask, and bolted across the street toward the wall. Capian's diversion had worked well. He and Darius leaped over the wide, thorny thicket with easy strength and agility, to land in the narrow space between the thicket and the wall. Thorns tore at their backs as they slipped down in between.

They then began to scale the wall, the sharp climbing claws finding the seams between the stone blocks with ease. They stopped just below the crenel of the battlement, hearing the tramp of booted feet returning to their posts. Another fireball erupted in the same area as the first. The guards above ran back to the source of the commotion, and Hamilton and Darius scurried up the rest of the distance, lit on the walkway for an instant, then leaped into the darkness below. Landing lightly on the grass, rolling to absorb the shock, they swiftly merged with the shadows of the foliage.

They were within the palace.

Lord Erastus was distressed. He had been preparing himself for bed when his captain-of-the-guard burst into his chamber babbling incoherencies about fireballs and sorcery.

Tall and slim, with coal-black hair and eyes and deep brown skin, Erastus looked down his long, aquiline nose, sniffed arrogantly at his captain's distress. "You disturb my rest to tell me this? Are you dim?"

The captain fidgeted uncomfortably.

"Poppycock!" Erastus muttered, apathetically tugging on his trousers and boots. Perhaps he needed a new captain-of-the-guard.

He walked up a ramp leading to the top of the wall behind the captain, his lightly tufted swarthy breast bare to the cool evening breeze. They stopped among a small cluster of men.

"It happened here, my lord," one fellow said.

"What did?" Erastus demanded.

"A huge ball of flame appeared out of nowhere," the fellow said.

Erastus twisted his pointed black mustache, and looked about at the area. It seemed burned, blacker than the surrounding stone, but he could not be sure in this light. "Bring some glows," he ordered.

A man raced away, and presently returned with a basket of glowcrystals. In their soft, yellowish light, he scrutinized the wall and walkway. Yes, there had been an intensely hot flame here. Then his eye caught a small glint near the stone of the battlement. He knelt and gently picked it up. He turned the small sharp object over and over in his fingers. A shard of glass. Then he saw another one, and another.

Erastus straightened up. "Fools!" said he. "There is no sorcery here, only someone playing us a joke." Throwing down the broken piece of glass, he commanded, "Back to your posts! Captain, tomorrow you will surrender your post." With that, he spun on his heel and strode gracefully down the ramp. He hoped that this was indeed only a joke, not something far more serious. He stopped beside the sergeant of the night watch. "After all this, double the guard, and have someone search the garden. Something is not right, I fear."

"Aye, my lord," the man said.

Erastus paused to look him over.

The man stood straight and tall as he was examined. "My lord?"

Erastus said, "Tomorrow, you will report to my audience. I have a new assignment for you."

The man saluted. "Aye, my lord!"

Erastus walked on, down the long, richly decorated, vaulted hallway toward his chambers. Pausing before the gilded, wooden doors, he reached for the latch, then stopped.

What had he heard? Something within? A stealthy footfall, a quiet shuffle? Instinctively he reached to his side for his scimitar. He cursed himself as he remembered it hanging sheathed on a chair near his bed. Moving to the wall, he took down an ornate saber from where it hung. Not a terribly effective weapon, but better than nothing. He returned to the door, and slowly turned the latch. With a shove to the door he leaped into the chamber, saber foremost.

The light in his chamber was all wrong. The room had been darkened. The curtains before his balcony window were drawn. The first thing he saw was a blazing white light, then the black figure etched against it.

"My Key!" Erastus cried, lunging forward.

A sharp clang suddenly sent his sword spinning out of his grip, and what felt like a sledgehammer buried itself in his belly. "Waugh!" exploded out of him, and he skidded to a halt face down on one of his lush rugs, gasping for breath.

"'Ware, Hamilton!" a voice hissed close by.

The man in the light whirled. In his hands he held a dimly glowing crystalline shape, three-pointed.

Erastus dimly heard the whisper of clothing

on skin move swiftly away from him. The door closed. The only light in the room came from the strange object in the man's hand, vaguely resembling his own Key, only larger, shaped like a dagger with one quillion missing.

Erastus tried to rise.

A soft boot pressed into the back of his neck, holding him down.

"Remain where you are, fellow," said a soft voice from behind him, "we have no wish to harm you."

"I am Erastus, Son of Abdallah, Lord of Allahn," Erastus said through clenched teeth, rage honing the edge in his voice, "I will not be treated this way."

"My apologies, Lord Erastus." The foot on his neck was removed.

Erastus immediately leaped to his feet.

"Do not call your guards," said the man with the glowing crystal, "or we will be forced to kill them. We did not come here for killing."

Erastus sneered, "Ah, then you came only as thieves to loot my very chambers! Replace the blasted glowstone so I may see your thieving faces!"

"Replace the crystal, Darius," said the man with the Key-thing.

A glowcrystal magically appeared, and was set in its sconce, revealing another figure clad in tunic and trousers of deepest black, hooded and masked.

"You certainly dress like thieves," Erastus said.

"We are Knights of the Eagles," said the man near him. "I am Capian, Son of Arnor."

"I know who you are! Valerion's oldest whelp! I thought the Eagle Knights were honorable men, not thieves!"

The man with the glowing crystal said, "We are not thieves, Lord Erastus. And please forgive our violence to your person. We did not know that it was you."

"So why are you here?" Erastus demanded. "What interest am I to the mysterious Eagle Knights?"

"I am Hamilton Corbin," said the man before him, "and I have come for the Key."

"You cannot have it!" Erastus hissed, "it has been in my family for centuries!"

The Eagle Knight's laugh was sharp, stinging, brief. "I am afraid it is too late for that, my friend, for I already have it." He held forth the glowing crystal object and tapped the half-guard with his finger.

"That section looks like my Key"

"It is yours no longer," Hamilton said. "It has been claimed by its brothers."

"What?"

Hamilton said, "Many people believe that I am The One. We are here in your palace tonight to claim this part of the Key to the Ivory Star."

It was Erastus's turn to laugh, harsh and mocking. "The One is a myth! A tale of hope-crazed housemothers to babble at their wide-eyed wards. 'The One will save us from the terrible, horrible, frightful Uhr!' A joke!"

Hamilton's hard blue stare silenced him, but his voice was calm and even. "I care not, sir, what you think. I know only what I believe, and may all the gods help me, I believe I am The One. I have been forced into this position by either the whim of circumstance and coincidence, or some cosmic web of fate. Nevertheless, I mean to see my task through to the end, even should it mean my own destruction."

"And what task is that? To kill Uhr I suppose." Erastus's voice dripped with sarcasm as he twisted his mustache, accenting his skeptical smirk.

"Yes, to kill Uhr."

The lord shook his head, and said, "You are mad." But the mocking edge was gone from his voice.

Capian said, "My father is now at war with Uhr. He needs aid."

Erastus burst out, "What of that? I care not for your reckless father! I have enough trouble with Uhr at present without involving my country in a hopeless rebellion."

Capian said, "Your problems with Uhr are only beginning. A legion of Slayers has already fallen upon Albreth's estate, and I suspect by now it has been destroyed, and everyone in it killed."

Erastus's eyes fell, and his voice was quiet. "I am sorry. Albreth was a good man."

"You know as well as I," Capian said, "that if Uhr has so much as a whim, he will not hesitate to raze Tejun, just to be sure you're not planning on throwing your bones in with my father. That legion of Slayers may already be on its way here."

Erastus's swarthy visage paled to an ashen gray.

Hamilton spoke up, "You may have no love for Valerion, but once I have killed Uhr, and the Slayers have been defeated, I would advise you not to antagonize him. He cares not for Uhr's adherents." He gestured to the masked Eagle Knight waiting by the window, who quickly opened the draperies and balcony doors, admitting a cool, fresh night breeze, alive with the smell of the sea.

The One said, "We will trouble you no longer."

Then with mind-numbing speed they were at the window and outside. In that same instant, Erastus dived for a thick rope hanging from the ceiling near his bed, his emergency alarm.

He did not see Hamilton pause at the bay window, the flash of silver in his hand. The instant Erastus's hand touched the rope, metal rang sharply on the stone above his head, and the entire length of rope fell to the floor. Erastus looked up. A small silvery crescent was embedded in the stone wall. The cleanly cut hand-span of rope dangled from its hole in the ceiling. He could not reach it. He looked at the window. The balcony was empty. Nothing remained to prove that the Eagle knights had even been there, except the talon-blade, if only he could get it down.

Erastus almost called his guards, but thought better of it. The Eagle Knights would be gone before his bumbling men-at-arms could ever reach him, or they'd be sliced to ribbons, if what he'd heard about Eagle Knights was true. He sank into his favorite chair, sighing over the loss of his Key. Could that man truly be The One of ageless legend?

"Bah!" Erastus spat. The son of Valerion a thief! They'd taken his Key. At least that's what his father and his grandfather had called it. Merely a bauble, but still it was his, a piece of his family history.

But if that man was truly The One, he needed it far more.

"Bah! The One! A fable spawned by lame priests and ignorant peasantry.

"Bah," he said half-heartedly, as he readied himself for bed.

Chapter 22

The Lakeside alarm bells rang as the first enemy banners appeared on the horizon. Mounting the foremost tower overlooking the wooden palisade, Valerion gazed out over the field of glaring snow.

Robinton took up a place next to him, and looked out over the whiteness. "I see it's finally happened, my lord. The Slayers are here."

Valerion shielded his eyes against the glare. "Those aren't Slayers."

Puzzled, Robinton looked again. "Who then?"

"Sneev," Valerion said.

Long green banners dangled from lofty poles. Coupling serpents writhed on an emerald field. No black armor, no gruesomely crested helms.

Valerion swore venomously, then said, "I expected as much out of that cur! Uhr merely leads him around by the nose."

Robinton said, "Ah, if only Lord Diomenes still lived, eh, m'lord."

"Aye, Robinton. When I was but a wet-eared youth, Diomenes and my father were close friends. Diomenes was a good man, and shared my father's views about Uhr. But he was old, and in his senility he took Sneev under his hoary wing."

Robinton mused, "I remember meeting Sneev

once, before old Diomenes died. He was a slimy rat even then. He wasted no time in bedding Prilla after old Diomenes finally died."

"There was no 'finally' about it, my friend," Valerion growled.

"What do you mean?"

"I've long believed Sneev killed him, or had him killed at Uhr's behest."

Robinton ran his fingers through his red beard. "A very likely theory, my lord."

"Aye," Valerion said, "what better position for a man of no noble blood to be in? Right hand man, and close friend to a noble lord. What better when the old lord gives up the ghost in his sleep? And by marrying Prilla with Tamarra but a babe, he further secured his grip on power."

Robinton added dryly, "With Uhr's full consent and filthy blessing."

Valerion's gaze grew far away, his hot blue eyes watching the approaching host. "My father always said that, anywhere in the world there might be two men who, upon meeting for the first time, recognize each other as natural foes, born enemies whose inescapable destiny is to clash. The clash might come at that instant, or a lifetime later. But nevertheless it is fated. I recognize such an enemy in Sneev. I have always known it. I knew as soon as Lord Diomenes died that the friendship between Ophidia and Armond was over." His eyes grew hard as steel. "And now the time for my fated clash with Sneev is here."

Neither of them spoke for a while, each absorbed in his own thoughts.

Then Robinton sighed. "Lately, my lord, I've been thinking about the old days, remembering when we were ravenous for the heat of battle and women, you and I and Fortine and Albreth. We fought the battles our families asked us to, and we loved every moment. The more I think about these things, the more I realize I no longer have the taste for the heat of battle, the lust for blood, like before. I only wish an end to't, that either I might meet my ancestors, or live my remaining years in peace with the world."

"Well spoken, man," Valerion said, clapping him on the plated shoulder. "We're of a mind, you and I."

Robinton continued, "My only regret is that I never loved only one woman long enough to keep her interested in me." Then Robinton realized the ground on which his words tread, and he was immediately sorry. He stammered, "My lord, I—"

Valerion reassured him. "It's all right, Rob. I was the luckiest man alive to have her as long as I did."

Robinton wiped at his eye, quickly. "Aye, my lord." And he rested his hand on Valerion's heavy shoulder.

They stood and watched the Ophidian army make camp far outside the widest trench, a trench now filled with frozen mud and glittering snow. Night brought dozens of cookfires, glinting out there like tiny orange firebugs. Robinton had gone away to tend to his duties, leaving Valerion alone on his perch, wrapped in his wool-lined leather cloak. The sliver of moon rose above the glimmering sheet of flawless white between Lakeside and Sneev's army. The wind whipped his heavy cloak about him, dusting his face with icy grains of snow.

It was then that his eye caught a movement, a black speck moving out there where no speck had business to be moving, coming slowly toward the fortress. As it came closer, Valerion saw that it was a man, wrapped all in furs, shambling easily along.

"Spy!" he hissed. Someone was trying to infiltrate the fortress!

Valerion saw the figure clearly enough to spot the puffs of steam escaping from the person's mouth. For an instant, Valerion thought he recognized the figure's gait, but quickly forgot this as the person approached the gate of the palisade, and spoke to one of the gate guards on duty. The guards and this strange figure spoke briefly, and Valerion could not hear over the hissing of the wind and snow. He quickly climbed down the tower, his curiosity burning. He intended to question the gate guards after they had turned this person away. But when he stepped out of the watchtower, he saw the gates were open! And with an invading army in sight! Rage boiled in him like lava. He'd have those guards in the stocks!

Valerion saw the fur-swathed figure walking through the open portal and down the street directly toward him.

"Speak your name!" Valerion demanded, unmoving in the dark.

The man gasped an oath in a rasping old voice. "Arnor's loins!" He sucked for breath, startled. "I am Garth, Son of Arnor."

Valerion leaped forward, eyes wide and staring in the dim yellow light of the street lamp. He saw the man's steely blue eyes stare at him in equal astonishment. Here was a man pounded but not vanquished by age. Long, black hair, profusely streaked with hoary gray, framed a strong weather-whipped face.

"My son!" the man exclaimed.

"Father!"

These words came simultaneously from both mouths. The two leaped at each other like bears, and they embraced.

As they separated and held one another at arm's length, Valerion managed to say, "I thought you dead."

A scratchy laugh brought a cough from Garth's ancient throat, and he spat a wad of phlegm onto the frozen ground. "As did most. As I so desired it."

"Why have you returned, Father?" Valerion asked quietly.

The old man smiled broadly, and answered, "How dull it is in one's old age to pause and rust unburnished like an old sword, and not shine in use! I would not miss this for all the gold on Irth."

Valerion chuckled heartily, and the two men regarded each other for several long moments, re-examining their memories.

Garth suddenly said, "Come, son, I know you have many questions. I know I do. So let us out of this damnable cold, to your house, where the fire is warm and the tal is strong. I've been trekking across that snow for days, not to mention skirting Sneev's force for miles out of my way. My hands and feet are well-nigh frozen."

"Aye," Valerion readily agreed, "we shall."

Valerion handed his father a tankard of warmed tal. Garth said, "Ah, just what these old bones need!"

"My lord! My lord Garth!" boomed a voice from the kitchen door.

"Little Tarl!" Garth grinned. "Gods, boy, you've grown!"

Tarl filled the kitchen doorway, his mouth agape. "I see a ghost!"

"Nay, my boy," Garth said, "'tis I, in the living flesh."

Tarl looked at Valerion, as if for confirmation.

Valerion smiled and nodded. "It is he."

"Wodan's Teeth, it is!" Tarl crossed a room in a few tremendous strides, and took the old man's hand in his gargantuan paw.

Garth returned the grip. "It is good to see you, my boy!" He managed to take his hand away while it was still attached to his body.

"Likewise, my lord. Are you back from the dead for long?" He grinned crookedly.

They laughed heartily. Then Tarl said, "I have duties, my lords, if you will excuse me. My lord Garth, I look forward to having you stay with us awhile."

"And I look forward to staying, if my son will have me.

Valerion said, "Of course, father. This was your house first."

Tarl took his leave then, and Valerion led his father to the sitting room. The halls were empty as they walked. Garth asked, "How is your family, son? All fares well, I hope."

Valerion drew a deep breath. "Uhr sent us a sickness...a plague."

Garth's mouth fell open and he stopped. "Everyone?"

"No," Valerion quickly answered, "not everyone. Just Ilone."

Garth's voice was soft and sincere as they resumed their way. "I am truly sorry, my son. She was a wonderful woman. A rare jewel."

Valerion said nothing, ushering his father through the sitting room door, closing it behind them.

"What of Madra and Capian?"

"You know of her?" Valerion asked quickly.

"News travels, son," Garth said vaguely, "but how are they?"

The lord choked back his rapidly rising grief, sitting down in one of the high-backed chairs. "Madra is dead. Capian, we know not."

Garth took a chair opposite him. "How came Madra's death? The plague? She was a pretty girl, I've heard."

"No." He leaned forward, hands on his knees, squeezing his eyes with two fingers.

"How then? Come, tell me."

Valerion's breath was deep and quivering. He lowered his hand and gazed at the empty corner of the room. "Uhr," he said, as if it were an obscene word.

Garth lowered his head in silence.

Valerion looked at him, his eyes glimmering with salty moistness. "You seek the whole truth," he quavered, "I shall give you the entire truth." He paused, resting his elbows on the table, and rubbing his red-rimmed eyes. "She was Great Master Uhr's loyal spy, and she betrayed us!" He spat the words like curses.

Garth paled, and appeared to have trouble regaining his breath.

Valerion said, "Are you well, father? You look ill."

Garth said, "I am fine, son. And sorry. I shouldn't have pressed."

"Uhr came here one night, at her summons, by sorcery. She told him where to find The One. Having no further use for her, he slew her."

Garth's jaw clenched. "Your own family. That bastard." Then he lowered his voice, as if to say only to himself, "He did it again." He looked at Valerion again. "Dare I ask of Capian?"

Valerion searched his father's face and manner, wondering what he had meant by 'again', but answered his question. "I sent Capian away to the

Knights of the Eagles soon after your…abdication. Earlier this winter, their Sanctuary was burned, their servants butchered. We know nothing of any Knights that may have escaped."

Garth remained speechless, absorbing all he had missed throughout his long hermitage. Then he said, "And Sorde?"

"Slain."

The door to the sitting room opened. A young lad stepped around the jamb, knuckling his eyes, square cut ebon mane tousled with sleep.

"And who is this?" Garth asked, turning to regard Valerion II. Bare feet shuffled on cold stone as Val crossed the room to stand beside his father.

Valerion rested a scarred hand on his son's shoulder. "This is my second son, Valerion." He said to the boy, "Son, this is your grandfather, Garth, Arnor's Son."

The boy looked up at Garth, and scratched his tousled black head in puzzlement. Val said, "Father always said you were dead. Are you back from the grave?"

Garth cleared his throat and stuttered, "Well, I'm not dead, or back from the grave, even though I may look like it." Then he cracked a wide grin. "I've been away for quite some time, and everyone thought me dead. But I have returned."

Val nodded. "Will you be staying with us? I never had a grandfather before."

"Have you any more offspring, my son?" Garth asked Valerion, "I've already taken a liking to this one." He grinned and squeezed the boy's wiry arm. "Well, my boy, I think I'll be staying awhile."

Val stood straight and strong and tall. "Good."

"A perfect image of his father when he was that age," Garth said.

"I have another daughter, Nessa," Valerion said.

"How old is she?"

"Just about eighteen. A perfect image of her mother."

"Then you are fortunate, to have had two such women in your life. I should like to meet her."

Val said, "You'll have to wait until tomorrow. She's sleeping now."

Garth laughed, "Impetuous boy!"

Valerion swiped the long hair out of his son's eyes. "She's taken her mother's death very hard. They were great friends. She sleeps a great deal now."

Garth nodded. "A tragic thing," he said. Then a sudden recollection grabbed him. "What of The One?"

Valerion sighed and shook his head. "We know nothing of him either. He was with the Eagle Knights when Uhr raided their lair."

Garth drew a deep breath. "It seems," he said, "that we stand in a rapidly filling manure pit."

Valerion could not help a smile. "Aye, father, so it seems."

"What of The One's large companion of the coal-black hair?"

"Angus MacTavish? He is one of my Red Dragons now. He's made a fine warrior."

"I thought as much about him. He has the spirit and temperament. All that remains for him, I suppose, is the final baptism of fire, blood and steel."

Valerion hugged his son close to him. "He will not have long to wait, now. My son, you go off to bed now. I'll see you on the morn."

"Aye, father." The boy kissed his father's cheek. "Good night, Grandfather," he said, and went away.

"A wonderful boy," Garth said, watching him go.

Valerion smiled. "Aye, but his mother always

says he's a little monster."

Garth exclaimed, "Hah!" Then he leaned forward, resting an elbow on his knee, his eyes dancing in merry recollection. "Your mother always said the same of you. 'The little hellion', if my old memory serves me."

And they laughed. The night passed quickly as they caught up on the many years since Garth's disappearance. But Valerion never asked why he had left. He hoped that his father would tell him, in time, when he was ready, but there was no reason now to cast a shadow over their joyous reunion. Someday, perhaps. Someday.

Chapter 23

With the silvery light of dawn came the brazen blast of trumpets. Valerion watched from the palisade gate the green serpent banners of Sneev, flapping and billowing in the morning breeze. A light sifting of snow had covered the field during the night, forming a perfect surface of stark, shimmering white, disturbed by not so much as a mouse's trail. The sky was a dazzling tapestry of sapphire and lavender in the morning light.

Sneev's ranks began to form as the blaring war horns sounded. Valerion's soldiers manned the top of the wooden palisade. Small arrow loops perforated the log joints, each manned by a well supplied archer. His bravest, most seasoned veterans and Red Dragons stood on the walkway.

Angus MacTavish stood on that wall, shield slung on his forearm with its blazing red Insignia. Robinton stood poised near the gate, his winged helmet polished and gleaming. His newly honed bastard sword rested point down in his gauntleted hand, padded chain mail coat stiff in the winter cold.

The ranks across the way swelled and matured. When they were complete, they began to move forward.

Angus sucked a quick breath. This was it. After all the waiting and training and preparation. Angus looked into the glorious sunrise, felt his breast swell with its beauty. He wondered if he would live to see another. He felt his heart begin to thump powerfully against his breastplate, heard the rush of the pulsing blood in his ears, and gripped his battle ax tightly.

The Ophidian host advanced slowly, steadily. Valerion and his father scrutinized the ranks of the enemy. The first rank was a bristling wall of shields and polearms. Behind these marched row upon row of swordsmen, followed by several ranks of bowmen. Officers mounted on snorting horses flanked these.

Somewhere behind those lines was Sneev, Valerion knew. His gauntleted fingers flexed as he imagined Sneev's vertebrae cracking and popping in his hands, collapsing his windpipe like a hollow reed. But that was a luxury he must wait for. It was now time for battle.

Garth took up a long bow, and joined the archers behind the arrow slits taking pot shots at the advancing enemy.

The advancing army trampled the virgin snow under their booted feet. Robinton and Valerion stood together above the wooden gate.

Robinton said, "Not an overly large force, eh, m'lord. Roughly two thousand, I'd say."

"Aye," Valerion said, squinting against the snow's icy glare. "But large enough to hold us here until the Slayers arrive."

Robinton said, "Every day we can hold out brings The One closer to his goal."

Valerion settled his mighty helm onto his head and strapped it underneath his chin. The polished steel helm snugly fit his head. The dangling camail draped his neck and shoulders. His face was partially concealed by a protective shell, with a T-shaped opening for the eyes, nose and mouth, and stout nasal dropping down between his eyes. His gauntleted fists gripped his heavy, notched broadsword, shield hanging on his opposite arm.

All around him, his men anxiously fingered and clutched their recently sharpened weapons.

Lord Sneev's army was close now, within forty paces. Then the Ophidian archers suddenly drew.

"Down, men, down!" Valerion howled.

The men atop the wall fell behind their shields, as a storm of arrows blasted toward them with the sound of swarms of angry hornets. From somewhere within the advancing ranks, men with ladders rushed forward, shields held high on one arm, ladders under the other.

The second volley of arrows swarmed from the Ophidian ranks, and several ladder crews burst from the ranks. Valerion behind his shield, looked over his shoulder at his own men behind the wall. None had yet been randomly wounded by a stray arrow, though the ground and nearby buildings were pincushioned. The wall bristled with embedded shafts. Valerion's own archers began to return fire from their arrow loops, decimating the Ophidian ladder crews to the last soul.

Suddenly, under another assault of razor-tipped arrows, the enemy's wall of shields rushed forward with a mad howl, followed closely by the pikemen. They snatched up the ladders and ran for the wall. Helpless, unable to move under the rain of arrows, the defenders could only watch them from behind their shields as they came.

Valerion cursed.

Ladders clacked up against the wall.

Arrows came down steadily now, a few at a

time, careful not to strike those climbing the ladders.

Valerion leaped up and thundered, "At them, men! To hell with the archers! Beat the bastards back down into the snow!"

With that, Valerion's warriors leaped to their feet, and with long-hafted forks shoved the ladders away from the wall and down. The ladders sprang up again, nearly a score at once.

Angus peered over the wall and stared down into the scarred face of a huge, bearded killer stalking up the creaking ladder. The man snarled and savagely thrust upward with a thick-hafted short spear. Angus reflexively dodged. The thrust glanced off his helm's cheekplate. He staggered back, dazed from the sudden blow. It was then that he fully realized he actually fought for his very life. He angrily grabbed the spear shaft, jerked it out of the man's hand, then chopped down with his wide-bladed battle-ax. Sparks flew as metal crashed down onto metal. The head of the ax split the metal helm, to stop at the victim's jawbone. Hot blood sprayed, steaming in the winter chill. Angus dragged his ax-head free of the crimson wreckage that had once been a skull, bringing the ruined helmet with it. He shook the helmet off just in time to see another antagonist climbing the ladder.

The ax again came whistling down, splitting the climber from shoulder to breastbone. The dead body fell backward off the ladder. The ax pulled free with a sickening squelch. In moments another attacker was scrambling up the ladder.

The ax in Angus's hand sang yet again. This man managed to raise his round, wood and steel shield in defense. Angus's terrible chop split the shield, and bit halfway through the man's arm. The attacker cursed savagely and stabbed upward with a wickedly barbed partizan. Angus caught the thrust on his shield, jerked his ax free, and struck his opponent's shield away. His sidewise return stroke sent the man's wooden helm spinning away, along with half his skull.

He no longer noticed arrows glancing off his shield and plated shoulders, caught up in the whirlwind of combat.

Nearly a hundred Ophidians already lay dead or wounded, while the defenders had yet to lose a score of men. Valerion and Robinton fought on either side of the gate. Fortine, Daarton and Tarl were spread across the wall, battling fiercely, while Sigmunnd, the Red Dragon bowmaster, with his finest bowmen, systematically picked off the attackers from behind their arrow loops. The men waiting as reinforcements behind the wall gathered arrows that had fallen, or dragged away the few dead and wounded.

The assault raged on until noon. Exhausted men on the wall were gradually replaced, one by one, by fresh warriors. Valerion refused to remove himself from the fighting, and, of course, no man was willing to press the point. The lord presented a fearsome sight indeed with his blood-spattered jupon ripped in a dozen places, revealing the scored armor underneath, blue eyes blazing with battle-fury inside the helmet, gore-smeared steel in a clenched fist.

The day wore bloodily on. The trampled snow became a scarlet slush. Corpses piled three and four high at the base of the palisade. The first breach of the defenses came near sunset. Angus was in his third shift of defense, and he had accounted for more Ophidians than he could remember or count. And he alone stood to hold the breach. An unnoticed arrow dispatched the man nearest him on the wall, giving an attacker a chance to leap up over the wall from his ladder, to alight heavily on the walkway and take a powerful sword stroke at Angus. Angus caught the blade on his mangled shield. Turning to face the man, he did not see another Ophidian leap up onto the walkway behind him.

The second man's spear head punched through chain mail, leather and flesh. Angus's clenched teeth held back the scream of raw agony that threatened to rip from his throat. He spun, hacking at the spear shaft. The wood splintered, as did its owner's skull with Angus's second stroke. He spun to face the first man just in time to see a huge club fall onto the back of the Ophidian's skull. In what seemed dreadful slow motion, the man's eyeballs burst from their sockets in twin sprays of blood. Meaty lumps plopped wetly against Angus's chest. He stared, dimly transfixed, watched the lumps ooze slowly down his front leaving bright red trails. Looking up again, he saw the man tumble from the walkway, and the huge, gore-splattered Tarl with his monstrous, dripping club. Angus foggily glimpsed concern in the giant's eyes, only for the briefest of instants before Tarl turned away, back to the battle. Another Armondian had filled the space next to Angus.

Angus's arms went limp. His forearm bumped the broken spear shaft protruding from his side. He winced. Then with grim determination, he dropped his ax and shield, grasped the splintered wood in both hands, and pulled, hard. The cold steel head grated across ribs and armor. A scream of agony tore from his throat like the spear head from his side. Instantly, he felt a hot gush.

Then nothing more.

Valerion did not see Angus fall, nor did he have

time to care. Sneev was becoming desperate already, throwing as much weight as he could against the wall in what daylight remained. Dozens fell repulsing this last desperate assault. Then a weary battle horn sounded somewhere, and the Ophidians withdrew.

Valerion, sucking for breath, let his sword point drop for the first time that day. He watched the enemy move back to their camp, dragging what wounded they could with them. The piles of corpses upon corpses against the base of the wall was incredible, almost tall enough for a man to climb and reach the top of the wall without a ladder.

Valerion could think of only one reason why Sneev was so desperate to take the castle quickly, when a wise strategist would wait them out. The only answer was that Uhr was pushing him hard, either directly or not. Perhaps he had done something to displease Uhr, and was now trying to regain face with his master. Sneev, however cunning in his evil way, was a stupid commander. Any competent commander would have burned the wooden wall from the start. But Valerion had no regrets about Sneev's stupidity. He saved his remorse for those men who had died. After sheathing his nicked, bloodied sword, he removed his helmet. Instantly, his sweat-soaked black mane stiffened in the cold wind. In the fury of battle, he had forgotten the cold of the air. His fingers and toes were long since numb.

Helm under one arm, shield on the other, he descended to the ground and returned to his house.

His helmet clunked down onto the floor, then his gauntlets. Unbuckling his armor, he removed it. His boots quickly followed, leaving him standing clothed only in leather breeks and tunic. The formerly white tunic was now sweat-stained and bloody. He pulled it over his head and tossed it across a chair, baring his broad, rippling chest.

Then all the strength that remained in him left his limbs like water from a sieve.

He sat down on a chair, elbows on his knees, head in his corded paws. A feeling of overwhelming loneliness swept through him, and he choked back a sob. "Gods, how this room is empty now!"

The canopied bed, the desk and chair, fireplace, bathtub, tightly shuttered window, and himself, alone. Part of him expected that any moment now he would hear the soft pad of Ilone's foot behind him, her soft, sweet breath on his back, her gentle caressing fingers massaging his knotted muscles. Another sob wracked him as he knew that he would never feel those hands again, nor feel her soft body in his arms, nor taste her sweet lips upon his.

A pair of soft, feminine arms suddenly encircled his chest from behind. A waft of familiar perfume swept into his nostrils. The glimpse of straight golden locks danced at the edge of his vision.

"Gods!" he gasped, leaping away, covering the madness glinting in his eyes. "Away, foul specter! Shade of what is no more! Leave me to mourn in peace, and bury myself in remembrance!"

"Father?" came a quiet, fear-filled voice.

"What?" he exclaimed as he spun.

"I'm sorry...I didn't...I meant ...I didn't mean to startle you so, Father," Nessa stuttered, eyes wide and staring, brimming with fear and concern.

"Oh, gods!" Valerion sighed, relaxing. He moved to embrace her. "Battle-weariness and grief have so made me mad that I cannot recognize my own daughter." He held her close, and said, "I am sorry, dear child. So caught up was I in your mother's memory, I didn't hear you enter."

She looked up at him with her large blue eyes. "I know, Father. I miss her, too. Sometimes I think I even see her, still walking the halls, or in here brushing her hair. Look." She pointed to the fireplace. "I heard you were coming, and had the servants stoke the fire, and warm water for your bath."

Valerion turned his eyes to the merrily blazing fireplace, and the simmering pots of water hanging above it from a bar. He felt its warmth spreading in his weary limbs. "Gods, a bath is what I crave! Cold and death have numbed me to the bone."

Nessa approached the fireplace, removed the steaming pot, and said, "Undress yourself, and I will bathe you, Father. You may tell me how the day went."

Valerion's breeks fell from him, leaving him clad only in a white loin cloth. He stepped into the fine porcelain tub. A breathless sigh escaped him as she poured the water over his head and massive shoulders. Relaxation seeped through him. He drew the rising steam into his breast, savoring the warmth.

"So, Father," she said briskly, "did you send Sneev scurrying back to his burrow?"

Steam roiling about him, Valerion smiled gratefully. "Aye, that we did."

"Did we lose many men?"

"Aye," he said, solemn now, "but not nearly as many as Sneev."

"How fared the mighty Red Dragons?"

"Well. Only a few casualties."

"That is good," she said, then asked innocently, "What of Angus MacTavish?" She poured more steaming water over him.

"He was—" he began, then looked in surprise

back over his shoulder at her. He raised a thick, black eyebrow. Her face betrayed nothing, but she was like Ilone, secretive in her feelings. Ilone had been that way when he had courted her. Emptiness gnawed at his guts again.

"He was what?" she asked.

Valerion answered with another question. "You have taken a fancy to him?"

"No," she said.

Valerion chuckled in spite of himself.

"Why do you laugh?" she asked innocently.

"You have taken a fancy to him."

"How do you know?" she demanded in protest, hands on her hips.

"You are like your mother, whom I knew better than myself," he said, "but be not too fancied, for he lies gravely wounded in the infirmary."

She gasped in spite of herself. The empty pot held in her hands clanged to the floor.

"Get you now to bed," he said abruptly, but gently, "I am refreshed. My deep thanks for the bath, dearest child. The hour is late, and I am weary."

"Yes. Good night, Father." She bent to kiss him tenderly on the cheek. Collecting her robes about her, she hurried from the room, her young mind thinking about the handsome Angus, and what she would do.

Chapter 24

Mist.

All-surrounding, all-encompassing gray mist. The mist was a solid thing, a living entity that held him, restrained him, kept him from walking, from living. He fought and thrashed, trying to find his way back to life.

But what if there, for him, was no way out? Could this be death? After all, hadn't a spear been driven into him?

Yes.

Angus MacTavish was dead. He was certain of it. But if he were dead, it seemed strange that he was still very much awake and aware. Was this the afterlife? If so, there must be other souls here. Forced to spend eternity alone, he would go mad. He resolved to find someone, anyone. But how? This damned mist denied all sight. He began to thrash about once again. Then he stopped fighting for a moment to listen, cocking an ear.

Angus vaguely heard muffled voices. But what voices! Cries of pain, moans of unbearable torment, screams of anguish. What manner of place was this, where all people screamed and wailed in torment? A single word crossed his mind in answer to his question: Hell.

"No!" he screamed, "I won't stay here! I won't!"

Then something touched him. Something cool and moist rested on his forehead. He heard more voices, like whispers in a fog, close by but unintelligible. Something soft and warm brushed his stubbled cheek, like slim fingers, stroking, caressing.

He strained to see. Look! Was the mist dissipating?

"Yes!"

But what did he see? Gold. Spun golden thread, in long flowing waves. He tried to touch it, but his arms would not obey him. No, it was not gold, but hair, long, silky golden locks that cascaded about a lovely face. The mist receded.

Bare, wooden rafters. A moist rag resting on his forehead. Furs covering his prostrate body.

The screams, the moans. He had not left them behind. They were here! But where was here?

The woman! The woman. Who was she? She was familiar, he was certain of it. He had seen her before, when he had been alive.

He parted his lips to speak, but only a dry rattle emanated from his throat. The woman squeezed cool water from a rag into his mouth. He gulped at it greedily. Finally he managed to croak, "Where am I, Heaven or Hell?"

She smiled, the full lips parting to reveal pearlescent white teeth. Lovely. "Neither, friend. You live."

He tried to look about, but his sore, stiff neck pained him. "Where then?" he asked.

"In my lord's stable, among the wounded," she answered. A sudden scream of pain from somewhere emphasized her statement. She glanced over her shoulder for a moment, then returned her attention to him.

"How long have I lain here so?" he asked. His

muscles felt knotted and weak.

"Nearly seven days."

"Seven!" he started, causing spasms of pain to shoot through him. "How goes the siege?"

She smiled a pretty smile. "Worry not about it now. We are safe. You must rest and recover. Your wound was most grievous, and must heal. We wonder that you still live at all."

Remembering the wound, he tried to move his hands to touch it, but found he could not. "What...? Why can't I move?"

"You are restrained," she replied apologetically. "You thrashed and fought so in your swoon that you reopened your wound many times." She began to untie the straps that bound him to the small bed on which he lay.

"Who are you?" he asked quietly, "I am sure I've seen you before, but I can't remember."

She smiled again—he liked that—and answered, "For one so lately awake, you ask many questions. I am a nurse, your nurse. Kavarius, the chief leech, felt you needed extra care, so I was assigned to you."

Even in his imperfect state, Angus could sense she was not telling the whole truth, but he left it alone. "Surely there are others more needful than I. Hear the moans!"

"All get the same care here," she said, "except those who need it no longer." She glanced off toward something across the room, and her voice quaked with sadness. "I will soon return to change your dressings and attend you." She smiled beautifully again, gathering her cloaks about her, and walked away. He tried to watch her go, but his stiff neck refused to twist.

Angus looked about as best he could. He could see other beds, some empty, some occupied. The scents of straw, sweat, blood and smoke combined into a single malodorous whole.

Blankets and furs covered him heavily, providing him with ample warmth. Glowing red coals heaped in black pots warmed the stable suitably. Wounded men groaned in pain. Angus himself felt little actual pain yet, just an ache below his ribs. He knew that the agony of mending muscle would be excruciating, if he lived that long. He could vaguely feel the blood-caked bandages encircling his midriff. A small stool, on which the woman had sat, stood near his shoulder by the bed.

A young boy came walking by, and Angus inquired of him, “How goes the battle while I have lain here, boy?”

The small, dark-haired lad stopped and answered, “Sneev and his army now stand idle on the banks of the lake, unable to reach us.”

“What, have we given up our mainland hold so soon?”

“Aye, five days ago. Sneev fired the wall with burning arrows the night after the first battle.” The lad turned to walk away, obviously in a hurry.

“Wait,” Angus pleaded, “please stay and tell me more.” The boy did so. “What happened after the palisade was burned?”

The lad scratched his head in remembrance. “The fire burned out the next day, and they sacked and burned Lakeside. But then they tried to come through the tunnel.” He smacked his fist into his palm. “Hah! What fools! We locked nigh a hundred of them inside it and got them through the killing holes. Then we withdrew to the castle.”

“And?” Angus prodded.

“Three days ago they tried to cross the bridge and assault the main gate, but…” He paused to giggle. “But Master Fortine collapsed it. Crash!”

He waved his arms in excitement. "Another fifty fell through the ice below." The boy was pleased, having outwitted Sneev. He paused, "Now they stand on the banks, frightened to cross the ice."

Angus gave them a smile, and thanked him gratefully.

The boy's eyes sparkled as he saluted, spun on his heel, and marched off.

The hours dragged slowly for Angus as he passed in and out of sleep. His wound began to ache more and more, stabbing blunt fingers deep into his bowels. He marveled that he was still alive. While he lay wake, he tried to recall where he had seen that woman before, but try as he might, he could not. He wished she would return. He craved company. This woman was not as beautiful as Madra had been, but she was still very pleasant to the eyes and ears, and even the nose in a smelly place such as this.

She finally returned, with a steaming bowl. Seating herself on the stool by his bed, she said, "I brought you some broth."

"I thank you, my lady, but I am not hungry," he told her.

"But you must eat," she said, "you haven't eaten in several days. Here, let me feed you."

He knew she was right. His aching head told him of his dehydration, so he acquiesced.

She took the spoon and bowl and began to lift the spoon to his mouth.

"No, let me do it," he said, "I am a man, not a child."

"You're a child to think so!" she scolded. "You're too weak to feed yourself."

"No, you're wrong," he growled, and began to slide back on the bed using his arms to prop himself up.

Spasms of pain wracked his left side. What strength remained in him vanished like a breath of stale air, and he slipped back down with an agonized groan. He refused to admit it, but, damn it, she was right again. Neither did he tell her he felt a moist heat spreading beneath his bandage. With a grunt of resignation, he allowed himself to be fed. She smiled smugly, secure in her victory, as she slowly spooned the broth into his mouth.

He could eat very little, so she set the bowl aside, and checked his dressing, scolding him thoroughly at the sight of the fresh crimson stain on the cloth. She immediately insisted on changing the dressing, and he instructed her on the best way to do it. He could at least apply some of his medical knowledge to saving himself.

To pass the time, they spoke to each other of themselves. She said her name was Ilia, and she was a merchant's daughter. She seemed reluctant to divulge more, even after persistent prodding, but he didn't care. He was satisfied just to get acquainted with her.

Days passed into weeks, and still Lord Sneev waited on the banks of Crystal Lake. The days began to warm with the coming of spring and pools of water began to form on the surface of the ice. Inside Lord Valerion's stronghold, food was little problem. Fish was brought forth daily from holes chopped in the ice, out of sight of the shore. Firewood, however, was dangerously scarce. If a warm spell did not come soon, the people would be eating food raw and sleeping unprotected from the cold. Dried horse and ox dung provided some alternative but was simply not plentiful enough to heat the entire fortress.

Angus meanwhile lay fuming in the makeshift infirmary, anxious to be up and about. Kavarius, the head leech, an old gnarled man, told him that if he was fortunate enough to have lived this long, he was probably out of danger. It was just a matter of healing now. The hole in his side slowly knitted, leaving a jagged purple scar.

Through this time, Angus and his nurse spent much time together, and during her absence he found himself counting the minutes until her return. If not for her, his time spent in recovery would have been unbearable. Several times she caught him up and staggering about, promptly ushering him back to bed with a tongue-lashing he hadn't had since the Academy. He was still weak as a kitten, and it pained him to straighten up and walk.

Valerion occasionally visited to hospital to review the men, inquire as to their well-being, and try to raise their spirits. There were men in the former stable with far worse wounds than Angus. They hovered on the brink of death. One man had to be put out of his misery due to a rampant infection in his chest from an arrow that had broken off inside his body. Sickening yellow pus oozed constantly from the puffy hole in his swollen chest. When touched, he screamed and screamed and his eyes bulged in utter madness. A quick dagger thrust finally ended his suffering.

Angus grew stronger. One particular morning, as he ventured outside for the first time in weeks, he was closing the stable door behind him, when the pat of small feet running toward him brought him around. Angus stared as his nurse stopped before him, standing with her small fists couched on shapely hips, glaring up at him half in anger, half in fear.

She demanded, "Where do you think you're going?"

Angus could not help but smile at her exaggerated expression. "For a walk."

"You," she said, stabbing a small finger into his face, "get back to bed."

He firmly replied, "You know as well as I that I am capable, and will never regain my strength unless I do something other than lay in bed." He turned to walk slowly away, leaving her fuming behind him. Then he looked back over his shoulder. "Of course, if you joined me, you could keep me out of trouble."

For a moment, she looked at him sternly, as if trying to decipher his strange tone. Then her eyes dropped, a faint blush spreading across her fair cheeks, and she shuffled after him.

They walked about the castle, keeping to the cobbled paths. The snow had melted in places and pooled into icy puddles of slush. The morning was pleasant, sun beaming down warmly, without a hint of breeze. They walked out to the outer ward, and climbed the battlement of the highest tower. They stood next to the monstrous ballista sitting unloaded, trained toward Sneev's army. She shuddered, and said, "Such a ghastly machine."

"A necessary instrument of war, my lady."

She sighed and looked out over the battlement. "I can't believe Lakeside is utterly destroyed. It just sickens me," she said.

He said nothing, looking out over the charred, blackened ruins where once had reposed a bustling town. Instead he laid a gentle hand on her shoulder. After a moment, she covered it with her own.

Angus noticed a dark speck growing on the horizon, behind Sneev's army. The speck rose steadily into the air, as if on a pole. Now, to Angus's utter horror, the entire southern horizon moved! That which he had seen was a coal black banner with a single scarlet eye glaring in the center of it. And the moving horizon materialized into thousands of mounted warriors riding into view. Countless grotesque black helmets bobbed on the ebon-armored shoulders of the mounted Slayers.

"God in 'eaven!" Angus gasped, unconsciously reverting back to English.

The women beside him sucked a breath of terror. "Come!" she cried, tugging at his arm. "We must tell my father!"

"Your father?" He looked at her askance. She looked at him with deep blue eyes, and his face lit with comprehension. "You are Valerion's daughter, Nessa!"

She looked away, eyes demurely downcast. "Yes," she said softly.

He turned away from her, to face the battlement, resting his hands on the cold gray stone. His eyes fell to the ice of the Lake below.

For a long moment, both were silent, until Nessa said, "We must tell my father."

"It is already being done," he said quickly.

It was true. Already, a pair of guardsmen ran away toward the ward gate.

"What is it, Angus?" she asked, her voice trembling. "Are you angry with me?"

"No," he replied, "I am angry with myself."

"But why?" she persisted.

He almost said something, but then cut himself short. Instead he said, "Come, let's go back. This tower will be busy shortly." Then he turned his back on her and walked away.

Chapter 25

The three Eagle Knights stared in grim apprehension at the monstrous effigy before them.

"It's huge!" Darius breathed, his breath forming a misty plume lost in the cold mountain wind.

"I can't imagine how we didn't find it sooner," Hamilton said.

Capian said, "Red Priest magic, no doubt. Theirs is more powerful than ours in many ways. They simply desire any unwanted visitors not to see it. So unless you fairly walk into it, you'll never find it. I'll wager it was sheer luck that got us close enough to see it in any case."

The huge carving rose above them as they hid among some fallen boulders a hundred paces away. The entire face of the towering cliff was carved in the likeness of a leering, fanged skull, perhaps a hundred feet tall. Bonfires blazed in the cavernous eye-sockets high above, casting smoky orange haloes into the night. The slim crescent moon provided little light as it rose just above the craggy Vicorian Mountains. Flickering orange torch light glowed from deep within the gaping fanged maw, silhouetting the vague, black-robed figures standing guard at the entrance of the mountain.

"The Key is in there," Hamilton said.

Capian looked at him in the darkness, took a deep breath, let it out again, looked at the skull. "This will be difficult," he whispered.

"Aye," Darius said.

Hamilton took a deep breath. "I must go alone."

His companions stared at him in disbelief, protests frozen on their lips.

"Once again, I must do this alone," Hamilton said. "One man has a better chance than three of infiltrating a place such as this. The Red Priests are looking for more than one man. The problem here lies not in fighting our way in and out again, but in getting past them and grabbing the Key before they know of our presence."

Capian sighed, "Once again, my friend, you're probably correct, much as it pains me to see you enter that adder's nest alone."

Hamilton tried to reassure them, sensing their frustration and worry. "I'll be fine. Besides, I sense that most of them are sleeping anyway."

"I didn't think they ever slept."

Hamilton said, "They are but men, Darius, however monstrous they make themselves up to be."

Capian warned, "Don't underestimate them, Hamilton. No one knows what power they truly possess. You say they are just men, but you may be wrong."

Darius said, "But how do you plan to get in?"

"Through the front door." Hamilton smiled grimly, as he reached out and touched the mind of one of the Red Priests guarding the entrance, implanting the suggestion that he had heard something, and must investigate.

"What are you—?" Darius began.

"Look!" Capian hissed.

Hamilton said, "He comes."

They watched the Red Priest warily approach their position.

"I'm not sure Sorde could even do that!" Capian said, staring in amazement at Hamilton.

But the Red Priest came, and when he walked around the boulder, out of sight of the entrance, they dispatched him quickly and silently.

As Hamilton quickly donned the black robes and scooped up the wooden staff, Capian said, "If you're not out by dawn, we're coming in after you."

Hamilton clapped him quietly on the shoulder. "I sincerely hope that will not be necessary. If I'm not back by dawn, it'll probably be too late."

They wished him luck, and he made the attempt.

He walked calmly, purposefully around the boulder toward the dark orifice waiting for him, hungrily it seemed. As he approached, he scanned the *jii* of the four men guarding the entrance. He sensed a variety of emotions from them, but predominantly boredom. He projected indifference at them as he neared. They must not ask him any questions, because, if forced to speak, his tongue would certainly betray him. He could not hope to simulate the vocal distortion caused by their split tongues. Therefore obscurity was his ally. Then it occurred to him that if he could read their auras, was it not possible they could also read his? A flash of panic quickly suppressed. One of the Red Priests cocked his head toward Hamilton at just that moment. His suspicions were correct. The Red Priests were quite aura-sensitive. He shackled his outward emotions into complete control, and projected boredom, indifference, to mask any deeper truths from them. If their suspicions were in the least aroused, his quest would be over before it began.

He stood with them for a few moments, resuming the original man's place. Then abruptly he winced outwardly, raising a hand to his belly, as if to signify a sudden bowel pain. He turned away, into the fanged mouth, and proceeded away from them, into the orange glow within. As he walked away stiffly, he sensed behind him that their reaction was mostly indifference, from one of them a flash of curiosity. Then he hurried away.

He was inside. The passageway sloped down into a wide, brightly lit tunnel, sconces of torches and glowcrystals spaced evenly along the finely cut stone walls. Stone archways of black and red marble supported the hewn ceiling. Once out of sight of the entrance, around an intersection in the corridor, he began to move more quickly. He did not even need to pull out the Key to tell him in which direction the other Key lay. It lay below, deep, deep into the roots of the mountain. The air was cool and dank, smoky from the torches. The hallways were empty. Hamilton had seen no one as yet except the guards outside. But he must be quick, or his absence from the guard post would cause suspicion before very long.

He found a spiral stairwell leading down, which he took, and found himself in another corridor like the one above, with several others branching from it. But still he felt the downward pull, like an instinctual urge. Far down the long passage, he saw a lone black figure walking, apparently oblivious to Hamilton's presence. Nevertheless Hamilton wasted no time in getting out of his sight until the man was gone down one of the branching tunnels.

As Hamilton traversed this passageway, he saw that the branching tunnels were quite narrow, lined with alcoves concealed by heavy cloth hangings. He spotted the lone Red Priest again as the figure stopped before one of these alcoves, stretched his arms as if preparing for sleep, lifted one of the hangings aside, and stepped out of sight. All these branching tunnels were the Red Priests' living quarters. Hamilton let out a deep breath. How many hundred of them could there be? He shrank to pose an answer to his own question, and hurried on, looking for another path downward.

He found what he sought, a broad, elaborately carved spiral stairwell leading downward, and passing into the next level down was like stepping into another world, part of Hell itself. The areas above had been rather surprisingly normal, but here, here was the evil he had envisioned, but he had had no idea.

Everywhere, skulls. Human skulls. Thousands upon thousands, covering the walls from floor to ceiling. The floor was flagged with blood red marble, worn into smooth trenches by the passage of countless feet. The air stank of blood and death and decay, and Hamilton's sensitive perceptions forced a shudder of nausea through him as centuries of leaden evil fell down upon him. He faltered for a moment, trying to regain his bearings, his sense of purpose almost lost in the wave of oppressive violence.

The sound of moans brought him around. He listened for a moment. These were not moans of agony, as he expected when he had recognized them. Moans of pleasure, faint cries of moist ecstasy. A horrified curiosity drove him to seek out the source of the sounds, and he found them.

The tunnel of skulls passed beside a great hall, with a high vaulted ceiling and stone columns of pure black. The floor of the great hall was a sea of brightly colored cushions and writhing bodies, naked and twisted into contorted beasts of pure lust. The miasma of musky smells was heavy in the smoky air. Scented oils and incense and carnal pleasure. Those in the room were completely oblivious to their horrified voyeur. The oiled bodies thrashed and shuddered and convulsed with pleasure.

Then Hamilton saw the chains, the shackles. Black robes lay scattered about everywhere, and the naked women were bound with fine silver chains. All of them. And as Hamilton watched, he saw their eyes, glazed, dull and emotionless. Their physical pleasure was real he knew, as he saw climaxes ripple across the features of several women, but he saw no life in them, and worst of all, he could sense none. Why this was he could only guess, but he knew that their bodies, these female receptacles of the Red Priests' vile seed, existed only for pleasure and breeding, with no lives existing outside this pleasure chamber.

Then he saw and scented the blood. Blood on some of the faces and the lips of males and females alike, on the breasts and limbs and organs, coming from the wounds caused by teeth or by tiny silver daggers they wore around their necks. Blood bright on the pale flesh, blood on the pillows. Hamilton felt bile suddenly rising in his throat, and his hand rose to his mouth. He restrained his impulse to leap into the room, killing everyone within, the Red Priests for their diabolical actions, and to end the misery of those poor women who were already lost.

He stared in horrified disbelief for he knew not how long. Then he saw on the far end of the hall several score motionless female figures, sleeping it seemed, recovering, and in another small area he saw several men shedding their black robes, preparing for their turns.

Two of the men noticed him suddenly, turning to fully look at him, their pale flesh gleaming in the smoky dimness. Another rush of panic. He quickly took his hand from his mouth, bowed to them and hurried away, trying to leave that chamber of horror behind him. Again his mind floundered for a purpose as his legs struggled to carry him away, and it was the final Key's insistent tugging that cleared his mind again.

He found himself at the entrance to another chamber similar in construction to the one he had just fled, with the tall black columns and high, vaulted ceiling. But this room was empty. The only furnishing was a black stone dais topped with an altar at the far end, with a scarlet tapestry hanging behind it. Glowcrystals lined the walls, brightly lighting the cavernous interior. The floor was a pattern of black and red flagstones, worn unevenly smooth by countless feet.

The Key was here. So close. The final piece. He could feel it calling him.

He padded softly into the cathedral, sending out his mind in search of the location of the Key and any Red Priests who might discover his presence, and he did his best to ignore the stored vibrations of centuries of death and torture that clung to the stone itself. The Key's call grew stronger as he approached the altar at the far end of the room.

Then the Red Priest was there.

"At last you bring the rest of the Keys to us," the Red Priest said, calmly, with a blunt edge of arrogance.

He had simply appeared, standing behind the altar as if he had been there all along.

Hamilton stared for a moment, saying nothing. Then Sorde's blade was in his hand, and he was moving swiftly, steadily toward the Red Priest. His robe was pure blood red, with strips of black leather hanging around his neck down the front of his habit. The deep scarlet hood obscured his entire head, and his hands were lost in the heavy folds.

"Stop!" the Red Priest said, his split tongue distorting the words. "You will never leave here alive."

Hamilton said nothing, but moved toward him warily, sword at the ready.

"Join us," the Red Priest said, unmoving, unfazed by Hamilton's approach. "Join us, and together we will topple Uhr, and you alone will be the new Uhr, ruler of Irth, god of all you survey. You have the power. You are The One."

Hamilton said, "I have no interest in godhood, or power. I want only what is right and just. The death of Uhr, and you." He was drawing closer, and now he noticed the symbol sewn into the tapestry directly behind the Red Priest. "You would use me to betray your all-powerful Master?"

The High Red Priest stood bisecting the black-slitted eye embroidered in the huge tapestry.

Hamilton sensed him smiling. The Red Priest said, "We use him as long as it suits us."

"Are you certain the great Uhr is not using you?"

"Silence. You have no idea the power he has given us. He asks little of us in return."

"Only fealty, subservience," Hamilton said. He was close now, almost within striking distance, and still the Red Priest had not moved.

"I shall ask you only one last time. Will you join us?"

"Never," said Hamilton, and he lunged forward to strike the man down.

His blade sliced deep into the crimson robes, and they dissolved into smoke, fanned by the passage of his hissing blade, instantly dissipating. Hamilton cast about, looking for his adversary.

"Here, One." The voice came from the other side of the dais.

Hamilton spun, and saw the crimson folds whirl with motion. His eye caught the flash of spinning silver in the air, and he reflexively raised his blade in defense. The singing silver ring glanced off his blade, whizzed a hair's breadth past his left ear. He almost breathed a sigh of relief until he felt the blood running. The weapon had not missed after all, and had been so sharp he had not felt the cut.

"Hah! You Eagle Knights think our martial skills have stagnated! You have not tasted the art of the gaebolg." The High Red Priest dropped into a crouch, and produced a wicked looking weapon from within his robes. It consisted of two half-staves, each about three feet long, connected by a foot-long chain, with vicious steel spikes and hooks bristling up and down the lengths of wood. "We have our own brand of killing."

Hamilton taunted, "Aye, a dagger in the back!" He sensed the Priest's emotions flare with anger at his words. So he decided to press. "You and all your order are nothing but scum. You enslave women to use their bodies. And you take their children, products of your vile seed, and you split their tongues and brand their heads. Do you perhaps eat them, too?"

The Red Priest leaped at Hamilton with his terrible weapon, his gaebolg. Hamilton shuffled quickly back, waiting to see what sort of technique the Red Priest would use with this bizarre weapon. The Priest struck first with one half, then the other in combination. Hamilton caught one half easily, but barely escaped being ensnared by the ghastly barbed hooks.

At close range, Hamilton was able to more closely examine the weapon, and his warrior's logic constructed a technique of use that went with the weapon's design. The long reach and flexibility of the staves was to use the hooks to their best advantage, by reaching for the enemy, embedding the hooks in his flesh, and drawing him closer for the finishing blow. The hooks and spikes could also be used to trap and break a bladed weapon such as a sword. This weapon was designed for killing Eagle Knights.

But he had little time to contemplate as the High Red Priest drove him back across the floor of the hall. The man's hood had fallen back, revealing his ghostly pale features. Eyes blazing with hatred and rimmed in red, mouth with its thin cruel lips twisted into a savage snarl. His face was old, gouged by the years with hard, deep lines.

Hamilton taunted him further, his blade dancing in defense as he writhed and dodged, careful not to be caught by the gaebolg. "What, have you not seen the sun in years? Do you fear it so? Does your depravity fear the light of day? You look dead already!"

They had fought back to the center of the chamber, the sounds of their blows echoing hollowly in the cavernous chamber. Hamilton heard the Red Priest's breath rasping in and out of him like an old bellows, and he knew that the man was tiring rapidly. His chance would come soon. The opening might last only an instant, but it would come.

Then the Red Priest stopped a few steps away.

He rested one half of the weapon on the floor as he slowly reached into his robe.

"Hah!" he shrieked, his voice shrill with the arrogance of victory. The dust hit Hamilton full in the face.

Searing pain on his flesh, in his eyes, acrid bitterness in his mouth. Tears burst like waterfalls from his burning eyes, and he heard the Red Priest coming. He was not ready. He was going to die unless he acted, so he did.

He ran. Spitting and spewing the vile taste of the dust from his mouth, he ran away, and heard the deadly whisper of the gaebolg in the space where his head had been an instant before. He sensed the Red Priest's furious pursuit, heard the roar of rage and frustration as he chased Hamilton about the subterranean cathedral, swinging the gaebolg madly before him. Hamilton managed to stay just out of his reach, rubbing at his blinded eyes. After perhaps thirty heartbeats, the pain was diminishing, but his eyes still watered so fiercely he could not see. He sensed his position within the room, sensed the location of the Red Priest, prepared himself for a brief moment, then stopped and spun, eyes closed, sword at the ready.

"Now, bastard," Hamilton said. "Come. Face the true power of The One."

The Red Priest stopped, stunned. Hamilton sensed him clearly, precisely, sensed his agitation, his fear. Then he attacked. Eyes squeezed shut against the tears, Hamilton leaped and slashed, danced and cut, feinted and kicked, driving the priest back, up the dais steps toward the altar. The Red Priest wheezed and gasped, desperately trying to fend off Hamilton's lethally accurate strikes. But his guard faltered for only a split second, then it was over. Hamilton's blade slipped under his defense. The incredibly keen edge Sorde had fashioned so long ago split the red robes with hardly a whisper, spilling the Red Priest's entrails in a deluge of gore. He groaned and fell, toppling down the black steps of the dais.

For a long moment, Hamilton centered himself again, regaining his breath, trying to see through his burning eyes. He spat more of the acrid bitterness from his mouth. As the heat of battle began to cool, Hamilton once again felt the pulling, calling of the final Key. It fairly screamed for him.

He walked up the steps toward the tapestry. Dimly through the tears he could see the blood red hanging, and with his mind he sensed the door behind it. Flinging the tapestry aside, he opened the door, sensing the passageway beyond. Orange torch light was a blurry flicker in his vision as he entered this passage. It ended quickly in a small chamber. Hamilton could use his eyes now to distinguish his surroundings. It was obviously the High Priest's living quarters. A small but luxurious bed, swathed all in silk and linen. A large wardrobe, filled with dozens of different robes. A chest at the foot of the bed. But the Key was not here. Not in this room.

Then he saw the narrow doorway, half-hidden by the shadow of the looming wardrobe. In an instant he had crossed the room, and passed through this doorway. Beyond the doorway was a tiny chamber with close, rough-hewn ceiling and walls. An altar sat against the far wall, and black candles burned bright red all about the smoky room. There on the altar was a grinning human head, long-since dead, staring into space with its empty sockets. A scarlet circle was painted around it on the surface of the black stone altar. Its mouth hung agape. Wisps of moldy hair straggled from the wrinkled parchmentlike scalp, and shreds of rotting flesh hung in loose tatters from the ancient face. The Key was there.

He looked down at his chest, and saw the other three Keys blazing inside his robes, their light shining out like a three-pointed star unwilling to be pent up any longer. They sought their final mate. Then Hamilton saw a glow emerge from the mouth of the hideous head.

He approached, and reached for the skull, closer, closer to that open mouth, those dreadfully sharp teeth. Nearer, nearer that terrible orifice. He suddenly withdrew his hand, taken by the feeling that those jaws would close upon his hand and bite it off if it entered.

Then with a snort of disgust, he whacked the head away with the back of his hand, off the altar. It hit the floor with a sound like old wood. There was a small cavity in the wall behind where the skull had rested, and into this he reached, grasping the small bundle of black silk that rested there. Then swiftly he slipped the final Key out of the silk and joined it with its companions. With a blazing flash of light, the Key to the Ivory Star was complete.

The light faded, leaving the four-pointed, dagger-like crystal resting in his hand. A whoop of joy rose in his breast, which died an instant later.

A faint word, whispered from behind him, caused his muscles to stiffen, and the familiar terrible paralysis gripped him once again, this time stronger than ever before. Slowly, involuntarily, he began to turn and face the person standing at the entrance to the shrine.

The High Red Priest stood in the opening, one hand outstretched toward Hamilton, his fingertips flickering with fiery red lightning, his other hand clutching at his dangling entrails, trying to keep them inside his wide-open belly.

"You will bring the final Key to me," he hissed, his voice cold and deadly.

Hamilton approached slowly, his body convulsing as he fought the spell. His sword fell from his hand, clattering uselessly on the floor. He clutched the Key so tightly its edges dug into his flesh. But as he approached, he slowly conserved and gathered his will. He would have perhaps one chance to break the Red Priest's grip, one chance to act. Perhaps.

Hamilton focused his vision on the flickering light at the Priest's fingertips, using it to focus his will. He was now within arm's reach of the Priest's clawed hands, and he acted.

His own will smashed into that of the Priest, smashed into it again, with all the force and will and purpose he could muster. The Priest's eyes bulged, and he staggered as if struck by a physical blow. Then his grip relaxed, and Hamilton leaped forward with the Key. The High Priest screamed in terror as Hamilton caught him by the throat, squeezing off the sound mercilessly, finally, and drove the long point of the Key into the High Priest's breast, piercing his putrid heart. The High Priest gasped his last breath and sank to the floor.

Hamilton wasted no time in secreting the Key within his own robes, snatching up his blade, and moving to get out. As he stepped out from behind the tapestry, two more Red Priests stood waiting for him on the dais, staves at the ready. He sensed their surprise at his escape from the High Priest as they stepped back onto their heels, and he used this opportunity to make quick work of them. As they fell, only then did he see the rest of them waiting for him on the outer floor of the cathedral.

All of them. A sea of black hoods.

A wave of hatred washed over Hamilton, dizzying him, sending him to his knees with nausea.

Then Hamilton saw a small trail of sparks arching through the air from the rear of the hall. Puzzled, he watched the lazy trail until it landed among the Red Priests nearest him, nearest the dais. In a moment of eternity some of the Red Priests turned to look at what this thing was that had fallen among them. Then the explosion ripped through the air.

Hamilton was thrown back against the stone altar by the force of the blast. A wave of heat struck him, along with stench of seared flesh and the screams of the dying. Stones and dust began to fall from the ceiling, striking down Red Priests left standing after the explosion. Chaos. They scattered, seeking shelter from the hail of stones.

And Hamilton ran. He ran through the smoke and flame and stench and dust, knocking disoriented figures blindly out of his way. He stood at the entrance to the cathedral now choking on smoke and dust, and skidded to a halt as two Red Priests stood in his way, completely unaffected by the carnage, destruction and confusion inside.

His sword instantly lanced out at the chest of the nearest one, and was struck aside by another blade similar to his.

One of them tore back his hood. "Hamilton, it's us!" Capian cried.

"Come!" Darius hissed before he spun and led their flight back down the tunnel of skulls.

Four Red Priests on the stairs up from this level died by Darius's hand, completely unable to stand against his expert blade.

Hamilton asked in amazement as they ran, "Where did you get such a thing as that explosive!"

"Eagle Knights have known about mixing brimstone and coal and such for centuries."

"And you never used it?"

"If we often used it, Uhr would have soon realized what we were doing and stolen it from us. He would have used it against us. Therefore, it has been among the most secret of Eagle Knight magicks..." He paused to cut down a bewildered Red Priest emerging from his sleeping alcove as they passed by it on the second level, barreling for the next passage up.

They reached ground level without another mishap, and headed for the way out. They were almost there. The fanged mouth was in sight now, with its eight guardians lying motionless on the ground in the opening. They leaped over the cooling corpses, out into the night, and Hamilton let out another whoop of exultation.

As their legs pumped fiercely, carrying them swiftly away from the chaos within the Red Priests' lair, Hamilton hollered and wept and whooped for joy. He had the Keys! Next, the Ivory Star!

Chapter 26

"Fool!"

The black-gauntleted hand smashed across his face like a hammer. The small, misshapen man spun completely around and fell backwards to the ground. With a tiny, gnarled hand he wiped the flow of blood from his crushed lips, staring up at his attacker, his entire body quivering with fear and rage.

"But—" Lord Sneev began, as the ebon-plated Slayer moved toward him.

The malevolent blood-red eye painted on the dull, black breastplate skewered him with its gaze.

"Silence, maggot," growled the towering Slayer. Two blood-shot stone-gray eyes flogged him from the cold eye-slits. A pair of mighty ram's horns curled away from the sides of the helmet. He was well over six feet tall, with spiked plate armor black as the depths of Hell, the flat blank faceplate slitted for eyes and mouth. A series of golden bands in the upper left corner of the breast plate designated his rank of general. His huge hand fingered the hilt of the massive bastard sword at his side.

The Slayer's voice sounded like gravel on old boot leather. "You are an imbecile, Sneev. Our master wants Valerion dead before the Great Conjunction, and you sit on your arse doing nothing." With a speed that belied the general's massive size and armored state, he reached down and snatched the trembling Lord Sneev off the ground, drug him outside, and pointed at the royal blue morning sky, at the three Day Stars which were now within a few weeks of convergence.

"But, Master," Sneev whined, squirming in the Slayer's grip, "weeks ago, I detached a dozen men after materials to rebuild the bridge! They haven't returned."

The Slayer general produced a coarse burlap bag crusted with a rusty brown stain, and tossed it at Sneev's feet. "Here is the head of your captain in charge of that detachment. We found it mounted on the head of a spear at the edge of Ryvan Marsh, along with all your men." The Slayer cast him away, sending Sneev sprawling in the dirt.

Sneev swallowed hard, breathing heavily. After a moment he struggled to his feet, his stoop more pronounced than ever. He said, "That bridge must be rebuilt to take the castle."

Stone-like silence was his answer.

"I'll send more men after materials."

"No," the Slayer general said. "Fortunately for you, the Master knew of this, and sent more materials with us. Your men will begin work on the bridge immediately." Then he spun on his spurred heel and stamped away, his heavy steel boots crunching the old snow and frozen mud. Then he paused, turning. "The Master grows very displeased with you, Sneev. I would advise you not to fail him again."

From the gatehouse tower Valerion and Garth watched the heavy wagons being drawn through the rubble of Lakeside toward the far side of the bridge, and unloaded of their cargoes of wood and binding materials.

"They're going to rebuild the bridge," Garth said.

"Not surprising," Valerion said.

"I suppose not. But what can we do to stop them?"

Valerion shrugged, stroking his mustache. "I wonder why they haven't tried to rebuild it sooner. Once that bridge is rebuilt, nothing but steel and blood will hold Uhr's dogs at bay."

They said nothing for a while as they watched wagon after wagon being unloaded.

Then Valerion said, "Father?"

"Aye, son?"

"Why did you leave, so many years ago?"

Garth stiffened, and spat over the battlement to clear his throat. He took his time answering. "I merely felt it was time to hand you the reins."

Valerion turned to him, "But I was hardly beyond twenty summers, newly married, with a baby son. I was not ready."

"No man is ever ready. Must we speak of this now?" Garth's voice was pleading.

Valerion looked back out over the shore, rubbing his corded forearms. "I have waited this long to know an answer to that. I had hoped that you would tell me on your own, when you were ready. Now I fear with the Slayers here, we may get little chance to speak again. I will not go meet the rest of Arnor's sons without knowing, knowing why you left."

Garth sighed. Then he said, slowly, "I thought you were ready. Besides, I was growing old and weak. You were young and strong. I felt you could rule better than I."

"Dung!" Valerion snorted. "You're as fit to rule

today as the day you left. The years have been kind to you. I am your son, and I deserve the truth."

Garth pounded his fist on the stone merlon in anger and shame. "Because I was afraid," he said quietly. Then he added quickly, "But I was not afraid just for me. Oh, nay! I feared for you and Ilone and Capian as well. That was why I did it."

Valerion looked at him.

He continued, "Do you remember Gervais, my old house master?"

Valerion nodded. "Aye."

"Then you remember how close we were, like brothers. There was no 'lord' or 'servant' between us. He served me out of love. I gave him and his family a home out of love." He paused. "Do you remember when Gervais disappeared?"

Valerion replied, "I was not there, but, aye, I remember the time. I was with your army chasing a pack of bandits across the Frontier. He disappeared without a trace. But what has Gervais's disappearance to do with yours?"

"I killed him."

Valerion stared at him, mouth agape.

Garth gazed at him evenly, eyes like gray stone. His voice cracked with anger as he spoke, "One night I was attacked while I slept. My side bears a nasty scar as proof. I fought with the man in the dark, took the dagger with which he'd tried to pierce my heart, and killed him with it. When I finally got the lamp lit, to my horror and shame I saw that the man on the floor was Gervais, my closest and dearest friend."

Valerion took a deep breath, looking away, "I am sorry, Father."

"I had just slain that man who had been like the brother I never had. When I removed the knife from his chest, I saw, etched upon the blade, a single slitted eye, Uhr's symbol, painted red by Gervais's blood. I wept until nearly dawn. Finally in the tender hours I wrapped him up in a blanket and threw both him and the wretched dagger into the lake. I threatened the watchman with torture and death if he ever spoke. From that day forward, I trusted no one, in constant fear for my life. If Uhr's evil could corrupt the love between Gervais and I, it could do it with anyone, even you. I knew that Uhr was merely taunting me, trying to provoke me. But I did nothing, for a while. I feared for you and your family, and I feared you as well, for what you could become. Ere long I was half-mad. That's no way to rule. I thought by leaving, Uhr would spare you and your family, and I could go somewhere to recover from the madness that ate at me. So I fled, while the fishes picked at Gervais's bones at the bottom of Crystal Lake."

Garth sighed, long and deep and quavering.

Valerion opened his mouth to speak, but thought better of it, and remained silent.

Both Sons of Arnor stood speechless for a long time.

Finally Valerion said, "Then why did you return?"

Garth thought for a moment before he answered, "I wanted to see my son once again before I died. I have lived in a secluded shack on the edge of Ophidia for a long time. Long, lonely years. And a long time to forget. I forgot about a great many things. But then The One came to me, and damn him, he brought it all back. I wanted to see my family again. I wanted to see Armond and Dynorr and Lakeside again. And I wanted to see the man my son had become. But above all, I wanted to see The One crush Uhr into the dirt, and my son and his allies do the same to Uhr's armies. What man would hide and miss the decision of a world's fate?"

Valerion smiled ironically. "Here we are," he said, spreading his arms, "my mighty army trapped within these walls, 'allies' no where in sight."

"Aye, I do see it."

Silence for a time.

Garth said, "I have decided that you are the better man."

Valerion stared at him. "How is that?"

"I fled when frightened. You did not. You stayed to protect your people and your family."

"True," Valerion said, "but then you must have been a magnificent father to have raised me so well." His eyes roamed the shore as he twisted his mustache.

"Oh," Garth said, surprised, "I suppose so."

They both looked out over the destruction on the shore.

They never spoke together like this again.

The Armondians watched helplessly from the fortress as the Ophidians constructed large mantlets and put them in place to protect the bridge-workers from bow fire. By midafternoon the mantlets were complete, and the reconstruction of the bridge had begun.

Fortine joined Valerion and Garth on the wall as evening neared. "Damn!" Disappointment was clear in his voice. "Uhr's Teats, but they're moving faster than I'd anticipated. At the rate they're going, they'll have a fully sound bridge in a couple of days."

Valerion clapped him on the shoulder. "Fear not, my friend. Your work was far from vain. It kept them from our gates for weeks. It did what it was meant to do."

Fortine grunted.

Garth said, "Look at that fog rolling in."

They turned to look at where Garth pointed, toward the western end of the lake. The setting sun turned the low-lying fog into a golden mist spreading swiftly across the surface of the lake, lying against the water like a foamy blanket.

"Boil my liver, look at that!" Fortine said, "I've never seen fog move so fast!"

Valerion stood and watched, and felt fear clutching his heart, the same fear he had felt when he realized that the terrible blizzard was Uhr's doing, the same fear he had felt when he saw his people, his wife, dying from the terrible disease that Uhr had inflicted upon them.

By nightfall the fog had engulfed them, blotting out all view of the bridge construction. The fog was so thick they could hardly see the ground from the top of the watchtowers. And a terrible chill accompanied the fog, an unnatural, bone-numbing chill that was not cold, but nevertheless sucked all warmth and comfort from their bones, leaving them shivering and scared. As the darkness thickened, the Armondians saw dimly the orange glow of the Slayers' watch fire near the bridge repair, barely visible through the thick mist.

The days passed with agonizing slowness. Never once did the fog thin. Sounds of construction echoed eerily through the impenetrable mist. What the Slayers were building Valerion could only guess. Catapults probably, or ballistae, Fortine thought, perhaps a battering ram, certainly ladders. The sounds of construction continued through the endless nights of waiting for something to happen.

Damn this waiting! Valerion thought. Every day the inevitable attack was delayed, was another day they got to live. But every day had become a hell unto itself, a hell of fear and foreboding and waiting. He was tired of waiting, and he knew his people were as well. Almost better to die and get it over with than face another day of waiting. He hadn't worn his armor so much in twenty years as he had in the last months. He had gotten used to it again, but it was heavy on him now, a burden. When he'd had his youth, it was nothing for him to wear it for days at a time, out on forays against the Frontier bandits. But that was a long time ago. And now he was just waiting.

Then, one dim and chilly morning, the waiting was over.

Valerion stood upon the wall, watching, waiting like he had done so many times before. Deathly silence lay like a shroud over the air itself. A sudden premonition thrilled through him, a chilly hand of foreboding whispering over the back of his neck.

Then he heard something, heavily muffled by the fog. He strained to hear, but it was like listening through a closed door. He cursed as he again heard it, but still could not identify it. Silence.

There it came again. Quietly he ordered ballistae and crossbows cocked and loaded. He sent a man for Robinton and Fortine, all the while staring into the mist, seeking some sign of movement. He ordered his Red Dragons to man the walls and towers above the gate. More unidentifiable sounds echoed from the shore. The Armondians' nerves drew taut like bowstrings.

Then came a muffled clangor.

"Sound the alarm!" he bellowed. "Archers ready!" He settled his helm upon his head, buckled it, shifted his shield down onto his arm, drew his faithful old sword.

Robinton stood next to him. "They're on the bridge."

Valerion nodded. "At last!"

"Aye, my lord," Robinton hissed. "Battle!"

Now there came a deep ominous rumbling, as if something ponderously large rolled across the stone. Valerion and all his men stared into the dense, impenetrable fog. White-knuckled hands clutched weapons with the strength born of fear.

Valerion felt the cold sweat running down his face inside the cold steel helmet. The mist was a shapeless, featureless gray wall. Then a huge black shape loomed in the emptiness, a vague, amorphous shadow that rumbled on the stone like a dragon's growl, moving forward like some dreadful juggernaut. Every man stood transfixed in fear and awe, when suddenly a storm of arrows, crossbow bolts and ballista-hurled javelins slashed over the top of the wall. Men screamed and fell, their bodies pierced by steel and wood. Splintering wood filled the air as the shafts flew apart against the stone battlements.

Then the shape on the bridge heaved into full view, as it crossed the creaking wood of the repaired section.

From somewhere in the gray mist Fortine's voice roared, "A siege tower! Bring the pitch, quickly!"

Valerion bellowed, "Reinforcements, ready!"

Robinton cried out, "Archers, wait for a target!"

They had not long to wait. The front of the siege tower opened slightly downward at the top, well above the highest point of the castle wall. Valerion's archers fired, sending a storm of arrows and quarrels into the small aperture. Another volley of missile fire from the shore raked the battlements.

The massive tower rolled inexorably nearer, pushed from behind by scores of men. It was a moving monolith, waiting to vomit its cargo of killers onto the wall.

"Burn that tower!" Valerion roared.

Flaming torches and pots of viscous black tar were brought swiftly. Archers dipped their shafts in the sticky pitch, and set them afire with the torches. Blazing arrows shot across the ever-narrowing gap to the wooden tower. When they struck, the dying flames told of how the wood had been soaked with water, and wet hides stretched across the front for just such protection.

Valerion's innards heaved when he saw what kind of skins they had used.

Human hides, nicely stretched and tanned and cured.

"Steady, men!" he cried. "Screw up your courage now! Get ready to fill the gates of Hell with Slayers."

The massive tower ground to a halt at the edge of the gap left by the castle's raised drawbridge. Then the top of the tower fell open, the door forming a perfect bridge as it clunked down onto the top of the wall, and Slayers bristling with spikes and weaponry poured across. Five of Valerion's men were pushed screaming from the walk with the first mad rush. And before Valerion could speak the curses, six Slayers stood on the gatehouse wall, hacking and slashing and bludgeoning and stabbing, clearing the way for more.

Valerion leaped toward the fray, bellowing like a bull. "At them, lads! Their blood is as red as ours! Let it flow like a cataract!" He bounded to the fore, chopped his broadsword into a chink between black helm and ebon shoulder plate. Blood gushed over the black armor, staining the stones of the walkway a dark crimson. Valerion's sudden kill brought his men alive. The five remaining Slayers did not last long under twenty swords and axes and spears.

But still more Slayers poured down onto the bridge, battling for purchase on the wall above the gate and drawbridge. Valerion's men died like flies before the rampaging killers.

Then through the fog came a distant cry. "Aieee! The boats! The boats! They come!"

Valerion shot a glance at the sound through the rapidly thinning fog. There, to his utter horror, he saw several black-spiked figures climbing over the wall of the middle ward behind them. Valerion roared a curse. Most of his men were at the gate. The Slayers over there dispersed quickly, unopposed, dispatching all they met with terrible ease.

"Robinton!" he cried over the din of battle. "Get some Dragons over there!" He did not bother to look and see if his order had been obeyed, involved as he was in tugging his blade from a Slayer's mangled throat. Almost immediately a score of Red Dragons stormed across the outer ward to meet this new threat; in fact, perhaps a greater immediate threat than the one they faced here, at the gate.

For a few seconds, the bridge from the siege tower was empty. Suddenly one of his men leaped up onto the ramp carrying a pot of flaming pitch. He rushed up the ramp screaming a wild Frontier war-cry, and flung the pot into the gaping mouth of the tower. The blazing tar spattered throughout the interior of the tower, burning viciously. The man looked back at his brothers in arms, astounded by his success, grinning. He whooped again in victory, and never saw the three burning spears shoot from the thick black smoke choking the opening. He screamed in agony and fell, clutching vainly at the flaming shafts protruding from his body. His killers advanced, ripping their smoldering weapons from his body, which they kicked into the lake below. Droplets of liquid flame clung like fiery leeches to their armor.

The defenders killed these last finally, at a tremendous price in blood. But no more Slayers came. The tower burned fiercely now, set irrevocably ablaze by that one selfless soul.

Valerion shook his head, immensely pleased that the tower was burning. And yet, he didn't even know that man's name. A small victory, he thought, then turned his attention to the distant wall of the middle ward, where Robinton and the Red Dragons fought desperately to stem the steady flow of Slayers coming over the wall. Even now the screams of women and children came faintly like wraiths from the distance as they were murdered in their homes.

Valerion raised his ensanguined blade to signal his orders, "Red Dragons, to the middle ward! The rest of us shall keep things here!"

Angus MacTavish sat up in bed, wincing. What was that noise? The clangor of battle! What, were they being overrun? He gained his feet, and saw a young page racing by. "Hold there, boy! What's happening?"

Wide-eyed and trembling and hardly able to speak, the boy replied, "Slayers…in the middle ward. Gates're closing."

Angus snarled a curse. "Fetch me my arms, lad! Be quick!"

The boy nodded solemnly, and off he went to get them.

Just as Angus was donning his chain mail coat, a small figure came running up to him. Nessa threw her arms around him, and pressed her face against his steel chest. She turned her gaze into his face, icy fear shimmering in her lovely eyes.

He read her mind in her beautiful face. "I must," he said softly, "I am a Red Dragon. I am needed out there, more than I need be here."

Her eyes glistened with crystal tears as she clutched him tight. "Forgive me," she said, "for everything."

He smiled, took her delicate head in his strong hands, and kissed her gently on the mouth. Her body molded to his for an exquisite instant.

Then he was gone, striding swiftly away, battle ax clenched in a mighty hand, battered shield slung on his muscular arm. She watched him, rooted where she stood. She had never been kissed like that before. *Her* man had never gone into battle before. Her heart thumped in her breast like a herd of wild stallions as she watched him go, tears of joy and fear streaming down her face.

Angus persuaded the guards at the gate of the inner ward to open the gates to let him out. He stood guard at the outside of the gate while they got the gates closed again. Then he ran across the ward, seeing the defenders battling fiercely against the ebon-armored invaders. Running as fast as his wounded side would allow, he made for the wall, but stopped upon hearing a woman's scream from a nearby cottage.

He saw the door ajar, and leaped inside, instantly surveying the scene. The old cobbler lay on the stone floor, his brains spilling out of his split skull. The Slayer now advanced upon the old cobbler's cowering wife, his blood-smeared mace upraised.

Then she glimpsed Angus creeping up behind

the Slayer. Her gaze betrayed him, and the Slayer spun. Angus's ax fell full upon the blood-shot red eye painted on his enemy's chest, cleaving apart the thick breast plate. Angus ripped the ax-head free, barely in time to avoid a devastating blow from the Slayer's mace. The two faced each other, blood gushing from the Slayer's terrible wound. The Slayer attacked, his mace moaning. Angus caught the blow on his raised shield and struck back. The ax-head rang on the side of the Slayer's helmet. The helm tore from the Slayer's head, and clanked onto the floor, bouncing away.

Angus stared at the man's face. He had been half-expecting some misshapen horror of a visage, but what he saw unnerved him even more. The man's face was normal in every respect, maybe even handsome, save that there was no life in it. No anger, no malice, nothing. The eyes were blank and dull, and the passionless expression was carved of pale marble. The Slayer's features did not twitch as he raised his mace for another blow.

Angus cried out in horror, and buried the head of his ax between those ghastly eyes.

Not stopping to acknowledge the old woman's sobbing thanks, he raced out the door, bound for battle. Running painfully up the parapet steps, he gained the walk, and barreled toward the melee. A towering Slayer suddenly struck down his combatant, and broke from the pack of straining muscle, running directly down the walk toward Angus. Angus did not slacken his pace as he raised his ax and set his shield. The two titans met with a resounding crash and flurry of staggering blows. They backed away from each other, heavy breath hissing, steaming in the cool morning air. The Slayer gripped a sword in each fist as he waited for an opening. Then Angus dove forward with a whirlwind of blows. Metal crashed and rang and groaned. When they separated, the Slayer's black plating was scratched and dented in a dozen places, and its wearer stood on shaking legs. Angus sensed his momentary edge, and leaped in once again. His next blow would have decapitated his antagonist, but the black spikes along the shoulder ridge deflected the blow. Angus failed to see one of his enemy's swords slip below his shield. The broadsword's point grated across the chain mail protecting his injured side. Bolts of fantastic pain shot through his body. Streaks of blinding light shot through his vision. He staggered backward, shield raised weakly in defense. The massive Slayer strode forward to finish the job, when suddenly a single arrow slipped beneath the coal black helm. The Slayer spun and collapsed in a heap. Angus glanced about for the source of the arrow. Sigmunnd, the Red Dragon bowmaster, saluted him from the ground. Angus returned the gesture.

Then he looked over the wall at the lake below. He saw three barges, laden with scores of Uhr's killers, grappled to the stone of the islet upon which the fortress rested. Hooked ladders stretched up the wall from where they rested on the decks. The thawing waters of Crystal Lake seemed particularly calm today, as if so just for this occasion.

Angus heard Robinton's voice from nearby, "Bring pitch, quickly!"

Angus, atop the wall, standing with a group of men above a ladder, waited for the next Slayer to make the attempt. A volley of arrows from the boats drove them to cover just long enough for a Slayer to gain the walk. Before he went down, he took five defenders with him, and another Slayer had gained the walk. Now another had gained purchase, and another. Defenders fell like wheat before the scythe. Suddenly a rush of reinforcements pushed the Slayers back and beat them down to clear the walk once again.

They battled at the wall until the defenders waded in thigh-deep piles of mangled corpses, black-armored and otherwise. For every Slayer dispatched, three good men were lost. They could not hope to beat those odds for long, when they were outnumbered already.

Finally, in a moment of respite, buckets of pitch were brought. The defenders set the pitch a flame, and cast the buckets down onto the wooden barges. The pitch plastered the decks, and splattered across the dark figures upon them. The Slayers made no sounds when iron and steel grew red hot, searing the soft flesh within. The stench of burning flesh rose with the cloud of noxious black smoke from below.

But still they came on, like unfeeling demons from the depths of Hell. They felt no pain. Again the defenders beat them back. At last the ladders fell as the grapple ropes burned through and snapped, allowing the floating infernos to lazily drift away from the islet with their cargoes of sizzling bodies.

Crimson waves lapped at the rocks below. The walkway was slippery with spilled gore, buried in corpses. The assault was over at last. The siege tower was a blazing pillar of flame. The Slayers had withdrawn to the shore.

Clouds and fog were gone now. The blazing white sun shone down warmly, and Valerion and his men cheered, raising their weary arms to the vaulting sky.

Valerion removed his helmet and surveyed the destruction, his clothing and armor in tatters, his body crisscrossed by numerous small wounds.

Slayers lay everywhere like piles of slaughtered spine-rats. Blood ran in congealing rivers down the walls, across the ground. His men wearily clutched at wounds, gasped for breath, searched for friends among the dead and wounded. He ordered the Slayers' bodies thrown into the lake with their armor. Weapons were in dreadfully short supply, so they would keep those, but the armor, no matter how useful it would have been, held too much evil. Valerion didn't think any of his men would have willingly worn that terrible armor.

Robinton stepped up to his lord. "There will be many mourning mothers and fatherless children tonight."

"Aye," Valerion said, "our losses were heavy. Much heavier than theirs. Do you have an estimate?"

"Perhaps a third of our number dead or seriously wounded, my lord."

"Kavarius and his leeches will be hard-pressed."

Robinton nodded.

"But those of us who still live have survived another day, at the expense of those who did not," Valerion said, leaning heavily on his blood-slick sword. Looking up into the uncaring sky, he stared at the Day Stars. They were almost touching now. He shook his head, and went to kill any Slayers still alive among the corpses, and speak to his men who clung vainly to life.

Chapter 27

Thick gray clouds and a cold clammy mist draped the sprawling city of Arnath like an unfeeling hand. A perpetual gloom infiltrated crack and crevice, street and alley, as if in unclean communion with the blight that now scourged this once-great city. Not a soul walked the streets. Doors were barred, windows boarded shut. Filth and refuse littered the streets and gutters, and that unnatural, warmth-sucking mist soaked everything.

The people that remained, those too poor and cowed to leave, huddled in their homes like half-starved sheep, waiting for the Slayers to come for them, too, as they had for so many others. The only movement was an occasional group of mounted Slayers who seemed to be searching for any spark of life to grind out under their spurred heels. Even rats seemed to stay in hiding. Once proud, populous Arnath was now a city of ghosts, with the devil Uhr malevolently watching over this desolate place, like a canker on scarred flesh.

But in this city of ghosts moved three black-swathed wraiths, silently, quickly, like flitting shadows, ever toward the towering palace in the center of the city.

Three black-cloaked forms stood just out of

sight of the palace, in an alley that opened into the large square before the gates. The three Eagle Knights surveyed Uhr's lair.

This once-beautiful achievement of art and architecture had long since fallen into differing stages of disrepair. The awesome edifice seemed deserted, except for the spiked black figures standing like statues at its towering iron gates. Chained beside them were four huge dark beasts, half-again as large as the Slayer's standing near them, vaguely canine, lying with their massive black heads resting on monstrous paws.

Capian muttered, "Are you sure it's in *there*?"

Hamilton answered, "It's calling to me, like part of myself."

Darius peered around the corner. "You have to chose the worst places, my friend," he said dryly.

Then, as if to confirm his statement, the clopping hooves and clangor of armor and accouterments echoed across the square, past where the three Knights of the Eagles stood plastered against the shadowed wall, and a dozen mounted Slayers rode slowly by.

"Have you any plan, Hamilton?" Capian asked.

Hamilton shook his head. "Do either of you know the layout of the palace?"

Capian and Darius shook their heads.

"Then let us circle the wall, and see what we find."

They kept to the shadows and alleys of the surrounding buildings, out of sight as they skirted the palace wall. A wide street, perhaps fifty paces across, separated the palace from the common streets and buildings. The wall was thirty feet tall, of thick dark stone. Four or five sentries could be seen at any one time patrolling the top of the barrier, and periodically a small patrol rode by down the way.

Capian said, "We should wait for nightfall before we try anything."

Darius said, "The sun only just rose. Must we wait outside all day?"

Hamilton said, "The longer we remain outside, the greater the risk of being discovered, no matter what precautions we take. We should search for a hiding place."

Capian said, "That shouldn't be too difficult. It seems every building in the city is boarded up and locked, ample places for us to hide until nightfall."

Then their noses caught the faint drift of wood smoke, too faint for anyone but an Eagle Knight to detect.

They looked at one another and nodded. Eventually they traced the smoke to its source. A tiny tavern, with its front door opening into a refuse-choked alley. Its hanging sign was broken and unreadable.

Hamilton stepped up to the small wooden door, and tried the handle. It was locked. Close to the door, Hamilton's nostrils detected the smoke strongly enough for him to decide that this was indeed the source of the smoke. He heard hushed voices within. The door was too thick for him to discern the nature of those voices.

He knocked lightly.

The voices suddenly stopped.

He rapped again.

After some shuffling within, the door opened slightly, a mere crack. A single blood-shot eye stared out at him in wide-eyed astonishment. A scratchy male voice asked timidly, "Who are ye?"

Hamilton answered soothingly, "Merely three weary travelers seeking shelter. Yours is the only open door."

The old man answered, still holding the opening to a tiny crack, "I haven't yet decided if my door is open."

Hamilton said in his most friendly tone, "Please, sir. We come in peace, and will leave in peace, after nightfall. We seek only the warmth of your hearth and concealment from the eyes of the Slayers."

Suspicion still tinged the old man's voice. "How do I know you won't rob me then slit my throat?"

Hamilton replied, "If we meant you harm, we would have done it already."

The old man sighed in resignation. "I suppose you're right." The door swung inward.

The three men in black quickly slipped inside, silently as cats. The room within was small, windowless, lit only by a single tallow candle flickering upon one of the half-dozen small tables, and a mound of coals glowing warmly in the fireplace. The burning candle cast huge dancing shadows on the plain stuccoed walls.

The old man stood before them, a thin bent shell of a man, who looked as if all will to live had been beaten from him. His haunted gray eyes were fearful, furtive. His clothing, little more than filthy rags, hung on his thin frame like the clothes of a scarecrow. He looked up at the three men, who towered over him in their black hoods and cloaks.

Hamilton did not need to sense his emotions. The fear in his eyes was plain. Trying to put the old man more at ease, he pulled back his hood. "Fear not, good man. We offer you no hurt."

The old man seemed to relax just a bit. Then they saw the small white face peering around the doorjamb to another room.

Removing his hood, Capian said, "Who is this?"

The old man's head whipped around. "Fitatric,

I told you to stay in the kitchen!" he scolded.

The young boy stepped into full view. "I'm sorry, Grandfather. I only wanted to see the guests. It's been so long..."

At the word "guests", the old man's face suddenly looked as if he were remembering what it was like to have them. He snatched a dusty apron from a hook on the wall, and swiftly tied it about himself.

"Sit!" he said suddenly. "Rest your weary feet beside the fire." They did so, and he tossed a small log upon the coals. It was the last one he had. "I haven't much more to offer ye than water and a bit of bread."

Capian said, "We have nothing to offer in return."

This changed his age-hewn face to a slight frown, but his features brightened. He said, "What the hell! It's been so long since I've had guests, it's on the house. Money is worthless in Arnath after all." His gnarled hand rubbed his bald, liver-spotted pate as he shuffled away. In his shambling gait, the young warriors saw a once proud man, once tall and strong, but now age and oppression and starvation had all but vanquished him.

The young boy was perhaps nine, with strong but haunted blue eyes in a once handsome face, now soiled and drawn by hunger. A filthy mop of straw-colored hair topped his round head. His clothes were little more than rags hung on his half-starved body like a sack.

"Come, Fitatric," the old man said, and the boy followed him obediently into the kitchen.

The three Knights looked at one another in grim disbelief that people so benign as these could live in a city as malevolent as this one. They sat in silence until the old man and the boy returned with three plates and three drinking jacks.

On each plate rested a piece of bread which would have been hard pressed to nourish a mouse, but the tankards were full of cool fresh water. The two set all this on the table.

"My name is Asric," the old man said, folding his hands, "and this is my grandson, Fitatric. May I ask who you be?"

Each gave Asric his name.

He said, "May I further inquire what three strong, young, able-bodied men be doing in a city as thrice-cursed as this one? After all, no outsider dares come here any more. You are my first guests in half a year."

Hamilton, resting his elbows on the table, folding his hands before him, stared into the old man's eyes. "We are after the Ivory Star."

The old man stood frozen in place. His face was blank.

The boy's eyes gaped open. He recovered first. "Are you The One?"

Hamilton's eyes flashed a steel blue. "Aye, I am."

The old man began to quiver and shake with joy. "I knew you would come!" he exclaimed. "The sun turned the color of blood, and you have come, no matter how much Uhr tries to deny it. But never in my wildest dreams did I imagine I would have this honor! Oh, gods, would that I had more to offer you!" Tears formed in his yellowed old eyes, and he sniffed, his lower lip quivering. "Forgive me, my lord, that we have nothing more to offer you!"

Hamilton reached out and squeezed his shoulder in comfort. "Do not fear, good Asric. Your hospitality has been more than enough in times such as these."

Fitatric piped up, "Are you going to kill Uhr?"

Hamilton smiled grimly, "I hope to."

"Will you kill him with magic?" The boy waved his arms about like an apprentice magician.

"No, Fitatric, I am not a magician, but merely a man."

The boy's eyes narrowed, and he studied Hamilton carefully. "Then how will you do it?"

Asric said, "Fitatric, that's rude to question The One so. He already said that they're looking for the Ivory Star. He will kill Uhr with the Ivory Star." He looked at Hamilton for confirmation.

Hamilton nodded. "That is true."

The boy looked at Capian and Darius. "Then who are you?"

Capian answered him, "We are Knights of the Eagles."

"Gods be praised!" Asric said, "I am doubly honored this day!" He lowered his head humbly.

Capian asked, "What has happened to Arnath? I was here once as a child. Even then it teemed with life and good cheer, despite Uhr's presence."

Asric sat down to speak. "For many years Uhr took one out of every fifty men of age eighteen to join his ranks of Slayers. But then, after the sun turned red, Uhr decided to take every man between the ages of sixteen and thirty-five, all those able to wield a weapon. All these soldiers needed food, so Uhr took every scrap of food he could get his filthy hands on. People went half-mad with hunger. Some finally rose up in a pitiful revolt." He closed his eyes and shook his head in sadness. "But the Slayers came, like everyone knew they would, and crushed this little revolt under hoof and heel. Thousands of citizens were slaughtered in the city square. Thousands more were taken as slaves, including Fitatric's parents and the rest of my children. Now, no one is left. My wife took sick soon after and died. She was never very strong, gods comfort her. Fitatric and I have been hiding for months. We get by, but our flour is almost gone now…" He suddenly broke into a fit of coughing. He spat into the fire. "This damnable mist has gotten into my chest again."

Darius asked, "Why do you not leave Arnath? Just get out."

Asric eyed him evenly. "We have no place to go. My entire family was lost to Uhr's slave coffles. Beside, we'd probably be ridden down before we took a hundred paces. Nay, we'll just stay right here, eh, Fitatric?" He clasped his grandson's shoulder. "Besides, now that you are here, things will get better soon."

Hamilton said nothing, staring into the fire, not at all in agreement with Asric's last words.

The boy said, "I'll bet you've had a bunch of adventures!"

The Eagle Knights laughed, and spent the balance of the day relating their experiences as both the boy and the grizzled tavern-keeper listened in wide-eyed wonder. Their journey from the Vicorian Mountains had taken fifteen days, even on the swift wings of the Eagles. And they had had no trouble with the Red Priests since. The eagles were hidden in a deserted barn a league or so from the outskirts of the city.

By this time, darkness had fallen. It was time for them to leave. Hamilton asked, "Do you know any way into the palace other than the front gate?"

The old man shook his head. "I am sorry, my lord, I do not."

"I do!"

All eyes turned on the boy. He continued sheepishly. "Balfor and me found a way once. We was playing by the sewer, and some Slayers came up, so we went between the grate bars, into the sewer tunnel, and hid from them, but they saw us, and tried to chase us, so we ran back to get away, and got lost. We found another grate that opened into the palace dungeons."

Asric said, amazed, "How ever did you get out?"

"There're lots of grates," Fitatric answered with a child's nonchalance.

"Could you show us the grating where you hid, lad?" Hamilton asked.

Excitement flashed in his large eyes. "Aye!" he said. "It's not far! I'll get my cloak!" He raced off.

Asric said, "But how will you find the dungeon in that rat-infested maze?"

"We will find it."

With that, everyone stood. Capian said, "Thank you for your hospitality, good sir."

"It is nothing, my lord," Asric replied, "but you did not touch your bread."

Capian said, "You need it far more than we. Here." He reached into his cloak, and withdrew a large leather pouch. "Take this in payment for your hospitality."

Hamilton and Darius looked at each other, and did the same, adding their bags to Capian's on the table.

Asric's eyes glazed over again with tears. "Thank you, my lords! Thank you! May all the gods smile on you and be gracious to you!"

Fitatric returned, wrapped in his ragged cloak. "I am ready."

"Fare well, Asric," Hamilton said.

"Good bye, Asric."

"Good luck, sir," Capian said. "Come, Fitatric."

The boy looked at his grandfather, his excitement overshadowed now by fear of going outside.

Asric said, "Now, you go help The One, my boy. But be careful!"

The Eagles Knights opened the door and disappeared, like silent ghosts. Asric closed the door against the chill, and returned to the table. He took one of the leather bags, emptied its contents out on the table. His mouth watered like a river as he gazed in joy at the pile of nuts, berries, strips of dried meat, wild vegetables. This was a feast such as he and Fitatric hadn't had in months. Asric then sank into a chair and wept for joy.

The gaps between the bars of the sewer grating were far too narrow for a grown man to fit through. The three Knights knelt about the rectangular hole at the end of the sewer gutter. They had sent Fitatric home as quickly as possible, bidding him to run fast and keep to the shadows. Meanwhile they crouched in the middle of the street, in full view of anyone's slightest glance. It was not yet fully dark. Wordlessly Hamilton grasped one of the rusty bars at its middle, and pulled. It would not budge. The other two men, realizing his intention, lent their own strength to his aid. Inside soaked black garments, under sweating flesh, the warriors' muscles bunched and corded like ropes. Teeth ground. The bar, unable to withstand the combined efforts of three steel-strong warriors, gave way with a grinding creak, and ripped out of its stone sockets with a resounding clang.

At the far end of the street came the echo of steel-shod hooves. In growing desperation, not daring to take time to look, each man squeezed himself in turn though the tight aperture. Capian, the last to enter, poked his head back out, and saw a dozen Slayers riding at a leisurely gate directly toward them. He quickly ducked back down, hoping they had not seen him, that their black clothing had camouflaged them just enough in the twilight. He judged that they must not have seen him, as they sounded no alarm, but he seemed to have trouble convincing himself of that.

The tunnel they had lowered themselves into was barely large enough to crawl on all fours. The floor and walls were slick with slime and filth. Water dripped incessantly. Small scurrying noises bespoke of rats moving at the edge of the light.

Almost immediately, the small tunnel rang with the clatter of hoofbeats on the street above.

Hamilton led them quickly down the tunnel a short distance, away from the grating. They felt their way along the cramped sewer passage for some time, filthy water dripping onto them, an ever-strengthening stench assailing their nostrils. Finally the tunnel emptied into a larger tunnel, tall enough for a man to stand upright. The stench here was almost overpowering.

Now, in this larger passage, Hamilton reached within his cloak and withdrew the four combined Keys. The star-shaped thing glowed brightly, more than enough to light their way in the black passage. And it led them, just as it had all the way from the Vicorian Mountains.

****

The empty palace halls rang with the step of heavy boots. A huge Slayer strode down the once-beautiful hallways, a pair of vulture's wings upon his helm. A dozen golden stripes emblazoned on his breastplate glinted in the lamplight. He came before a thick, steel-bound door, and struck it thrice with the pommel of his jeweled dagger.

After a brief pause, a small window swung

open, and a pale, glassy-eyed face regarded the stark, black faceplate. Inside the helmet, the Slayer snarled in disgust. How he hated these mindless servants of his Master.

General Stakkarr rumbled imperiously, "I would speak with the Master."

The weasely servant said in a dream-like monotone, "The Master wishes not to be disturbed."

"This is a matter of utmost importance, you sniveling cur. Open this door. The Master will feed you to the devil dogs if he hears not my message." The Slayer's voice grated like stone wheels on a cobbled street.

Without another word, the servant closed the window, and the door swung inward. After General Stakkarr stepped inside, the servant led him across the large, high-ceilinged room beyond. Four great white pillars stood in the center of the room. As they passed these, the Slayer disregarded the caked rusty-brown deposits on marble surfaces. They moved past gorgeously frescoed walls, mosaicked floors of exquisite design, fantastic tapestries, all faded with age, dusty, misted by cobwebs. Finally they traversed a long, torchlit corridor that ended in a thick, oaken door.

The weasely servant tugged a hanging rope near the door. The door opened without a sound, and a thunderous command rolled out, "Enter!"

The rat-faced servant went in first, followed closely by General Stakkarr. The room within hung in gloom, lit only by the huge blood-red jewel in the center of the chamber. As his eyes adjusted to the light, the Slayer saw the inhumanly large, black and crimson robed creature couched in a tall ebony throne near the far wall of the room.

Uhr's voice was like the roll of distant thunder. "Speak!"

The servant fell prostrate at Uhr's feet, and cried, "General Stakkarr to see you, O omnipotent Master. He would not be turned away."

"Leave us," Uhr said.

The servant leaped up, and ran out.

"Stakkarr, you try my patience. What have you?"

General Stakkar bowed deeply. "My Master, they are here."

"At last," Uhr said. "All my sorcerous surveillance was in vain. The Power of The One held my mystical eyes at bay. But now I can dispose of them once and for all time!" A sudden roar of furious pleasure blasted the Slayer's ears. "Where are they?" he said in anticipation, his voice seeming to echo from the pit of hell itself.

"They were seen entering the sewer tunnels, my Master."

"You have done well. You may choose a fresh woman as your reward. Now leave me to my work. The One shall receive a fitting welcome."

Chapter 28

The Key held before him like an everlasting torch, Hamilton led them through the seemingly endless stinking sewer passages. The white light shone on glistening slime that blanketed the walls, and reflected off the knee-deep sloshing brown filth. The splashing sewage echoed thunderously down the long tunnels, driving thousands of rats before them. The sewer system was a labyrinth, but the three warriors had the ever-trustworthy Key pointing the direction. And Hamilton felt the nearness of his goal. The Ivory Star did not call out to him as the Keys had, but by some instinctual feeling, he knew that his quest was nearly over.

The tunnel began to slope slightly downwards, and the sewage deepened. They pushed their way through the chest-deep muck. Something splashed in the water not far ahead. Something large, just outside the sphere of light.

They froze. Their steel slithered from scabbards.

Again, silence. The only sounds were the faint dripping of water, and their slow controlled breathing.

Hamilton reached out with his mind, trying to sense anything that might threaten them.

The sewage exploded before them in a blinding torrent.

Unable to see, they spat and wiped frantically at their eyes, trying to clear the sewage out of their mouths and eyes. When they did, the sight of the thing thrashing toward them made them yearn for blindness. Something huge and bulky thrust up out of the filth. A giant, misshapen head, at least they took it for a head, although it was not the head of any sane or normal creature. They saw a great toad-like face, the features of which were as vague and unstable as those seen in the mirror of a nightmare. Two great circles of light glowed redly in place of eyes. It was a form blacker than the cosmic depths of space. Its outline seemed to waver and shift as they stared at it, yet its substance was real enough as it pushed through the water. The thing's details were obscure and indistinct. Their eyes could not discern where shadow ended and the beast began. It was a black blot of shadow on the face of sanity that the pure, cleansing light of the Key could neither illuminate nor dissipate.

Hamilton felt a tentacle-like member encircle his torso. Instinctively he slashed down through the muck, and gasped when he felt no resistance. But he must have cut it! Yet the tentacle was still strongly wrapped around him, now pulling him nearer.

A talon-blade sliced the air, and disappeared into that large toad-like head. Bright blue sparks struck from the ceiling above as it passed clean through.

It towered above them like a clinging black cloud, seemed to flow toward them, engulf and envelop them. Capian and Darius leaped to the fore, slashing and stabbing at the nightmarish mass. Hamilton's madly slashing blade tore through it again and again. He was deluged with a slimy something that must have been the creature's blood. The men were tossed about like dolls in a tidal wave in that awful battle, unable to distinguish if they were being pummeled, clawed, bitten, or crushed. Fangs and talons rent their flesh, flabby tentacles as hard as iron cables wrapped them, crushed them.

A tremendous blow to his shoulder numbed Hamilton's arm, and he dropped the Key. He helplessly watched it disappear into the filth. Capian thrust his sword upward, hilt deep into that mass of unearthly flesh, ripped and tore, to no avail.

Then hope.

Darius stabbed his blade into one of those terrible eyes. The pool of light suddenly disappeared, and the entire being began to thrash and writhe as if in cosmic agony. The tunnel shook violently. Capian leaped, thrusting into the other eye. The monster spasmed, giving forth no sound. It heaved up and struck the ceiling, and bits of slime and stone rained down onto their heads. Suddenly the beast disappeared below the water with a tremendous splash, such a splash that the Key, having fallen to the bottom, flew into the air with the rest of the muck. Hamilton lunged out, stretching, praying to grasp it in time. He had it.

The monster was gone, vanished as quickly as it came, leaving them panting, pummeled, exhausted.

Hamilton said, "We have to get out of this muck and clean our wounds! They'll putrefy if we don't!"

His companions quite readily agreed, and they pressed on, even though their bodies ached with every step. The tunnel sloped upward gradually, and the water level dropped to their waists. They passed several branches and intersections, any one of which the great beast could have taken.

Then they saw a faint light up ahead from around a bend in the tunnel. The passage ended abruptly. Dim flickering torchlight shone through a small aperture near the ceiling on the wall before them. Hamilton stepped up, pocketing the Key, grasped the sill of the opening, and pulled himself up. A long corridor stretched beyond, lit by a guttering torch at the far end, one wall lined by strong, wooden doors. Seated below the torch on a stool near a small table, was a Slayer.

Hamilton lowered himself down and whispered, "We're here. Uhr's dungeon is up there. There's a long corridor with a Slayer sitting at the far end, perhaps thirty paces away."

The opening was barely large enough for a man to slip through, and only then with considerable difficulty.

Hamilton withdrew a talon-blade.

Capian shook his head. "At this distance and angle, we cannot throw with a enough force to penetrate his coif."

From somewhere Darius produced a small bow, which he quickly strung. He nocked the small arrow and said, "Capian, let me on your shoulders." He climbed onto Capian's shoulders, level with the hole. He took aim and fired.

The Slayer reeled off the stool, clutching at the arrow in his throat.

"Quickly," Capian urged, squeezing himself through the hole. They followed him without a word.

A low moan drifted from within one of the cells, proving that at least one of them was occupied. They moved on, reluctantly. They dared not take the time to loose a prisoner that would only hinder their quest. But as they passed, Hamilton silently vowed to return soon and free them all. After Uhr was dead. They raced down the hall, rounded a corner past the dead jailer, and slowed their pace up the flight of stone steps beyond, to be ready for anything.

At the top of the steps was a thick wooden door. They stopped, waiting for Hamilton to sense any possible danger on the other side. Sensing nothing, he quietly pulled the door open, checked the corridor outside, and motioned them to follow him. The door formed the end of another long corridor, similar to the first, with rows of cells along both walls. No Slayers were in sight.

This they traversed speedily, gaining the end to find a left and right fork. The Key pointed vaguely toward the left, so they took the left one, down an unlit hallway perhaps seventy paces in length. This ended in a heavy steel door, obviously well-used.

Hamilton again tried to sense anything perilous on the other side. Nothing immediate, just an all-encompassing sense of foreboding. The latch opened with a well-oiled click. He peered cautiously out, surveying the room outside. The floor was of black flagstones. Four huge marble pillars supported the high-vaulted ceiling. Seeing no one, he opened the door just enough to step out.

The instant he did so, he remembered the tale Sorde had told him of Arnor, how Uhr had clung to the wall above the door, waiting for Arnor to step through. And Hamilton felt eyes on him, malevolent, drilling eyes. A cold sweat burst out all over his body. He hardly dared turn around, but he knew he must. All this flashed through his mind in a tiny fraction of the time it takes to tell of it, and he spun to look up at the wall above the door. Uhr was not there. Capian and Darius looked at him curiously as they stepped into the room behind them.

Hamilton's mind reached out to sense anything he could. What he felt sickened him.

Centuries of pain, anguish, suffering and death pounded at his subtle senses like a horde of screaming devils. The lair of the Red Priests had been horrible, but even the horror of that place paled in comparison to the utter blackness that prevailed here. Evil saturated the musty air, soiling the palace itself and all the magnificent works of art that adorned the walls and floors ceilings. But after his terrible experiences at the Red Priests' lair, he was better able to shut it out once he had let it in, and shut it out he did, before it drove him mad.

They moved warily toward the center of the room, silently as stalking panthers. Still Hamilton felt as if malevolent eyes watched them from somewhere. The room was empty. He then noticed the numerous rusty-brown and sticky red splotches staining the bases of those four great pillars. They moved closer to examine them, and found some of the blood to be only hours old.

Suddenly Capian spun. There stood a few paces away a small, weasely, rat-faced man in a black robe, his head shaven clean, his eyes like glassy chips of ice, his face a dead mask. Then his mouth opened up into an earsplitting shriek that reverberated through the hall, down the adjoining corridors. A flicker of Capian's movement and a glinting flash of silver cut that scream short with gurgling finality.

Somewhere a door crashed shut.

Capian quickly retrieved his talon-blade from the man's throat. "Hurry, Hamilton! Which way?"

"That way." He pointed, Key in hand, as they ran for one of the six exits. Their soiled black boots, crusted with sewer filth, passed noiselessly across the beautiful floor, down a long, torchlit corridor that ended in a thick wooden door, bound in steel. A small rope dangled from a hole to the side of the door. There was no visible latch or handle.

"Through here?" Darius asked.

Hamilton nodded. He felt around the door with his mind, finding it heavily bolted from the inside.

Then they heard the running stamp of many booted feet with a jangle of weapons and armor in the distance, growing louder. They glanced nervously at each other. The door appeared strong enough to withstand a battering ram. Several black-armored warriors came running into view at the far end of the hallway, bared steel in hand.

Capian reached with his cloak and pulled out two small vials of some clear liquid. "Hold them off, while I open this door."

Darius loosed an arrow from his short bow. A Slayer toppled in mid-stride with it lodged in his eye slit. Hamilton put the Key away, drew his sword, and stood to meet the rush of enemies, unaware that Capian was pouring the contents of those vials onto the steel bindings of the door. Darius flung another blade, then drew his sword, standing placidly in wait for the attack. The Slayers were upon them. The passage was wide enough for only two men to fight abreast, thus Hamilton and Darius were able to easily hold off the dozen Slayers. Two of them were already down, choking on their own gore. Blades flickered in and out like serpents' tongues.

Hamilton and Darius could not see the steel bindings of the door bubbling and melting away, or Capian, his hands folded, in a meditative trance.

The Knights' swords danced a ballet of death. Slayers crumpled, slipping in their own spurting blood. Finally the last fell. Darius tugged his scarlet blade free, as the last corpse fell heavily onto one of his dead companions.

As they turned to regard Capian, he came out of his trance, his eyes steel-cold with determination. Facing the door, with its steel rivets and bindings melted away, the wood scarred as if by a great heat, Capian braced himself, and lashed out at the door. Hands and feet pummeled like a whirlwind of hammer blows on the stubborn barrier as the wood splintered and cracked. Then it was over, and Capian stood motionless save for his heaving chest. The door hung in shattered ruin from its hinges. Another sharp kick broke the bolt completely loose inside and sent the door swinging inward. Capian seemed to take a moment to recollect himself. He recovered slowly as Hamilton led them into the chamber beyond. The room was lit by an odd red glow. In the center of the low-ceilinged chamber on a black pedestal was an enormous red gem that glowed like a small sun. The faint stench of rotting flesh lingered in the air.

Hamilton held the Key for a moment, and pointed toward a tall ebony throne near the far wall. "That way."

Approaching the chair and examining it, they discovered nothing. Then Hamilton said, "There is a concealed door here." He pointed behind the chair, and began to feel around the base of the chair, the back, the ancient arms of wood splitting with age, the wall behind it, looking for some sort of hidden opening mechanism.

He wondered where Uhr was, but was more concerned with finding the Ivory Star. It was close.

Suddenly a section of the wall behind the chair fell back, revealing a hidden passage. They gaped in amazement.

"Who found the mechanism?" Hamilton asked.

Capian and Darius both shrugged.

Hamilton said, "Must be some delayed-action mechanism."

They all three looked at one another, not quite believing that explanation.

A cold sense of danger whispered across the back of Hamilton's neck, but he couldn't afford to succumb to it. The end of his quest was too near.

They stepped inside the narrow passage barely wide enough for a man to walk abreast. Hamilton led the way, Key upraised, lighting the way. Cobwebs choked the ceiling. Dust caked the stone floor. In the dust was a single set of footprints that moved in the same direction as they. The passage was long and straight, then began to slope upward and curve slightly.

The smell of decaying flesh was slightly stronger now.

The slope and curve of the passage steadily increased, until Hamilton could no longer see more than a couple of steps ahead before the cramped passage curved up and out of sight. The slope still increased and finally changed to steps.

Hamilton's heart pounded like a piledriver. He felt the birthmark on his chest tingling as if in anticipation. Somehow he knew that the object of his long search waited for him at the top of the stairs. Still up the Knights spiraled, almost squeezing themselves up the narrow way.

Hamilton stopped short. Blood lashed like whips in his veins. Sweat slicked his palms. His entire body quivered, and his breath came in short, quick gasps. He licked his lips with a dry tongue. The Key almost squirmed in his grip.

"This is it," he whispered.

The stairs ended at a small landing. They stood before an ancient, time-worn door. A four-pointed star was burned into the wood.

He reached for the latch. It protested with an aged creak, then opened. Hamilton pushed the door open and held up the Key.

With a deep breath he stepped inside.

The stench of rotting flesh was strong here. Could there be a corpse here somewhere...

Insane laughter boomed like Hell's Bells in his ears. A tremendous impact drove his breath from him and bore him heavily to the floor. The Key tore from his hand and skidded across the floor. He felt a hot, stinking breath on his neck. The stench of death reeked in his face. Huge claws ripped and tore at his flesh like a thousand fiends.

A voice roared in his ear like living thunder. "You are mine, mortal worm!"

Hamilton tried to writhe free, but was unable to break the viselike clutch. He managed to wriggle around onto his back and face the monstrosity. He shoved with all his considerable might against the red and black robes falling over him. What was beneath felt like old wood, but infinitely stronger. Iron claws dug into him and pulled his throat nearer the source of that foul breath which was still hidden within the dark recesses of the hood. He gasped and fought, but to no avail.

From behind them came a wild, fearful cry of rage.

Hamilton heard the slither of a drawn blade and felt a terrible impact shudder through Uhr's steel-strong frame. Capian's sword hardly sank into that woody back. He chopped again and again, without effect on Uhr's unnatural vitality. Uhr's unseen fangs inched nearer and nearer Hamilton's bared throat.

Hamilton managed to free his hand, and reached into that awful hood, finding Uhr's throat.

His powerful fingers clamped around what felt like a small sapling sheathed in flaking, moldering flesh that hung loose like an old sack. Bits of Uhr's rotting flesh fell into his face, into his gasping mouth. He retched, but kept control of his thrashing guts. His entire will was focused on keeping those teeth away from his throat. Uhr growled like a rabid beast. Hamilton felt a hot gush down his side as Uhr's claws raked his ribs. Then he managed to cock his legs under the monster's belly. As hard as he could, he kicked. Claws shredded his skin trying to maintain their hold as Uhr flew backward and struck the wall with a dry thud. Hamilton scrambled to his feet, gasping, and whipped out his sword.

Uhr merely stood there facing them now, all three, and laughed a terrible, earth-shuddering laugh that sent shivers of icy fear through them.

"Puny mortals!" Uhr said. "You have no idea of the power you face here. I am older than a thousand of your ancestors. Your blades are as gnats to me."

Hamilton raised his voice in defiance, "The Ivory Star!"

Uhr's roar cut him off and momentarily deafened them. "The Ivory Star is an overblown legend, a baseless wish of a worthless populace! You are nothing to me. You are like sheep to be slaughtered, and that is my intention." He slammed the door shut with such force the edges splintered. "As for this trinket..." He gestured toward the Key. It whisked off the floor, through the air, into his outstretched hand.

Suddenly he roared in pain, and the Key clattered to the stone floor at his feet, bits of smoldering flesh clinging to the smooth surface. Uhr momentarily clutched his sizzling hand in agony, then pointed at the three warriors with his smoking claw. Two red beads gleamed in demonic fury from within the dark hood. Uhr leaped toward them, and his hammer-like fist sent Hamilton spinning across the room. Hamilton smashed into the wall with bone-shattering force. Blazing streaks of light split his vision as he slid to the floor, unconscious.

He awoke after what must have been mere moments. Uhr's back was turned to him. Uhr faced Capian on one side, Darius on the other. The two razor-sharp blades gleamed in the crystal clear light of the Key.

Groggily Hamilton gained his knees. The Key lay but a few feet away. He began to crawl dizzily toward it. His vision swam, and he thought he might pass out again. Every inch was an eternity of agonizing motion. His abused body threatened him with senselessness at every movement. The Key was before him. He reached for it.

Uhr spun. "You live!"

He had it.

Capian darted in during Uhr's momentary distraction. The blade sang, arcing upward, slicing through the hood.

Uhr's head fell to the side, hanging by mere shreds of flesh and cloth. The body staggered backward, arms floundering, but did not fall.

Capian's sword slashed again, and Uhr's head tumbled to the floor.

Still Uhr's headless body did not fall, but blindly began to shamble toward the half-covered head lying nearby.

Hamilton snapped to his senses and cried, "Get his head away from him!"

Darius leaped forward and snatched up the fallen head. The body turned and came for him, swinging its long arms violently, claws raking.

Capian lunged and grasped the shuffling feet, pinning them together. The body toppled heavily forward. Darius gasped and cried out in horror and pain, flinging that awful head away from him. He clenched his badly bleeding hand.

"It bit me!" he cried.

Uhr's severed head struck the far wall with a dry smack. The remnants of the hood fell away, revealing the monster's abominable visage. A leering skull, with flaking, yellowish-brown skin stretched tight across it, mouthing viciously at them from where it lay. Piercing, stabbing eyes burned with an evil red intelligence. Cracked, yellowed fangs snapped behind the stretched, decaying lips.

On the floor lay the body, thrashing and struggling to crawl toward its missing head. Darius leaped down beside Capian to help hold the thing down. A flailing arm swept back and struck Capian across the head. He fell back, stunned, and Uhr's body almost gained its feet. Darius again pinned its feet together.

Capian gasped, "Is it here?"

Hamilton shook off his horrified stupor and nodded. He could feel something here, somewhere in this room. The room was circular, perhaps fifteen paces across. A small dais rose against the far side of the room, on which rested an altar-like block of silvery metal, now coated with the dust of ages. In a half-trance he approached it.

Darius panted, "Hurry!"

In a daze Hamilton stepped up to the block. Carved upon the top of the block was a large four-pointed star, roughly the same size and shape as the Key. He hardly realized what he was doing as he laid the glowing star into the carving. It fit perfectly. There sounded a low hum of escaping air. The top of the block slid slowly back, revealing the interior of the case.

In the bottom lay a bundle of white cloth. He reached down and picked up the bundle. The yellowed silk fell away, revealing a strange-looking weapon. A sword. Its blade was dull and colorless, appearing to be made of some weird stone. The hilt however, gleamed like polished silver.

Darius and Capian cried out as Uhr's inhuman body flung them off and away, and began to crawl toward its horribly mouthing head.

As if guided by an unseen hand, his finger found a catch under the crossguard. He slid the mechanism down, over, up. Hilt and blade sprang apart, splitting the quillion.

Blindly grasping claws found the abhorrent head.

Hamilton saw a diamond-shaped hole in the base of the blade, another in the top of the hilt, and matching grooves along the insides of the split crossguard. He took the Key from its place in the carving, and slid the long point into the opening at the base of the blade. The fit was flawless. The shorter points of the Key fit into grooves carved inside the quillion. He fitted the hilt back up to the blade, the opposite point of the star sliding perfectly into the matching hole in the hilt.

All came together.

The blade of the sword burst alive. The dull, gray substance of the blade flashed into a thousand scintillating colors, like every color of every star in the universe had suddenly some together. The dazzling hues faded slowly, leaving a softly iridescent white.

"No!" wracked the room like an explosion. Uhr stood, again whole, against the wall, hands raised in defense. "It's too soon!" he screamed. "We shall meet again, human. I'll find you when I'm ready!"

Uhr's black and crimson robes lost their substance, dissolving into smoke, dissipating. Gone.

Chapter 29

The Ivory Star gleamed brightly before him. Hamilton stared, mesmerized by its alien beauty, its shimmering blade. He saw the Key glowing within through a small, diamond-shaped window at the intersection of the quillion and grip. Then the light began to dim.

Capian said, in the deepening darkness, "Let us hurry! Uhr may yet be about! We could catch him!"

Hamilton said, "No. He is gone. Somehow, I can now feel if he is nearby, but...he is not here. He has fled."

"Then let us give chase!" Darius exclaimed. The exhilaration of having Uhr on the run was sweeping through them all.

Hamilton smiled. "Aye!"

Down the spiraling steps they raced with the little light the Ivory Star now gave. Soon it dimmed altogether, and forced them to feel their way blindly. Then they burst into Uhr's chamber from behind the throne. One glance told them the glowing red stone was gone.

Through the chamber they dashed, down the hallway, and into the great hall, where they skidded to a halt.

Fully a score of warriors surrounded them, weapons of every sort gleaming in black-gauntleted fists.

Hamilton slid the Ivory Star into his belt, and whipped out his sword. Darius dropped into a crouch with a talon-blade in one hand, sword in the other. Capian waited, sword ready.

The Slayers did not move. These were armed differently than any they had seen thus far. They wore chain mail coats, instead of the bulky suits of black, spiked plate. Their heads sported plain black heaumes, with none of the gruesome adornments, over chain mail coifs. Padded cuir-boulli protected their legs. These men wore nothing but the bare essentials of armor and weapons, implying a more deadly threat.

Darius flung his talon-blade. With an almost imperceptible motion, a Slayer deflected it away with the haft of his battle-ax. It echoed loudly in the deathly silent hall. The very air was taut as a drawn bowstring.

The Knights watched and waited like cornered panthers. Hamilton glanced at Capian and made a small gesture toward the nearest open door, just beyond the circle of enemies. Suddenly Capian loosed a wild cry and bolted toward the line of Slayers. They set their weapons to meet him. A mere pace out of their reach, he leaped high into the air, somersaulted over their heads, landed behind. Hamilton and Darius followed him a split second later, meeting the warriors rushing toward them. Up, over, behind.

Now all three Knights barreled for that closest door and escape. With break-neck speed they raced down that corridor. The Slayers came hot on their heels, baying as they came like devil dogs on a hot scent. The corridor ended abruptly at a single wooden door. Capian flung it open, waited for his companions to follow, then slammed it shut and threw the bolt. They spun and surveyed the dimly lit room.

A huge man leaped out of the canopied bed, naked, snatched his sheathed bastard sword from where it lay nearby, ripped it from its scabbard, and threw the scabbard away. His thick muscles writhed like serpents under his scarred flesh. His blood-shot eyes glared at them with pure hatred from under thick black-tufted brows.

His voice grated like gravel on old leather. "You yet live!" He advanced, his battle-notched sword brandished. "It seems General Stakkarr must kill you himself!" His scarred face twisted with fury. Here was a merciless beast of a man.

Darius leaped forward, smooth and quick.

With speed that belied his tremendous size, Stakkarr met him. Their swords crashed, and Darius's blade shattered like glass. Stakkarr's blade crunched deep into Darius's body. The Eagle Knight sank to the floor without a sound.

"Hah!" Stakkarr exclaimed, wrenching his blade free, and kicking Darius's body back toward them. "Like cattle to the slaughter!" He advanced again.

A crash broke the shocked silence, and the door groaned under a great impact.

Stakkarr sneered, "There is no place for you to go, worms."

"Bastard!" Capian growled, drawing a talon blade. "Son of a bitch!" he cried, as he took aim.

Stakkarr stomped forward, raising his sword, bloodlust twisting his cruel features.

"Die, dog!" Capian hissed. He let fly.

Stakkarr's head snapped back with the impact and a hard thunk. Then a horrible sneer ripped across his face, as his gaze returned to them. Blood poured down his right cheek from the talon blade embedded in his eye socket. Stakkarr glared at them with his remaining eye blazing a feral red, and bared his teeth like a beast. His sword came up again.

Capian's second talon blade split his throat wide. The Slayer's jugular burst open in a scarlet stream, spewing gore across the floor as he fell.

They surveyed the room. A luxurious canopied bed squatted along one wall. A padded chair and a large bureau reposed at opposite sides of the room. A dimly burning lamp rested on a small table near the bed. Shutters covered the window.

Capian moved to examine Darius. He was very dead. Stakkarr's heavy sword had cleft him from shoulder to navel.

Something crashed into the door again. The wood groaned in protest, but the steel bolt held.

Then came a soft sound from the bed, the gentle sound of a woman weeping. Hamilton stepped up to the bed, and flung the curtains aside. The naked woman cringed.

"Please do not hurt me," she whispered, her face buried in the silk pillows.

"You have nothing to fear from us, lady, unless you are loyal to Uhr," Hamilton said.

She looked up at him, her face and body bruised and battered.

Hamilton's heart skipped a beat.

"Who are you?" she asked, staring up into his eyes, all that was visible on his fearsome, black-swathed form.

The door cracked.

"Your salvation, lady," Hamilton answered her.

"Let's go!" Capian hissed.

"She comes with us."

Capian stared at him in disbelief. "Are you mad?"

"Not at all. She comes with us." Even as he spoke, he was gathering up the woman's torn clothing. "Dress yourself, quickly now!"

She suddenly remembered her nakedness and clutched the sheets about herself. He could not help but admire her exquisite feminine beauty. His heart raced like a herd of horses, and his mouth went dry as an autumn leaf. He found himself staring and quickly turned away, his face reddening.

Capian flung the shutters open and thrust out his head, looking for a means of escape. He produced a coil of thin cord and proceeded to secure it to the heavy bureau near the window. The ground was twenty feet down the flat stone wall below the window.

The woman tugged the remains of her clothing about herself. Hamilton stepped up to the window, and gestured her nearer. "Hold on to me tightly," he told her. She brushed her disheveled auburn hair out of her eyes, and clutched his shoulders and neck tightly. He looped the cord about their waists and climbed out the window. "Do not let go," he soothed. He felt her entire body shivering as she clung to him. He quickly began his descent.

He heard a tremendous crash on the door above. They were halfway down. Splintering wood. Almost down. An ebon blur flashed from the window, and Capian landed lithely on his feet, collapsed and rolled to absorb the impact. He sprang to his feet, wincing, favoring his ankle. Hamilton let go of the rope and they dropped the last five feet to the ground.

"Now what?" Capian said.

They were in an alley perhaps ten paces wide

between the palace and wall.

"Run!" Hamilton exclaimed, as a javelin from above struck the pavement a hair's breadth from his foot.

They bolted down the alley, out of range of missile weapons from the window. Capian limped slightly as they ran. The woman stumbled and nearly fell, and Hamilton clutched her arm tightly, half-dragging her along.

Then, for a moment, they were alone. They stopped, and Capian said, "We must separate, and reach the eagles however we can."

Hamilton nodded. "You're right. Escape will be more likely that way."

Shouted commands echoed down the alley.

"Conceal yourselves," Capian said, "I'll try to draw them away. If one of us does not meet at the eagles' hiding place by sunrise tomorrow, the other should assume the worst." His voice was hard as he glared at the woman. How could Hamilton jeopardize the fate of the entire world for the safety of one palace slave woman?

Already the coming of day began to brighten the deep gray sky.

Hamilton nodded in agreement.

The sound of heavy, stomping boots filled the alley.

With that, Capian quickly affixed his climbing claws to his hands and feet, leaped up the high palace wall, and began to scale it like a great black spider.

Hamilton again took her arm and ran down the alley along the wall. The alley abruptly widened into a broad courtyard. They skidded to a halt and backed into the shadows.

A hundred paces away was the front gate of the palace. He could see four Slayers to his left at the locked gate, four on the wall above, two at his far right on the great set of sprawling steps leading up the huge palace doors. At his immediate right was what looked to be a stable, a long, low, stone building with several sets of wide half-doors.

He heard Slayers behind growing nearer, and Capian's taunting cry. He darted for the stable, dragging her with him. Inside, the stable was dark, but its great size was evident. Scores of horses were stabled here, just now beginning to stir from sleep. Hamilton cast about for a hiding place. A commotion broke out in the courtyard. Then in the darkness he dimly saw a pile of straw at the back of a nearby stall. He led her swiftly toward this, bade her crawl in and cover herself, while he did the same.

In the quiet darkness, he heard her whisper, her voice quaking with fear, "Who are you? Why do you risk your life for me?"

"I know who you are, my lady," answered he, through the straw. "Although you don't know me yet, I assure you we have met. Now please remain silent and motionless. We may yet escape."

Within moments the stable was buzzing with activity. Slayers hurried about, carrying tack and saddles. Horses jumped and whinnied and fidgeted at this unexpected activity. Stable doors were thrown open, and the mounted killers sallied forth. A cacophony of orders were shouted just outside.

"...seen just outside the walls..."

"...search the alleys and houses within a mile of the palace wall..."

"...a woman with them so they can't have gotten far..."

"Open the gates!"

The gates rumbled ponderously open. The drum of hoofbeats faded as the horsemen mounted and rode through the palace gates. All was quiet again.

For several long hours, they remained concealed in the pile of straw. He heard her quiet breathing, sensed her fear, her curiosity. And he smiled. He tried to formulate a plan that would grant both of them freedom. He quickly realized just how much of a burden his female charge was. She could do none of the physical feats in which he had been trained, severely limiting his options for escape. Eventually he decided to wait until nightfall. Their chances would be best then. For a while, he even dozed, having not slept for three days. He was awakened by voices just outside.

"...two new horses, lad. These are weary. They've come all the way from Armond." A man's gruff voice.

"I'll get them for you," said a youthful voice.

Footsteps came into the stable. Hamilton heard the horses being prepared and taken outside.

The stable boy said, "I suppose you have another long journey back to Armond with these supplies."

"Aye, I'm already loaded." Creak of the wagon seat. "I only need two fresh draft horses to get me there. The rest of the caravan has already left, but I should be able to catch up to them in a couple of days. Toss on a bag of oats, can you? The beasts will fare better on that than the scrub grass that's still too short for eating."

"I don't know..."

"Oh, come on, lad! It's only one bag. The great Master can't have his horses dying of starvation now can he?"

"I suppose..."

"Excellent, lad, you're a true loyal servant to the Master!" The man's voice dripped with sarcasm.

The lad shushed him hurriedly. "We're in his very palace!"

The man waved him off. "I care not, although my throat may be slit for saying so! I only crave an end to it all. Valerion holds on still, tenacious as a cornered swamp cat, and may Arnor give him comfort when the Slayers finally take him. Why, if the other lords would just show some backbone, they could kick Uhr's moldy arse all the way back to Arnath! How about those oats, boy?"

"Of course."

Hamilton seized upon a fresh plan.

He crawled from the straw, crouching out of sight behind the side of the adjoining stall. He peered through a crack between the boards. "Come, lady! We're going now."

She removed herself from the straw pile and knelt beside him.

A lad of perhaps fourteen years tossed a full bag onto the back of the wagon, and pulled the tarpaulin over the cargo. It was just as Hamilton had hoped. He motioned her to follow him, and silently moved to crouch just inside the stable door with her close beside. The lad moved up toward the front of the wagon with the two fresh horses and set about switching them with the gaunt animals harnessed there.

Hamilton cautioned her to utmost silence, then jerked her after him toward the back of the wagon, where he quietly lifted the tarpaulin, thrust her under, and followed.

Hamilton sensed the wagon driver glance back at the small noise made by the fluttering tarpaulin. He opened his mouth to speak, but Hamilton projected calm indifference upon him. He kept silent. The boy harnessing the horses had not noticed. Hamilton settled himself between the sacks of flour and a barrel of salted fish. The man's own emotions were a mixture of fear, surprise, curiosity. All tangled into a jumble of conflicting urges.

What would he do? His words betrayed his disloyalty to Uhr. But would he go so far as to help half-seen strangers escape from Uhr's palace?

"All hooked up!" the lad said.

"Thanks, boy. Watch your back, and fare well!" The reins slapped.

The boy called after them, "Farewell!"

As the wagon rattled across the courtyard, Hamilton squeezed the woman's arm in comfort. He could feel her paralyzing terror. Lest it distract him, he closed his mind to it. He carefully lifted the tarpaulin a mere crack, so that he might see out. The wagon slowly rattled through the massive palace gates. Hamilton felt the driver's urge to call alarm to the guards at the gate. He did his best to stifle the driver's urge, but clutched the hilt of his sword, ready to fight or flee instantly.

But the wagon kept rolling, and the driver did not call the alarm.

"Courage, lady," Hamilton whispered.

After they had left the gate some distance behind, the driver said quietly, "Be you a Knight of the Eagles?"

Hamilton was stunned. Finally he replied, "Aye, I am. And you have my thanks for not turning me over to the guards."

"Don't thank me yet. I'm simply not scared enough to turn you in at this point. Whither are you bound?"

"Out of this city."

Hamilton felt the fellow smile. "That's simple enough. So am I. I feared you'd force me to take you somewhere."

"No, just outside the city."

"For that, you have my thanks."

The wagon wobbled down the street. Hamilton risked another peek. The day had brightened. The mist and fog were gone. The heavy black clouds dispersed.

By nightfall, as the old wagon trundled on, stars bared their sparkling faces through the rapidly thinning overcast.

Suddenly a voice called out in an emotionless, dreamlike monotone, "Halt!"

The horses whickered, and the wagon slowly slid to the stop.

"Is there a problem, my lords?"

Iron-shod hooves trotted near. Armor and accouterments jingled in the crisp night air. A dead voice droned, "What is your cargo?"

Hamilton caught his breath. He felt the woman tense, and gripped her forearm in both reassurance and control. His hand fell onto his sword hilt. He sensed the driver's pure terror, but his respect for the man grew when he heard the driver's voice remain calm and steady, almost friendly.

The driver said, "Supplies for the gallant troops sieging Valerion's filthy stronghold."

"Your caravan left yesterday. Why did you not leave with them?"

"A broken wagon wheel, my lords, forced me to extend my stay just a bit."

There was a moment of tense silence as the Slayer absorbed this. "Carry on."

"Thank you, my lords. Farewell!" Reins snapped lightly, and the wagon lurched forward again.

After a bit, the driver said to Hamilton, "That's the good thing about Slayers. The soulless whoresons are none too bright."

Eventually the street on which the wagon

traveled changed to a dirt road as the last houses and buildings of Arnath were lost in the darkness behind them.

Hamilton whispered to her, "Prepare yourself. We're getting off. It's better if he doesn't know we've done it."

The clouds were gone now. Stars shone brightly above as he helped her gently out of the slowly moving wagon. He pulled her quickly into the ditch beside the road, and there crouched out of sight until the clattering of the wagon had passed far away. When the wagon was gone, he led her into the thick grove of trees a few paces from the ditch. This proved to be just a strip of growth as they soon broke through into a wide grassy plain, with a few close-growing clumps of trees scattered across it. Across this huge field for perhaps a league they walked. Dry grass rustled underfoot. Hamilton was forced to stop twice to allow her to rest. Neither of them spoke, although Hamilton badly wanted to speak to her. He could sense her curiosity about him, her puzzlement, but he said nothing. He preferred to wait.

Finally they reached their destination, an old stone barn gutted by fire but still standing, in a clump of trees near a little-used path meandering across the plain. The charred stone walls of the building stood not far from the blackened ruins of a burned farmhouse.

A flickering light shone from inside the barn.

Capian looked up at them as they entered. His mask and hood lay at his feet. "Greetings! I had almost given up hope."

As they fully entered the barn, the woman gasped in outright fear. The two eagles glared at her in distrust with their platter-sized brown eyes, from where they nested in some old straw in the back of the barn.

Capian had already released Skyrider.

Hamilton felt a twinge of sadness. Darius had been a good friend, and a brave warrior.

"What are they?" she whispered, staring at the monstrous birds.

"Fear not," Hamilton said. "We are Knights of the Eagles. They are our steeds."

He felt her unease as she split her gaze between Hamilton and Capian. "Who are you?"

Capian answered, "My name is Capian, Son of Arnor."

"Lord Valerion's eldest son," she said. "I am in company of friends then, at least. And you, sir?" Her beautiful gaze speared into Hamilton's heart.

He removed his mask and hood.

She stared into his face, her eyes wide. "It is you!"

"Aye."

Capian said puzzledly, "You two have met?"

Hamilton said, "Once, briefly." He smiled at her.

She fumbled for words.

"What is your name, lady?" Capian asked.

She stuttered, "I am...Tamarra, daughter of Lord Diomenes, step-daughter of Lord Sneev."

Chapter 30

"What was the step-daughter of Sneev, the Snake on the Crag, doing in Uhr's palace?" Capian asked, his face an immobile mask, suspicion harsh in his voice.

Tamarra snarled at him. "What, did you not see? I was a palace slave!"

Capian, startled by her venomous response, stepped back and stuttered, "I am sorry…"

Hamilton said, trying the salvage the situation, "My lady Tamarra, if I may ask, what happened that you became one of Uhr's slaves?"

She looked down, turning away. Her voice was quiet and shuddering, "Uhr took me and my mother as slaves to punish my step-father."

"To punish him for what?" Hamilton said.

"Allowing you and your friend to escape."

For a long moment, no one said anything. Hamilton stared at her, with mixed guilt and outrage filling his bosom. Months of suffering had taken a terrible toll on this beautiful woman. She turned and sat gracefully before the crackling fire. Her face was drawn and haggard from malnutrition, and bruised from Stakkarr's abuse. Her auburn hair, once long and flowing, was cut short, undoubtedly for catapult cord and bowstring. Hair as long and thick as hers was a valuable commodity in wartime.

Capian said, his voice softening just a bit, "What of your mother?"

Her reply was terse and painful. "Dead."

Hamilton said, "My lady, I am sorry. My freedom was not worth the cost to you and your mother."

She said nothing at first, just stared into the fire rocking back and forth slightly. Suddenly she said, "Ooh, the things they made me..." A sob choked her off.

Hamilton regarded her. This woman was very different than the one who had slapped his face so long ago. She was still shaken from Stakkarr's rape, traumatized. He wanted very much to comfort her somehow, touch her shoulder in reassurance, but he knew that right now probably the last thing she wanted was the touch of a man, so he made no move toward her.

Abruptly she looked up at him, the gratitude shining brightly in her tear-filled eyes. "Thank you, sir, for freeing me," she said, her deep voice husky with emotion.

He smiled at her, warmly. "The least I could have done for you, my lady."

She wiped a tear from her cheek with a trembling hand. "So," she said, trying to regain her composure, "what were you doing in Arnath?"

Hamilton pulled the Ivory Star from where it hung in his belt, more a burden than anything in the course of their escape. "We came for this."

"A sword. I noticed it before." She looked up at Hamilton. "That is all?"

A smile touched his lips again. "It is the Ivory Star."

She looked away, almost laughing. "Surely you

jest! That would mean..." Her voice trailed off as her hand rose to her lips. "Dear gods!" she whispered, "I struck The One!" She stared again at Hamilton. "You're The One. How can this be?"

Capian harumphed, obviously a little disgusted. "How can the sun rise? How can the grass grow? My lady, how can he be The One? He simply is."

Tamarra gazed at Hamilton, not speaking.

Hamilton sensed her jumbled emotions, her tumultuous consciousness, and realized that she was so traumatized she was still not thinking clearly. "Come," he said, "let us rest. Tomorrow's journey will be difficult."

Capian glanced knowingly at Hamilton, having sensed the same thing. "Aye," he said, "Hamilton, you're right." He turned away, and Hamilton sensed his remorse for having been so terse with her.

Hamilton said to her, "You may use my cloak for warmth. What's left of your clothes will do nothing to keep back the night's chill. Please, try to sleep now. You need it very badly."

She looked up at him again, obviously surprised by his kindness. "Thank you, sir, you're very kind. It's been so long since I've seen kindness..."

"Please, call me Hamilton."

"If you'll call me Tamarra. Agreed?"

He grinned at her. "Agreed."

Capian had taken a place away from them, nearer the birds, to sleep for the night. He lay on his side with his back to them.

Tamarra wrapped herself tightly in Hamilton's cloak. "You were right, I am very tired. But I'm not sure I can sleep."

Hamilton tried to project soothing calm to her, ease her suffering. "Please try, Tamarra. There is nothing to fear. No one will harm you while I am near."

She looked away. "Thank you." A crystal tear shone on her flawless cheek, sparkling in the fire-light. As she lay down next to the fire with her back toward Hamilton he heard her whisper, "...such a wonderful man..."

Hamilton's heart caught fire with those words. How he'd longed to know this woman these long months, never once believing that he actually would, but somehow knowing, knowing that he would.

He felt sleep coming on him again. But the excitement of the moment kept it at bay for the time being as he seated himself near her on the ground. He sensed her emotions again, felt her immense pain, and reached into her with himself, and tried to heal her pain with his mind. He did his best to put out the fires of guilt and rage and pain and disgust and shame that burned within her, eating at her. After a time, her deep, regular breathing told him that sleep had befallen her and he was, at least in part, successful.

Then he took a deep breath and began to examine the warm piece of metal resting on his lap. Excitement rippled through him again. He scrutinized the weapon. The blade was perhaps three feet long, with a hilt long enough for both hands. The hilt was fashioned from a strange silvery metal with those crystal windows through which the Key shone coolly. The blade was ivory white, about four fingers wide at the hilt, tapering to a sharp point. It was made of a substance he had never before seen, polished to mirror smoothness. He tested the edge. It was sharp, razor-sharp. It was an Eagle Knight's edge.

He grasped it firmly and tested it for balance.

A weapon with a blade as large as this one should have weighed more than it did. Its balance was perfect. Strangely, it seemed to flow naturally in his grasp. It felt like a part of him already, a natural extension of his arm. Its glow was gone now. Perhaps that was the Key: Uhr's presence triggered the surge of its power. He examined it with his mind, as well, and felt power waiting there, just for him, power beyond anything he had ever felt so intimately. And it was flowing into him, feeding his strength.

He tried setting the sword down on the ground, and immediately the exertion of the past three days overtook him. Exhaustion swept over him like a gigantic wave. The deep gashes made by Uhr's claws burned over his ribs, and the bruises and wounds inflicted by the monster in the sewer began to ache and throb. It was too late now to stop any infection. He began to wash the cuts and lesions with water and a clean cloth. His eyes began to swim and fall shut, and before long he was asleep, a deep, dreamless, bottomless sleep.

****

The second massive assault had begun. Valerion stood watching on the wall near the front gate. His men were ready. Flaming javelins shot toward them from the shore. Great balls of blazing pitch, hurled by catapults on the bank, struck the wall or sailed over, splattering liquid fire everywhere. Suddenly the raised drawbridge exploded into flame.

Robinton's voice roared above the melee, "Water! Water to the gate!"

Slayers stormed across the stone bridge, carrying heavy wooden planks, like massive ants. Valerion's archers sent a storm of arrows and crossbow bolts down at them, to little effect. Another volley of arrows and javelins from the shore raked the men on the wall.

Valerion cursed. He was too damned undermanned. Over a third, nearly half of all his fighting number had been lost in that first terrible assault. Now the Slayers threatened to overwhelm them.

He went down to the barbican. A fire brigade desperately threw buckets of water on the burning drawbridge. Valerion shook his head. The drawbridge already burned too fiercely to be saved.

"Leave it," he finally said.

Robinton came up to him. "What now, m'lord?"

"Lock the portcullis down, and let us retreat to the middle ward. We can't hold this one any longer."

Robinton nodded. "We're simply too blasted thin."

He called a retreat, and the Armondians ran back to the bridge leading to the middle ward.

Robinton and Valerion waited for all of them to get out of the outer ward before they swung the heavy, double-bolted gates closed after them, and threw the thick iron bolts locked with levers on the bridge side of the gates.

Then Valerion picked up a big sledge-hammer and four long, steel pins from where they lay on a four-foot wide ledge along the wall stretching away from the bridge. This was Fortine's latest defense. It would prove little more than an inconvenience to the Slayers, but every inconvenience bought the defenders a little more time, time to live.

He fitted one of the steel pins into a newly drilled hole in the stone about the same level as the bolts. Then with the sledge hammer he drove the pin into the hole and through the bolt beyond, pinning the bolt into place. Now the bar could not be moved at all.

Valerion hoped this would prove an effective barrier for a while. Time was precious, because once the Slayers had prepared for another full assault, the Armondians would not last much longer. He joined his men in the middle ward as the gates were closed.

Chapter 31

The wind howled like wolves in their ears, as the level shafts of the setting sun inflamed the clouds still lingering about them. Clutching Hamilton's waist like a noose, Tamarra stared wide-eyed over Skyking's magnificent black wing, down at the sprawling green carpet far below. Hamilton could sense that she was afraid, even after two days of continuous traveling.

She spoke in Hamilton's ear, pointing to the bright blue ribbon meandering through the trees below, "Beyond that river lies my step-father's domain."

"That is the Saxon River?" he asked, remembering Sorde's lessons in geography.

"Yes," she replied, "may we rest, Hamilton? I am fordone."

"Aye," he said, giving Capian the signal to land, and sending Skyking into a plummeting dive that brought their stomachs into their throats. With a single beat of his tremendous wings, the great bird lit on the grassy strip between the bank of the Saxon River and the forest.

The deep gurgling of the river came like music through the air as Hamilton dismounted and helped her down. Her legs went rubbery from disuse, and she nearly collapsed. He caught her, supported her with strong arms. He felt her body mold to his momentarily.

Then she said, "I can stand."

Reluctantly he released her.

Starjumper then landed also, and Capian unbuckled the strap to jump down. The two men began to make a camp for the evening, while Tamarra went to the river to bathe.

Capian said, "I'm going to fetch some supper." Then he disappeared into the forest.

Hamilton watched him go. Since their escape from Arnath, Capian had been in a decidedly dour mood. He spoke little, and never to Tamarra. Hamilton wondered if Capian held resentment toward her, though he was not sure why.

Capian stalked through the forest, fuming once again. He was appalled at how Hamilton could think her of such importance as to jeopardize both their lives and the very fate of the world. His life's training taught him that women held the power to sway men's minds from their duty, to distract at the most crucial times. For these reasons Eagle Knights took their vows of chastity upon initiation of their training. He saw now these truths first hand. And worse, Hamilton's heart had been snared by a woman of Sneev's immediate family, and Sneev was their mortal enemy.

Hamilton, meanwhile, had unsaddled Skyking. He ran his fingers through the bird's thick black and white feathers. The beast relaxed to receive this attention. Hamilton patted the massive hooked beak that could have nearly bitten him in half. During their long journey, he had become very attached to his ferocious mount. He could sense the animal's complete trust in him, perhaps love, if such a wild, savage beast could feel love.

Skyking screamed deeply.

"He is a magnificent creature," Tamarra said.

Hamilton spun. He had not heard her approach, and silently scolded himself because he should have. He said, "Aye, he is."

She approached, wrapped only in Hamilton's cloak, carrying her torn, tattered garments in a bundle. In the failing light her soft skin gleamed with droplets of water, her emerald eyes sparkled, and her short auburn hair glistened like burnished copper. She was the most beautiful sight he had ever seen, and his heart raced.

"He still frightens me," she said, stepping nearer, "but I trust him."

"I trust him with my life." He looked into her eyes.

"And I trust you with mine." She looked away, as if surprised at her own words.

Hamilton's tongue caught in his throat. The urge to kiss her suddenly landed on him like a pile of bricks. But fear of being slapped again stayed him.

"I'll make a fire," he blurted. He averted his eyes, stepped away, and went to gather wood. All too soon for his comfort, a nice fire crackled warmly at his making.

Tamarra sat down opposite the fire and eyed him strangely.

He stood up abruptly. "I'm going to bathe. Cry out if you need help."

He walked off into the darkness toward the river, removing his clothing as he went. As he waded out into the river, the crystal-clear water engulfed his body in its cool embrace. He dove and swam, naked as a babe, invigorated by the clean, clear, cold stream. The stench of sewer, blood and sweat that had clung to him for three days was gone. The ache seeped away from his wounds and muscles, and he swam and splashed about joyfully, like a child. His whole body tingled with life as he stepped onto the sandy bank.

He then took his filthy clothes and rubbed them on a rock in the shallows, to cleanse the filth and blood from them. He examined the gashes in the fabric made by the thing in the sewer and Uhr's terrible claws. His tunic would need mending. Finally he returned to camp, feeling like a new man, wearing only his soaked black breeks. The cool night air raised invigorating gooseflesh on his chest and back and arms. His wounds itched and tingled.

Tossing the rest of his garments down on the grass near the fire, he sat down opposite her.

Tamarra looked up at him, admiring the rippling of his hardened muscles. She spied the terrible gashes criss-crossing his torso. She gasped, "Where did you get those dreadful wounds?" She stood and skirted the fire to kneel beside him, staring at them.

"Uhr gave me most of them," he replied, "others I got in the sewers from some beast he conjured up from Hell itself."

"You survived a fight with Uhr!" she exclaimed. "Even Arnor of old did not. You are truly The One!"

"Aye, survived, but barely," he said, "I'll bear the scars until I die." He stared into the dancing flames, not wanting to look at her, turned his eyes toward his mangled tunic, poked his fingers through the gashes uncomfortably.

She moved around the fire to kneel behind him, and began to rub and massage his bruises and gouged back, further admiring his trim, hard body.

He could not help relaxing under her expert touch.

She said, "I learned well how to do this as one of Uhr's slaves. I waited on many a Slayer officer until...until they made me a pleasure slave."

He found himself speaking, his voice quavering with nervousness, "Would you like to take a walk by the river with me, until Capian returns, that is?"

He sensed her surprise, and immediately cursed himself for being so forward.

Then she answered him, "Yes, I would like that very much."

Hamilton felt his face split by a schoolboy grin. His mouth opened to say something stupid, but she cut him off.

"But first I must clothe myself. A simple cloak will not do."

He kept his back turned as she slipped into her fire-dried clothes. His heart leaped as he stood, and she took his arm for him to lead the way. They walked along the bank of the giggling stream for a short distance, until they came to a beautiful bush that was fairly exploding with white flowers. The large, drooping blossoms scented the air so sweetly they decided to sit beside them for a while.

"What lovely moon roses!" she exclaimed. "My mother used to grow these in her garden, and put them in my hair when I was a little girl."

He picked one and handed it to her, his heart racing. She smiled at him as she put it in her hair.

He said, "Do you hate me for what happened to you and your mother, because of me?"

She stared at him, astounded at his question. She said, slowly, "I...did. I did for a long time. Now, just now, I know that I don't anymore. I did hate you, but not anymore."

He said nothing, with his knees drawn up to his chest, resting his arms and chin on them as he stared at the moon-dappled water.

She continued, "It was for the good that you escaped. If my step-father had killed you, no one would have been able to stand against Uhr. If my suffering and my mother's death was the price of that escape, so be it. I am still alive, and healing, and my mother would have given her life willingly for the greater good." Then her voice hardened, "You had to live so you could avenge her."

"I am truly sorry," Hamilton said, touching her hand.

"I know." She sighed heavily. "Thank you for rescuing me."

"You've thanked me already."

"I know, but I'm more happy than ever that it was you that did it."

His heart fluttered, and his stomach danced. Their eyes met, and Hamilton felt himself drawn to her, and he knew she was drawn him. He trembled like a leaf. He was moving toward her, lost in the depths of her eyes. She leaned to meet him, almost imperceptibly.

He jerked himself away.

"What is it?" she asked, bewildered. "Do I not please you?"

He stared at her, realizing at that moment with her choice of words just how deep her conditioning as a pleasure slave had been driven. He quickly said, "No, no, that's not it. It's just that, ever since the escape from your step-father's fortress, I've had these dreams about you and I. In the dreams we're sitting next to this very river, beside this bush, these flowers. It's all the same." He heard her gasp, but continued, "Then I move to kiss you, and—"

She interrupted him. "I slap you."

His jaw dropped open.

She said, "I had the same dream." She looked

into his eyes and smiled. "Except I didn't want to strike you, I told myself I would not, but I always did. I'm sorry."

He shook his head in disbelief. Then he gazed into her lovely eyes that glittered like jewels in the moonlight. "I apologize, for my audacity so long ago."

She smiled again. He liked that. "I was a different woman then. I know that now. Your apology is most enthusiastically accepted. And I would ask you, in return, to forgive my foolish response to your audacity."

"I accept," he said, elation swelling like a balloon in his breast.

Then, exactly as in the other dream, the one that had ended so abruptly, their fingers intertwined. His heart was going to burst out of his chest in a big mess. The starlight shone softly on her fair cheek. The moon splashed a silvery blaze across the rippling water. He swallowed hard. Somewhere in the water a fish splashed. Night creatures chirped and skreeked. He moved to kiss her again.

She would not strike him this time. Her soft, full lips parted.

And they kissed.

An explosion. Her lips were sweet, sweet honey. Her body soft, firm as he clutched it against him.

Hamilton's world reeled about him. He poured his very soul into that one kiss. Stars exploded behind his closed eyelids. He knew not how long they remained locked in that passionate embrace, but when it ended his soul sighed for joy. They sat looking deep into each other's eyes as if searching for affirmation that it had been real, a long timeless while. They kissed again, tenderly this time.

And they sat together in joyous silence, just content to be together.

Capian knelt holding a spitted rabbit over the crackling flames. He did not look at them as they approached. The eagles were gone, off to search for prey.

He did not speak to them as they ate the rabbit he had caught and prepared. Hamilton could feel Capian's resentment burn him like scalding water. He thought about this for the duration of the meal, after which Capian immediately left to bathe in the river.

Tamarra sensed the tension between them. "He's angry at you, isn't he?"

Hamilton nodded. "And I'm not sure why."

She said, "It's about me."

"You think so?"

She nodded. "I think so. Why not go speak to him? I'll stay here. I don't wish to hear what he has to say about me."

Hamilton nodded, got up and walked toward the river. He heard Capian splashing out in the water, so he sat down on the rock to wait for him. Eventually Capian waded out of the river. As he approached the bank, he saw Hamilton, and stopped, waist deep in the water.

Hamilton said, "What is it, Capian?"

Capian looked away, up the boundless night sky before he answered, "You won't like it, what I have to say."

Hamilton shrugged.

Capian took a deep breath, then said, "How dare you jeopardize both of our lives, our mission, the fate of the world, and the lives of thousands of people, for one woman? We could have both been killed trying to escape, especially you, trying to free her. We knew when we went through Uhr's dungeons that we couldn't save all the poor wretches imprisoned there. But you, completely on impulse and at the worst possible time, decide to burden us with a woman. A woman who is, no less, kith and kin to Lord Sneev, our mortal enemy."

"My friend," Hamilton said, "I'm in love with her."

"Then you should have loved her enough to go back for her, after all this was over."

"Capian, you've never known the love of a woman, therefore you don't know the feeling. You don't know how powerful those emotions can be. And there was no guarantee that we would be successful in our mission. I simply could not leave her there. If either of us, she or I, had died, I would have never known if it had all been real or just my imagination. And that would have been torture worse than any I can imagine. However, perhaps you're right. Maybe I shouldn't have gambled so severely with so much at stake, and for that I truly am sorry. But nevertheless, we did not die. We accomplished our mission in spite of having her as a burden. And she is not of Sneev's blood. She is not Uhr's lapdog, as her step-father is. Trust me when I tell you this."

Capian looked down, standing waist deep in the water, swirling it about with his hands. "Your arguments are as sound as mine. I know that. But still..."

"What is it?" Hamilton sensed Capian's emotions. Anger, fading, sadness. What was that, envy?

Capian shrugged. "I don't know. Something still pains me, but I'm not sure what it is." He waded out of the water, up onto the bank, picked up his garments and began to wash them, saying nothing. "I am sorry, my friend. I shouldn't have been so angry with you."

"Friends again?" Hamilton said.

"Aye." Capian looked over his shoulder at him as he scrubbed his breeks on a rock in the water, and smiled wanly. "Now go watch her, make sure she doesn't get away."

Hamilton smiled, and did so. As he approached the fire, he saw that she was now sleeping soundly. He laid down not far away, and was soon himself asleep.

The morning came swiftly and unwelcome in their exhaustion. The eagles had returned, their breast feathers stained with dried blood. Capian sat staring sullenly into the dying coals as they awoke. Before long, they were on their way, floating high above the green forests of Ophidia. The end of the day found them only a few leagues from the lofty Crag, on which perched Sneev's fortress like a great gray vulture in the hazy blue distance.

Hamilton craned his neck to speak to her over the keening wind. "There is your home."

"Yes," she whispered, barely audible. "How I have longed for it! But now I have no desire to return. It's an empty place now. I only wish to stay with you."

He smiled at that. His love for her grew with every passing moment, every touch, every glance. For them to be apart now was unthinkable. Her touch thrilled him. Her voice at once soothed and impassioned him. Her scent excited him with almost animal desire. And he had never been so happy, so utterly content and wild at once. Even though his tremendous task, finding Uhr and defeating him, still loomed ahead of him, he could die now if necessary, happily, his existence complete with experiencing the love that burned and crackled in his breast.

Capian's voice brought him down to more

earthly ponderings. "We should land soon. The eagles are weary," he shouted.

Hamilton nodded in agreement, but looking down, he saw the thick growth of trees prevented it.

"We must find a clearing then."

Tamarra pointed. "There lies the village of Saxonsand, just down that road."

Hamilton relayed this to Capian. The narrow road afforded an adequate landing site, even though the eagles' wing tips lashed at the outermost boughs stretching over the road. They concealed the birds in the heavy trees walling either side of the dirt path. Deciding to seek an inn, they walked the few hundred paces into the village. The road cut straight through the hamlet, forming its main thoroughfare. Log buildings lined the street on both sides. The forest had been cut back for other houses back from the main way. A few lights still burned along the way, but most of the inhabitants had turned in for the evening. The scent of roasting meat seized their attention, wafting from an open door shining with a subdued light. Loud voices echoed from the doorway out into the night. A wooden sign with a forester's ax painted on it creaked on its hangings above the door in the soft twilight breeze.

Hamilton stepped into the light, Tamarra beside him, Capian behind. Light came from wall-hung lanterns and the crackling blaze in the fireplace. They entered the place, surveying the room. The tavern was small, perhaps fifteen paces on a side, but it was packed with patrons. Their threadbare clothing and toil-drawn faces proclaimed them poor woodsmen and serfs, washing down the day's sweat with a meager cup of ale. About forty eyes took stock of the newcomers before returning to their own affairs. Except for the four armed men sitting at a table near the back wall. Yellow snakes intertwined writhed on their green surcoats. The soldiers eyed them with outright suspicion.

As they claimed the last empty table, one near the door, Capian and Hamilton removed their sword belts from their shoulders and laid them on the floor, but careful to keep them within easy reach.

A young lady weaved her way among the patrons to their table. "Greetings, folks," she said, smiling brightly, genuinely. "What would you?"

Her womanly curves wrapped tightly in her low-cut brown frock did not match the youthfulness of her face. Her face was girlishly pretty, with large sloe eyes, freckles lightly sprinkling her pert nose, straw-colored hair dancing about her shoulders.

They ordered a meal, and Hamilton noticed with a smile that her gaze lingered overlong on Capian, who apparently had not noticed her attention, engaged as he was in a rather foul mood. She soon returned with plates of meat and bread. Again Hamilton watched her eyes as her companions began to dine, and again her eyes seemed to caress Capian with their desirous touch. This time he did notice, and he seemed somewhat taken aback.

As she spun and weaved away with an extra swing of her sweetly curved hips, Hamilton watched his gaze follow her.

Hamilton chuckled.

Capian looked at him sourly. "What is it?"

"She is pretty," Hamilton said.

"Aye, she is," he agreed, his frown softening somewhat.

Tamarra said, "She likes you, Capian."

"She does?" he said, genuinely surprised. "How

do you know that?"

Tamarra told him, "It is obvious, especially to a woman."

Capian looked down at the rough, stained table. "I don't know of such things. Women are enigmas to me. Few lived at Sanctuary."

Hamilton said, "When she returns, talk to her. That's what she wants. What harm?"

"We'll see," Capian shrugged.

Hamilton grinned. He could see Capian's nervousness without sensing it.

They finished their meal in silence, savoring the hot meal. The serving girl returned and gathered their plates. This time she averted her pretty eyes, apparently discouraged by Capian's lack of response, and a little embarrassed.

She turned away, and Capian blurted, "What is your name, girl?"

She spun, a gigantic smile plastered across her lovely face, eyes sparkling. "My name is Lina, good sir," she replied. She turned away again with a wink, as if to say she would return.

The hour began to grow late, and the other patrons slowly took their leave, gradually emptying the tavern.

Eventually Lina came back with four foaming jacks of ale, pulled up a stool next to Capian, and said, "Good eventide to you, folks. Mind you if I sit for a while and rest my weary feet?"

Hamilton answered her, "Not at all, Lina. We would welcome your company."

"Did you stable your horses? They must have been tired."

"No," Hamilton replied, "we are on foot."

"Strange that there is no dust of the road on your clothes," she said, without a trace of suspicion in her voice.

They said nothing.

She continued, "I will not bother to ask you your names. Some of Lord Snake's guardsmen sit over there. These are troubled times. No need to stir up any more."

Hamilton noticed the guardsmen were in a heated discussion. As the soldiers argued, they eyed Hamilton and his companions. He returned his attention to the conversation at hand, holding back another grin as he saw Lina's ripe cleavage, more visible than before, thrust up for Capian's benefit. Capian's face was flushed red.

Lina said, "This is my father's inn. But he is gone to fight in the war, so I am left here with my mother to run this place." Her eyes were glued to Capian as she spoke.

Hamilton watched him try to maintain some semblance of composure, and laughed inwardly.

Their conversation continued until the ale flagons were empty, when Lina went to get more. Capian had grown progressively more confident, and his mood was improving, probably due to the strong drink, and the fact that Lina was such a gregarious conversationalist.

Now the only other patrons were the four soldiers at the far table. While Lina was gone, all four of them stood up and began to move toward the three strangers. Hamilton and Capian slid slowly back from the table to give them more room to act, if necessary. The guardsmen stopped before them. Much to Hamilton's alarm, he saw Tamarra's eyes light with recognition as she looked at the guardsmen. She quickly looked down at the table top.

One of the soldiers stepped forward. "My lady, are you or are you not Sneev's step-daughter? I know you look like her, because I was one of his house guards for a time."

Tamarra fairly jumped up. Capian and Hamilton tensed for the attack.

She stammered and finally spoke, quickly, her voice high-pitched and nasal. "No, sir, I am not, although there may be a resemblance. What would the Lady Tamarra be doing here? I am but a poor traveler."

The man's face twisted with distaste upon hearing her speak. He turned to his associates. "No, I told you that's not her, dolt! Tamarra had at least a pleasant voice!" They wheeled drunkenly about, and staggered for the door.

Tamarra's hand fell to her breast where her heart thumped like a rabbit's and her breath came in quick gasps.

Lina returned with fresh draughts. "Ah, they finally left, drunken sluggards," she mumbled. She seated herself again, this time very close to Capian, and stared wistfully into his face as she couched her chin in one palm. The other hand disappeared below the table.

With a surprised yelp, Capian jumped off his stool. He then regained his composure, and resolve hardened his features. He reclaimed his seat, gently took her hand and placed it back on the table. "Dear lady," he said, "you are very pretty, and a wonderful companion, but I am a Knight of the Eagles, and we take no women. I have never regretted being one until just this moment, because I must ask you to quench your fires..."

Hamilton heard no more. He had leaped to his feet and bounded for the door. His mind, nay, his entire being, burned, seethed upon four loathsome words. "We take no women." He jumped around tables and stools, his companions' queries falling on deaf ears. He had to get away, away, away from them, from her, alone, into the night. He was a

Eagle Knight, and he had known it was too good to last. Far too good.

A lifetime's worth of pain and anger boiled out of him like a cauldron of molten lead, scalding his very soul. Tears streaked his cheeks. She was too good, too wonderful. And he couldn't have her.

"We take no women." He heard it in his head over and over, again and again, beating upon his brow like a battering ram.

Outside, he ran, he didn't know how far. Finally he stopped, knelt, curled up in the shadows, and wept quietly in the dark.

Chapter 32

Uhr's power was growing. The Great Conjunction drew near. Soon the heavens would be in alignment, and then this puny mortal resistance would no longer matter. Until then, however, they must be dealt with, stamped out, lest they somehow gain a victory. He could hear the preparations outside for the next assault on Valerion's fortress. The tactician's most devastating error is to underestimate his enemy.

He picked up the sorcerously carved silver bowl from the black stone table. In the bottom of the bowl lay a few bits of torn skin and dried blood, The One's own flesh, which Uhr had dug from beneath his nails. The bowl he carried to the center of his private pavilion, where the Bloodstone burned upon a jet-black pedestal. He laid a rotting hand on the stone, holding the bowl in the other. Arcane syllables began to drip from his mouth like acid. The red glow strengthened, filling the large tent like a tiny sun. Flashes of crimson lightning crackled and snapped around his hands and bowl with its gruesome contents.

Outside, the grass around the tent wilted and blackened. Nearby night creatures stopped chirping. The two Slayers standing guard at the entrance fell over, dead. Birds stopped their flight and fell to the ground, the life-energy drained from them.

The bottom of the silver bowl began to fill with fresh blood and a thick, clear mucus.

The Ophidians in the camp watched the red light brighten the fringe of their encampment, tried not to look. The Slayers ignored it.

On the wall of the fortress, Robinton cursed, and felt his stomach knot up, his legs unsinew slightly, as he watched this scarlet brilliance grow. He did not bother to pray to his father's gods anymore. He was convinced now that they were deaf and dumb and blind. Robinton and his countrymen were alone now, it seemed, abandoned by their gods and allies to face the Evil One himself. The glow out there began to throb and pulse, like a heartbeat. He looked out at the hundreds of cook fires dotting the shore of the lake among the ruins of Lakeside and beyond.

Uhr's voice avalanched across the camp as if a thousand times amplified. Sneev's men cried out in pain, clawing at their ears. It was the tongue of madness that swept men's souls into the realm of black insanity. Agonized screams filled the air.

Inside the pavilion, the beast that was Uhr blasted out the chant's last horrid syllables. Thunder rolled across the cloudless sky. The blinding sorcerous light slowly faded. The Ophidians collapsed and wept, or stared dumbly into their cook fires with glazed eyes, or lay drooling on the ground, or ignorantly mumbling the syllables that had just been blasted into their minds.

Uhr pccrcd cxpcctantly down into thc bowl. Scarlet arcs crackled across the warm surface. There, in the bottom of the bowl, in a pool of mixed blood and fluid, lay a human fetus. It pulsed with a new-given life, and even as Uhr watched, it grew.

438

In minutes it swelled into a mewling, sandy-haired infant.

Uhr's ghoulish laughter roared across the encampment.

Angus MacTavish scowled in disgust. After three sleepless nights and days, he had pulled guard duty. His exhaustion merely served to magnify his foul mood. He paced monotonously back and forth across the wall above the inner ward's gatehouse. The hour was just past midnight, and three hours still remained in his watch. Even now he felt himself on the brink of collapse. Only his own iron will kept him going. Two other Red Dragons walked their own stations on this section of the wall. Only Red Dragons guarded the inner ward, now that the outer ward was lost.

As he patrolled, Angus thought about how Valerion's mood had darkened of late. He seemed to have fallen into a fit of deep despair. Who wouldn't? Angus thought. He had seen Valerion at about sunset, and the lord looked as if he hadn't slept in days. Valerion had sent a messenger dove to Lord Skaand in desperation, but had received no reply. And what about Hamilton? What of The One? Angus wondered if his long-time friend was dead, or rotting in a dungeon somewhere. Or maybe he had the legendary Ivory Star by now and was on his way to kill Uhr. If so, could they last long enough for Hamilton to get here?

As Valerion wandered through his house, these same questions ate at his brain, denying him the comfort of sleep. His house was empty now. His wife and daughter long dead left a hollow feeling in his guts. The unknown fate of his son, Capian still a mystery after these eternal weeks, did little but turn his thoughts toward dark depression. Even the presence of his long-lost father failed to help. He spent every night pacing the halls of his house, deep in melancholiac thoughts. Often he even thought he saw, out of the corner of his eye, Ilone gazing sadly at him. But when he spun and tried to look, she was always gone. He longed for her comfort now more than ever. He could almost feel her caress on his skin, and the grief of it was driving him mad.

It was late now, and everyone was asleep, except the guards outside, and himself. And he sat in his meeting chamber alone, eyes filled with tears.

Angus yawned and rubbed his eyes. His body screamed for sleep. Then he spied a wraith-like black figure moving swiftly, silently through the night toward the inner ward's drawbridge. The drawbridge was lowered, but the portcullis was closed. The figure appeared to have the intention of entering the inner ward.

Angus raised his voice in challenge, "Hold there! Who goes?" He hefted his loaded crossbow.

A voice came up from below. "I must speak with Valerion."

Angus lowered his crossbow. "I know that voice!" he exclaimed. "Hamilton is that you?"

"Aye," the voice said, "open the portcullis. It's urgent that I speak with Valerion."

Angus flew to the winch, a huge grin splitting his face. He single-handedly did the work of two men in cranking it. Opening the triple-bolted gates ook him several minutes. He sent another Dragon o fetch Robinton, and inform Valerion of the new rrival. When the gates finally opened, the man arbed in black robes slipped inside.

Angus grasped his shoulder. "Hamilton, it's

good to see you."

The man with Hamilton's face pulled back his black hood and gazed at Angus. No trace of recognition in his blue eyes as he smiled. "It's good to see you, too," he said, "but I must see Valerion. It's quite urgent. Uhr's planning something special."

A chill brushed Angus's spine like a glacier's breath. "Of course," he replied, puzzled, but not yet suspicious.

Robinton came running across the courtyard. "What's going on here?" he demanded. "Why are the gates open!" Then he saw Hamilton regarding him, and nodded. "I see." He turned then to another Dragon, and said, "Close the gates, Tolby." He said to the stranger, "I will take you to Valerion."

Angus said, "With your permission, I will accompany you."

Robinton saw Angus's strange expression "Aye, follow me."

They followed the Red Dragon commander int the house. Valerion awaited them in the meetin room. As the three stepped into the room, a singl lantern cast huge shadows on the stone walls. A Valerion looked for a moment at the man wit Angus and Robinton, his eyes brightened, and the he sighed as if a tremendous weight had been lifte from his soul.

"At last!" Valerion said. "We have awaited you return."

"Aye," the man said, "I have come."

Valerion sat facing him on the edge of the t ble in his night-clothes, a soft white tunic and tro sers. "Have you the Ivory Star?"

"Aye," the man said. "Here it is." He reach into his robes.

Angus saw the man's muscles tense. With a warning he leaped forward.

Steel flashed.

Angus plowed into the black robes and bore the man heavily to the floor.

Valerion grunted in surprise and pain.

The man underneath Angus thrashed and growled and screamed like an animal.

Valerion staggered back, blood spurting.

The blood-smeared short sword in the man's hand stabbed up at Angus. Only his mail coat saved him from evisceration. The force of the blow flung him off, and the man with Hamilton's face leaped to his feet, eyes blazing maliciously. Angus's ax jumped from his belt into his hand as he stood. Robinton dragged Valerion away from the fight.

The simulacrum coiled in the corner like a caged beast, short sword brandished.

"I suspected," Angus said, "but I wasn't sure. I will send your head back to Uhr in a bag."

The simulacrum smiled maleficently.

Angus attacked. His ax slashed brightly in the lamp light. His enemy knocked the blow away and leaped aside.

Robinton jumped back into the room, sword foremost.

The simulacrum laughed, swinging his sword at the lamp on the table. The lamp crashed aside, and the light disappeared, plunging them into inky blackness. Angus felt a shape brush past him in the dark. Blindly he lashed out, and missed. There came a hard "thud" at the door and a whoosh of breath.

Robinton gasped from the floor, "He got past me."

For what seemed an eternity, Angus groped

about the room, finally stepping into the adjoining torch-lit corridor, and cast about for the impostor. There, almost to the far door, ran the enemy. In a moment, he would be gone. Almost without thinking, Angus flung his battle ax with all his might. The simulacrum's hand closed on the door latch.

The ax spun across the distance. The door was opening. Then it slammed shut again with the force of the simulacrum's body smashing into it, with the head of Angus's ax buried in the back of his skull. The impostor's body slid slowly down the door, to the floor, as Angus bounded down the hallway. He stopped before the body, and a dreadful shiver raced up and down his spine as Hamilton's dead blue eyes stared up at him from the grossly cocked head. Angus tore the ax head free of the smashed brain case with a squelch of gore and brains. With a single blow he separated the mutilated head from the neck. His hand trembled as he picked it up by the blood-soaked hair, and carried it back to throw at his lord's feet.

As he walked away, he gasped as the head in his hand dissolved into smoke, and disappeared. He spun in time to see the headless body do the same. It was all gone, even the blood on his hands and ax. But he was willing to bet that Valerion's wound had not disappeared.

He found them in the meeting chamber again, with Valerion couched in a chair, and Robinton pouring vegetable spirits over the deep wound in his left thigh. Valerion hissed in pain as the spirits poured over the bleeding gash, adding to the pool of crimson on the floor below.

Angus said, "He is dead, my lord."

Valerion said, gritting his teeth, "My thanks, Angus. Had you not jumped him, he would have gutted me."

Angus nodded, saying nothing.

Tarl burst into the room, shouldering past Angus. "What commotion is—! My lord! You're wounded!" he bellowed.

"Aye," Valerion said, "but not gravely."

Tarl blustered, "By whom? I'll—!"

Valerion gestured him to calm down. "Ease yourself, my friend. It's already over."

Then Garth hurried in behind Tarl. "What's happened!"

Valerion sighed. "It's over, I tell you! Some impostor fashioned by Uhr came to assassinate me...! Damn it all, man, use not so much of that brew! It burns like fire! Someone summon Kavarius. I need a real leech."

After Angus had completed his guard shift, he lay in his bunk, hands behind his head, staring up at the black ceiling. In spite of his exhaustion, he could not sleep. How could Uhr have made such an exact copy? he wondered. What if that man really was Hamilton? He shuddered at the thought. Hamilton was like his brother. Had he slain the real Hamilton? But even if Uhr had somehow captured Hamilton and enslaved him, he was still a man, a man left a corpse, and he had watched the corpse dissolve to smoke before his own eyes. But then he remembered the Red Priests, how they disappeared after they died. Perhaps Uhr recalled the husks of his own servants, when their usefulness was gone. It was nearly dawn when the final answer finally hit him. The man he had slain nearly assassinated Lord Valerion, his lord, whom he was honor-bound to protect at all cost, even sacrificing his own life if necessary. If that corpse had been the true Hamilton, so be it. His truest friend would not have wanted his body to be one of Uhr's puppets.

After that somewhat painful resolution, he drifted off into a short, troubled sleep.

A terrified cry rang out, and the alarm bell began to clang from the gates of the middle ward. It was mid-morning, and everyone quickly converged there to ascertain the cause of the commotion. Fear struck deep into what hope remained in them.

"Gods, what a sight!" Garth breathed.

The massive gates that separated the outer ward from the bridge leading to the middle ward were gone, burnt to ashes with hardly a wisp of smoke. The stone around where the hinges had been was blackened and sagging from a tremendous heat.

And now there stood in the gaping hole a frightening figure, one that towered head and shoulders and chest above the armored Slayers standing behind him. He was clad in black and silver plate armor, fit perfectly to his gaunt frame, like a beetle's spindly carapace, eight feet tall. The armor moved with him, easily, perfectly, quite unlike the way natural armor should. A long flowing cape the color of congealed blood flared from narrow shoulders. A black helm topped the figure. The faceplate was blank and flat, save for two narrow eye slits blazing with an obscene scarlet glow. The sides of the helm were adorned by two leathery wings the likes of which mortal man had never seen. Hanging at the figure's armor-encrusted hip was a huge sword in a black lacquered scabbard. The blade alone was nearly five feet long, a hand's breadth wide. The hilt was a plain black handle, unadorned, without a quillion.

Uhr was the embodiment of Evil.

All felt it, and shuddered to the depths of their souls.

Uhr walked slowly, menacingly, halfway across the bridge, and stopped. His gaze raked the terrified faces staring at him from the battlements.

His voice slashed hollow from the terrible helmet. "Lord Valerion, I would speak with you. I see you are there."

"Speak, devil!" Valerion snarled. "And be done!"

Uhr's voice boomed, "I would be merciful this day. Send out your civilians, and they will live."

Uhr's words grated on Valerion's conscience, with the memory of the butchery at the Eagle Knight's Sanctuary haunting his reply. "I have seen your mercy, monster! My people would better die quickly than in your slave coffles!"

"Who are you, one man, to decide the fate of thousands? Perhaps you should let them decide! After all, this battle is between you and I, not them. I will give you until noon to decide. After that, the bones are cast."

Uhr spun on his black heel and disappeared among his soldiers, leaving Valerion in a dilemma. The men around him watched him expectantly, wondering what he would do. He looked at his father, "Father, have you any advice?"

Garth cleared his throat and shook his head. "I don't know, Son. His words make sense, to men like us. But Uhr is not a man. Who knows if he means what he says, that he'll let them live."

Fortine scratched his paunch, and spat. "Oh, he'll let 'em live, at least for now. He needs the slaves. My guess is he's running out of Ophidians to do the Slayers' dirty work. You know, cooking, patching up the wounded, sharpening weapons and such."

"I hardly dare open the gates for a second," Valerion said. "He might seize the opportunity to overrun us. But he's right in that I can't condemn all the helpless women and children to certain death. Better to let them decide. Robinton, spread the word. Call out everyone, women, children, everyone. I have to speak to them."

Before long, several thousand people had gathered in the crowded yard near the gatehouse to hear what their lord had to say. Men and women, young and old, the infirm, the wounded. Their faces bore the invisible scars of long hardship and utter despair. Valerion's heart wept for them. He stood above them on the wall not in glory this time, but in dismal resignation. He leaned on Robinton's shoulder, his wounded leg throbbing painfully.

He raised his voice. "There will be no brave speeches today, no glorious oratory. The time for that is drowned in a sea of our blood. Uhr..." He spat the word contemptuously. "...has given you a choice. Those among you who wish to leave here may do so and live, albeit as Uhr's slaves. But it will be life, a life to carry on the legacy and memory of those of us who remain, and will most probably die here.

"The choice is yours. There will be no judgment upon you if you decide to leave."

A man's voice cried out from the milling crowd, "I would sooner die than give Uhr the satisfaction!"

Then a women spoke up, "But I have three fatherless sons. I would see them as men!"

The throng exploded into uproar.

Valerion raised his hands, and they eventually silenced. "As I said, there will be no judgment upon those who wish to leave. Those wishing to go, gather your belongings and wait near the gate." He looked up at the sun. It was nearly noon. "It is time."

And they did, widows and children for the most part. Possessions were gathered and tearful farewells exchanged.

As they did so, Valerion called out across the bridge. "Uhr! They come!" That was all he said.

He gave orders for the sentries to watch and be ready to slam the gates shut in an instant, lest the Slayers try to rush them. As a precaution, he sent out only as many people at a time as would fill the barbican, with either the portcullis or the gates closed at all times. He watched as the first group shuffled across the bridge, and were herded away. Several groups followed, until all were gone that wished to be, amounting to about half those unable to fight: women, children, the aged.

Then, only after the last of them had gone, did the horrible sounds began to drift from the shore. Anguished screams and the cracking of whips floated like ghosts across the water, and in agony Valerion hurled roaring curses to Uhr in return.

But the end was coming, Valerion knew. He hardly bothered to look at the sky anymore, or hope. Uhr's power was growing. All day Valerion stood at the battlement. No one spoke to him, or approached where he stood, and he watched the weary sun drown in a sea of bloody mountains, as if finally giving up the life of day for the death of night.

Valerion found it fitting, as the attack began.

Chapter 33

"But why?" Tamarra demanded, fists on hips.

Hamilton answered her as he saddled Skyking, "There will be heavy fighting. We will be in the thick of it. And Skyking flies faster with only one rider." His face was a mask of emotionless iron, concealing the pain that ground at his heart.

"But I don't want to go home!" she shouted.

Hamilton said, "Then I will bind you and leave you in the courtyard."

She gazed at him, straight in the eye. "Worse has been done to me."

Hamilton winced.

Capian piped up, chuckling, his voice mischievous, "Then you would not mind." He led Starjumper out of the forest beside the road.

A ghost of a smile flickered across her lovely mouth, then swiftly disappeared in her anger and confusion.

Hamilton kept his back to her, unwilling to even look at her, fearing it would only cause him more grief, and waver him in his conviction.

"Let's go," he said grimly, climbing astride Skyking's broad shoulders. Without bothering to buckle the safety strap, he hauled back on the top rein, leaving Tamarra standing open-mouthed on the ground.

She wiped at the tears trickling down her cheek. "Why? I thought..." her voice trailed off.

Capian looked down at her from his perch on Starjumper's back, and his eyes softened at her anguish. "I don't know what's gotten into him, my lady," he said, offering his hand to her. "Climb aboard. He seems to be in a hurry."

As Starjumper leaped into the air and gained a cruising altitude, Capian said, "It is better that you remain with your people until this is over."

She sniffled, wiping at her eyes. "I know that." A sob cracked her voice. "But why did he have to be so...so cold?"

"I don't know that, my lady, but I do know something. He loves you more than his own life, and he was willing to risk everything to see that love fulfilled. What he feels right now, it will pass, I think."

She hugged Capian tightly from behind, saying nothing more.

An hour later they were circling the Fortress on the Crag. They landed on the grassy strip between the Crag and the surrounding forest, opposite the rock from the town of Cragmoor. They dared not pass too close lest an overzealous sentry shoot one of their mounts from under them.

After Tamarra dismounted Starjumper, she quickly circled to stand at Hamilton's stirrup.

He didn't look at her, staring straight ahead, his face hard.

She said, "Please, promise me you'll return for me."

Then he looked at her.

She gazed up into his face, and his carefully built facade crumbled into dust. The agony poured out of his eyes, and then, in that moment, she understood.

"I cannot," he said, and with that ambiguous reply, he hauled on the straps, and Skyking leaped into the air. Gone.

Capian said, "Farewell, Lady Tamarra. I will try to keep him safe."

She nodded, and looked away. "Thank you."

"And if necessary," Capian added, "when this is all over, I will bring him back to you myself."

Then he too pitched into the air, and was gone.

High above the two eagle riders, the Day Stars were so close they shone as one, a single bright point of light in the azure sky. The sun had already passed them on its celestial path.

The Great Conjunction was tomorrow! Hamilton realized, with a sudden sickness in his heart. Would he be in time? He cursed his dalliance with Tamarra. His foolish emotions may have already doomed the world. And all for naught, because he could not have her anyway. He was an Eagle Knight. He forced all such thought of her from his tortured mind. He must concentrate on the task at hand.

They crossed the border into Armond at the time Valerion's people left the safety of the fortress and passed into slavery. They stopped at sunset for one last rest before the last desperate leg of their trek.

The attack had begun shortly after sunset. Valerion had decided to abandon the middle ward now that most of the non-combatants were gone. With the number of fighting men still remaining, the inner ward and Keep were more easily defensible. Even now the preparations for withdrawal were underway. A small contingent of Red Dragons were holding the gatehouse, to keep the Slayers at bay long enough to herd the civilians to safety. After the civilians were safe, Robinton and his men would quietly retreat.

That was the plan.

Robinton and his men watched the gatehouse. The buildings in the outer ward were ablaze, and the wall was a crenelated silhouette in the smoky orange glow. The Slayers made a few seemingly half-hearted thrusts at the gatehouse with some ladder crews, but were easily beaten back. Robinton scratched his beard, eyes narrowed in thought. He said, "Daarton, I don't like this. That was too easy. They're up to something."

The swordmaster answered him, "I think you may be right."

Robinton said, "Aalok, how is the withdrawal proceeding?"

"Nearly finished, sir," the short man answered from behind his loaded crossbow as he glanced back at the compound.

"Oh, no!" came a furtive whisper. Robinton wasn't sure who said it, but he looked nevertheless, and the blood chilled in his veins.

Uhr was crossing the bridge, coming toward the middle ward gate, carrying something. A bowl. A metal bowl, full of something dark and thick in the light from the fires burning in the outer ward. Aalok took aim with his crossbow and fired. The hurtling splinter of metal exploded into sparks a few inches from Uhr's helmet. Aalok whistled in surprise and fear.

Daarton grasped Robinton's mailed arm and looked him in the face, "Sir, we must withdraw."

Robinton said, "Is the evacuation complete?"

Someone answered him, "Not yet, sir."

"Then we stay." Robinton sighed, and raised his voice, "Crossbowmen, load and fire at will!"

The Red Dragons did so, sending a volley of bolts at the towering figure standing obliviously below them. He ignored the quarrels bursting into fiery nothingness about him as he dipped a brush made of virgin's hair into his bowl, and began to splash the hot congealing blood on the heavy wooden gate, creating a large arcane sigil.

The defenders could only watch in helpless horror from the wall, as Uhr, with his painting done, dipped his hands in the blood, and stepped back. He flung the blood away from him in a hot spray as he bellowed a single terrible word the likes of which human ears had never heard. His rotting fists blazed with scarlet brilliance as he lashed out at the thick portal. The blow roared like thunder under the Red Dragons' feet, and the massive gate exploded into a deadly barrage of wood and metal splinters. He did not miss a step as he strode through the smoke and destruction, into the gatehouse.

"He's at the portcullis!" someone cried.

Uhr's hands were still glowing as he stepped up to the iron bars of the portcullis, touched them and uttered another sorcerous phrase. Instantly the portcullis flashed white hot, and collapsed into an orange puddle at Uhr's feet.

Uhr roared, "The way is now open, my pets!"

Robinton said, "We have to get down there and hold them, men."

But it was too late. Something was coming across the bridge. More swiftly than human feet could move.

Uhr strode unchecked into the middle ward, standing in triumph below the horrified Red Dragons. A phalanx of close-ranked Slayers marched in at his heels.

Aalok cried, "We're cut off!"

"Aye," Robinton said, "but we'll go out like Dragons..."

He was cut off by the terrible cacophony of snarling and growling from below. Into the courtyard below stalked four huge beasts. Feral eyes glowed like red stars and tiny pointed ears were laid back against the massive midnight-black heads. Thick spiked collars encircled the bull-like necks. Huge slavering jaws lined with dagger teeth chomped and gnashed. The monsters stood six feet tall at the shoulder, quivering blocks of taut, rippling muscle and death.

One of the men whispered in barely-checked fear, "Devil dogs!"

The sight of these almost mythical incarnations of primal unfettered savagery squelched all thoughts of a last defiant stand. It wouldn't be a stand against beasts such as that. It would be a massacre. But they had to act quickly. Robinton cast about for a means of escape. The only possible path was along the rampart. Motioning his men to silence he led them towards the walkway. Perhaps if the devil dogs didn't notice them immediately...

Suddenly white light exploded from Uhr's hands, shooting a blazing white ball high into the air, illuminating the scene like a miniature sun. Uhr's chilling voice boomed through the smoky air, "There, my pets!" He pointed with a black steel claw at Robinton and his hapless band. "There is your prey!"

With roars of savage glee, the devil dogs sprang into pursuit. The Armondians broke into terror-stricken flight. In two bounds one of the dogs had gained the walk and bore down on them in slavering blood-lust.

Robinton did not look back as he broke into a

dead run, hearing the gurgling scream and rending of flesh. He heard the clicking of nails on the stone walk, drawing nearer. Another scream ripped from a savaged throat, the popping of rivets torn from armor, the crunch of bone, the splash of blood on stone. He glanced back as he ran and saw two monstrous shapes overtaking his men one by one, slaughtering them like cattle.

His legs were mired in a thick bog, it seemed. No matter how fast he ran, the dogs gained on him. He did not know how many times he stumbled and nearly fell, awaiting the hot breath on the nape of his neck, the sharp fangs.

His goal was in sight, but he skidded to a halt. He stood at the edge of the walkway, before it fell away twenty feet short of the wall of the inner ward. The moat was just below him. The inner ward gates were closed, and wide-eyed white faces stared at him from behind the safety of the battlements just above. He heard their cries of mixed encouragement and terror, helplessness and anger.

And two more dogs waited for him below, at the edge of the moat, red eyes blazing hungrily.

His sword came with a well-oiled whisper into his hand. He turned and awaited his fate. The nearest dog on the walkway pulled its muzzle out of Daarton's chest, its mouth full of dangling entrails, glaring at him, stabbing him with its merciless gaze.

He was alone now. He would meet Death now, but not helpless.

The beast's black muzzle glistened wetly in the dying light, its teeth stained scarlet.

It seemed to smile at him.

It leaped.

His sword clove a flashing arc as he threw himself to the side. His blade bit deep and a hot gush sprayed his face. A tremendous weight glanced off him, throwing him heavily against the battlement.

The dog's severed head splashed into the moat below, and the hulking carcass skidded to a halt against the battlement, twitching spasmodically.

An icy howl of mourning rose from the throats of the other dogs, a howl which quickly turned to roars of hatred.

Robinton staggered upright. The dogs below padded nearer, hackles standing like spikes, eyes fixed on Robinton. "Come, you bastards!" he snarled. "Taste of my steel!"

He saw the muscles of the nearest beast bunch for the spring, and braced himself.

With a bone-chilling roar the devil dog leaped straight up from the ground below.

Robinton thrust. The point stabbed deep.

Fangs locked on his throat.

The monster's terrific momentum carried them both through the crenel in the battlement, over the wall, into the cold water below.

Lord Valerion watched in horrified immobility from his perch above, and he wept.

The middle ward was lost.

Orange flames shot up from the houses, throwing eerie light into the dark sky.

Valerion watched the tall, armored figure striding down the way toward the inner ward gates. Houses burst into blazing conflagrations at Uhr's mere passing.

Uhr stopped a few paces from the moat. His voice rose, "Tomorrow is the Conjunction. By then, I will not need all these Slayers to destroy you, for you will be but dust in my divine wind. I give you the night to pray to your gods and use your women. Prepare yourselves to die, mortals!"

He turned and glided away.

Angus MacTavish, standing at the battlement, heard Uhr's words. He had watched his friends and brothers in arms die in the fangs of the devil dogs. A great emptiness opened up inside of him, sucking away all feeling. Uhr's words rang true, Angus thought. And the emptiness inside of him howled to be filled. And he knew that there was one person in the world now who could fill it.

A knock sounded lightly on the door of Nessa's chamber, where she sat idly brushing her flaxen hair. Sleep had refused to find her. A single lamp burned on the night table.

"Enter."

The door swung inward. Angus stepped inside. The brush fell from her fingers, and an astonished stare was his greeting. Then she leaped up and threw her arms around his armored body. He held her in a strong, gentle embrace.

As she reluctantly released him, he said, "Uhr has generously given us the night to contemplate our deaths."

Her sparkling blue eyes met his coal black eyes.

"I love you, Nessa," he said. Those strong eyes plumbed her very soul.

Her heart raced. "I love you," she whispered. She reached out, but he stopped her.

He said, "I wish nothing to separate us, not even this armor." He unbuckled the straps of his chain mail coat, and pulled it off, revealing the sweat-soaked green tunic beneath. His belt fell at his ankles. She reached up and touched his clean-shaven cheek. Tears streaked her face. Then he took her and squeezed her close. She wore only a long, silk night gown that did little to contain her full, firm breasts. The closeness of her soft, sensual body sent lightning through his veins.

"These could be our last moments together," he said.

"I know," she said, her voice quavering.

He could feel her heart thumping against his chest, her body shivering.

"You are frightened," he said.

She nodded, and gulped. "I have never…known a man before."

"I know," he said.

He stepped back and pulled off his tunic, baring his broad black-furred chest, hard rippling belly, corded thews. She swallowed hard and ran her fingers through the thick tufts of black. His hands caressed her shoulders.

He kissed her then, a long, deep, soft, wet, passionate kiss, and her body melted against his, like hot living wax.

His fingers toyed with the laces of her gown. She gasped in surprise, and jumped back.

His eyes fell. "I am sorry," he said sincerely. "Truly sorry."

She looked down for a moment, then returned to his arms. "No, be not sorry when I should be." Her voice came in soft quick gasps as she gently kissed his breast, and herself unlaced the front of her gown. "Now is not the time for chastity."

Their lips met again, and her fingers snaked through this wavy, jet-black hair.

Then she stepped back, allowed the gown to slip down over her shoulders, held up now only by her womanly abundance. With a slight wriggle that set Angus on fire, she let the gown fall down into a glistening white pool at her feet.

A long deep breath escaped him as his eyes feasted. "You are so beautiful!" he breathed.

A pink flush spread across her cheeks, and

gooseflesh rose on her flawless skin. He slipped out of his boots, unbuckled the narrow belt that supported his leather breeks, and slipped out of them. He stood now naked, in all his manhood.

Her eyes widened. "Oh, my!" She gasped. "I had no idea! Angus, I'm frightened."

He approached her, rubbing her shoulders soothingly. "Fear not, my heart. I swear I'll not harm you." He smiled and kissed her lightly on the mouth. Suddenly he scooped her up in his mighty arms.

"I love you, Angus," she said, as he carried her to the bed, "and I trust you with my life."

He smiled and kissed her.

With new-found gentleness, he laid her down on the bed, and they made profound, tender, gentle, passionate love.

Chapter 34

Dawn came reluctantly, as if dreading the coming day's events. The first silver rays of sunlight glanced from the lofty peaks of the Viderian Mountains, and Uhr raised his hands to the brightening sky. He was alone in the mountains, save for the violently quivering young girl who lay bound by human sinew on the ground several paces away. Her use would come later.

His work complete, he surveyed the results. He had leveled the peak of an exceptionally tall, narrow stone projection, a task that would have taken a hundred men years. He had done it in a few hours, and, of course, he had only used up the lives of twenty of his new slaves. Their remains lay below, far below down the side of the mountain where he had cast them. The flat top of the mountain was flawless black stone perhaps a hundred paces across. A waist-high altar of the mountain's stone, just large enough for a human body, stood directly in the center of the platform. The site was prepared. Now the spell must be readied for his ascension to godhood. He glanced at the cowering slave girl, and laughed, a dry, terrible sound.

From the plain leather satchel he slipped the

Bloodstone. It pulsed with a dull, red glow. Uhr felt its growing power, and he basked in it. For centuries he had awaited this day. He was ready, ready for life, not this sickening half-existence, trapped in the shell of a hideous, rotting corpse. Only the total consumption of humanity, the blessed union of flesh, blood and soul, had sustained him in his wretched existence for the last thousand years. On that last Great Conjunction, he had been given immortality, and power beyond his wildest imagining, but he had been robbed of his humanity. Now he would have it back, his humanity. The eternal exuberance of a youthful body, a body such as it had looked a thousand years ago. But now that form would be coupled with power such as he had never dreamed.

He wondered with smug amusement if he even remembered how to be human. Then he thought, no he wouldn't remember at all. He wouldn't even try. He would learn to be a god.

The Bloodstone would be of use one last time.

****

Angus quietly clothed himself, watching his beloved Nessa sleeping peacefully. So like a child in many ways, he thought, yet such a beautiful, wondrous, loving woman. He knew now that he loved her more than his own life, and he wanted to be gone before she awoke. He wanted her last memories of him to be of their love, not of his goodbye before he went to die. Silently he picked up his sword belt and chain mail shirt, wincing at the tell-tale jangle. Stealthily he opened the door and stepped into the hall, closing the door quietly behind him.

"Who goes there?" came a deep voice, quiet in these last sleeping hours.

Angus tensed, knowing the voice well. He turned.

Valerion stepped into the light of the single, flickering torch.

"It is only Angus MacTavish, my lord," Angus said, standing straight and tall. He saw Valerion's fists clench, he braced himself for the coming storm. Valerion was no fool.

To Angus's great surprise, he only said, "It seems you have a way with my daughters, Angus MacTavish." His lips were drawn into a tight line.

Angus stiffened. "I fully intend to ask you for her hand, should we, by fate's freak, live through tomorrow."

Valerion nodded. "You don't surprise me. Under different circumstances, I would have sooner expected it." He paused. "It's good. She should love before she dies. I only wish..." His voice trailed off.

"My lord?"

"If we somehow survive, I wish you only the greatest happiness. And I wish my own happiness still lived."

"We all have many wishes, my lord."

"She is so like her mother, Angus. I never want her to leave my side. I know she must someday, else I leave hers." Valerion paused again. "And I see so much of myself in you, Angus. I was much like you when I was young, hungry for battle and glory, thirsty for strong wine and sweet women, hot of temper as well. But age and responsibility temper the raw steel of youth, man. You'll find that."

"Is there a purpose in this speech, my lord?"

"Hah! Impetuous as ever, eh?" Valerion looked away, shaking his head as his visage darkened. He sighed. "Nay, no purpose. Just a tired man's last lament before he meets his ancestors. Go now.

Sleep maybe. Uhr will be upon us before long."

Angus saluted him. "Thank you, my lord." He moved past Valerion, then stopped and turned around again. He said, "My lord Valerion, I have but one thing to say, while I yet may."

"What is that?"

"My lord, in your service, my life has been given meaning, whatever the outcome of all this. I just wanted you to know."

Valerion smiled grimly, saluting Angus. "Thank you, Angus MacTavish. I hope I am worthy of your service."

Angus bowed and departed.

Lord Sneev sat up from his sleeping mat. Cold sweat soaked him. His small misshapen frame quaked uncontrollably. The familiar cold emptiness still sucked at his soul. He swung his feet out of the blankets, into the chilly air. The interior of his private pavilion was beginning to brighten with dawn's coming. His hand wiped the cold sweat from his bald pate. The message from the Master was coming to him...

The final assault!

It was time.

He hurriedly dressed himself. He abusively roused his pages from their exhausted slumber to arm and armor him. Then he sent for Brudge.

The fat man limped into the tent rubbing sleep from his piggish eyes. "Yes, my lord?"

"Sound the reveille and the battle trumpets. See that General Antrax gets this." He handed Brudge a piece of rolled up parchment, containing Sneev's transcription of Uhr's message. "The fortress falls today!" Sneev hissed.

Brudge yawned, and Sneev's gauntleted fist clouted him on the side of the head. "Waken, lout!"

he bawled. "Now be quick!"

Brudge bowed and stumbled out.

Sneev's tiny fists clenched in anticipation. After today, Valerion's fortress would be rubble, his people either slaughtered or scattered to the four winds. He would enjoy seeing Valerion's bloody corpse dragged through the encampment, and he would spit on the grave.

A hundred battle trumpets blared in the dawn light

The defenders clutched their weapons with desperate strength. The Slayers gathered and formed ranks in the middle ward.

Valerion stood alone on the watchtower, surveying the enemy gathering below. A step behind him caused him to look over his shoulder. His father stood there, clad in mail and breastplate. His gray-streaked black hair fell out of his polished steel helm covering his head. A shield hung on his arm and a longsword hung at his hip. The old lord stood there nobly, proudly.

Valerion regarded him quizzically.

Seeing his son's expression, Garth said, "When I first returned, I told you the old sword wanted to shine in use. Well, the old rusty sword will shine one last time. He will fight and die beside his countrymen, and his son."

Valerion smiled. "As you wish, my lord. It is an honor."

Now a great commotion in the middle ward gained their attention. Teams of straining horses drew large carts and wagons into view, bearing loads of sticks. Whatever the sticks were for, they boded no good. Before Valerion could call for him, Fortine came huffing up the tower steps.

"My lord!" Fortine puffed. "See you that?"

"Aye," Valerion answered, "it looks like bundles of sticks. What are they for?"

The master engineer swallowed hard. "They mean to fill the moat."

Valerion said softly, "This is it then. We die. We don't have the numbers defend this wall for long, once they cross the moat."

They watched helplessly. The carts were maneuvered into position at the edge of the moat and dumped, pouring the bundles into the water.

Fortine scratched his stubby chin, and said, "Eventually they'll fill it. Normally all that wood would float, but it's already been soaked with water, and weighted down with iron. The bundles will settle, and the Slayers will have a path to the wall."

A few arrows managed to down some of the Slayers approaching with the wagons, but their supply of arrows and bolts was nearly gone.

Valerion fumed and cursed, helpless to stop or even slow them. The pitch was long since gone. There would be no burning this time.

After a few hours, the two bridges the Slayers had created were complete. Valerion had sent word to his house that Tarl should move everyone into the Keep, and be prepared for the defenders' retreat. He had joined his men above the gatehouse, looking about at the stalwart fighters surrounding him. They had trusted him, and now they were going to die. He saw many of them were already wounded from previous assaults, but they had taken their place among the defenders. They would die on their feet, not on their backs.

And the Slayers came, a howling horde of black-spiked demons, weapons bristling and glinting in the midday light. Valerion's men shrank in fear, but stood fast.

At each bridge, the path was wide enough to

support three ladder crews. The Slayers stormed across the makeshift bridges, set the ladders, and climbed. The defenders' polearms sent them tumbling back again. Then a hail of arrows blasted the defenders. Men staggered and fell, clutching at the black shafts. Another volley lashed at them, sending them behind the merlons for cover.

Then a Slayer leaped onto the walk, then another, and another, wreaking hurricanes of death among the startled Armondians.

"At them, lads!" Valerion roared. "Beat them back into Hell."

But it was too late. Too undermanned and disheartened, the desperate defenders could not stem the tide. Blood gushed and ran and dripped, slicking the stone.

Thus occupied with this last desperate battle, no one saw the cloud of dust rising in the west. Most of the Slayers had gathered inside the castle for the final attack, leaving what was left of Sneev's men and the wounded on the shore. And the cloud of dust grew.

A noise began to build with the dust cloud, a low rumble. The Ophidians in the encampments looked toward the sound with little excitement, thinking it was just another contingent of Slayer reinforcements arriving.

A roaring regiment of mounted warriors suddenly burst over the nearest hill, flew down the slope, and swept through the Ophidian camps like a howling tornado. Sneev's men snatched at their weapons, but fell crushed under unshod hooves. Bellowing, bearded berserkers ripped through the camp. The Ophidians were slaughtered like cattle. Chain mail glinted beneath the great fur cloaks of the savage horsemen. Nasal helms gleamed dully in the afternoon sunlight. Their shrieks of bloodlust whipped the Ophidians who remained into quick surrender. The horsemen whirled about the camp, swinging their flails and battle axes and spears above their heads, whooping and roaring with victory.

But the Slayers had seen them, and were gathering, preparing to retaliate.

The horsemen saw this, and began to raze the rough, scattered groups of Slayers as they tried to form defensive ranks. The horsemen wreaked havoc among these pockets of defense, broke free, and turned about to harry them again. These tactics delayed the Slayers, but they were slowly but surely gathering their wits, making defensive formations of pikes and spears to keep the horsemen at bay.

Now, from over the same hill that the horsemen had appeared, came another roaring mob. Hundreds of foot warriors barreled down the slopes, weapons waving. The men were bearded, like the riders, with long, braided hair, and a minimum of armor. Fur cloaks and kilts flapped with the churning of corded legs. Mail shirts and nasal helms, some sporting bull horns. Round, iron-bound wooden shields, savagely adorned with human scalps and horse tails, slung on knotted arms. Battle-axes, broadswords and spears. The wave of warriors washed over the outer fringes of the camp, drowning all vestiges of Ophidian resistance.

Then a towering standard hove into view over the crest of the hill. The white cloth and heavy brown barr-skin flapped and rippled in the breeze, and the massive white skull of a northern barr topped the lofty pole.

A battle-horn blasted from inside the fortress,

and the Slayers began to sally forth from the fortress. A black-bristling column rumbled across the bridge toward the shore to meet this new threat. Before long, this seemingly endless column began to merge with the scattered groups of Slayers on the mainland, forming the beginnings of a massive wall of pikes and spears and shields.

The Armondian defenders only realized what had happened when the steady flow of Slayers up the ladders ceased. Few defenders remained, but those that did, managed to dispatch the abandoned Slayers who remained. Only then could they turn their attention to events on the shore.

Valerion saw the banner atop the distant hill. "Arnor be praised!"

Garth stepped up to him, "The Barr of Tyberia!"

Fortine allowed his bloodied blade to drop, and he breathed a sigh. "Lord Skaand has come at last!"

Valerion scowled, breathing heavily. "We owe him our lives, and that's certain. But I fear Skaand's army alone will keep Uhr's dogs from our doorstep only a little while. They are too few to deliver a killing blow to a horde such as that."

The Slayers formerly assaulting the inner ward withdrew, and now merely stood and waited a few dozen paces from the gate, keeping watch over the trapped Armondians.

On the shore, the attacking horse warriors wheeled and thrust hither and there, forming shifting bands, charging about, trying to keep things in an uproar until the Tyberian infantry could reach the battle. Before long the cavalry were succeeding only in spitting themselves on the razor-sharp points of the Slayer pikes braced against the bloody ground.

Now, with their ranks complete, the Slayers began a slow advance towards the Tyberian infantry.

Valerion's eager eyes devoured the scene on the land. The Tyberian footmen formed a ragged line, then dashed forward, swatted the pikes aside, and engaged the Slayers with ax and shield. The black line buckled, but held. Then the fur-swathed warriors ran away, before the Slayers could recover and fall upon them with full force.

"Fortine," Valerion said, "what would you estimate to be the number of Lord Skaand's force?"

Fortine rubbed his stubbly chin with a leathery hand. "Oh, Wodan's Jewels, but I'd say three thousand, all told."

"And the Slayers?"

Fortine snorted. "Ten thousand, at least, damn 'em."

Valerion said, "All our men able to fight number slightly over a hundred, a paltry sum, at best."

A dozen times the Tyberians rushed in, traded quick blows with the enemy, then fled, always leading them on.

Fortine chuckled. "Those Tyberians lead them away a little farther each blessed time!"

Valerion nodded with a faint smile. "Skaand is a shrewd tactician."

Garth said, "Even with an army as untrained as his."

Fortine said, "Underestimate them not, my lord. Ill-trained in organized battle perhaps, but hearty warriors all. I lived in Tyberia for a time, and I know their ways and mettle. Tor's Teeth, but those Tyberians'll gouge the livers out o' those Slayers and eat 'em!"

Repeatedly the Tyberian horsemen dashed in and harried the Slayer flanks as they engaged the infantry. The Slayer officers bellowed orders as they charged about on black coursers.

Most of the enemy's horses had been scattered

in the first charge, another tactical victory for the Tyberians. The Slayers could not gain the advantage of horseback now. They could only follow the Tyberians, who were more fleet of foot, unweighted by so much plate armor. Eventually the skirmish moved away perhaps a thousand paces to the south, raising such a billow of dust that it hid another cloud rising farther to the south.

Valerion watched in wonder as the Slayer force suddenly broke into a tight fighting withdrawal. The large force hurried back toward the lake, screaming Tyberians in hot pursuit. And then Valerion saw the reason for the Slayers' unexpected retreat.

Dozens of brilliantly colored banners rose from the dust-clouded southern horizon. Sunlight glinted from spired helmets and polished armor. The thunder of hooves rose in the air like the sound of a distant storm, as two thousand dazzling knights bore down on the retreating Slayers. Trumpets and drums thundered on both sides like instruments of perdition. The Tyberians stared wide-eyed for startled moments, then scrambled to get out of the way. The mounted lancers overtook the retreating Slayers and clove through their ranks like an ax through flesh. Screams of anguish ripped from the tortured throats of both horses and men. Gore soaked the trampled earth.

Valerion roared a jubilant cheer, echoed by all his men.

Garth breathed, "Allahnians, by all the gods!"

Valerion clutched Fortine's arm, "How many?"

Fortine gulped. "Not enough, I fear."

But now the Allahnian infantry came into view, marching out of the dust cloud pounded up by the knights who preceded them. Scores of regimental standards rose like deadly flowers from the dust cloud. A close-packed shield wall emerged from the roiling veil, with a row of wickedly shaped pikes bristling out from between the shields. Ranks of longbowmen followed the pikemen. Next came rank upon rank of swordsmen, razor-sharp talwars and scimitars shining like curved icicles in the sun.

"Hah!" Fortine exclaimed. "Now, broil my gizzard, but we've a chance, m'lord!"

The pulse of drums quickened, and the foot soldiers matched pace. The Allahnian host stretched in a line across the horizon at least three hundred paces long, approaching steadily, inexorably.

Meanwhile, the Allahnian knights formed, charged through the increasingly disarrayed ranks of Slayers, reformed, and charged again. The Tyberians somehow managed to stay out of the way, and still cause massive amounts of damage before darting away again. These combined tactics effectively kept the enemy from completing their defensive formation.

However, each attack invariably left a litter of Tyberian and Allahnian corpses behind. Slashed and screaming horses and men kicked and thrashed on the ground, whipping their blood into a froth, gutted by Slayer pikes. Allahnian knights and fur-swathed Tyberians groaned and died beneath black-armored feet. But lifeless mounds of dull black armor covered the field in staggering numbers, like piles of slaughtered porcupines.

All the while, more Slayers poured out of the castle, across the bridge, to the land, and the mass of them expanded like a bladder.

Little remained of the former encampment. Tents and pavilions lay in trampled puddles of soiled cloth, splintered poles and sticks jutting like dark bones. Corpses oozed on the trampled earth like squashed fruit. Small blazes licked here and there.

Somewhere among this, a small figure groaned and stirred. Tiny misshapen hands scrabbled at the dirt as Lord Sneev struggled to sit up. He found that he could not. The last thing he remembered was the sudden uproar. He had been in his pavilion with Brudge, as the Slayers assaulted Valerion's last bastion of defense, when suddenly the barbaric war-cries had filled the air. His private tent had collapsed on top of him, and a blow to the head had sent him reeling into darkness.

Now awareness had found him. His head swam, and his bald scalp felt warm and sticky. His beady eyes opened, and he found himself lying under his collapsed tent. He vaguely heard the sounds of battle far off in the distance.

"Must get to safety!" he whispered.

Somehow. But how? Weakly he tried to raise himself up, and found again that he could not. The tent fabric was too heavy. He could only drag himself along the ground beneath the thick cloth.

He froze at the sound of movement nearby, and gruff voices speaking in the guttural Tyberian tongue. Sneev lay as still as a corpse, but his breath was wheezing so loudly that they must have heard it. An uncontrollable shuddering seized him. Fear paralyzed his every muscle. Finally the Tyberian warriors moved on. And he could once again breathe and move.

For what seemed an eternity, he struggled beneath the collapsed pavilion, trying to free himself. Then he met an obstacle. It was soft and heavy, and he could not move it. When he lifted the tent cloth to observe it, his stomach heaved, and he retched uncontrollably. Brudge's dead, blood-caked face watched him spew the contents of his stomach onto the ground. Brudge's head, crushed and bloodied, lay twisted at an unnatural angle. Clotted blood covered a dozen wounds, oozed from his pulped nose. Splintered bones speared through battered flesh in several places.

When Sneev again controlled his innards, he looked past the corpse, and saw daylight brighter than the light filtering through the tent cloth. He forced himself to crawl over Brudge's mangled corpse toward the light. It squelched and gave way under his weight, and his belly heaved again.

Finally he peeked out into the noonday sunlight. He cautiously glanced about for the enemy. He saw no one near. Where to find safety? The fortress. There! If only he could get to it, he would be safe. Uhr's forces held almost all the castle, and would not likely lose it. His decision was made. He moved as swiftly as possible on his still wobbly legs, trying to keep a low profile and remain unnoticed. Hundreds of Slayers were pouring across the bridge to where their ragged formations grew, perhaps a hundred paces from the shore of the lake. The bridge was a hundred and fifty paces away. Among the fringes of the Lakeside ruins, Tyberians and Allahnians stormed within fifty paces of him, ignoring him because he did not wear black armor.

Then, gathering his strength, he dashed for the bridge, darting among the smashed, charred buildings. Amazingly he reached the bridge unscathed. The blood rushed in his frail body, his heart thumping like a rabbit's. His breath wheezed in and out of him. He was forced to wait until the tide of Slayers from the fortress slowed sufficiently to allow him room to cross. He cringed every time the enemy dashed in, fearing they would break through and get to him. He would be a prize for

DALTON BOOKSELLER TUKWILA, WA
5-246-4373
605.02.10 10/21/97 15.35 13094

1-55197-361-8 5.99

SUBTOTAL	5.99
Book$aver DISCOUNT	0.60-
SALES TAX	0.46
TOTAL	5.85
CASH	10.00

Book$aver 1147726492

OTAL SAVINGS $0.60

---------------- THANK YOU ----------------

the rebels indeed! Was he not Uhr's second-in-command?

He approached a mounted Slayer officer standing near the bridge, barking orders at his subordinates crossing the bridge. Sneev hailed him. "Ho there, Colonel Harkilon! Can you spare a squad of men to escort me into the castle?"

Colonel Harkilon spun, and the blank, black faceplate speared him with contempt. The warhorse snorted, and snapped at him. "Out of the way, worm!" the Slayer snarled, and returned to his business.

Sneev, dumbfounded, took a step back. Well, he would just have to wait until there was room enough to cross.

Valerion and his men watched the Slayers guarding the inner ward disperse and march toward shore. They could see the Allahnian infantry drawing ever nearer. The Tyberian and Allahnian cavalry harried the Slayers to keep them from organizing completely.

Lord Valerion stamped his feet and clenched his fists. "There must be something we can do!"

The Allahnian infantry drew within range of bowshot. Storms of arrows from each side filled the air, raking both armies. Then a battle horn sounded from within the Allahnian host, and with a screaming roar of chorused war-cries, the Allahnian army rushed forward. The wall of shields and pikes crashed into the ragged Slayer line with a sound like the smith god's hammer and anvil. Shrieks of pain mingled with bellowed war-cries.

And the battle raged.

The Slayers had formed up almost completely until now. But this attack flung their ranks back into disarray. The battle surged and gave back as the lines shifted. Neither side could gain or lose ground now, but Death ran rampant over both sides.

The Tyberians had withdrawn temporarily to the hillside occupied by the ruined Slayer camp, to rest and tend their wounded. The Allahnian shield wall had assumed the shape of a crescent moon, with the concave side encircling the Slayers. But the crescent was thin, and the Slayers still far outnumbered the Allahnian host.

Most of the Slayer horde had gained the shore now, leaving the fortress relatively unoccupied.

As Valerion realized this, he struck upon a bold and desperate plan.

No one saw, far, far above, two dots circling this bloody scene. Hamilton could feel Uhr's proximity. The Ivory Star pulsed and throbbed within its cloth wrapping, strapped to his back.

Hamilton and Capian looked down over the scene far below. Hamilton saw the expression of pain and sorrow on Capian's features. The fortress looked gutted, empty. It appeared that the Slayers had already taken it, and were now fighting to keep it.

"We're too late," Capian said.

"Could your father still be alive?"

Capian shook his head, "I doubt it. But I must find out for certain."

The battlefield rippled and shifted. The ground was scarlet with lakes of spilled blood, hazed over by the dim clouds of rising dust and smoke. The battle appeared to be in a temporary stalemate.

Hamilton said, "But who are the Slayers fighting?"

"I can't tell from this height."

Hamilton looked up at the sky. It would be noon

shortly, and the sun and Day Stars would be in conjunction. "Capian, look!" Hamilton cried. "The Great Conjunction is almost here. I must find Uhr. He is not here."

"And I must know if my father still lives."

Hamilton waved to him as he began to veer away. "May we meet again, Capian Arnor's Son!"

"May we meet again, Hamilton Corbin!"

With that the two friends parted. Capian sent Starjumper plummeting downward toward the fortress. Hamilton nosed Skyking toward the Viderian Mountains, where he could feel Uhr's presence festering like an unholy canker.

His destiny was at hand.

Chapter 35

The Armondians were gathered in the courtyard, leaving the battlements unoccupied save for one sentry.

Garth, Valerion and Fortine conversed in low tones, apart from the rest of the men for a moment.

Garth exclaimed, "Arnor's Loins, Son! Are you mad?"

"Nay, Father! Don't you see?" Valerion's eyes were bright with excitement as he hefted his sword.

Fortine said, "Aye, my lord, it just might work!"

Valerion smiled grimly. "Aye, it will work. We have enough men! We can retake the castle!" He turned towards his men and raised his voice for all to hear. "Hear me, brave warriors of Armond. I have a plan to regain our lost honor, revenge our dead, and reclaim our home. With Arnor's help, we will sweep the Slayers from within these walls. There aren't many left. But if we take our fortress back, we will leave the Slayers on the shore with nowhere to flee!"

"You plan to attack?" said a voice from the rear of the throng.

"Aye!" Valerion said, with a steely glint in his eyes, the glint of youth, one that had not dwelled in those azure caves for a long time.

The same voice said, "If you plan to attack, you'll need more than Arnor's help."

A man was walking through the crowd of men standing around Valerion. He was hooded, clad all in black. A sword hilt protruded above his left shoulder.

The men at once parted and encircled him, voices tense with suspicion.

"We don't recognize you."

"Aye, who are you?"

"Where did you come from?"

The questions came rapid fire from the men surrounding him, and their blades drew closer.

"Hold, friends," the man said, raising his empty hands to pull back his hood.

Valerion slammed his sword into its sheath in amazement. "Gods, Capian, is it you, my son!"

The handsome young man smiled. "Aye, Father. It is I."

The crowd around Capian parted to allow Lord Valerion through. "My son!" he exclaimed, laughing joyously as he clapped Capian into a warm embrace. "I have long thought you dead!"

Capian said, clutching his father like a child, "I feared so about you, too, Father."

As they separated, Garth rushed up and clasped them both. "At last! Three generations of Arnor's Sons together! Uhr barely defeated one of us. How can he hope to stand against three!"

At that a mighty cheer rose from the throats of the men around them. "Hail the Sons of Arnor! Long live the Sons of Arnor!"

Angus approached Capian. "You're a Knight of the Eagles?" he said, hesitantly. "What of Hamilton Corbin?"

Capian smiled and outstretched his hand.

Angus took it, and Capian said, "You must be Angus. Hamilton spoke much of you in our journeys. The One was perfectly fine when I left him a few moments ago."

Garth said, "Well, where is he, lad?"

"He's gone to destroy Uhr."

A moment of stunned silence. Could it be true? Had The One come at last?

Valerion clasped his son's shoulder, and turned his body to stare directly into his eyes. "Capian, it's true...?"

Capian beamed, proud and delighted to be the messenger of the news. "Aye, Father!" He raised his voice. "The One has come to destroy Uhr, and he is ready. Uhr's time is nearly over!"

A thunderous cheer roared from the men around them, hope swelling once again in their long-despairing breasts like sails in a mighty wind, and it would carry them to victory.

"Father," Capian asked quietly, "what of Mother? I would like to see her after this is over. And my brother and sisters."

Valerion's face darkened in his helm as he looked away. "I was hoping you wouldn't ask that until later." He sighed heavily.

"What is it?" Capian asked.

"Your mother is—"

"Look! Look at the sky!" A terrified cry cut him thankfully short.

They gazed up, and gasped collectively when they saw the blazing white slash splitting the brilliant blue sky, spearing down from the sun directly above.

"The Great Conjunction!" someone cried.

The Day Stars and ivory sun shone as one in the heavens, and a continuous dazzling white beam shot straight down from the sky, and seemed to strike the ground somewhere in the Viderian Mountains. From this blazing white column of light exploded swarms of millions of sparks and shards of luminescence of a million different hues. The battle on the land diminished as men on both sides stopped fighting to watch this event, enthralled by its power and beauty.

Lord Valerion seized the moment, whipping out his battle-notched broadsword. This was the sign! "Open the gates!" he bellowed, "*Victory!*"

"*VICTORY!*"

Roaring with desperate strength, the Armondians poured through the opening gates, across the drawbridge toward the waiting Slayers.

Hamilton could feel Uhr's presence, his evil strength. It screamed out at him like a siren. Skyking sensed it too, Hamilton knew, for the bird shivered beneath him, and there was a tenseness, an anticipation, in his normally effortless flight. The massive predator dipped and soared unerringly among the towering peaks, as if he knew precisely their destination without Hamilton's guiding hand.

Then a blinding flash of light suddenly split the sky wide. Skyking blinked and tried to look away. Hamilton shielded his eyes. When he dared to look, the brilliance of the sun itself seemed to be pouring down in a column of pure ivory light directly before them.

The sky was alive with countless shimmering shards of iridescence, all around him, swirling and coalescing, dispersing again, passing through him with a vague warmth. He marveled at the incredible beauty swirling around him. The Ivory Star came alive on his back. He could feel it quivering, pulsing against him like a living thing. It seemed to cry a challenge of purity to Uhr's corrupt malevolence.

Then his mind snapped alert. The Great Conjunction! Was he already too late? Had all his long quest been for naught? Fear clutched at his heart like an ice-cold claw, and he urged Skyking to greater speed. The massive old eagle, sensing his urgency, beat his huge wings ever harder, faster.

The top of the crag was bathed in brilliant white light, nearly blinding. The moldering claw gripped the wickedly curved dagger with the strength of inhuman anticipation, and the blade rose and fell, plunging into soft, yielding flesh. Gore spurted and flowed, brilliantly crimson, staining hand, steel and stone. Uhr laughed, and licked his rotting hand with a black tongue, savoring the tang of the blood. The girl had not even screamed. How disappointing. Regrettably her mind had left her a gibbering husk long ago, but her spirit was still in tact as he reached out for it, snatching it as it tried to escape, dragging it back from the edge of Beyond. In a half-trance, he touched the Bloodstone and projected her soul into it, trapping it there. Like an animal, growling with pleasure, he ripped into the hot flesh with his strong yellow teeth. He devoured the corpse gleefully, feeling power and life course through him like a mighty cataract, and he turned to where the Bloodstone rested at the head of the altar.

His eyes blazed with a savage scarlet light. Blood steamed in the cool mountain air as it dripped from his bony chin, his sickening hands. He touched the faceted scarlet stone, wherein was trapped the cowering soul of the slain virgin. He began a slow, deep, guttural chant. His voice chopped the isolated silence like an ax.

The column of light, the sun and the sky turned bloody red as Uhr began to draw life from the very spirit of the sun itself, stealing its energy for himself.

On the battlefield the men cried out in terror as the sky shifted to a bright crimson, momentarily forgetting the heat of battle. The spiked ebon armor looked blacker still in the eerie, blood-red light. The field took on a strange surreality. Screams of agony. Clash of arms. Thunder of drums. Brazen blare of the trumpets. The very air was pregnant with energy. Crystal Lake was a sea of fire. If ever there was Hell among the living, it was here.

The stoic Slayers took immediate advantage of the rebels' lack of action, and almost overwhelmed them in a sudden surge. The engaging Allahnians and Tyberians were hard-pressed at best to contain them. The front two ranks of Allahnians crumpled beneath the black onslaught, but a powerful surge from the rear held the ranks fast, pushing the Slayers back.

Lord Sneev meanwhile had made his way into the fortress. He now watched the battle from a tower adjoining the first gate. His heart still raced wildly from his flight from the battlefield, and his slight frame quaked with fear and exertion. A drop of blood fell from his brow. Startled by his own blood, he cringed. The droplet splattered on the cold stone, and the small pattern was black in the red light. He decided to try to find water to cleanse himself. He made his way down to the ground, finding himself within the outer ward's compound, and looked for a well or fountain. Finding none readily, he cautiously crossed the bridge to the middle ward, noting that no Slayers were about.

They must be guarding the Armondians, making sure they were contained. He surveyed the results of Uhr's sorcerous breach of the fortress's defenses, and he shuddered at the raw power that Uhr now wielded, and at how much more Uhr would soon have. Then, as he stood near the gate, he heard a great commotion somewhere ahead.

Moving on down the street, the sounds of battle ahead asserted themselves over the general din. A fight? Here? Hadn't most of the Slayers taken to shore to deal with the treacherous Tyberians and Allahnians? Weren't Valerion and his men trapped within the inner ward? Curiosity led him onward, toward the sounds as he drew his rapier. Rounding the corner of the cottage, he saw the gates of the inner ward standing open. He watched as Lord Valerion and his men overwhelmed the small contingent of Slayers left to guard them. The victors stood among the spiked heaps, and cheered.

What a motley lot! Sneev mused. These ill-equipped, bedraggled men had beaten back the legions of Slayers Uhr had thrown at them? Sneev watched them, these thoughts working through his mind, failing to realize that he stood in full view.

Valerion, gore-spattered, bloodlust raging in him like an unquenchable fire, cast about for more enemies. He happed to glance the lone figure standing down the way, watching them. He stopped, staring. Could it be?

A mighty bellow blew like a catapult stone from his raw throat. "*SNEEV!*"

Forgetting all, eyes blazing a mad steel-blue, Valerion launched himself at the diminutive man standing perhaps seventy-five paces away.

Sneev, abruptly realizing his danger, bolted away, flying back down the path. Valerion rounded the corner of the cottage in hot, roaring pursuit. Sneev's stunted body could not hope to match Valerion's great stride, even as he limped with the wound in his thigh. The distance between them had already been halved.

Sneev's mind raced along with his legs. If only he could make it to the shore, he would be safe. The Slayers there would crush this insignificant bunch like a rotten fruit. He risked a glanced over his shoulder. Valerion was right on him like a snarling hound.

"Turn and face me, Sneev, you craven bastard!"

Sneev ran blindly now, his fear-filled gaze glued to Valerion. Thus he failed to see a small pile of stones near a wrecked hovel. A stone turned under his foot, twisting his ankle and sending him sprawling face-first on the cobblestones. His sword skittered away.

Valerion stood over him, panting, favoring his wounded leg. "Get up, cur!" he growled.

Sneev rolled over to face him, wiping at the blood pouring from his hooked nose, and looked fearfully up at the towering warrior-lord.

"Get up, farrac, or I'll skewer you where you lay," Valerion rumbled. The point of his great notched broadsword dropped to Sneev's throat.

Sneev gulped, and shakily gained his feet.

"Only one of us shall live out this day, Snake. Retrieve your weapon. Arnor knows, I should kill you like the serpent you are. But I can't bring myself to do it in cold blood."

Sneev turned to pick up his sword. A cunning half-smile flickered across his features as he drew his dagger.

Valerion raised his sword and shield. His eyes were blue chips of ice in the open-faced helmet.

The duel was short.

The two combatants circled each other once, then Valerion charged, roaring like a lion. His broadsword clove the air, and Sneev darted in, a blur of snake-like speed. Valerion's blade sheared through Sneev's neckpiece, and his head jumped from his narrow shoulders, to hit the cobbles with a wet smack. Sneev's bloodied dagger fell from dead fingers, and his decapitated body staggered and collapsed, twitching. Valerion winced and staggered back. He sank to one knee, clutching his side.

Capian was the first to reach him. "Father, are you well?"

"Aye, my son. 'Tis but a scratch. Help me up." The fire in Valerion's eyes was extinguished. Capian helped him to his feet and supported him. Blood dripped on the flagstones.

"Father," Capian said quietly, squeezing his shoulder, "it is bad?" His voice implored a truthful answer.

Valerion answered him quietly, so the men could not hear, "It is bad enough, but not mortal."

Angus stopped beside them. "Sneev is dead!" he exclaimed.

"Aye, but his dagger slipped past my guard and under my breastplate. Nevertheless, I shall live. Help me to the house, son." Valerion said nothing about the poison from Sneev's dagger that burned like liquid fire in his veins. Looking at the rest of his men gathering around him, he raised his voice, "Your work is not finished. The outer ward now! Take it back! Reclaim our home."

Angus looked knowingly at Valerion's face. Something was wrong, but the rest of the men mustn't know. He raised a cheer, "Long live Lord Valerion."

The men took it up and changed it to a battle

cry, as they charged down the street to the bridge, trampling Sneev's corpse underfoot.

Hamilton caught sight of the tall, craggy spire of rock, whose flattened peak seemed to support the towering column of light which had suddenly turned a blood red. He saw a tiny speck at the very top, and he knew that this was Uhr. He urged Skyking to greater speed, but the bird already pushed the limits of his strength. He unslung the Ivory Star from his back and unwrapped it from the cloth. He hefted it, tested the edge. The blade blazed now a shimmering iridescent white, the color the pillar of light had been mere moments ago. He clutched it now, grim determination chiseling his face.

Uhr chanted in a tongue that was ancient a thousand years ago. He could feel his power growing like a lightning cancer.

Then he felt the presence. So strong it could only be The One. And the Ivory Star.

No! Not yet!

He must hurry now. He snatched up his helmet from the ground and thrust it back onto his head. Then he picked up the dagger from where it lay beside the half-eaten remains. Clutching the weapon with both hands, he plunged it through the armor, into his own chest. He ripped. His ribs broke and separated like dry twigs, and he felt no pain. When he removed the dagger, a gaping black hole stood open in his chest. Armor and dead flesh immediately began to mend. A red glow pulsed like an obscene heart from within that awful wound, in place of where his heart would have been. Quickly he reached inside and plucked out the blood-red crystal the size of a fist that glowed with the same hue as the pulsing Bloodstone. The Bloodstone's Child. He faltered, his life-force in his hand. The strength left his knees like water. Already he could feel himself dying. His chanting grew ever louder as he raised the small crystal and smashed it against the top of the Bloodstone. A flash of light erupted, and the small stone was gone, without a trace. The altar next to him shook with the strength of his chant. The last staccato syllable blasted from his leathery lips as he snatched the cowering essence of the slain girl out of the Bloodstone, and instantly devoured it. A thunderclap smote the skies, and Uhr reeled like a skiff in a hurricane. A tremendous wind lashed the top of the crag, bowling him over like a rag doll, blowing him across the nearly polished surface, threatening to throw him over the edge. But then the wind subsided, and a shimmering scarlet aura surrounded his body. He stood up, weaving unsteadily.

He looked about in wonder, bathed in this reddish luminescence. His sorcerous black and silver armor healed like a carapace across his chest. He could feel his body that had been a rotting cadaver for so many centuries changing.

Changing...

As The One swooped ever nearer the towering crag, the speck he saw grew arms and legs, leathery wings sprouted from a blank, black helmet, and a darker red glow formed around it in the strange red light.

Suddenly the figure spun. A needle-thin spear of crimson brilliance lanced from Uhr's hand, straight toward the hurtling eagle and rider. Hamilton gasped as smoking blood and brains splattered his face. Skyking's carcass, the head half-blown away, plummeted. The beast's momentum carried them to the top of the crag, where the massive body crashed and rolled to a halt. Hamilton, confined by the safety strap, was pinned beneath the heavy carcass. Somehow he managed to retain his grip on the Ivory Star, and used it to cut the leather strap holding his bruised and battered legs against the quivering feathered shoulders. Frantically he struggled to free himself. He could feel Uhr's malevolence coming nearer, an awful presence that chilled him to the core.

Then Skyking's carcass flew into the air and away, over the edge of the crag. Fortunately Hamilton had extricated himself, and now scrambled to his feet. He faced his nemesis, with the Ivory Star brandished as both weapon and shield.

Hamilton blinked as he stared at Uhr's horrific silver and black figure. Did he look shorter somehow than before? The blank face plate regarded him with passive malignance. The red glow surrounding him pulsed and rippled, throwing eerie reflections from the unearthly armor.

The Ivory Star blazed like a sun between them.

Uhr's aura of raw, primal evil washed over Hamilton's highly tuned senses like a tidal wave, and his knees turned to water. He watched in stunned amazement as Uhr's form shrunk before his eyes. The terrible armor he wore shrunk like a skin to fit his frame, as did the black lacquered scabbard at his hip. His inhuman height had diminished to about the same as Hamilton's. His gaunt limbs thickened, became more manlike, his chest deeper. The blood red glow began to fade.

"You are too late, pitiful mortal," Uhr said in a soft, not quite human voice, a voice that carried a cosmic overtone that would make stars and planets quiver in fear. "Look you upon the face of God," he said. His helmet evaporated in a wisp of black smoke, and Hamilton looked upon Uhr's face.

Full golden hair fell to his shoulders. Finely chiseled features, with a strong chin and straight nose. He would have been quite handsome, if not for his eyes. Those eyes.

They were black, with no whites, blacker than the depths of the deepest cavern, the farthest reaches of space. And those eyes reflected all the abysmal lust, raging greed, cruelty and monstrous evil that had existed since the dawn of Mankind's race. In those grisly orbs were mirrored all the unholy things, the vile secrets that Man had feared and loathed since he crawled from the muck pools of ageless antiquity.

Hamilton's blood turned to ice, and Uhr laughed. The One's body trembled like a leaf in a mighty wind. The point of the Ivory Star sagged.

Uhr took a step forward.

"No!" Hamilton cried, suddenly regaining his senses. The sword-point came back up, and Uhr stepped back.

Was that the glint of fear in those terrible eyes? They watched the shimmering blade with caution.

Hamilton, careful not to look directly into Uhr's face, advanced. "Now, beast, you will die."

Uhr's gauntleted hand lashed out, and a scarlet flame shot toward him. But as the flame licked nearer, it died without a wisp of smoke.

Hamilton smiled mockingly. "Your power has no effect on me."

Then a growl issued from Uhr's throat like the rage of some otherwordly leviathan. His metal-encrusted hand flew to his hip and drew his own blade.

If Uhr was the essence of Evil, then the sword was his minion. The blade, long and straight and double-edged, was as black as his eyes. Hideous runes glowed scarlet along the length of the blade, runes that even in their mystery sent cold terror like frost through Hamilton's nerves, and at the base, near the hilt, shone a bloodshot red eye that blinked and moved with full, fiendish intelligence.

"Can you do battle with Gōd, mortal worm?" Uhr said, "Soul Reaper and I shall show you agony as no living being has known since the birth of the cosmos."

Hamilton said nothing, his white-knuckled fist grasping the silver hilt with the strength of barely-checked terror. Then he felt the Ivory Star come to life in his grasp. It seized his fear with a powerful guiding hand. It took his fear and bridled it, reshaped it into strength. And then sent it surging back into him. This strength galvanized him. His thews turned to steel, and his heart became a raging furnace of power.

The One leaped to attack, the Ivory Star an iridescent streak. Uhr parried with his own terrible weapon, and the battle for the fate of the world was joined.

Black and white arced and glittered, crashed and sang, in a flurry of blows that would have dizzied any spectator. The Ivory Star danced. Soul Reaper thrashed. All across the top of the crag, god and man battled, back and forth, round and round. Uhr's blows carried strength beyond belief, each one jarring Hamilton to the marrow of his bones. He found himself constantly giving ground to Uhr's terrible assault. Uhr's was the strength of his evil. The One's was the strength of his soul. Mortal swords would have long been shattered by the force of those titanic blows. Unnatural metal struck and smote, hacked and hewed.

For what seemed an eternity Hamilton attacked, parried, counter-attacked, all to no avail. The battle ranged over the entire surface of the crag as the combatants charged, gave ground, circled, spun. They fought near the altar now, where the gory remains of the sacrifice oozed blood and offal down onto the smooth surface of the crag. Uhr loosed a tremendous cut at Hamilton's head. The One lithely ducked, and Soul Reaper crashed into the altar, lodging deep in the stone. Hamilton seized the instant of opportunity, and darted to the side like a striking serpent. The razor-sharp iridescent blade found the crease between the upper-leg plate and the knee-plate. Uhr shrieked in agony as his leg crumpled beneath him, hamstrung. The wound sizzled and smoked as if scored by a hot coal.

But as Hamilton tried to back away, he misjudged the slickness of the bloodied stone. His foot shot out from under him. Uhr's own fall had wrenched his black blade free from the stone altar, and he hacked awkwardly. The terrible blade clove clean through Hamilton's ankle, striking sparks on the stone below, and Hamilton screamed to the depths of his soul. An icy chill and pain such as he had never known racked his physical body, and he crawled, whimpering, dragging his leg behind, around the altar away from Uhr.

He looked back at his tortured leg, expecting to see a bloody stump pumping his life onto the stone. Instead, to his astonishment, he saw his leg, ankle and foot intact, apparently unwounded. But the tremendous agony paralyzed him, and that cosmic chill crept like venom up his leg.

He heard Uhr cackle. "Now you know the agony of the soul, the torment of the spirit," he said, "Soul Reaper wreaks the true, complete death, the utter destruction of everything that is you."

Hamilton could feel that part of him missing now, not a vital part, but a part of his very essence. He tried to stand weakly, and found that he could. His leg was nerveless wood, but it supported him. He staggered back around the altar and saw Uhr standing on his one good leg.

Hamilton said, "And the Ivory Star wreaks upon you the true death, the one you should have died a thousand years ago."

And The One leaped forward with speed that denied sight. He feinted at Uhr's other leg. Soul Reaper dropped to block the cut, and the Ivory Star arced up and buried its point below Uhr's chin, driving into his braincase, and out the back of his head.

A flash of light exploded like a sun, and Uhr dropped as if struck by a thunderbolt. A recoil of energy enough to level the nearby mountains flung Hamilton away. That was the last thing he saw before blackness engulfed him.

Chapter 36

The sun was a scarlet coal in the flaming west. It glowered like a Cyclops's bloody eye across the silent battlefield. Silent as death, strewn with the wreckage of war, the field stretched grim and still and sullen in the lurid rays. Here and there amidst the sprawled, mangled corpses, crimson pools of congealing gore lay like calm lakes reflecting the scarlet streamered sky. Dark, gaunt, furtive shapes moved among them in the deepening dusk. Their ugly, dog-like snouts marked them as farracs, the carrion-eaters of the Armondian grasslands. This would be their banquet. Carrion birds wheeled and circled in the flaming sky like silent ghosts. The grisly kites settled to earth with the rustle of dusty wings

But for these, nothing moved.

Lord Valerion lay in bed like a corpse. His face tinged with a ghost's pallor. His breath wheezed like an old bellows. A fever burned hot on his brow, and sweat ran from him in rivers. Only his iron constitution had sustained him thus far. Nessa sat holding his hand at one side of his bed, Valerion II at the other. Garth and Angus sat quietly on stools along the back wall. The door opened and a man Nessa had never seen before entered the room. His black raiment was torn and stained with blood.

Capian traded his gaze between them all, saying nothing.

Valerion's eyes opened, and he spoke, "Capian, come here, my son."

Nessa's mouth fell open, and Val simply stared.

"Valerion, Nessa," the lord said, addressing his children, "this is your older brother, Capian. Capian, meet Nessa and Valerion II."

Capian came forward and reached for Val's hand to grasp it. "I am honored, Brother," he said, smiling.

Val was speechless as he stared at his elder brother in fascination and admiration.

Capian then circled the bed to Nessa. She stood up and embraced him. "I'm happy to finally meet you, Brother."

"It's good to meet you, too."

They released each other, and Lord Valerion said, "The battle, Son?"

"It's over, Father."

"Well, what happened?"

"It seems hard to explain..."

Valerion's hoarse voice was sharp with anticipation. "Well, explain!"

"The Slayers...they just...they just stopped fighting."

Valerion propped himself up on his elbows, clenching his teeth in pain. He echoed Capian, "They just stopped fighting?"

Capian nodded. "Just stopped. One minute the battle was fierce, and the next minute they stopped and simply stood there. No amount of screaming by the Slayer officers could make them start again."

"What happened then?"

"After they became more certain it wasn't a ruse

of some kind, the Tyberians and Allahnians took their weapons away, and stripped them of their armor."

"I'll wager they're quite a sight indeed without all their armor on."

Capian shook his head. "They're just men under all that. Their eyes are the most frightening. All the tales told of how Uhr stole their souls must be true, because their eyes are as empty as glass."

Nessa asked, "But why would they just stop fighting?"

"Without souls they have no life of their own outside serving the will of their Master."

Valerion interrupted, "Then if they are no longer being controlled, that must mean..."

Capian said, "Uhr is dead."

Val leaped up, shouting, "Hooray! Hooray!"

Lord Valerion said, "Has anyone else realized this yet?"

"I'm not sure. Right now all the soldiers are too busy tending their dead and licking their wounds to think about the reason why they've won."

Lord Valerion nodded in agreement, then said to his youngest son, "Valerion, my son."

The boy was beaming with joy. "Aye, Father!"

"Spread the news. It must be true. Uhr is no more."

The boys eyes shone with pride. "Truly, Father? I can spread the news?" His fists clenched with excitement.

"Aye, son! Cry it out in every corner. It must be true."

Valerion II laughed with ecstasy and ran from the chamber as fast as he could, crying out at the top of his lungs that Uhr was no more.

After he was gone, Valerion whispered, "A thousand years Uhr has ruled the Four Lands. What now? Do we know how to be free?" Then he turned to Nessa. "My dear, would you open the window? I'd like a fresh breeze."

She did so, and the last crimson rays of sunlight streamed through the open window, falling across Valerion's body. He said, "But what of the Slayer officers? They're a nasty lot, even without the regulars."

"The Tyberians quickly singled them out and executed them all."

At that moment a heavy knock at the door filled the room.

"Enter!" Valerion croaked.

The door swung open, and a veritable giant of a man ducked his head to enter. He stood a couple of inches shy of seven feet tall, with broad, thickly muscled shoulders, barrel chest, thick battle-scarred arms, legs like tree trunks swathed in leather. Long, yellow braids hung down his armored chest. Ice-blue eyes blazed in deep sockets above broad, stubbly cheek bones. And on the blood-stained white surcoat crossing the vast chest was embroidered the silhouette of a brown northern barr.

Valerion exclaimed, "Skaand, you old war-dog!" He managed a wan smile, and lifted a weak arm.

Lord Skaand grasped Valerion's hand in his own corded paw. "Wodan and Tor be praised, you still live, old friend," Skaand rumbled. "But what was it laid you low?"

"Vile treachery," Valerion said. "Even as Sneev's foul head went apart from his shoulders, he slipped a poisoned dagger past my guard. The serpent's severed head struck one last time."

"I regret that I could not aid you sooner, old friend, but Slayers had barricaded all the mountain passes. We couldn't break through, and were trapped within our own land for most of the winter. Finally they simply left. We came as quickly as we could."

"Aye, and good you did," Valerion said, "else we'd all have died today."

Another knock, and another man entered. Dying sunlight glinted from polished, laminated steel armor. Lord Erastus carried his turban-helm under his arm. Sweat-soaked black hair plastered his swarthy forehead. "Lord Valerion," Lord Erastus said courteously, "we have never met. I am..."

"I know who you are, Lord Erastus," Valerion said, "and you have my thanks, and the gratitude of all my people for your actions today. It was a brave gamble. Had Uhr not been vanquished, your own land would have been forfeit."

Erastus's teeth flashed under his black mustache. "But look how well the gamble paid!" As his black eyes scanned the others in the room, they lit upon Capian, and his eyes narrowed.

Capian flashed him a sly smile, and Erastus said nothing.

A haunted smile crossed Valerion's features. "Any may the souls of those who paid the price in blood find rest in the Halls of Ancestors."

Skaand said, "You've paid a price higher than any man should, my friend."

Suddenly recollecting, Valerion asked, "Lord Erastus, did you pass Albreth's fortress and settlements on your journey here?"

Capian's fists clenched, and he clasped Nessa's shoulder. She glanced at him, saw him bite his lip in pain.

Erastus's chin fell. "Aye, Lord Valerion. We stopped at his fortress, after your son and The One had informed me that his fortress was under siege.... We found it burnt and pillaged. Not a soul remained alive. I am sorry."

Valerion's face, a face that had known pain beyond understanding, registered fresh grief. "He was my cousin, and well-loved. Did you find his body?"

"We...could not distinguish one from another."

A grief-pregnant silence reigned.

Garth's old voice quavered as he spoke. "Albreth was a fine lad. And, aye, well-loved."

After a long-silence, Valerion said, "And Arnor's Dagger is lost as well."

Capian reached into his tunic. "No, Father, it's here." He held forth the ancient, wide-bladed knife.

Valerion said, "So you saw him before..."

"Aye."

"Let me hold it once more," Valerion said. Capian offered it, and Valerion took it in a trembling hand, his eyes caressing this ancient symbol of their lineage.

Skaand said, "Long live the Sons of Arnor."

The room echoed with the words. "Long live the Sons of Arnor."

"Long live the Sons of Corbin."

Everyone turned to the voice that had spoke. Angus, who had been sitting unobtrusively along the back wall, elbows on his knees, spoke again, "Long live the Sons of Corbin, should he still be alive to bear any. You all seem to forget that it was he who probably slew Uhr, and pulled your fat out of the fire."

Capian's eyes widened as he remembered. "Aye, and we must find him! He should have returned ere now." He moved like a cat for the door, and the two powerful lords found themselves stepping aside for this man in black.

"I'm coming," Angus said, "I'll saddle my horse."

Capian held up his hand to stop him. "Hold, Angus. Where I'm going, you cannot follow."

"Then bring him back," Angus said, "alive or dead, bring him back."

****

Somewhere he stirred.

He saw nothing, only blackness. He could not tell if his eyes were open or closed. A dream. Like a dream. He thought he might be lying down, but was not sure. Blackness. A void without form. Engulfing him. But then he saw a bright light forming around him. What could that be? The light began to coalesce, touching him. Healing him? Was he alive? Or dead?

You are alive, Hamilton Corbin.

"Is someone speaking to me?" His own thoughts were vague and indistinct. Difficult to understand, to make anything coherent.

Yes.

"Who are you?"

We are part of you. At least for now.

"What do you mean, 'for now'?"

Our time with you is now over. You have fulfilled your mission, therefore you do not need us any longer.

"Mission, what mission?"

To end the physical existence of the being known as Uhr.

"I am The One."

Yes. You are The One, chosen by us for this task.

"Who are you? Why did you choose me? How did you choose me?"

A thousand years ago, a terrible mistake was made.

"What sort of mistake? I have many questions."

The mistake was made in the creation of the being called Uhr. He was created by some of our brethren, and the rest of us were obligated to make amends for that mistake. We waited for you, searched for you. You are the culmination of a thousand year search. We waited and searched, and you were born. You were chosen from that moment to be our instrument, to restore the balance.

"What balance?"

The balance of this world. Uhr's presence destroyed the delicate balance of development on this world.

Hamilton's thoughts were slowly gaining clarity. "You said you were part of me? What did you mean?"

He felt a warmth, a tingling on his left breast, a sensation he was so accustomed to he hardly noticed it.

We gave you the power to destroy the physical existence of the entity known as Uhr.

"So it was your power all along that destroyed Uhr, not mine."

Incorrect. We merely unlocked the power within yourself, the power that exists in all of your species. Most of you simply lack the knowledge and skill to use it. We helped you do all the things to strengthen your power and manifest itself. The power that was yours all along. We merely caused its release. But beware, although you destroyed Uhr's body, he has had a thousand years to grow in power and knowledge, and the Ivory Star does not destroy the spirit as did Uhr's vile weapon. The physical form of Uhr is gone. But his spirit can only live on. He may choose to return. He may not. If he chooses to do so, you and your descendants must be ready.

Hamilton's memories slowly began to return to him, like rain seeping through a leaking roof. And the thought that Uhr might still exist somewhere chilled him to the soul. But his many long-held questions began to form in his mind, demanding answers. "Was it your ship that brought all these humans here?"

We cannot answer that question.

"Why not?"

Because you are still part of our greatest experiment.

He felt the presence around him fading, the bright light clothing him slipping away like ethereal silk. "Wait, don't leave me! You've been with me so long."

Your entire lifetime. But you don't need us any longer. We were always there without your knowledge. You are still the same person. You are still The One. Your powers are yours. Use them wisely. Use them well.

"Wait, who are you?"

Farewell, Hamilton Corbin, Savior of this Irth. We are always watching.

Then the light was gone, leaving him in darkness. Only darkness.

And there was no Time. How long before he felt something? Touching him. Moving him. A mighty wind whipped about him, but he didn't know from where. Then the wind was gone. More hands touched him, handled him, moved him.

Curious, he thought, as all consciousness left him again. Merciful darkness.

****

He heard a voice now. The dark had given way to gray. The voice penetrated the gray as if from a great distance. But it seemed to draw nearer.

"Hamilton," it said. It seemed somehow familiar to him, but it was a voice he had not heard in a very long time. Ages. An eternity.

He felt himself lying on something soft. And his entire body ached. He tried to move, and found he could, but his arms were like lead. He opened his eyes. The face before his slowly focused.

"Angus?" he croaked.

Strong hands clasped his shoulders. "Aye, my friend! You are alive after all!"

"Barely," Hamilton said, his clouded mind slowly gaining clarity once again. He twisted his head and surveyed his surroundings. Stone walls, small room, table and bench. He did indeed lie upon a soft couch, and Angus sat beside him on a three-legged stool.

"We have feared you as good as dead. You've been here unconscious for three days," Angus said, reaching for a tray of food on the table. "Here, eat." He brought a small bowl of broth to Hamilton's lips. Hamilton levered himself up on his elbows, and took the bowl, unsteadily. As he took a tentative sip, hunger suddenly erupted in him like a raging lion. He gulped thirstily at the tepid liquid.

"Easy," Angus said, "it's been awhile. You might get sick."

Capian entered. "Ah! The One lives!" He smiled warmly at Hamilton as he knelt and grasped his arm. "It's good to see you alive, my friend!"

"And you," Hamilton said, smiling. "Where are we, by the by?"

"My father's fortress," Capian said, "I brought you here. I found you on top of a flattened mountain. I should say Starjumper found you. He knew just where to go, it seems."

"What else did you find up there?" Hamilton asked.

"An altar with some ghastly remains on it, some strange armor lying amid a pile of black dust."

"You found no trace of the Ivory Star?"

Capian shook his head.

"That pile of dust was Uhr's remains."

Capian said, "And I left it to be scattered to the Four Winds."

"Good," Hamilton said, "Uhr is gone forever, and the Ivory Star with him." He took a deep breath and sighed deeply. "I can be just a man again. Is there any more of that soup?"

Over the next couple of days, Hamilton regained his strength, bruised, battered. He quickly noticed that the birthmark on his chest had faded, changed color to a rusty brown, and it no longer tingled when he used his mental abilities.

Before long, Capian and Angus noticed that Hamilton's mood was dark, strangely brooding. In fact, he spent most of his time sitting in Valerion's garden next to a large clump of budding moon roses. His friends were sure something was eating at him, but they quickly became too concerned about Valerion to think much more about it.

There had been no victory celebration as yet. Everyone waited and watched Valerion's deteriorating condition. He had been bedridden since his injury, and his condition had slowly worsened over the five days since. Both Skaand and Erastus had postponed their departures to see this through, however it might end.

At sunset of the fifth day, the mighty lord growled a curse, and with gargantuan effort slung his feet off the bed. He nearly passed out from the pain. "I will walk or die!" he grated. "Enough of being an invalid!"

Nessa and Kavarius, unable to stop him,

watched him collapse to the floor, blood streaming from the wound in his side, soaking his white bedclothes. The two rushed to aid him. His face was graven as pale granite as he rolled onto Nessa's lap. Her tears pattered against his face as he looked up at her.

"Dearest daughter," he said, sighing like a lost soul, "how I love you. But my time is over, and I must leave your side. Marry that Angus MacTavish, my dear. He is a good man."

"You will not die, Father!" she sobbed. "You will live to see your grandchildren grow and marry."

"Nay, my dear," he answered her, "I go to join your mother. I miss her so."

And Lord Valerion, Son of Arnor, leader of a world, died.

A gigantic funeral pyre was built on the side of a mountain overlooking Crystal Lake, now named Valerion's Peak. A Tyberian priest of Wodan, Lord Skaand's patron god of strength and power, recited the funeral eulogy. Thousands attended the funeral, noble and warrior and peasant alike. All loved him, and mourned his passing. When the leather-clad priest had finished, Capian thrust a torch into the bier and set it ablaze. Valerion's polished armor, gilded with gold and silver, glittered as the flames licked up around it. His battle notched broadsword rested on his chest in a gauntleted hand.

Garth said, "I never thought to outlive him. Arnor knows I had no right."

Nessa wept and buried her face against him. And Garth held her, tears streaking down his grizzled face.

Capian said, "He is at peace now, at last."

Val clutched his brother around the waist, bearing the grief with a boy's stoicism. Capian ruffled his thick black hair, trying to control his own tears.

The fire burned high, far into the following night, high enough to be seen for leagues. Capian, Hamilton, Val, Garth, Angus and Nessa stood on the mountain long after everyone else had filed down the rocky path, watching the flames lick the twinkling heavens.

Capian said, “A blazing path for his soul to walk to meet Arnor. It is worthy of him.”

The following day was all business. Capian called the other two lords to meet him in the council chamber. They sat around the table, morning sunlight beaming in through the window. Angus and Hamilton stood observing along the wall, near the door.

After they had settled themselves, Capian said, “Friends and allies, Lord Skaand, and Lord Erastus, what now?”

Erastus looked puzzled. “Lord Capian, can you explain? What do you mean?”

Capian hesitated, momentarily taken aback by the sudden use of his new title. “I mean, what of us now? Uhr is dead, after a thousand years. And I say good riddance. We all do. But what of us now? Do we want a new ruler? And if so, who shall it be?”

Erastus jumped up, eyes blazing. “This is why you called us here, to discuss putting another tyrant in Uhr’s place? We did not destroy Uhr simply to replace him with someone else! We will master our own affairs!” He put his hands on the table. “Lord Skaand, what say you?”

The huge, yellow-maned man in leather vest and green broadcloth tunic spoke slowly, choosing his words. “I tend to agree with Lord Erastus.

Now is our chance to be truly free."

The two lords turned to Capian, and Skaand said, "What say you, Son of Valerion?"

Capian replied, "I withhold my opinion until the arrival of the ruler of Ophidia."

"Say," Skaand said, "who rules Ophidia now that the Snake is dead?"

"I do," came a rich contralto voice from the doorway.

Hamilton felt his heart shrink at the sound of that voice.

Erastus said, "And you are?"

"Lady Tamarra, daughter of Diomenes," she said, stepping into the chamber.

Hamilton wanted to look at the floor, but could not help staring. Soft doeskin boots covered her feet and shapely calves. Brown riding pants gloriously accented her lower curves, and a loose, exquisitely embroidered green tunic hung from her high, firm breasts like a gorgeous drapery. Her short auburn hair shone in the sunlight.

Hamilton's breath and heartbeat quickened.

"Wodan's Loins, girl! I've not seen you since you suckled at your mother's breast!" Skaand said. "You've become a beautiful woman since."

She bowed graciously. "I thank you, Lord Skaand." But her eyes were on Hamilton.

Capian said, "We were discussing the futures of our respective lands, Lady Tamarra. Lords Skaand and Erastus feel we should remain independent, governing our own affairs."

Tamarra regally circled the table and seated herself in the empty chair, listening intently. She clasped her fingers in front of her, confidently.

Capian continued, "I have withheld my judgment until we hear your opinion. I feel our decision should be unanimous, for the good of the Four

Lands."

Tamarra regarded each lord in turn, her deep green gaze scrutinizing them. Then she said, "I wish to know the thoughts of The One."

"Excellent idea, lady," Skaand said, running sausage-like fingers through his thick beard. He turned toward Hamilton.

All eyes were upon him. Hamilton's heart pounded, and he did not speak for a moment. Then he said, "I think we should re-establish the Council of Twelve, as it was before Uhr, and restore Arnath and its palace to their former glory."

His eyes locked with hers again. She stiffened in surprise. The power in those eyes was that to lead armies and melt the hearts of the coldest women. But her heart had already melted, burning within her breast. She could read no emotions from him. He was keeping them under tight rein.

"I..." she started, "I feel as does Hamilton Corbin."

Skaand exclaimed, slapping the table, "Tor's Bones, man, what a grand vision! Let us indeed return to the days of glory before Uhr."

Capian nodded. "We are more powerful when we stand together. I agree with Hamilton. Lord Erastus?"

The dark, hawk-faced man looked at the others in turn, uncertain, cautious. "Let us proceed with details. When we have a solid scheme, I will decide."

They spent the rest of the day drafting their plans. Scribes scribbled busily at their parchments, taking notes and writing documents, often amid heated debate. They re-established the Council of Twelve as supreme rule over the League of Lands. Each Land would choose three council members, and each Land would select the manner of appointment for their three council members. And all pledged to help restore Arnath as the capital, and rebuild the palace to its former glory. They detached soldiers to take any remaining Slayers into custody, and free the thousands Uhr had enslaved where ever they might be, fields, camps, mines, quarries, across the Four Lands.

When the meeting ended at dusk, the four leaders had formed a solid pact of alliance and friendship with one another. And they all shook hands across the table to informally seal the pact.

Hamilton quickly left the chamber, before all the formalities had been finished. He had tried to avoid her eyes all day, and found it difficult. He walked hurriedly down the corridor, trying to flee the possibility of having to speak to anyone, especially her.

Angus called after him, and trotted to catch up.

Hamilton did not turn and wait, his mind centered on getting away. Then he heard a language he hadn't heard or spoken in many months.

"Hey! Wait!" Angus called.

Surprised, Hamilton turned. "What?" he answered in English. The word felt strange on his tongue after so long.

Angus stopped beside him. "We're not friends anymore?"

Hamilton looked away. "Of course we are."

"Then what's the problem? You haven't spoken much in days."

Hamilton kicked a crack in the stone floor absently, trying to avoid having to answer.

"Well, man, spit it out!"

Hamilton sighed. "Do you remember when we first met Tamarra?"

"Yeah," Angus chuckled, "she nearly tore your

face off!"

"Well, slapped or not, I'm in love with her. And I know she loves me."

Angus slapped him on the shoulder. "That's great! What's the problem?"

"I..."

"What is it? Do somethin' aboot it!"

"I can't!" Hamilton hissed. "That's why I've been such poor company lately."

"Wot, for the sake o' all th' bloody saints?"

"I'm an Eagle Knight. Eagle Knights don't take women."

Angus suddenly turned angry. "An' wot's wi' that! Ye just saved th' bloody world. I'd say yer entitled t' th' woman o' yer choice!"

"Angus speaks the truth, Hamilton," Capian said. In English.

The two men started. Even Hamilton had not sensed his approach. Angus exclaimed, "You speak English, lad!"

"I speaketh many of the languages from which our own hath sprung," Capian said. "But methinks it strange that thou speakest it as well, albeit with a strange accent."

"We'll discuss that later," Hamilton said, hurriedly, "you said I was wrong. About what?"

"Hamilton, I was but a baby child when Master Sorde started me as an Eagle Knight. As I became a man, I took vows of chastity, honor and bravery. I am now a true Knight. Master Sorde trained thee as an Eagle Knight, but thou art not a true Eagle Knight."

"Why?"

"Thou wert already a man when thy training began. Thou spakest no such vows."

Slowly, timidly, a grin cleft Hamilton's face. Then he clapped Capian on the shoulders. "Capian, you are a true friend! And you, Angus. Thank you for slapping me in the face, both of you. But if you'll excuse me, I have rather pressing business." He shouldered past them, and ran back toward the council chamber. He almost collided with Tamarra, who was just leaving the empty room as he burst in.

His joy washed over her before he even spoke. He took her up and kissed her hard and long and deep. She eagerly molded to him, returning his kiss. When their lips parted, he spoke in a rush of breath and feeling. "I have loved you with all my heart and soul since the moment I first saw you." He dropped to one knee, holding her hands in his. "Lady Tamarra, would you be my wife?"

He waited, surprised by his own audacity, but without regret.

She looked at him in stunned silence, mouth agape, unable to speak. Her eyes shone like emeralds as she whispered, "Yes."

Hamilton stood, clutched her to him, laughing like a child, like a man in love, and their mouths melded for an eternity, and their joy knew no bounds.

Epilogue

Hamilton Corbin married Lady Tamarra of Ophidia alongside Angus MacTavish and Maid Nessa of Armond in a double wedding ceremony amid friends and the flowers and fountains of Valerion's garden. That night a tremendous feast was held, with food brought from the far corners of the Four Lands.

Lord Erastus and his retinue brought an entire caravan of food, spices, exotic animals and birds, silks and fineries from Tejun, Jewel of Allahn, for gifts and celebration. Lord Skaand brought fifty fine horses, furs and cattle. The retinue from Ophidia came bearing monstrous barrels of tal, wine, beer, baskets of fruit, sugar and meal. It became a celebration as there had not been in a thousand years.

The newly-weds paraded through the middle ward in a gilded carriage drawn by eight snorting white chargers through a mob of cheering onlookers and well-wishers. A phalanx of Allahnian knights in polished armor and rich bright-colored trappings followed in their wake. The ten remaining Red Dragons, in finest silk and astride prancing war-horses, followed them, and a group of flowered maidens laid a carpet of moon-rose petals behind them.

The gigantic feast was held that night in the middle ward, under the twinkling stars. The newlyweds, the lords and ladies and their families, sat at the high table, which was at least fifty paces long, built especially to accommodate them all.

Hamilton was greatly pleased and amused to see a certain flaxen-haired former serving girl sitting next to Capian at the festivities.

Musicians from all corners of the Four Lands piped up a grand dance that lasted for hours and hours. The festive mob danced and sang and drank far into the night. They were celebrating many things. Two grand weddings, the death of Uhr, the defeat of the Slayers. The new Council of Twelve. The glorious plans for the restoration of Arnath and its palace.

And late that night, Capian set Starjumper free. The monstrous bird voiced a single sad scream, and launched itself into the air, heading for the mountains. Capian, leather harness in hand, watched his faithful mount and beloved friend dwindle to a speck in the silvery moonlight. The great bird would be sorely missed, but if he ever would have need of Starjumper again, he would find him. But for now, Capian, Son of Arnor, was Lord of Armond, with all the attending duties and responsibilities.

The four newly-weds spent the night in the House of Arnor, although they slept little, and when morning came, Hamilton was pleased to see Capian leave his room with Lina at his side. Hamilton smiled at them, and Capian blushed terribly, while the pretty woman on his arm merely laughed with joy.

A huge caravan prepared for Lord Erastus's journey back to Tejun. Lord Skaand left that same morning, with his soldiers and retinue, bound for the mountainous lands of Tyberia.

Amongst all the commotion, Hamilton pulled Angus aside. "Let's go for a ride," he said, with a twinkle in his eye Angus had never seen before, "we have much to talk about."

Angus readily agreed, and they quickly saddled two spirited black mares. Soon the bank of Crystal Lake was at their side as they rode at a leisurely walk.

"So what are your plans now?" Hamilton said, in English for old times' sake.

"My wife and I," Angus answered, rather liking the sound of that, "are off to the Frontier to oversee the restoration of Albreth's estate and lands, and serve as regents until young Valerion is old enough to oversee it himself. After that, who knows? That'll be a few years down the road anyway."

"And I," Hamilton said, "have a land to help rule." He grinned. "And children to bear. She says she wants dozens."

Angus laughed deeply, shoulders shaking. "Who'd have thought it?"

"What's that?"

"Us. We graduate from one of the finest naval academies in the known galaxy, and we were practically nobody. Then we land on some remote, uncivilized world, where we've both married princesses and saved the world. Hell, man, we're lords of all we survey! God, it's a rammin' fairy tale!"

Hamilton nodded, grinning, watching the splash of a fish leaping into the air after a spring insect. Then his face grew serious. "Have you missed Earth, Angus?"

"I missed home a little at first, but then I realized that I love this place. This." He raised his arms to the endless azure heavens, to the glittering lake, to the emerald hills. "This is Earth as it once was. As it should have remained. Let's hope these people, in the centuries to come, take better care of their world."

"Maybe that's why they were brought here in the first place," Hamilton said. "I've often thought about what this is all about, what it means. This world, these people, why were they brought here? Who did it? 'A great experiment', they said. It's all a mystery. I plan to visit that derelict ship again someday. When I do, are you with me?"

Angus answered him gravely, "Do we really want to know what secrets that ship holds?"

Hamilton thought for a moment, then nodded. "Exploration. Discovery. That's what being human is all about."

Angus nodded his head, rubbing his smooth shaven chin. "You're right. When you go, whenever it might be, I'm in."

And the two rode on for a while, into the rising sun, trading tales of high adventure.

About The Author

Travis Lee Heermann was born in 1969, and grew up on a dairy farm in rural Nebraska. He received his bachelor's degree in Electrical Engineering from the University of Nebraska at Lincoln. He currently resides in Omaha, Nebraska, with his wife, Cheryl, and Virgil, the mobile feline carpet.

He started writing when he was twelve years old, after reading *Swords of Mars* by Edgar Rice Burroughs. He promptly moved on to devour Robert E. Howard's tales of Conan the Barbarian. These two authors became his soul and inspiration as a writer. He finished writing his first novel at the age of fourteen.

He enjoys reading, writing, hunting, studying paranormal phenomena, war games and role-playing games of various genres, and painting fantasy miniatures.